"THE 14-YEAR-OLD MEXICAN-AMERICAN
POINT OF VIEW IS AUTHENTIC, FUNNY AND
TRAGIC . . . STREET-WISE DIALOGUE AND
VIVID DESCRIPTIONS CRACKLE OFF THE
PAGE." —PITTSBURGH PRESS

"Few things are more cheering than to pick up a first
novel by an unknown author and see immediately that
the new novelist is a natural . . . a writer endowed as
though genetically with the sure, pure sense of how to
shape his material . . . with not just a keen eye but a
keen ear, a keen wit. . . . It is cheering to report that
Danny Santiago is a natural. . . . His *Famous All Over
Town* is full of poverty, violence, emotional injury
and other forms of major disaster, all vividly and
realistically portrayed, yet, like a spring feast-day in a
barrio, it is nevertheless relentlessly joyous. Best of all
is its language . . . a rich street Chicano English that
pleases the ear like sly and cheerful Mejicana music . . .
Famous All Over Town is a classic of the Chicano
urban experience. And Danny Santiago is good news."
—THE NEW YORK TIMES BOOK REVIEW

DANNY SANTIAGO grew up in Los Angeles. His stories
have appeared in a number of national magazines, and one of
them, "The Somebody," was chosen for Martha Foley's
annual *Best American Short Stories* and since has been widely
anthologized. *Famous All Over Town* is his first novel.

Famous All Over Town

Danny Santiago

A PLUME BOOK

PLUME
Published by the Penguin Group
Penguin Books USA Inc., 375 Hudson Street,
New York, New York 10014, U.S.A.
Penguin Books Ltd, 27 Wrights Lane,
London W8 5TZ, England
Penguin Books Australia Ltd, Ringwood,
Victoria, Australia
Penguin Books Canada Ltd, 10 Alcorn Avenue,
Toronto, Ontario, Canada M4V 3B2
Penguin Books (N.Z.) Ltd, 182–190 Wairau Road,
Auckland 10, New Zealand

Penguin Books Ltd, Registered Offices:
Harmondsworth, Middlesex, England

Published by Plume, an imprint of Dutton Signet, a division of Penguin
Books USA Inc. This is an authorized reprint of a hardcover edition
published by Simon & Schuster.

First Plume Printing, April, 1984
20 19

 REGISTERED TRADEMARK—MARCA REGISTRADA

Library of Congress Cataloging in Publication Data

Santiago, Danny.
    Famous all over town.
    I. Title.
PS3569.A545F3   1984   813'.54   83-22020

Printed in the United States of America

The palaces, how spacious and well-built they were, of beautiful stone work and cedar wood, a miracle to behold. Great canoes passed through the gardens from the lake, and all was very splendid, with many monuments with pictures on them which gave much to think about. . . . As I stood there looking at it, I thought that never in the world would there be discovered another land like this one, for at that time there was no Peru or any thought of it. But of the wonders that I then beheld, today all is overthrown and lost and nothing is left standing.

Bernal Díaz del Castillo (1517–1521)

Tr. A. P. Maudslay

(George Routledge & Sons, Ltd., London, 1928)

Chapter

1

SLOW, LAW-ABIDING AND DRUNK, I cruised down North Main Street toward the river. It was way past the middle of the night. Frankie Martin's bar was dark, the last drinker long gone home. I passed by old familiar Eastside Brewery, took a left into Shamrock Street and switched off my headlights. I planned to dig up various long-buried corpses and didn't care for company.

Up ahead, one long block ahead were the S.P. tracks. I watched the signal tower blink red and green as it angled south toward skyscraping City Hall beyond. When the two of them lined up just right, I coasted to the curb. This would be the place exactly. I got out and looked and listened. Not a truck, not a car, not a sound. My patriotic bumper was the loudest noise in sight.

"CHICANO POWER," it yelled. "BROWN IS BEAUTI-FUL. FULANO FOR SHERIFF."

"Shut up," I told my bumper. "Be quiet."

I stood face to face with the enemy, a long line of trailers boxcar size with S.P. Railroad on their rumps. Nothing be-tween me and them except a 10-foot chainlink fence with two strands of friendly barbwire at the top. I planted my feet and spoke the magic word.

"114."

Trailers and chainlink went up in flames. In their place a certain saggy picket fence sprouted from the ground, a certain squeaky front porch rose up behind, and the skinny little

house where I lived half my life. Down the block up popped
number 112 and 110 and all their brothers. Old Shamrock
lived again and I was home.

Before the S.P. rolled us under asphalt we were the best
street in all L.A. with cozy little homes on both sides solid.
Maybe they weren't too new or too fresh-painted but they
were warm and lively, and when the trains passed by, how
those little houses used to shake, rattle and roll. Strangers
would ask, How can you stand it? But to tell the truth, we
barely noticed. It was like rocking a baby and very good for
the circulation of the blood, people used to claim.

"Gimme the pelota, Stupid." "Pítchala, pendejo!" "En-
rique, vente p'acá or else you're really gonna get it." My ears
tuned in ghost voices and murdered Spanish and my father's
well-known whistle that used to bring me running home.

One hour I stood there listening to the dead and gone. It
was a bad time in my life. I couldn't see my next step, should
it be Left or Right, or Up or Down? Maybe if I relived my
yesterdays I could be surer of my tomorrows. So I spread out
old memories like hopscotch on the sidewalk, took a running
jump and landed in the square of my fourteenth birthday,
which was the last I spent on Shamrock Street, and that's
where let's begin.

It took place on a hot Saturday in September.

"Here's your present."

My father slapped his chicken-killer knife into my hand. It
was ground down thin as a needle and had a razor edge. Nobody but him was allowed to touch it.

"Huh?" I asked.

"Fourteen years makes a man, so prove yourself."

"Me?" I asked.

"Why not?" he said. "You seen me do it often enough."

"When?" I asked.

"When I tell you to," he told me crossly, "and quit looking
so green in the face."

My father was quite famous for his chicken killing. People

came from up and down the street to watch. He made a regular rodeo of it, jumping up and down like a cowboy with chickens running every which way. He'd grab and miss in a dozen comical ways till his watchers ran out of laughs, then he'd make one quick snatch and there was his chicken-of-the-week scooped up in his arms with a cord whipped tight around her legs. Next my father would make love to that chicken, whispering in her ear, and she'd arch her neck and wink at him as flirty as any señorita while he waltzed her round the yard singing. Then the music would stop.

"Buenas noches, mi amor," he'd say. "Go to sleep, little chickie dear."

The American Way of twisting necks off or chopping heads never pleased my father. It left the meat tough and angry, he claimed. So, Mexican style, he hung his chicken from her feet and slipped the blade into her neck so nice and easy she never felt it. She'd flop her wings once or twice and her eyes would blank out very peaceful while she bled to death with a pan underneath to catch the blood.

That was my father's style and I only hoped I could do as well. In one way I was proud he trusted me, but in another way, Who knows? So then the mailman came with the insurance check for his shortened pinkie finger. That cheered my father up and he slapped me on the shoulder.

"Let's go cash it," he suggested, which was a wonder because my father always preferred to cash his checks in private. So we climbed into our famous '55 low-mileage Buick and away we went to García's Short-Change Department Store to check on the merchandise.

"You call these things boots?" he hollered in that bull-voice of his. My father is very loud in stores when speaking Spanish but in English you can barely hear him. "What you make them of, worm skin?" he asked and the clerk ran to bring the best boots money could buy, and triple-soled. My father dropped them on the floor. They hit like sledgehammers and he was more or less content.

"Fit my Junior here," he ordered. "Good heavy boots will

put meat on those matchstick legs of yours," he preached for all who cared to listen, "only don't leave them around where your mother will trip on them in her condition."

"Si, señor," I said and stomped my boots around the store. I was crazy to wear them home but my father said, No, put neat's-foot oil first, and peeled off a 20. As usual they tried to short him a dollar, my father's arithmetic is not the best, but I caught them at it. So from there we stopped by the Brewery for a keg and rolled home at five miles an hour to keep the foam from rising.

What followed was a little argument. My sister started throwing little indirectos like "What a thoughtful present for a fourteen-year-old and will you invite his hoodlum friends?" And, "How charming for our mother to have a gang of drunkards in the house with the baby due any minute now." Her smart remarks failed to please my father. In our house it was the pants that ruled so when Lena said Shit right out loud in English, my father hit her. In the right way of course. He never closed his fist on any girl or woman, like some, or slapped in dirty places. But even so he had a heavy hand and Lena marched out swearing she would never enter my father's door again. Personally, I expected her back for dinner. She had the biggest appetite in the family but on her it didn't show. My sister was as skinny as me except here and there, but what a temper.

On Shamrock, like most other places, people drank privately in backyards, not my father. He set up his beer on the front porch for all the world to come help him drink it. He stood the keg in a tub with ice around and threw an old rug over for shade, then he shoved in the tapper. It stuck up shiny as a sword.

"Free blood," my father shouted to various passing friends and slipped off the bandage for all to admire his stump. Myself, I didn't care to look at it.

"How much they pay you?" was asked.

"Hundred-fifty," my father said, which was not bad for one tiny knuckle on his pinkie finger's end.

"What's your fat finger worth?" they inquired.

"The S.P. Railroad don't have that kind of money," my father bragged. Quite some crowd soon collected. Virgie's Arturo and various others from S.P. and of course Chuchu Madrigal that was in Construction. My father settled his big pile-driver butt onto his Superchief silver train step which he bought it for twenty-five cents. There are always good bargains on Shamrock if you don't ask too many questions. He sat there solid as a fireplug with little brown eggs of flesh poking out through the holes in his famous air-condition T-shirt, enjoying his beer and king of everybody.

Up and down the street the paychecks had been cashed. Saturday night lay ahead, and after, Lazy Sunday. My father and his friends were in the mood to laugh at everything and I was proud to laugh along with them while I sat sunning on the steps. They were soft to sit on, spongy and not like new lumber, only you had to drive the nails back in once a week which was my regular job. So I sat there working the neat's-foot oil into my new boots. My fingers slided slick and smooth over the leather and deep into the creases till I found myself wondering if a girl or woman might feel like that.

"What you dreaming there boy?" my father asked. Maybe I jumped because the men couldn't quit laughing. "You got a little window in your head," my father told me, "and oh what I can see in there. You keep your hands out of your pockets, hear? or else we'll see hair growing on your palms."

I was ready for the subject to get changed.

"Still," my father said, "this Junior of mine, he's a pretty good boy, smart too, his teachers claim, with prizes for his handwriting. So stand up, son, and let's drink him a toast on his fourteenth birthday."

"Hey, look where he's taller than his dad," Chuchu pointed out.

My father doubted it so they stood us back to back. I had an easy quarter-inch on him, so Chuchu gave me a dollar, and everybody cheered except my father. "It's all in that skinny goose neck," he complained and gave my head a friendly shove that nearly tore it off, then preached barbells for my self-improvement while he went back to sharpening up the chicken-killer knife.

Out on the street my friends were busy shoving Fat Manuel's car in hopes to get it started, Gorilla, Hungryman, Pelón and a couple others. Los Jesters de Shamrock was our name and in those days we were Kings in Eastside, nobody cared to mess with us.

"Esé, Chato," they called, which was my street name, from being flat-nose like a cat. "Give us a hand, man," they hollered but I shook my finger No.

"What's this 'Chato'?" my father scolded. He hated that name. "You're Rudy M. Medina, Junior, and be proud of it."

"Sí, señor," I quickly told him and hoped to be forgotten, but Pelón was a genius for trouble and here he comes with his decorated shoeshine box, all silver stars and red reflectors.

"Buenos días, Padrino," he tells my father. "No quieres un free shoeshine?"

I sweated. Of all my friends Pelón was my father's least favorite. Three years back when the guy was orphaned, my father took him into our house and slept him on the couch with me like twins. Till that bad day when my father caught us doing something.

"Come on, Godfather," Pelón begged, on the sarcastic side, "I'll give you a real fine shine and you could lay back and tell us all about your cowboy days in Mexico when you were captain of one hundred horses."

"Get out of my nose, mocoso," my father shouted and started down the steps.

"Oh, indubitably," said Pelón, which was his favorite word, and off he went like a rabbit. My father knew better than to try and catch him.

"No-good hoodlums," he complained. "Where's Respect? Fight, steal, rob, make trouble, that's all those rat-packers know to do, light their pimpy cigarettes and blow the smoke in their fathers' face. When I was their age I was already doing a man's work down there in mi pueblo. And any time I came in the house I kissed my father's hand and any time I went out too. But when I come home these days who kisses my hand? Not even a dog or cat."

"They're all too educáted," Arturo agreed, "with their twelve years in school and their television. But down there in my village we had our advantages. We were poor as dirt but there used to be a certain little dark-skin girl, a fine plump little morenita she was. We all went to school on her and nobody whined about their homework."

To hear my father's friends tell it, there was a girl like that in every village and always she seemed to be dark-skinned and generous. And while my father's knife sang on the stone, his friends' Spanish words came rolling out like on rubber tires and they all turned patriotic Mejicanos. Yes, they admitted, there was hunger down there but the food had such a taste on it. The beans themselves were better than the best prime steaks of the USA. And yes, maybe it was chilly sleeping nights on those little mats of straw, but the mornings, hombre, when you stood outside shivering against the adobe wall and then the big round Mexican sun came up to warm you. It was the blanket of the poor, they all agreed, and tequila was the other poor man's blanket. To hear them talk, you wondered why they ever left the place.

And the snakes, man, those snakes of Mexico which always raised their head by beer number 5, snakes that whipped you to death with their tails, and others that rolled after you like wheels, tail tucked into mouth. And still others, nighttime snakes that came sliding down out of the grass roof while your compadre's mother's cousin's wife was sleeping, and sucked her nipples till her baby pined away to skin and bones, but that snake grew fat as a fire hose and over 12 feet long. I found myself especially interested in that nighttime snake and its strange way of life, while I sat there on the steps working on my new boots. By now they had soaked up all the oil they could hold so I put them on and laced them up very carefully to keep the tongues from wrinkling.

"Stand up, son," my father told me.

My time had come. Everybody had their eyes on me. I was the Main Event.

"You're fourteen years today," my father said. "And old enough to be my right hand. Now for once don't mess up. And be sure you catch all the blood." He slapped the chicken-killer knife into my hand. I gripped it tight.

"Con permiso?" I asked.

"Pass," they told me in a chorus.

My new boots marched me like an army round the corner of the house, along the side fence and up the back steps to the kitchen. My mother with her swollen belly stood leaning on the stove. Her braids hung tired and heavy down her back and she didn't notice when I came in. Since last month she'd been like half-asleep with her eyes turned inside out to watch the baby grow inside her.

"Hey, where's the pan at?" I asked her.

"What pan?" she wanted to know.

"The one for the blood naturally," I told her and flashed my knife. She looked at it and looked at me.

"You?" she said.

"Why not?" I told her.

My mother groaned when she bended down to rattle the pan out from under the sink. What if she should die? flashed through my head. What if this giant baby killed her while my father and his friends sat drinking on the front porch?

"See you don't cut yourself," she said and tuned me out.

Our backest yard was where the chickens lived. We had nopales solid along the fence reaching up their prickly paws higher than your shoulders. Our tumbledown shed took up one corner. I stood by the gate, knife in hand and watched the stupid chickens peck-peck-pecking through the gravel and complaining about the hard life they had. It was our old red hen I wanted. She used to be a steady layer but now only gave eggs when in the mood.

"Hey Junior, you gonna kill the chickie?"

"Make a circus like your daddy, Junior, huh?"

It was those pesty little kids from next door. I ignored them.

My plan was to imitate my father exactly. I opened the gate and started clowning but those dumb kids never laughed even one time. So then I got disgusted and went after that old hen for real, but she turned track star on me. Twice I missed her and fell against the nopale cactuses and tore my shirt.

"Should I call your daddy, Junior?"

Junior this and Junior that. "Shut up," I told those snotnose kids. Maybe I even threw my knife at them, I don't remember, anyway they left there running. Then I really grabbed that chicken and hit her a good one too, to learn her a lesson. The rope kept tangling. It took three tries to get her legs tied up. Next, I hung her upside down where my father always did and put the blood pan under. With my left hand I stretched her neck out long for the knife, but it felt very funny to me, like something I had possibly felt before, only with feathers on it.

I creeped the knife in till it just barely touched skin. Only one inch more, a half-inch even. But my muscles froze on me. My hand started in to shake. Out front the men were waiting. Out front my father trusted me. He had generously put his own special knife into my hand. There was no way in all this world I could possibly go back to the front porch with that chicken still alive.

We hung there, me and that old red hen, how long—who knows? Till suddenly it came to me: What's so great about my father's crazy Mexican way of chicken killing? Why not try something new for a change, something more up-to-date? In his closet, in a shoe box, my father had a revolver which he kept loaded just in case. It was another one of those Shamrock Street bargains and he paid $10 for it. For years my father always warned me, "Don't you ever touch that thing," but today I was fourteen years old which was a man, so I went for it.

God was good to me. My mother didn't notice when I sneaked through the kitchen with the .45 under my T-shirt. It seemed heavier than I remembered, and wanted to wave around when I took aim. So I steadied the barrel on the trash can just 6 inches away from that old chicken's throat. It was quite important not to miss. I might be criticized.

"SSAAAAHHHHSSS!"

It turned out to be the Shot Heard Round The World.

On Shamrock people can tell pistols from firecrackers any day, having heard plenty of both from time to time. No doubt they asked each other, "Did she finally shoot him? Or him her?" There were several well-known trouble spots. So they all came running to see the corpse. But of course it was my father that got to me first.

"Here's your chicken," I told him and held it up.

Nothing in this world was ever deader than that old red hen. It was a perfect shot, just one tiny thread of neck left and the head hanging down. I expected my father to be quite pleased with me. Instead he yelled. He grabbed the pistol. He slammed the chicken in the dirt. He slapped for my face but I ducked under.

"Hey," I told him, "what's wrong with you?"

"You wait!" he shouted and slung me into the shed and banged the door.

"What happened?" somebody outside asked. "Who's dead?"

"Medina's kid just shot a chicken."

"With a GUN?"

Then somebody hollered, "Yaaay, chicken-shooter!" It sounded like Pelón that used to be my friend. Others took it up. I heard that ugly word race up and down the block like a fire engine. But I ask you, "What's the difference how you kill a chicken as long as that chicken gets dead?" Possibly I was the first in history to use a gun. But that's people for you, try anything new and different and they're sure to criticize, my father especially. You had to do every least thing exactly his way or he blamed you for it.

I laid there in the dirt. The sun was shooting blades of light between the boards. There was a big new hole where the .45 blasted through. My hands were all over dirt and blood. My boots were bloody too. Who cared? Let it rot there. From outside I heard my father chasing people from the yard. I heard Chuchu arguing with him till my father ordered him out too. It got quite quiet. I heard the noise leather makes when you slap it on a wall. And then my father pulled the shed door open. His well-known belt squirmed in his hands like a snake.

Let him kill me. I'll never make a sound.

But behind him, through the door I saw my mother. She came waddling down the back steps. If she argued with him it would only make things worse. She didn't. Instead, she grabbed her belly and screamed a scream like no scream I ever heard before. My father dropped his belt and ran to catch her. I ran too, but it turned out to be a false alarm. The baby took two more days in coming. And I could almost swear I saw my mother wink at me while my father carried her inside.

Chapter
2

THAT WAS A SATURDAY. On Monday night I'm sound asleep on
my couch when a mad bull charges into the living room. It
bangs the table. It hooks a mean black horn at my belly. I
woke up yelling. The horn turned into the telephone and the
mad bull into my father, busy with the dial. His finger was too
stubby for the holes. Twice he had to start over again. It could
be four in the morning, or three. From across the room the
television stared at me dead-eye and empty. When I fell
asleep it was full of cowboys.

"Baby coming!" my father shouted in the phone. "Shamrock e-Street hundred catorce—"

He was practicing that speech for days but now his words
went Spanish on him and he shoved me the phone.

"Please repeat the address," it said politely. "Does anybody
there speak English?"

I couldn't find my tongue in any language.

"Dummy, what's wrong with you?" my father yelled.

"I got the bellyache."

"Then go to the damn toilet!"

He slammed down the phone and ran for Lena.

The toilet was where everybody kept sending me all day,
or the toledo, or basement, or restroom depending on their
mood. I told them in the morning I was too sick for school but
with my reputation who believed me? In Social Studies it hurt
to sit up so I folded myself across the desk and got in trouble
with Mrs. Milner who claimed I was only acting. Lunchtime,

I couldn't eat. What felt best was sitting on the steps with my head between my knees. The Yard Teacher sent me to the nurse. The nurse said "Gas," and sent me to the restroom. I sat and sat and nothing. Except son of a bitch Wolfie de Sierra slapped me around in public and I was too weak to hit him back. So I went back to the nurse who fired me questions. How late did I watch TV last night? What did I eat for break-fast? Or did I have special worries on my mind?

Stupid me, I told her my mother was expecting. "Oho," the nurse decided, then what I must have, no doubt, was sympa-thetic nerves. Didn't I recall those movies in Life Science which showed how neatly kittens got born and puppies? So why worry for my mother? She would be tended in a germ-free hospital where every day doctors and nurses worked mir-acles with modern medicine, nurses especially. That lady preached on and on. To pass the time I read the eye chart on the wall. "E O P," it said and "f l d g e," and I didn't bother to mention that my mother would be giving birth in her own bedroom because of money. When I got home they gave me yerba buena tea but I threw it up on the kitchen floor, which bored my mother. Who was supposed to be pregnant around here anyway, she asked, her or me? And that was my charm-ing day.

Lena came banging out of the back room with blue curlers in her hair like dragon feathers. She snatched the phone and her fingers raced round the dial like spiders. It was a pleasure to watch her after my clumsy father. The phone rang and rang.

"Answer it, you lazy bitch," Lena yelled. Tranquilina she had been baptized but before she was seven months old the Tranquil half was dropped. Finally, finally they answered at the hospital, either the Lazy Bitch or somebody else, and Lena rattled off our name, address and how fast the pains were coming.

"Hold the line please," they told her sweetly. "I'll see if we have a doctor available."

Lena raved. If our name was O'Toole or Shitzenheim the damn doctor would be on his way already, so she claimed.

But Medina? End of the line, you dirty Mexican. They came back on the phone again. Could the patient possibly be driven to the hospital?

"What if my mommie flops out the baby in the car?" Lena bawled. "Who knows where my father is? And I don't have no driver license."

They asked how old are you, dear?

"I'm gonna be twelve," Lena lied.

They said hold everything. The doctor would be there in five minutes. My sister hung up and grinned at me.

"They never believe you if you tell the truth," she said and off she clattered in her slip and slippers and started crashing pots around the kitchen to boil the water in. Scary noises came from the bedroom. My mother had warned me not to pay attention but who could help it? I put fingers in my ears. My father stood by the door dressed but helpless. Always he had been master of the house but he didn't look it now. The women had taken over. Each time my mother moaned he flinched. I never saw him scared before.

"Going down Main," he stuttered. "They might miss our corner."

My mother should never be having this baby, but it shamed my father to have a two-kid family where on Shamrock six was usual, or five at least. And people used to tease him over it, those that dared. So for years my little mother patiently did everything to get pregnant, ate and drank one million crazy herbs which my grandma that was some kind of witch down there in Mexico sent up to her. Time went by and my mother wasn't getting any younger and more and more she spilled those little dimes and quarters of blood on the linoleum. Till finally last January this baby seemed to take. My father was in heaven and ran to borrow 200 for the hospital, but then to our surprise my patient little mother turned tiger.

"No hospital," she told him fiercely.

My father got very hot. Was he some dumb Indian down there in the swamps of Yucatán to have his son born unscientific like the cucarachas?"

"Who says it's a son?" my mother asked.

My father said. He was very positive about it. And the son's name would be Rigoberto and his color would be coffee-and-cream with green eyes which was my father's color and my sister's. Me and my mother were more on the dark-brown side.

"You're going to the hospital!" my father swore, "and don't think of money. To me $200 is nothing!"

"To me it's something," my mother said. "And since you're suddenly so generous you can just put that two hundred in my hand or else I'll have this famous son of yours by knitting needle."

My mother was not what you might call the motherly type, and she threw my father such a scare he gave her the money. Next day she bought a bus ticket to visit my grandma in Mexico which my father broke promises on for years.

In the argument I personally was on the man's side, but Lena stood with my mother. She was all excited about having the baby at home because it would be good experience for her in days to come.

"Now everybody please quit worrying," my mother told us. "All I do is wait till the pains start, then call the hospital and they send a free doctor because it's the law. Look at my co-madre, Virgie, she had her last two at home and it never costed her one penny."

For once the women won and I was sorry. Sure. Look at Virgie. She was built like a baby factory. You barely knew her pregnant till here comes the baby as easy as firemen sliding down a pole. But my mother was a tiny little woman and that thing inside her was giant-size. From under my blanket I said a prayer for her. And after, one for me because my belly was starting in to ache again.

"Hey," my sister shouted. "Don't be so lazy. Go bring the papers."

That was my job, to spread them on the bedroom floor and squash the germs. The papers were stacked on the back porch 1,000 miles away but who could say no to Lena? I swung my feet off the couch but the blankets twisted round my legs. They were hot and sweaty and hung on like wrestlers. I went stumbling through the kitchen. When I bended down for the papers, my stomach took a bounce. I grabbed my mouth, yanked open the door to the toledo and fell on my knees to vomit. Nothing came and I was burning up. I leaned my head across the water to rest it on the bowl, which was the only cool thing in all the world. I pulled my T-shirt out of my shorts and pressed my aching belly to the near side of the bowl. Slowly, slowly I could feel the pain creep away. It was like medicine. That good old toledo where people had all day been sending me to would cure me after all and I hugged my arms around it till Lena came banging in.

"What are you doing, you pig? Making love to the toilet?" She pulled me loose.

"Get out quick. My mother has to go."

Lena might be a good nurse but her heart only had room for one patient at a time. Back on the couch I snuggled under the blankets. I was cold and shivery. I touched my belly. It felt tight like my mother's. Could you catch a baby the way you catch the measles? Life Science said, No, impossible. But what else could it be? God's punishment for shooting that chicken? But if God was on the chickens' side why hadn't He punished my father for all those slit throats?

Then I remembered something. Back there in July I ate watermelon. "Don't swallow the seeds," they told me, "or one might sprout in you." But I was careless and now I was paying for it. That watermelon would no doubt kill me, and the baby would kill my mother. Then they could hold a double-barrel funeral and save money, possibly $200. Bury us in a single coffin and save more, but it would be very spooky down there in the ground with a skeleton beside me, even if it was my mother's and I was one myself.

Something heavy dropped onto the couch. Bony fingers squeezed my ankle. Death's come for me, I thought, but it was only my mother when I dared to open up my eyes. She had a blanket round her like an Indian and her hair she was so proud of hung down any which way.

"Ai de mí," my mother sighed. "This one takes forever. The little rat's hanging on with all four paws. And who could blame him? Cozy little home, no rent to pay, free meals, no school, no work, no worries. And what could we give him better on the outside unless it's the television?"

Her head snapped back. I saw her teeth.

"Eeeeho, this one must be an acrobat," she moaned. "Don't I ever have any luck? Upside down is how you came and the doctor had to squash your little nose to turn you round." She petted my foot. "My poor little Chatito, what a sickly little worm you were, I never thought we'd raise you. And asthma? Every breath sounded like your last. And now here you are, taller than your father, no thanks to all those crazy doctors."

Dr. Everhard was the name of one. My father heard his ad on the Mexican radio, Cured or Your Money Back. His office was downtown at 4th and Main, up a long flight of stairs with his name in gold on every step. Underneath, they sold switch-blades and scissors. Dr. Everhard was loud and bald and glad to see us. His treatment was the latest thing, all electric. He strapped me in a chair with silver knobs to grab and threw the switch. The chair went Buzz, lights flashed like Frankenstein and electricity fizzed through my blood. Each time I went, that chair kept count, 24 treatments and I would be cured, then 23. The trouble was, nobody but that electric chair was smart enough to notice any change in me, so after $50 my mother started spending the doctor's money at the Million Dollar theater where she took me to the Mexican movies, and we never told my father, which was how I learned to keep a secret back in those good old days when my mother was such a pretty lady and I was the baby of the family.

"The bedroom's ready," Lena called.

My mother tried to get up but fell on her knees instead. Air hissed through her teeth and her fists pounded on the floor.

"Grab her arm," Lena yelled.

I was scared to touch her.

"Quick, or she'll have it on the floor!"

We dragged her to the bedroom moaning. Lena had put down my newspapers. They bunched and tore under us. My mother hollered. We couldn't lift her. The candle lit up our two virgins, La Candelaria with her kind white face which was my father's favorite and black Guadalupe for my mother. Neither one seemed to be on duty. My father came in running.

"Her water's broke," Lena noted.

I didn't care to hear about it. I went back to my couch and pulled the blankets over my ears.

"Get a towel," I heard.

"Where's the shitty doctor?"

"Any towel, any rag, anything!"

Possibly I fell asleep, because suddenly there's no more noise in the house. I'm all alone, except my mother. She's in the bedroom dead, all torn up and bleeding. But something is in there with her, something I don't care for at all. And now it comes crawling out at me, something like a giant blond baby acrobat with green eyes and ugly bubbles coming out its mouth. It's got red tights on and swings a barbell and scuttles at me like a cucaracha and starts slugging at my belly. A siren yelling up the street is all that saved me, and feet pounding on our porch.

I tuned in human voices and pulled the blankets off to focus on the picture. Anything would be better than that baby acrobat waiting inside my eyelids. Two doctors is what I saw, in white suits, one very tiny, the other big and red-haired.

"Does she understand English?" they asked, then closed the bedroom door in Lena's face. My mother was yelling again now and my father hit his head with both fists.

"Let it be quick," he prayed. "Let it be anything, a girl even, but quick!"

The little doctor came back out.

"Has she seen a physician?" he asked.

Nobody cared to answer.

"Won't you people ever learn?"

My father looked at the floor. Not Lena. "What you mean, you people?" she answered back. "We got our rights, I hope. We pay our taxes."

"And your taxes bring you one scared redheaded intern on his first delivery."

He scared my sister good, and me too.

"But my mother's gonna be okay?"

The doctor yawned a very big yawn for a man his size.

"Oh yace," he said on the sarcastic side, "since you've got wide-awake little me in case Red makes a mess of it."

His voice was cross and tired. His face looked dipped in flour except for black moons under his eyes. He had a long sharp nose and when he pointed it round the room everything got uglier. The cracks in our old plaster turned into gulleys and the bare patch in our linoleum looked like a swamp. The doctor inspected our long framed photo of the S.P. round-house crew with my comical father standing at both ends. It was hanging crooked so he straightened it. Next he checked the wedding picture taken in El Paso when my parents crossed the border, the one they tinted so my mother came out almost a blonde. Then he dropped into my father's arm-chair and shut his eyes to sleep, but his fingers stayed awake. They found the hole in the arm and picked out stuffing, rolled it into little balls and dropped them on the floor. My mother's yelling in the bedroom didn't seem to bother him.

"Can't you give her a shot?" Lena begged, "or some kind of pill at least?"

"Not here," the doctor said. "In the hospital we could. Do you have water boiling?"

My belly kept on hurting and it got worse. Every time my mother yelled I wanted to yell too. But what would my father say? Since Saturday his favorite name for me was Coward. I tried to pray. Nobody listened. I gritted teeth. I bit on fingers. Then I made up a little game. Every time the pain hit I scored myself a touchdown for not yelling. It wasn't much of a game but what else was there to do? I stuffed the blanket in my mouth and chewed it. From the bedroom the yells were coming faster. I was sorry for my mother but I had problems of my own. I scored touchdowns by the dozens and field goals left and right but the noise kept building up inside me too big to hold. Maybe if I let out just one little yell, and timed it with my mother's, maybe it might not be heard. For a while it worked. Then everybody was staring at me and I had lost the game.

"What's wrong with him?" the doctor asked.

"The bellyache," my father said disgusted.

"Oh yace?" the doctor said. "That's very interesting. There's even a name for it but usually it's the husband, not the son."

"Shut up, crybaby-coward!" my father told me in Spanish.

Lena came and looked at me.

"You know something?" she said. "What if he really is sick? What if he's caught the Asiatic flu or something?"

She grabbed my arm like pliers.

"You little pest," she told me, "tell the truth now or else I'm gonna hit you. Are you sick or only faking?"

"I'm okay."

I grinded it out between my teeth and it sounded funny. The little doctor came over and stared down at me with those dead-and-buried eyes of his. He stripped the blankets back and slid his hand under my T-shirt to where I hurt. His hand felt nice and cool, till suddenly he pressed it hard into my belly. Then I really hollered.

"Jesus Katie Christ!" the doctor said.

Then everything started taking place at once, a needle in my arm, a stretcher, straps across my chest. "I'm sorry," I kept telling them. Then the ambulance screamed and away we went.

Chapter

3

CURTAINS CAME ROLLING on squeaky wheels, then swung out to make a fence around my bed, I wondered why. It was dark and there were snorers outside the curtains. Inside was a big white bear that stood beside my head and a black bear that moved around and talked.

"Has he been confirmed?" the black one said. "It makes a difference."

If he meant me, the answer was yes but I didn't bother to tell him so.

"Poor little lad," he said, "did you call the family?"

That black bear talked very funny. I could barely understand him.

"Pity not to wait for them," he said, "but I've another one on Seven."

Another what?

He snapped open a little box that smelled of church. He lit a cigarette or maybe it was a candle. I heard dishes clank, then Latin. He touched me here and there, on my foot and on my head, and mumbled. If I still hurt I couldn't feel it. Possibly they had given me something because I was flying. All of us were flying, me, the bed, the rolling curtains, the black bear and the white one. Where to, who knows?

The next I remember, those rolling curtains were gone and I was in a tall bright room with eight beds of strangers, which was no doubt a hospital ward, and how are you supposed to act? I wondered. Do you wave and say Hi to everybody or only speak when spoken to? To be on the safe side, I shut my eyes because who can criticize you when you're asleep? I was hurting but like very far away. Mostly what I felt was uneasy. Something was very very wrong down underneath the covers. I slided my hand down under very slow and sneaky so nobody would get any wrong ideas, and found a big fat bandage on my belly. That I had expected because no doubt they operated me, but lower down felt very unfamiliar. I went exploring You Know Where. My fingers touched something and I jerked my hand away like bitten. What was it?

A snake?

Like that milk-sucker in Mexico? No. Too skinny.

A worm then?

Which had crawled into my thing to feed on my insides? Except it didn't squirm. Possibly it died in there.

A wire?

Some mad scientist could have me hooked up to a big machine like on the television, to change me to a monster, with lights blinking and needles whipping around on various dials.

Or was it a lesson to me?

For certain little sins I might have committed down there. Like that bad day with Pelón. "Puto," my father yelled at me, "do you let him use you for a woman?" And wouldn't listen when I told him No, no, no.

Or wait!

It could be a mistake, something they forgot to take out after the operation. Everybody knows how they treat Mexicans at County Hospital. Like that little lady on Milflores Street, she went there to get cough medicine and came out a corpse, I forget her name.

Should I ask a nurse? They were trotting in and out, but they were white ladies and if I called attention to myself Down There, they would be sure to scream and slap my face. No, whatever that thing might be, I had to get rid of it by myself. Slowly, slowly I started pulling. It came out inch by inch, slick and slimy, I could barely stand to touch it. It came

out forever, till finally I felt it loose and squirmy on my legs.
I quick kicked it out of bed and it flip-flopped on the floor.

You might think I had burned down their hospital.

Nurses came scolding from near and far.

"Look what you've done, bad boy!"

"I told you we should of tied his hands."

"Call the Resident!"

He turned out to be that same tiny doctor which came to
our house last night or whenever. The one that possibly saved
my life, and for a wonder he took my side against the nurses.
It was time for The Thing to come out anyway, he said.

"But it's ordered," the boss nurse said. She had a cap with
horns like a bull, and brass hair. "Dr. *Wenty* ordered it," she
said.

"I'm changing the orders," Dr. Penrose said which seemed
to be his name.

"And what if he wets the bed, doctor?"

"Then you will change the sheets, nurse."

They didn't love each other. She stomped away broadcast-
ing her twenty years nursing experience. Dr. Penrose sat
down on my bed like an old friend and explained me everything. That snaky thing was to piss through while asleep, he
said, and Catheter was its name. Next he drew a picture of my
operation. It seemed my appendix busted which poisoned my
insides and they called it Peritonitis. Later he would show it
to me in a bottle. I was three hours on the table, Dr. Penrose
said, while surgeons swabbed me out. They barely pulled me
through. Another hour and I would be dead, it seemed, but
now with ten days bed rest I would be as good as new. Dr.
Penrose, who had been quite cranky in our house, today was
very cheery and even combed me with his personal comb.

That afternoon my father was admitted with the news. My
mother got well half an hour after they took me to the hospital,
he reported.

"How's Rigoberto?" I asked.

"Dolores," he said disgusted.

After that he couldn't find too much to say. Mexican-style

he kept his hat on but he didn't seem real happy about it and kept taking it off and putting it on while he searched the ceiling for conversation. I wished I could see my mother but of course she couldn't leave the house till her forty days were up.

"Where's Lena?" I asked.

"Down in the Buick praying for you."

Then I remembered. When Li'l Angel got knifed she went to the hospital to see him, he was like a boyfriend almost, and she found him quite lively and cracking jokes, but next morning he was dead and after that Lena never dared to visit the sick, especially not in County Hospital.

My father handed me her Get Well card. "Thanks be to God I never get sick," he said. "No sir, never been in one of these places except to visit friends so see you get well quick and come home soon."

He kissed me loudly and left, still fiddling with his hat. My poor father, he might be King of the Aztecs' club but here in County Hospital he looked uneasy and out of place for all his coat and tie. Every day he came to see me after work, and I appreciáted him, but the high point of my hospital days was when Dr. Penrose visited the ward.

Where other residents and interns looked as if they wore their clothes to bed, Dr. Penrose was always spotless in his white doctor-suit with earphones dangling casual from the pocket. He had that real sharp Ivy League look which I only wished I had myself and his trousers were recut by his personal tailor. They fitted him so tight he had to unscrew his feet to take them off, he said. The whole ward cheered up when Dr. Penrose marched in. He always winked at me first, then passed on to his graver cases, never too impatient to listen to all their troubles, even those poor old winos they had in there. With the needle, nobody else could find your vein like him, the others poked you like a pincushion. Everybody was crazy about Dr. Penrose except the nurses.

"Why hasn't this bed been changed?" he'd ask. "Who wrote

this idiot chart? Fill that man's water jug. Where's the ice packs I ordered?"

He really kept those nurses hopping, and then after he'd checked the ward he would perch on my bed which he seldom if never did on any others.

"What's new?" he'd say like any other guy, "how's the aches and pains today?" He never once discriminated me. In fact, Mexicans seemed to be his most favorite class of people, and last year he flew down there to Acapulco with his friend Colin for vacation. He showed me their pictures on the beach, all very tanned and more muscley than you might guess. They had more or less adopted a shoeshine boy around my age, it seemed. Personally I didn't care too much for the guy's looks. He smiled too much. In every snapshot there was old Pepe with all his teeth on display. Dr. Penrose said they really had a ball in Acapulco except somebody stole his gold wristwatch worth $400. I could guess who but naturally I didn't say anything. You can't trust those Mexicans down there. They aren't like us. I would never steal from a friend, never, even if I could get away with it.

Dr. Penrose found a lot to talk about. He told me about the rare and interesting cases they had there in the hospital, and about those hotshot staff doctors who look so saintly when they come cruising through your ward with a dozen interns following along like mice. You might not believe it, but a lot of those doctors are drunks, and others cheat on their wives and they all blame each other for butchering up the patients, just like anybody else. Then too, Dr. Penrose explained me all those hospital words like OB, RN, EKG and ETKM meaning Every Test Known to Man, which doctors call for when they run into puzzling patients. Dr. Penrose was very pleased how fast I learned that language. We could talk together like a couple of pros.

The priest dropped by to see me too, the one that ministered me my Last Rites. He talked football mostly, the way they do, but later turned quite solemn.

"You're a very lucky boy," he told me. "Do you go every Sunday to mass?"

"Sometimes," I confessed.

"You should, laddie. You owe God a big debt. The doctors gave you up for lost. They left you in God's hands and in His mercy he chose to spare your life. Perhaps he has in mind some great work you'll do in this world."

What type of work? I wondered.

The father mentioned Altar Boy and left me with a Rosary. The beads felt friendly to my fingers and I tried out a prayer or two. My life was a real mess. I was sinning more than my share both by thought and act, and getting very poor grades in school besides. Why would God bother to save me with my record? I thought quite a lot about what that priest said, and asked Dr. Penrose if it was true God brought me back to life? He told me possibly but blamed penicillin more.

I thought about it. Could it be He spared me to cure the sick? "How do you get to be a doctor?" I asked.

That same day Dr. Penrose brought me a Book of Bones to study. It had a spooky fold-out skeleton which you could dance the arms and legs around. Your ear was on another page with tiny bones inside almost too small to notice. A lot of bones have names as long as freight trains but Dr. Penrose taught me how to say them and it sounded quite a lot like Spanish. I promised to learn two bones per day. After I got them all by heart I could start memorizing my muscles and my inside organs, and after that a Book of Germs, and then I would be in business.

But I would have to graduate too and Audubon Junior High School stood in my way. In Social Studies, Life Science, and Spanish Language my grades were pure C's and D's, and I had a gang of U's for Unsatisfactory in Cooperation, Personal Hygiene and Habits of Thrift.

What happened to me?

Back there in 6th grade everything came so easy. Mrs. Cully was my teacher then. She was a chubby red-haired lady, very motherly but with bad breath, and she really made you learn.

I even got some 100's in arithmetic, and how that lady used to love my handwriting! She made me the official writer for Open House when parents were invited to see our work, except mine always failed to show up.

I was quite sickly with the asthma in those days so while others played baseball, she got me into marble-shooting and introduced me at the Boys' Club where Ernie Zapata coached me every day. That was the year I came in runner-up in the All-City Playgrounds Marbles Championship, twelve and under. Mr. Zapata helped me a lot but not like Mrs. Cully. I'll never forget the day I graduated. "Rudy, Rudy," she told me. "You're so darned gifted but what's going to happen to you in Junior High? Will you get lost like all the rest?"

How right that lady was! She hugged and kissed me too, in front of everybody, but when I dropped by last spring to say hello, it seemed they had moved her to another district.

So anyway, I worked very hard on my Book of Bones, and when they let me walk I started practicing a little medicine on my own. I used to crank beds up and down when the nurses were busy gabbing at their station. I brought fresh ice water and helped the patients to drink, those little old winos especially which their hands were all the time playing the guitar. I emptied forgotten bedpans and sometimes even, I translated Spanish-speakers to the doctors which my own father never trusted me to do. Lena was always interpreter with us.

Another time they brought in a colored kid around my age and he had caught his hand in a meat-grinder so they had to chop it off. He was quite upset and hollered around Why not die better?

"Cheer up and make the best of it," I told the guy. "They'll put a hook on you, man, with a real sharp point on it so nobody would ever dare to mess with you."

It failed to cheer him up and when I loaned him my Classic Comic about Dr. Jekyll and Mr. Hyde which Dr. Penrose gave me, the guy didn't even return it, which shows you how those people are. Then too I read charts when nobody was looking so I could inform my friends if their temperature was up or down. I got quite popular up there in ward 1017 and several said they didn't know what they would do without me, grown men too. But forget about those nurses. They were not one tiny bit like on TV. Fat and ugly was their style and they seemed to come in two colors only, Alabama black or silver blondie with never a Mexican in the crowd. And were they ever bossy? You should have heard them when they caught me reading charts.

"You're the limit!" they yelled. "Back to your bed, you little snotnose. You know the rules."

"So throw me out of the hospital," I suggested. "Report me to the District Attorney."

I stood there two weeks. Most people might get homesick, but me never. Except maybe once or twice in the middle of the night, like the time I got restless and climbed out on the fire escape for fresh air, ten dizzy stories up. There was old familiar Eastside spread out under me. I felt like God or an angel at the very least. Shamrock I couldn't see. It was in a puddle of black between the brewery and the S.P. tracks, but there was the river, and beyond the Civic Center with lights climbing City Hall to the sky. There was Sunset Boulevard curving off toward the ocean, and Wilshire like a chain of Xmas lights. The whole city stretched out under me and there was no end to it, my L.A. which I was once almost marbles champion of. It made me proud and I pitied guys from poor little Oxnard and El Centro and all those towns they have to keep apologizing for.

A low humming and a buzzing came up from all those snoring people, and from dishwashers coming home by bus, night shifts changing, trucks bringing in tomorrow's groceries and the latest styles. So many millions of people and only one of me. How easy to get lost down there, one tiny ant chasing around with all those other ants. Was that all that God had spared me for? He had given me a second chance but what could I possibly do with it.

"Why don't you jump?" came to me suddenly. "Jump and

all your worries will be over." My knees shook so hard I had to hang onto the railing. And then the iron door swung open and there was Dr. Penrose.

"Looked for you everywhere," he said. "Thought you flew the coop."

His voice was quite muddy. Possibly he'd been drinking, or did he take some kind of pill? Anyway he took my hand.

"Trust me?" he asked.

"Cómo no?" I said. How not?

"Then let's fly," he said and flapped both arms.

"Hey!" I grabbed the railing.

"Coward," he told me. "Time for bed."

He bolted the door after us, then led me along the hall. Nobody else in sight.

"Wrong way," I informed him.

"I'm promoting you to a private room," he said.

The bed was made up in there so I laid down on it, wondering what next?

"Now," he told me, "I'm going to give you a back rub to raise the dead."

"Since when do doctors give back rubs?" I asked.

"Since tonight."

He untied my neck strings and peeled the gown off my shoulders. His hands were just right, not too hot and not too cold. He held the alcohol in his palm to warm it, and not like the nurses. And let me tell you something. In all my nights in the hospital I never had a back rub like that one. Dr. Penrose seemed to know each tiny bone and muscle from my neck all the way down. Mine wasn't the first back he ever rubbed, you could tell. Right away my eyes got heavy and I started floating into sleep, till he folded back my covers and I was naked to my heels.

"Hey," I said embarrassed.

"Never be ashamed of your body," he told me. "Your body is a beautiful thing."

"My legs are too skinny."

"So are a deer's," he said.

"Don't you feel anything?" he said.

What should I feel? He stood looking down. Then he gave my butt a friendly slap, pulled up my covers and left before I could even tell him thanks.

As it turned out, that was the last night I spent at County Hospital. Dr. Wenty checked me over in the morning and gave me my release. I could finish getting well at home, he said but no school for the next few days which didn't break my heart. I was hoping Dr. Penrose would drop in and say goodbye but he didn't, and when I packed up, along with various other things I took his Book of Bones, only hoping it was a gift and not just a loaner.

Chapter
4

"HOW COME THE WHEELCHAIR?" I asked the orderly. "I been ambulating all week."

"So you don't bust your leg and sue the County," he informed me. "Anything can always happen," he said, "and especially with Mexicans."

He was black and limped.

"What-all you got in this sack, boy?" he asked. "Steal your bedpan or what?"

He wheeled me down the elevator and out the basement door. I saw the friendly Buick.

"Handle him like soft-boiled eggs," he told my father.

My father nested me in the back seat with pillows from his own bed. The parking lot was clogged with black-and-whites and ambulances. He eased us through, and down the ramp to bumpy Zonal Street, up the rise to Mission Road and across on Griffin. I couldn't see enough. Nothing was changed but everything was new. The trees were like fresh-painted green and dingy old brick buildings bloomed like roses. My eyes climbed telephone poles to where their crosses raked the blue blue sky and I fell in love with those long suave valleys where wires sagged from pole to pole as far as you could see. They'd been there all my life but today they seemed a miracle, and how could I ever get bored again when the world was so loaded with fine things to look at? Later, I tried to catch that mood again, but I could never bring it back. Possibly it only takes you when you come back from Death.

The bell rang at the crossing. The striped arm dropped just in front of us. My father shook his fist and blew his horn at the block-long locomotive. Seldom did I ever see him so bothered by the trains.

"Pinchi S.P., he yelled, "busted Tony Torres' back at the roundhouse, son of a bitches! Think you'll bust mine too, hah?" My father threw chingazos at every freight car as it rumbled past. This was something new. In the old days he always bragged of working for the S.P. Railroad. When the arm went up, my father took off like a shot, then remembered me and inched his way up Griffin, and drove down Main slower than a hearse.

By the time we passed the brewery my father got his good mood again and reached his big hand back to pat my knees. "My good old Junior," he said, "soon's you're cured we got to see more ball games, me and you, go more to the parks for picnics. And hey, I just remembered, they got the fights tonight on television. How 'bout that now?"

This man was my father, I proudly thought, his big round head with hat on top, his curly brown hair well-barbered with little tips of gray, his big square face with jaws like a rock-crusher, arms thicker than my legs and what a pair of fists! No wonder he was King of the Aztecs' club whenever he went there to drink his beer.

We swung left off Main and cruised up Shamrock, my Shamrock. Familiar cozy little homes drifted past my window, so close together they seemed to be holding hands. Well-known doors and windows made smiling faces at me and I was welcome in every one of them, excepting two or three. It was around eleven o'clock, the women's time of day, men off to work, kids in school, you could see ladies old and young leaning on fences or perched on porches while the latest gossip flew back and forth. Their pesty little ones were out practicing 100 easy ways to break your neck. "Don't leave the yard, you hear me? Or if you do, don't cross the street or else I'll murder you." There was Elva sitting on the front-porch bench they made her out of 2-by-6's to hold up her 300

pounds. More men were after her than you might believe.
Pelón lived there in the cellar and his twin sister upstairs.

And now here comes the Milagro Market with its five padlocks on the door so it took them a half-hour to open up in the
morning. Their prices were possibly the highest in the city,
but credit was easy and you went there when the paycheck
was spent or when too lazy to walk to Main Street, but most
of all for conversation. And I could see a big gang of mothers
telling each other about all the world-shaking events that happened since they saw each other two hours ago. Up ahead I
stared down the dark tunnel under the tracks where my father
went every day to work. I used to dream that tunnel quite a
lot, in nightmares especially. And then, finally, we slid over
to the curb, tires scraping on it like always. Number 114.

My little mother stood waiting on the porch. She had her
pretty shape again and her hair which I last saw so ratty was
pulled back neat and tight with her fine fat braid hanging
down below her waist.

"Well," she said, "Señor Bellyache!"

My mother was not the crying type but she cried on me.
She seldom cared to be touched but now she hugged me tight,
both arms round my neck. My father said, Quit bawling, but I
caught him wiping off a tear of his own. It was a big moment
for me and possibly I cried a little too.

"You might at least show off the baby," my father ordered.

"What baby?" my mother asked. "Oh, that one!"

They took me in the bedroom to inspect Dolores. She was
a tiny picture of my father, rock-crusher jaw and all. It was
quite comical.

"Who's she look like?" my father bragged.

"King Kong," I told him and he had to laugh. Next, while
he dressed for work, here comes Virgie from across the street
to wish me Welcome Home. With Virgie in your house who
needed newspapers? She dished out the day's disasters till
the kitchen bulged with them, sick babies, jailed fathers, lost
jobs and broken homes, but today Virgie's big headline was
about herself.

"Guess what, comadre," she told my mother, "we just sold our home. And we got a good price too, considering all that talk about how S.P.'s gonna gobble up the street. Yes, comadre, it's adiós Shamrock for me and Arturo."

This was bad news for my mother. Virgie was her closest friend, in and out of the house five times a day. They were exactly opposite, my little mother soft-voiced and stay-at-home where Virgie was a gadabout with a tongue that wagged 1,000 times per minute. She dyed her black hair bright red which fooled nobody and was born back there in Chicago or one of those crazy states back east so when Virgie started off in Spanish she might switch to English and back a dozen times before she caught her breath. As a friend she couldn't do enough for you, but oh how that woman talked.

"We're gonna buy us a new home out in the tracts," she rattled. "And comadre, I won't be sorry to leave. It scares me every time my Debra leaves the house, what with marijuanos, Asiatic flu, rapers running wild and quién sabe qué. I'm telling you, comadre, Shamrock's no place to raise a family any more."

"What do you mean?" I told her. "Shamrock's where it's at, man. Sure it may be a little rugged here and there but that's good for you. It teaches a guy to take care of himself."

I threw a couple of left jabs to demonstrate but they seemed to land on my incision, so I sat down.

"You should move out too, comadre," Virgie preached. "It's so pretty out there in the tracts with everything brand-new and lawns. And another thing, comadre, it could keep certain people out of trouble, if you know what I mean."

"What people?" I wanted to know.

"Get that boy to bed," my father ordered from his bedroom.

I was promoted into Lena's room which she decorated in my absence. What a shock! It was like stepping into the television tube. The floor was dazzling white, the walls were black, the ceiling was white again and the window trim, so of course the curtains had to be black for contrast. Lena wanted to blacken the sheets too, my mother said, but they told her

No on account the washing machine, so she settled for black pillowcases to be done by hand in the kitchen sink. And on top of the black dresser my sister put a white vase with black plastic lilies in it. Lena was never the type to go halfway.

I slipped into bed but sleep didn't come to me. What had gotten into my sister? Before, her room was like anybody else's, all colors but mostly brown and her junk used to be piled here and there sky-high. Could it be she fell in love? If so, her diary might give me answers. It was taped to the back of her number 3 dresser drawer for privacy, so she hoped. I eased the drawer out very slow because it had a yell all its own which might bring my mother.

Panties. Nobody in the world had more. On top were my sister's favorites, one for each day of the week with its name sewed on from White Sunday to Black Saturday, with a rainbow of colors in between. I'm ashamed to say I caught myself petting those silky things like kittens before I remembered and untaped the diary.

"IF ANYBODY READS THIS I WILL KILL THEM" Lena had printed on the cover. Taking my life in my hands I opened to my sister's scraggly handwriting.

September 22. I dream Carlos last night and today didn't he touch my leg in the chili dep't, the rat. I use to like him when I thought he was what he wasn't . . . After work my Dad scoled me about too much legs and lipst. He called me a H. and I had my tears rolling.

My father never cared for X-Cell Packing where Lena worked packing spices and I didn't like it either. It was not only low pay but too many free-and-easy men around, the most of them TJ's from Mexico. Everybody knows how they are with girls and women. Lena claimed she never socialized but her diary proved her liar.

September 23. Early to bed but late to work. I had a nice conversation with Teddy. He's the serious type to make a good husband, but on the chubby side.

September 24. Geronimo that use to be Annie's boyfr. talked to me quite well. He says I have a good personality and very shapy legs, the rat. He is muy handsome, something like Marlon Brando and Montg. Clif too.

Carlos, Teddy, Geronimo, Montg. Clif! My sister was so man-crazy it made me sick. And what if she got pregnant? Or left home? Or got married? I couldn't stand to think about it. The house would be a morgue without her. And, all my life she was my protector. As number 1 girl fighter of Shamrock, when she told the older guys to lay off me, they listened. And the protection even followed me to school because in 4th grade when Mrs. Eagleburger slapped my face, Lena came charging into my classroom. "Don't you ever hit my little brother or even touch him," she told that teacher. Mrs. Eagleburger grabbed my sister by both shoulders and shook her for insubordination but that was a mistake because Lena called her big fat sloppy whore in front of all the class and dug her fists into that Mrs. Eagleburger's belly and slugged her on the face even if she was twice Lena's size. It took two teachers and one nurse to pull my sister off that howling teacher.

The trouble was, that little incident went down on her record and trailed her into high school. Everywhere they had it in for my sister because there's no worse crime than hitting a teacher, unless maybe it's hitting a principal or possibly a custodian. So as soon as the law allowed, Lena quit school and went to work.

I turned the page in my boy-crazy sister's diary.

September 25

It was pure stars and hearts and moons and flowers. The only human word was potato salad. Why? What happened? Was that the day some son of a bitch nailed her? While I studied it over, the front door slammed and shook the house, which could be nobody but my sister coming home. I slipped the diary back, jumped into bed and pulled the covers up.

"I wanna see my brother *now*," came through the door. "Why can't he sleep at night like other people?"

I heard my mother shooshing her, then heavy silence. I

watched the doorknob turn very sneaky and quick shut my
eyes to look asleep. The new-painted floor gave out its usual
old squeaks till I knew Lena was standing beside the bed,
noisily holding her breath. I kept her waiting quite a while
before I generously opened up my eyes.

"Well," she said. "Some people sure have life easy!" She
gave me a cross little kiss that landed on my nose, then went
fishing. "How do you like my color scheme?" she fished. "I
spose you hate it."

Of course I raved. What else? The idea came from how fine
guys look at weddings in tuxedos, Lena said, but to me all that
black and white suggested was L.A.P.D., the Los Angeles
Police Department. Either way it was no doubt the only room
of its kind in all the world or anyway in Eastside. "So don't
mess it up," Lena scolded. "And see you don't piss the bed
like you used to do."

"Only when I'm too lazy to get up," I promised.

"Just once and I'll murder you. Hey!" my sister suddenly
remembered. "How did you do it at the hospital?"

"Do what?" I innocently asked.

"You know!"

"Oh, you just do it in the bed," I casually informed her.

"Eeeeee, how filthy!"

"In glass bottles of course," I explained.

"Well," she said, "that's better."

"And then you ring for the nurse to take it away."

"You mean she sees it? Oooo, how embarrassing."

"You get used to it. Everything's very free and easy over
there at County, like nursies giving you your bed baths."

"Do they wash you all over? Even your You-Know-What?"

"Naturally," I lied.

"They must be whores," Lena shouted.

I tried to get Lena on the subject of that moony September
25th but she switched back to the hospital. "That night you
were so sick, did you see Death?" she asked. "Some claim
you do."

"You mean old skull-face?" I said, "the one that stretches out his bony fingers for you? Sure I saw him. Close like I am to you."

Lena broke. She held my hand and kissed it and spilled tears all over me. "I prayed for you," she sobbed. "All that night I stood on my knees for you praying." So I filled her up with deathly details, squeaky ghosts flying round in sheets, angels calling from the chandelier and devils under the bed.

"Weren't you scared?" she asked and held her breath.

"Not too too much," I said. "After all, we're here today and gone tomorrow and if your number's up, what can you do about it? And besides," I told her, "I had this real cute blonde nursie holding my hand, so what a way to go."

"You and your blondies," Lena raged. "They sure spoiled you rotten over there. Only if they loved you so much, how come they wouldn't give you a haircut at least? You look like an Indian." She grabbed scissors from the bureau and snapped them in my face. I hollered help and buried my head under the sheets but she snatched them off. "Sit up! I'm not gonna scalp you." Lena propped pillows behind my back and wrapped a towel round my neck and while she snipped away she filled me in on the local news, which was mostly Espie's wedding down the street that Lena would be bridesmaid in. "And my name's printed on the invitations too," she bragged, "qué cute con rosas y wedding bells and it's gonna take place next month."

My sister's comb made little shivery tracks across my skull and her breath in my face was sweet to smell. Her fingers moved over my neck and ears as if they owned me. Warm loving rivers started running in my chest and my heart beat so loud I was sure it shook the house. When trimming my far side, Lena pulled my head against her and through her blouse I felt her little chichis on my cheek. I breathed deep to taste that pretty smell of her. Was that a deadly sin? If so, I couldn't help myself. Not that I would ever touch her the wrong way. I would die first. But I only hoped she wasn't guessing all the crazy things that raced around inside me. Or maybe she did, because suddenly she shoved my head away like a basketball, pulled off the covers and start snip-snapping scissors at my shorts.

"Hold real still now," she ordered. "I'm gonna make a little girl of you." I fought to cover up myself. "Wouldn't you love to be a dainty little girl?" she teased, "then you and me could sleep in the same bed like we used to do."

Finally she remembered I was supposed to be sick, scolded me for not relaxing, and stomped out and slammed the door. I laid there trying to get my breath back. For all her new tuxedo room, my sister was the same Lena she had always been. I called back ancient history when we used to sleep in the same bed and she told me fairy stories in the dark, witches mostly with long bloody fingernails and hair made out of snakes. At the last minute a fairy named Halloweena always just barely saved me. I remembered too how I used to complain because my sister was always crowding me in the bed. I wouldn't complain today.

I wriggled down into the cozy valley in the mattress that my sister's shape had made. There was nothing like this in the hospital. Lena loved me, my mother loved me and my father too, it seemed. Safe from Death at 114 Shamrock Street, I was everybody's Man of the Hour for a change. So I shut my eyes and slept like a grizzly bear all afternoon.

Chapter
5

TEMPTING LITTLE SMELLS came sneaking through the keyhole. I slipped into my L.A. County bathrobe which by chance followed me home from the hospital, then cruised into the kitchen. For all its cracked plaster that threw sand in the food when the trains passed by, it was the happiest room in the house. Old friends greeted me, my mother's pet stove that stood so tall and proud on its skinny legs, the one-of-a-kind kitchen sink which Chuchu handmade it of blue cement, the shiny-new refrigerator we paid Sears $20 a month for, and the round table from Goodwill where I did my homework, if, as and when.

My mother was busy cleaning birdcages and putting fresh paper. It was her habit to talk and whistle to her canaries and hold birdseed between her lips for them to kiss.

"Those dumb birds," Lena scolded. "You love them better than your own kids."

"Naturally," my mother said. "Can you sing? Or fly? What good are you anyway?"

It was an old familiar argument and I sat there enjoying it, while Lena slapped her angry mop around.

"Look at this dirt," she yelled. "Just look at it!"

"Which dirt are you talking about?" my mother inquired. Lena pointed her mop at it. "Oh, that dirt. Don't touch it. That's my very favorite dirt. We have a little understanding, that dirt and me. I leave it in peace and it minds its own business. And besides," my mother said, "I'm thinking of growing corn there in the Spring."

Nobody was fiercer than my mother with the washing machine. We wore the cleanest clothes on the street, but mops never appealed to her and babies less, especially when they howled.

"Meal time," my sister pointed out.

"Not again!" my mother complained. "Don't they ever fill up?"

"I could feed her," I said to my surprise and to my mother's too.

"Qué milagro," she said, "what a miracle," and fished Dolores from her basket and handed me a bottle from the stove. I was extra careful to keep my sister's head from falling off.

"Don't be so nervous," my mother instructed, "they're made of solid brass, those little rosebuds."

The baby made angry little faces just like my father's till I squeezed out a drop of milk and smeared it on her lips. Then she clamped her gums onto the nipple and sucked so hard she almost pulled the bottle out of my hands. With the fingers of my free hand I touched her eyebrows and her tiny ears. She didn't seem to mind. And when nobody was looking I squeezed her tight.

"My little chicken," I whispered to her, "my little egg." I made wild promises to my baby sister. How I would protect her all her days and if any guy ever got smart with her, I would kill him, no matter if it costed me my life.

"You'll give her gas." Lena snatched the baby. She was the jealous type. "And I suppose you know the hospital phoned about the bill while you were snoring and probly we'll end up selling the house to pay it, if not the Buick too. And don't blame me if we don't got paper streamers for your welcome party. The damn scissors went and broke on me."

Things broke on Lena. Glasses crumbled in her fingers. Plates jumped out of her hands, and the pull-chain in the toledo snapped for her too often. Nobody could quite explain it.

My father came late from work and grouchy. He threw his six-pack in the refrigerator, then pulled a half-pint from his pocket and helped himself to a jolt, which wasn't usual. Whiskey was for holidays. "Damn S.P. and their insurance forms," he grumbled. "Why not send your boy to the railroad hospital in San Francisco? Son of a bitches, and he'd be dead by Glendale! And swear to Junior's birth certificate, and that damn hospital too, $178 for pills and drugs not covered."

"I could earn it working Saturdays," I quickly said.

"Just like you earned your bicicleta," he pointed out from ancient history.

"I could help out," Lena offered, "except those weeks I pay on the roof." She kissed my father's cheek and massaged his neck for him which usually cheered him, but not tonight. "Relax yourself, Papa, you're all knotted up, and besides we're making my brother his party so let's forget our troubles, huh?"

He tried.

In my family we seldom if never all sat down together. My father ate when he came from work. I ate around 5:30 or 5 or whenever my father's well-known whistle called me home. Lena ate when in the mood, and my mother served us all, nipping little bites of this and that while standing by the stove. Tonight Lena took her by the shoulders and forced her into a chair and there we were, the four of us, dining like Americans, and what a dinner. It was the sister of that chicken I messed up on my birthday floating in thick brown chocolate sauce and beans refritoed on the side with my mother's famous rice with tomatoes in it, real Spanish-style. It was my first real food in two weeks and I ate and ate.

I also talked and talked which wasn't usual for me but the words came bubbling out. I explained my operation and drew its picture on a napkin. I wrote out Peritonitis with every letter right, and showed off my Book of Bones. And while on seconds, I told about all the patients I'd seen vomiting or spitting blood or oozing pus down there at the hospital. Meantime, my father drank beers like he had a fire in his stomach. He had very little to say till I possibly started bragging too much about Dr. Penrose and what a good friend he was to me.

"That's his job," my father interrupted, "and don't forget I pay for it with my taxes." So then he got up crossly from the table and went in the living room to turn on the fights.

"Oh boy," Lena whispered, "pray the Coloreds don't win tonight."

Because it was the policy of those wide-awake promoters at the Olympic Auditorium to match Coloreds and Mexicans when possible, which guaranteed a sell-out gallery full of browns and blacks plus a ringside of American sportsmen anxious to back the Mexican race in hopes it might give the Coloreds a good stomping, but it seldom if never did except in the flyweight and banty divisions.

"Socko! There's a solid right to the bean basket of scrappy little Corky García and that one really hurt, folks."

The crowd came roaring into our living room.

"Quit running, coward," my father told our brother Corky. "Knock his son of a bitch head off!"

Evidently Corky didn't hear him. I sat on the couch propped up by pillows but far from comfortable. Every fist seemed to land square on my incision.

"The Panther's working on the midsection. Ouch! How much longer can Corky take it?"

"Break loose," my father urged. "One-two! One-two! Give him, give him!"

Our race was not doing well tonight down at the Olympic. It got saved by the bell. Corky came back with a rush in the next round but ran into too many fists. The crowd was screaming and right then of course our phone had to ring. My father glared at it. I hoped for a wrong number but it was Dr. Penrose and for me.

"Be damn quick about it," my father ordered.

"Sí, señor."

"Corky's down! Yes. On the canvas. No, he's getting up. Four, five, six . . ."

"How does it feel to be home?" Dr. Penrose asked. "Are you being careful about your diet?"

"Oh, yes," I promised him.

I could barely hear his voice, even with my finger in the other ear. It was something about my hospital bill. "What?" I asked. "Could you speak louder?" You can't ask a medical doctor to call back later. I begged my father to turn down the sound.

"Yes, captain," he told me. "Right away, chief!"

He turned the knob like twisting off a chicken head. It seemed to take Dr. Penrose a year to explain about the welfare office at the hospital. All that time my father glared at me and now they were counting Corky out for the third time. It took three helpers to carry him from the ring.

"Coward," my father shouted at the TV. "Gallina!"

"Did you memorize your bones today?" asked Dr. Penrose. I recited two long ones. My father tuned in on me.

"What's that spatoola and badooka?" he asked. "Is it that same little chickenshit doctor?"

When finally, finally Dr. Penrose hung up I tried to explain to my father how he'd fixed our hospital bill for us but my father failed to appreciáte it.

"I don't take their damn welfare charity," he shouted. "You tell that puny little son of a bitch to mind his own business."

Maybe I got a little hot.

"You better not call him puny. You should see the arms on him."

"Do they run around naked up there at the hospital?" my father inquired. "To show off their muscles?"

"I saw him in a swimsuit. In a snapshot picture," I quickly added.

"Was that when he won some beauty contest?" my father asked.

I couldn't stand it.

"Dr. Penrose is my friend!" I hollered. "He takes an interest in me. Is there anything wrong about that? And besides, didn't he save my damn life?"

The next bout at the Olympic was between two Coloreds. Heavyweights. My father didn't bother to watch. Let those niggers murder each other and who cares? was his point of view. So he gave me his full attention.

"Who says that doctor saved your life?" he asked.

"Didn't he just barely get me to the hospital in time?"

"The ambulance got you there," my father stated. "Did he operate you?"

"No," I admitted. "That was another doctor."

"Then another doctor saved your life."

My father was famous for his arguments both at home and at the Aztecs' club. Once started nobody could stop him.

"Or maybe nobody saved your life," my father said. "Let's inspect this question. What did those doctors do exactly? They put you on the operating table, yes? And then cut out your What-you-call-him?"

"Appendix," I said and right away regretted it.

"Thank you, chief," my father told me, "with my lack of education I'll try to remember the name. But! How do you know they cut it out? Were you awake at the time? Did you see them do it?"

"How could I be awake? They told me after."

"Then can you prove they were telling you the truth?"

"They showed it to me in a bottle," I yelled. "You even saw it your own self, all busted up and ugly."

"Yes, chief," my father said. "We both saw it, but how do we know it was yours? Did you ever see it before to recognize it? Did it have your name printed on the side, or initials even? How do you know it wasn't somebody else's What-you-call-him?"

"I got the scar to prove it, that's how!"

"Nobody denies they cut into you," my father said. "That's all they know to do up there at the hospital, cut into people, sick or well. That's how they make their money. But suppose they cut into you and all they found was just a little gas or something. Do they admit their mistake? No, señor. They'll sew you up and then they'll rustle through the corpses they killed yesterday and find a spare What-you-call-him and claim it's yours. And how would you know the difference? Answer me that."

My belly was starting in to ache. I looked at the silent tube. The two Coloreds were petting each other with their gloves and dancing around the ring like there were roses growing on the ropes.

"The answer is, you don't know the difference," my father crowed. "You believe those smart-ass doctors because they wear white suits and went to college. What do you know about the dirty little tricks they play on people? And how about Alfonso Plasencia? Answer me that!"

"Who's he?" I grumbled.

"His friends shot him in the leg, that's who. And took him to the hospital, that's who. Yes, with his leg all swollen up and turning green. So then what do your doctor friends do? They put him to sleep and get out their little saw and cut off his good leg by mistake. After, of course they got to cut off his bad one too. So now Alfonso's coasting through the streets of L.A. with roller skates strapped to his ass, a very big man in the pencil trade."

My father was very pleased with himself. He threw his belly a solid one-two. The one was whiskey and the two was beer. "Or was it Alfonso's wrong eye they cut out? I forget the details, but anyway there's doctors for you."

"For your information," I shouted at my father, "I plan to study and go to college and be a doctor myself. And Dr. Penrose is gonna help me."

"That desgraciado little puto?" my father shouted back. "Help you what? Play stinky finger?"

I buried my face in the pillow and bit on it and pounded it with my fists while my father raved and raved. What finally stopped him was a pile of plates smashing on the floor.

"I can't take it no more," Lena yelled. "My brother's sick!

You want him to die or something? That doctor saved his life. Is this how you thank him for it?"

She stood there waiting to get slapped. Instead, my father gave her a long, long look, then went to the bedroom for his jacket. Lena massaged my neck.

"He don't really mean it," she said. "You know my father, how he is. He's only jealous. Relax. You're all knotted up."

My father came back with his jacket on. He opened the front door, then looked back at me and Lena.

"One certain night those doctors maybe saved your life," he said. "But who kept you alive all those other nights and days of your fourteen years? Who gave you to eat? Who put the roof over your head? Shoes on your feet? Some dumb Mexican, that's who. No white suit, no big words, no college education. No, he slaves for the S.P. Railroad and every day they shit in his face. What's his name? I forget. Who cares anyway?"

My father left the house with the door well slammed. Lena rolled me into bed and sat a while holding my hand. When I pretended to be asleep, she left. But I was wide-awake. My incision hurt, had it opened up? My head hurt too.

How about that back rub? Which Dr. Penrose gave me?

How about Acapulco and Pepe the shoeshine boy?

Dr. Penrose saved my life. But he also touched my naked butt, was it in the wrong way? "Puto," my father called him, could Dr. Penrose be one of those? And what did that make me?

How could I be so dumb?

I lay there hating myself and hating him and his Book of Bones and his white suit from the Ivy Leagues.

Or was it like he couldn't help himself? Was that what he tried to tell me when he loaned me that "Dr. Jekyll and Mr. Hyde" which my colored brother stole off me?

Chapter
6

"BUY ME SHADES," I begged Lena in the morning. My father had stomped my old ones because he claimed they made me look like a hoodlum but today I felt I would rather go out on the street without pants. Long lazy hours stretched out in front of me. I took my time eating my Corn Frosties which before I always ate on the run, then played with Dolores till she needed changing, which I pointed out to my mother.

"So change her," she said. "A little peepee wouldn't kill you."

"She's a girl," I said. "It wouldn't be right." And turned away to give my baby sister privacy while my mother changed her pants. "Are you really going down there to Mexico?" I asked.

"In exactly seventeen days and four hours." She waved her bus ticket at me to prove it, which she wore down her neck next to her heart.

"How long you gonna be gone?"

"A month, maybe two."

"Eee," I moaned. "What about us?"

"Lena will feed you, don't worry."

"Poison us, you mean. All she ever thinks about is her damn boyfriend." I tried a little fishing. My mother claimed she never knew of any boyfriend of my sister, but who can trust a woman? They always stick together. I gave up and switched back to Mexico. "Was my father really some crazy kind of cowboy down there?" I asked. "Did he wear those bullet-belts like in the movies, crossed over in front?"

"His real name was Pancho Villa," my mother said. "Didn't you know?"

Never try to get straight answers from my mother. It's impossible. I inspected the picture of my grandma on the wall which in seventeen days my mother would be seeing in real life. A fierce plump lady stared back at me. How she must have hated that cameraman. She looked ready to tear his leg off, and mine too. But she had my mother's nose exactly, and Lena's.

"How come everybody's got better noses than me?" I complained. "I might even be quite some handsome guy if it wasn't for this squashed potato. Did the doctor butcher me or what?"

"Nothing's wrong with your nose," my mother told me. "You breathe."

Which was what everybody always said.

"At the hospital they claimed they could operate and make me real sensational for $500."

"You bore me with your nose," my mother said. "Hold the baby while I go to the store."

"What if she does caca in her pants?"

"Call the Fire Department."

You can make conversation just so long with a 23-day baby. I tried TV. Nothing. I looked out the window. Nothing was doing on the street. The guys wouldn't get back from school till after three. And even when they did I wasn't sure about showing myself. Nobody had bothered to visit me in the hospital which could mean they had it in for me. You know how people talk behind your back. They could of at least sent me a Get Well card. I didn't care to think about it.

To pass the time I did something I hadn't done for ages, fished out my old sack of marbles. I set up a glassie on the linoleum and knuckled down with my faithful shooter, winner of 1,000 victories and only one defeat. I let fly and missed by a mile. "Just a damn minute," I told myself and tried again, a medium-hard shot, five feet away. This time I connected like a cannonball and the glassie flew out the door. "Magnífico, perfecto, estupendo," I crowed. Which was how Ernie Zapata used to congratulate me over at Boys' Club in the good old days.

Three o'clock finally rolled around. It was time to show myself outside. If only Lena could bring my shades first, but that was impossible, so I went out anyway and sat on the porch steps, wearing my County of L.A. bathrobe to inform the public I was still not a well man. By bad luck my first passer-by was stupid Kiko. He was in my class at Audubon but he came rattling a stick along the picket fence like a kindergardener.

"Hey traitor, where you been?" he yelled at me.

What a reception!

"Where do you think?" I asked, with my bathrobe staring the guy in the face.

"I pity you, man. You're really gonna get it for that Wolfie, man."

Down the street he went, rattling fences all the way. Wolfie was the rat that slapped me round my last day at school. There were witnesses and I was criticized. "Sick or not, you're Shamrock, man," they told me. "And Wolfie's Sierra and Shamrock don't take shit from Sierra Street." That might be true for colds or even the Asiatic flu, but peritonitis? Forget it.

In front of Elva's house Kiko was pointing at me and various Jesters were staring. I only hoped Pelón was absent. Lately he had been cutting me to pieces with that tongue of his. A few months in Juvy will do wonders for a guy's oratory.

And now the Jesters came cruising up the sidewalk in good old Shamrock style, knees swinging high and loose and shoulders muscling free. Being War Minister, Gorilla led the way.

He had brown curly fur all over his face because as everybody knows, if you shave too early your beard will come in very wiry later on. His arms were long and his legs were short. You might not call him exactly handsome but those sad little eyes of his could see right through you to the heart. Buddha

rolled along beside him, then came Termite, Hungryman and
Kiko. No Pelón was good news, but the guys' faces were blank
as ice cubes. They froze my blood, till finally Gorilla cracked
a friendly smile.

"What you say, Chato?" he told me. "How you feeling,
man?"

"We tried to see you in the hospital," Buddha reported.
"Only dumb Pelón bust their cigarette machine so they
chased us."

"Oh yah," Kiko remembered, "you was in the hospital,
huh?"

They all pounded him. He howled and everybody asked me
questions. It was Chato this and Chato that. Before, I was
never what you might call too popular in the Jesters. By
chance I had missed several of their punch-outs and my police
record was pitiful, but everybody respects you when you return from the dead.

I showed off the bandage on my belly and brought out my
sack of hospital souvenirs, the half-moon dish you vomit in,
and a surgeon knife some doctor left on the next bed by mistake, and my thermometer and enough rolls of tape and bandage to last a lifetime. I had tried for a stethoscope but they
never left any laying around.

"Give that Wolfie a message from me," I announced. "The
first day the doctors give permission I'm really gonna stomp
him."

But it seemed they had already attended to the guy. And
the old war with Sierra had started up again after a six-month
truce. For the benefit of those who might not know, Sierra
Street is an ugly little cowpath up in the hills. They're Mexicans, but very low, pure drogadictos, and their sisters are
mostly whores, it's said, and who knows about their mothers?
Since before anybody can remember it's been War between
Sierra and Shamrock, with quite a few corpses from time to
time. A full-scale punch-out had been scheduled yesterday for
after school, only the cops got there first. And anything could
happen over the weekend.

So we talked of this and this and that till everybody got bored of my front steps.

"Let's sit in the Buick better," Kiko suggested, so we piled in. As usual Kiko got left outside but Gorilla let him hang his face in through the window and pass out cigarettes, and we sat there sucking in the good smoke and holding it in our lungs like it might be something more interesting, and cracked jokes and cooled our elbows out the windows of my father's Buick ready for anything, but no key for the ignition.

"I could jump the wires," Hungryman thought.

"And I could pay for your funeral," Buddha said. He had a lot of respect for my father.

Eventually it got quite boring.

"If only Pelón was here, he'd think of something."

"Pelón, shit, I need a woman, man."

"How 'bout that cross-eyed chick over in Dogtown?"

"Where you been, man? They got her in a Foster Home."

"Maybe we could stir up something at Forney Playground."

"She-it."

We checked over all the old familiar if's and maybe's. Everything either costed money or else you needed wheels. So there we sat and sat.

"Going someplace?" Lena teased us from the sidewalk and handed me my new shades. Gorilla blushed. He always blushed when Lena came in view, what you could see of him through the fuzz.

"They're the wrong color," I complained. "I told you black."

Gorilla nearly slugged me for ungrateful.

"See you later, hoodlums," Lena said. "Don't forget to send me a postcard when you get there."

Gorilla's eyes followed her into the house. It was pitiful. For years Lena was the movie star of his dreams. And now he pulled me out to the fence for privacy. "I hate to say it," he said, "but your sister's been seen going with a TJ."

"By who?" I asked.

"By me and not just one time neither. You're her brother,

man, and you better straighten her out, even if you got to
knock her round some."

That would be the day. Me and what army? But before I
could answer the guy, here comes Pelón on a dead run from
Main. He skids to a stop beside the Buick. You could smell
burning rubber from his tennies. Bad news never comes in
singles on Shamrock Street.

"The Sierra," he gasped and blew. "They gonna Pearl Harbor us. I just barely got away."

The Buick emptied.

"Four cars packed solid, man. Cholos, low-riders. I seen a
shotgun in Robot's Chevy."

"Dig up the arsenal!" Buddha yelled.

"Clear the street!"

"Wait wait wait," Gorilla ordered and turned his sad little
eyes on Pelón. "Where'd you spot them?"

"Parked opposite the brewery."

"Why would they want to advertise themself up there?"

"Maybe they had car trouble."

"Peló—on," Gorilla singsonged. "You're lying, Pelón. Remember last time when we believed you? And called out the
allies? And threw roofing nails in the street? And all we
caught was the welfare lady? And Sierra's laughing at us yet."

We were all set to murder that little guy till we got interrupted. It was a noise nobody could doubt, motors racing,
horns blasting, backfires, or was it guns? The Peewees dived
for cover. Ladies snatched babies off of porches, screamed
and ran inside. It was shots, now definitely. We ducked behind my father's gunboat Buick, all except Pelón.

"What's wrong with you?" he yelled at us. "It's only a fairy
story. I made it up."

We pulled him behind the fender. The Sierra screeched
their brakes, blasted horns.

"Chickenshit Shamrocks! Pinchi cabrones. Come out and
fight, you putos!" And sprayed lead from zip guns, you heard
it smash against the Buick. Buddha's kid brother ran for the
courts. A shotgun blasted and he went down yelling. The big

front window crashed at Miracle Market. I saw Wolfie in the second car. We scrambled in the dirt for rocks, gravel, anything to throw, and screamed and raved.

Less than a minute and it was over.

"Viva la Sierra," they yelled and their tires spinned screaming on the asphalt and away they went. Gorilla pounded his fists bloody on the Buick. It had three bullet holes, two in the fender, one in the door.

"Fucking cowards," Fat Manuel called us. "Nobody never dared raid Shamrock in my day," he added, which is Veteranos for you. Buddha's kid brother was yelling on the sidewalk. I grabbed my First Aid from the porch and ran to him. The kid's pants were all over blood, the seat especially. I sliced it off with my surgeon knife while Kiko held him down, and Buddha's mother screamed and screamed.

"It isn't vital," I explained, "but he can't be moved just yet." And carefully mopped up the blood with cotton. People crowded in. "Stand back," I ordered. "Let this man breathe." They paid attention. Buddha's mother grabbed Gorilla by the T-shirt and slapped his face. "You killed my baby," she kept screaming. I tried to calm the woman down. "It's only flesh wounds," I pointed out. "He'll recover."

I had just barely finished bandaging the kid when sirens screamed down Main Street. I wanted to discuss my patient with the police but Lena dragged me in the house. We watched through the window. As usual the cops shoved people here and shoved people there. "Keep moving! Break it up," they ordered.

"Who made this crazy bandage?" one yelled, possibly from jealousy. They grabbed Gorilla and Pelón who were well known to them.

"Did you get their license plates?"

"I didn't see nothing, man," I heard Gorilla say. "I was too busy ducking, man." The cops threw him in their black-and-white with Pelón for questioning. Answers they would never get. No Shamrock rats. Not even on enemies. We have our own little ways of getting even.

The street was still boiling when my father came from work. The bullet holes in his Buick got loudly commented on. Lena put me in her bed while she argued with him on the porch.

"How could it be Junior's fault?" she said. "He was in the house resting all the time." But my father wasn't pacified.

"If I ever catch you with those rat-packers, I'll tear you apart," he stormed in and said, then stormed back to poke his finger in the Buick's bullet holes. I almost had to laugh.

"It isn't funny!" Lena yelled at me, then bursted into tears. "I thought it was you got shot," she wailed. "I was washing my hair and I think I fainted."

"Quit worrying," I told her. "I can take care of myself, man."

Looking back over the last half-hour I was more or less contented. My first time under fire and I didn't panic, and tended the wounded like a pro. All that blood hardly bothered me at all. Naturally I was raging at the Sierra, still there was no denying they brought a little spice into our life and we would pay them back double, don't worry. If not over the weekend, then Monday morning at school.

Audubon would be a battlefield, no doubt, full of cops and double patrols of teachers in the halls and on the grounds. Still, you can catch a guy between classes or at Nutrition or in the toledo. Thirty seconds and too bad for him. But a certain picture came into my head, an ugly picture and I still can't forget it, that time four of us stomped Blackie. There he was on the pavement while we worked him over with our boots. He might be Sierra and no denying he once busted a baseball bat on Kiko from behind, but all bloody on the pavement and screaming and begging for his life like a baby, it made me sick. I had to kneel beside the telephone pole and vomit in the gutter. What was wrong with me that win or lose I couldn't feel good about it either way?

I laid there on the bed while Lena lectured me, wondering Did God spare my life at the hospital only to see me die in battle? And from outside listened to the Miracle Market howling over their busted window.

Chapter

7

IN ALL MY LIFE I never saw so much heat as Monday morning
on the way to school. Black-and-whites, foot cops, paddy wa-
gons jammed Avenue 26 at the bridge where we crossed over
to Audubon. TV had their trucks there too, and cameras. And
there were pictures of the bullet holes in my father's Buick in
the Sunday papers. RAT PACK STRIKES AGAIN was the
headline. We were quite famous.

"One at a time," the cops ordered on the bridge, and patted
everybody down.

"Careful! I got a loaded doughnut in there," Pelón yelled
when they went through his lunch.

"Move on, clown," they told him and kicked his ass.

Boxer was next in line. She was Captain of our Auxiliary.

"No frisking girls," Pelón pointed out. "It's in the Consti-
tution." They chased him but passed Boxer through. And then
here came the Sierra.

"Well well if it isn't the Boy Scouts of America," some
wisecrack copper said because Sierra was all in uniform, with
those black knit watchcaps pulled down over their ears like
helmets, real menacing. "Are we any match for them?" I wondered. Gorilla could take Robot, possibly. Buddha was fat and
fearless. It he charged you, watch out. It was like getting
runned over by a tank, and Kiko when he got mad used to
froth at the mouth. Nobody cared to be around him. With
Hungryman you could never be quite sure. He had his off

days. But thank God for Termite. Still, in numbers the Sierra had us, and how much good could I ever do with my incision which was already starting in to hurt?

"We don't talk," Gorilla told the TV camera when it asked questions and we passed on through the gates of Audubon Junior High. Boxer whispered to me she had her brother's zip gun taped to her chest so tell Gorilla, which I did. She worshipped the guy but he only had eyes for my sister, which is life. So around then the last bell rang and we trooped off to our various classes, Sierra next to Sierra and Shamrock next to Shamrock with strict orders, "Don't go to the restroom except in threes."

"Underline every noun," my workbook instructed me. Nouns are said to be the names of persons and things.

"(1) Oscar," I underlined him, "at sixteen was already the best football player in his school." My workbook was quite sports-minded. Next, I underlined "sixteen" which was the name of how old this Oscar was. Or could it be a when-where-how word? I casually glanced around at my neighbors. Nobody's paper was in view. I erased my underline.

A messenger came in and handed a green slip to Mr. Millstone who was our home-room teacher. I inspected her. She wasn't much to look at but not as boring as Oscar the sixteen-year-old football hero, or was it sixteen?

"Medina, Rudy!"

I jumped.

"Counselor's office."

"Oh-oh," somebody said.

Counselor is not as dangerous as Vice-principal but bad enough, and when I went up front for my pass, friends flashed me sympathetic faces and enemies slit their throats with fingernails.

The schoolyard empty looked twice life-size. It was solid blacktop, not clean healthy blacktop but blotchy gray from all our dirty feet. There were lines painted for basketball and numbers 1 to 12 to line up behind and wait. Today the sky looked blacktopped too and where it met the yard you saw chainlink fence. All we lacked was machine-gun towers.

I took a long look round for Sierra, then started off for the Administration building. I felt like an ant walking across that monster yard all by myself and when I tripped on a crack expected the whole world to bust out laughing at me. Where the steps went down, somebody had pulled the handrail loose. I gave it a healthy shake to do my bit, then went wading through plastic cups and dirty napkins by the picnic tables. A squashed Baby Ruth wrapped its loving arms around my shoe. I peeled it off.

"Tsssss! Chato!" somebody hollered in a whisper. It was Boxer coming from the Girls'. "Gym's next period and they search us. Act real lovey-dovey, huh? They're watching."

I snuggled over to her. She stroked my hair like going steady. And with her other hand slipped me the zip gun. "Get it to Gorilla," she said and left me running. And no time to tell her I was going to the counselor. And no chance to run her down because here's a yard teacher.

"Show your pass," he tells me.

I did. He followed me into Administration and down the long hall, with Boxer's pistol burning up my pocket. The barrel was a curtain rod with a rubber band-type trigger. It saw a lot of duty among the Veteranos, and once went off in Fat Manuel's pocket. And here I was carrying it into the lion's den. I said a prayer and knocked, what else?

"Come in, come in," somebody sang.

The previous counselor was your typical wrestler type, but this one was a fat bouncy little man with blue sparkles in his eyes and wild white hair fuzzing out around his head. He didn't look too dangerous, but then you never know.

"Rudy Medina? Pilger's the name, Max Pilger. Sit down, son. One million years and you'll never guess why I called you in. The principal just received a letter about you."

Now what? People usually complained by phone.

"Dear Sir," Mr. Pilger read. "One of your eighth-graders,

Rudy Medina, was recently under our care at County Hospital." Oh-oh, their missing thermometer, I thought, but it was Dr. Penrose and he praised me till I didn't know where to look, but suggested special counseling. "So, Mr. Rudy Medina that wants to tack an M.D. on his name, sit back and relax while we talk it over." Relax? With The Goods in my pants pocket? But this new counselor didn't look to be the suspicious type, and he even beamed a smile across his desk at me.

"You realize, son, it won't be easy. You need to be tops in every subject, the sciences especially, biology, chemistry, physics. How do you spell gastrointestinal hemorrhoids? You've got to spell them before breakfast. In your sleep you've got to spell them. But God love you, Rudy, thousands of bright boys in your shoes make doctor, so why not you? Let's take a look at your track record."

He opened my folder. Every year they keep a record on you and it follows you like a wolf from school to school.

"Ai-yi-yí," Mr. Pilger said when he saw page one. "C-minus average with a D in Spanish? In *Spanish*, Rudy Medina?"

I didn't mention it but Miss Helstrom's Spanish was from Spain. If you talked Mexican, forget it. Only Anglos got A's with her. Mr. Pilger sighed over every page till he got back to Mrs. Cully and 6th grade at Hibernia. My A's there cheered him up but what surprised him was a certain test they gave that year and IQ was its name.

"135!" he exploded. "Why, son, you scored right off the board."

"Just lucky," I apologized.

He said there were no luckies on that IQ test, then fired me questions. Did I get sick next term? Did anybody die? Or lose their job? Or how could my score drop forty points in one short year?

"Well," I more or less explained, "my seventh-grade teacher claimed Mrs. Cully cheated on my score."

"A teacher told you that?" Mr. Pilger picked up his pen to make a fiery note of it. "What was her name?"

"Miss Kaplan."

"Kaplan?" It seemed to take the heart out of him. "God love you, son," he finally said, "teachers have their bad days like all the rest of us."

The bell sounded off for 5th period. Classroom doors banged open, guys hollered at each other, girls screamed and laughed and happy feet went stampeding down the hall. I wished I could be out there with them, but with that time bomb in my pocket maybe I was better off with this Mr. Pilger. I felt almost safe.

"Rudy," he said when the noise outside quieted down, "in Junior High a lot of bright boys and girls get lost and it's Max Pilger's job to find those buried jewels and bring them to the light."

Could he be meaning me?

"Tell me, Rudy," he asked. "How do you honestly feel about Audubon?"

"It's okay, I guess." Who was I to tell him?

"Doesn't it bother you that your class is reading at fourth-grade level? Doesn't it bother you that every youngster with a Mexican name gets shunted into Metal Shop or Carpentry?"

"Not the girls," I pointed out. "They take Home Economics."

Mr. Pilger sadly shook his head at me. "Hurray for them," he said. "Now tell me frankly, are you learning anything? Do you enjoy *any* of your classes?"

"Maybe sometimes," I admitted.

"Rudy, Rudy, what am I going to do about a boy that one year cracks genius level and next year drops to dull normal?" I looked out the window. Questions like that bother me. "Son, to get two words from you I need a can opener, and it just happens I have one in stock."

He rustled in his desk and came up with a flat green box. It had the ugly word "test" written on it. No doubt he saw my disgusted look.

"It won't be graded," he quickly said. "This is strictly between you and me, and nothing to write down." He handed me the craziest picture I ever saw. It looked like some kinder-gardener spilled a bunch of paint, then folded the paper over.

"Huh?" I asked.

" 'Huh' is right. Now look close and tell me what it's a picture of."

"A giant man-eating butterfly," I said. "It's got wings fifty feet across and look, here's blood dripping from its mouth. Bullets couldn't kill it, so it goes flying around the world eating everyone in sight."

I was pleased with my answer but Mr. Pilger seemed upset. He said there were no rights and wrongs on this particular test but happy dancing girls was what most people seemed to see in that picture. Personally I don't know how they could unless they were either blind or sex-minded. So Mr. Pilger put away that test and handed me another. It had pictures too but more like photographs, and I was to make up a little story to fit them.

"Easy! They broke the poor guy's guitar," I said.

"Where is it broken?"

You couldn't exactly see the place but there was this sad-face kid staring at it, so what else?

"Couldn't the boy be daydreaming?" Mr. Pilger asked. "Maybe about the concert he'll some day give at Carnegie Hall?"

"Where's that?" I asked.

"And isn't that a violin in his hands?"

To my surprise it was. Mr. Pilger handed me more pictures, and I made up stories for him. They were good stories too, with lots of action, but Mr. Pilger wondered why no happy endings?

"That's a sad bunch of pictures," I told him, "so why lie about it?"

"The sadness is in you, son," he told me. "I don't see them sad at all."

"You're not a Mexican." It popped out of me just-like-that.

"Well," he said. "At last. The sleeping giant talks."

He looked at me a while.

"No, Rudy. I'm not a Mexican. I'm a Jew. Do you know what that means, son? You think you have it tough? We've been discriminated against for two thousand years. You should see the street Max Pilger grew up on. Tenements, son, five stories high and we lived on the top floor. Did the roof leak? It did. Did the landlord fix it? He did not. Toilet? Oh yes, run through the garbage two flights down."

Mr. Pilger bounced to his feet, his wild white hair all flying.

"Son, you think Audubon is bad? P.S. 153, New York City, was worse. Our teachers hated us. They made fun of our Jewboy haircuts and our oiyoi accents, but we fought those teachers, Rudy. We fought them for good grades. By being two times twice as smart as other kids. We won our A's in spite of them. We made it, Rudy. Through high school, through college and beyond. From my own building came two medical doctors, one now a famous specialist with a very fine practice. Lawyers? By the dozen. Two judges, one of them respected. Yes sir, Mr. Rudy Medina, we made it and I'm going to see you make it too."

Mr. Pilger sat down and caught his breath. "Are you willing to cooperate?"

I think he really meant it. I think he took an interest. Maybe I had a friend on the other side at last.

"I'll try," I told him.

"Tomorrow is your new leaf. Come early. Seven A.M. I'll have a ninth-grader there to tutor you. We'll work on English first, and God love you, Rudy, we'll lift that C-minus to an A before the term is over."

I believed in him, almost.

"Write me out a pass," I reminded.

Mr. Pilger clapped his hand on his forehead. "Passes! Fences! Policemen in the restrooms!" he exploded. "What are we running here, a penitentiary?"

"More or less, maybe," I told him, and left his office, with my pass in hand and Boxer's zip gun in pocket.

Chapter
8

NEXT DAY I WOKE UP before the alarm clock. Daylight Savings was almost over, the sun was tardy and the house was black but I woke up happy because today I would turn over my New Leaf. I was disgusted with the old one.

What about that zip gun, man? you might be wondering. Did it go off in my pocket? Did I get caught with it, or what? No is the answer. Did I get rid of it in the nearest trash barrel? And throw away a valuable piece of Shamrock hardware? And be a traitor to Boxer that trusted me? No, señor, I lived through two periods with it burning up my pocket and even carried it home, which won me merit badges with the Jesters even if it costed me two years' growth.

So anyway, I ate breakfast in the dark and went out back. The yard looked very different and misterioso at that time of day. A crouching leopard chilled my blood, which turned into an up-ended washtub. The moon hung low over City Hall. My neighbors were all asleep and I was temporary King of Shamrock Street, till I heard my father talking with the chickens. He was always the early bird of the family and preached for us to do the same but when he spotted me in the moonlight he seemed quite cranky that anybody should trespass on his private time of day.

"Qué milagro!" he growled and went in the toledo.

Shamrock mostly walks to school by Broadway to show our face to the public and because the chicks go that way too, for window-shopping, but today I went by the S.P. tracks which was the shortest road and safest from the Sierra. A steady little breeze blew on my back to help me on my way, which was a hopeful sign. The rails by now were turning pink, night was behind my back and day in front of me and my feet wanted to run. The railroad ties were spaced just right to land on every third one and I ran and ran as if I could run forever, and jumped up in the air and happy little yells and screeches came out of my mouth. Lucky for me, nobody was around to hear. Possibly my father was right, this was the best time of day after all and all my life I had been missing out on it.

It was 6:30 when I got to Audubon. The gates were still locked but I got in through Administration where the custodian was mopping halls. Out back the picnic tables were new-washed and the ground too. The place looked naked, not a single candy paper or Dixie Cup in sight. I dropped a crumpled page out of my notebook to dress it up, then sat down and waited for my tutor.

Who could quite possibly turn out to be some chick. They got better grades than the guys. It might even be some Paddy 9th-grader with blue eyes and a stately shape, why not? which would be a new learning experience for me and maybe just what I needed to straighten me out. Besides, they claim blondies often get quite interested in dark-skin Latins like myself, though I never quite saw it happen at Audubon Junior High. Whatever, I couldn't afford to show myself a dummy so I opened up my English assignment which slipped my mind last night.

Our text was supposed to be about a certain Mexican kid named Pancho which his father worked for the railroad and his sister María cleaned house for rich old ladies. The story started out in New Mexico where this Pancho specialized mostly in killing rattlesnakes under the baby's crib. They seemed to follow the guy around like a dog, but now Santa Fe has moved the family to Elmsville, Kansas. It's Pancho's first day in his new school but the blondie kids discriminate him and won't let him play on their ball teams so there he is, sitting on the bench. Except Miss Brewster proves very understanding the way teachers are in books and in the ninth inning with bases loaded she gets the bright idea to send him in to pitch. That's where our assignment began so I started reading:

As Pancho advanced to the "mound," a howl of disapproval arose from his teammates. "Who ever heard of a Mexican pitcher?" the shortstop grumbled. "I quit." "He doesn't even have a baseball mitt," exclaimed the catcher. "Then someone can lend him his," Miss Brewster retorted. "Thank you, Miss Brewster," said Pancho, "I'd rather do without."

Billy Jasper stepped into the batter's "box." He was the best hitter on his team. Pancho hurled his pitch. Billy swung his famous home run swing. But lo and behold, the ball twisted around his bat like a corkscrew.

"Steerike one!" roared Miss Brewster in tones a Big League umpire well might envy. New hope came to Pancho's teammates.

"Oh boy," cried one of them. "Did you see that "sinker?""

Pancho pitched again. A sharp crack like a pistol shot was heard. It would be a "three-bagger" at least. But Pancho leaped high in the air and caught the ball bare-handed. He then ran nimbly to third base. It was a double play unassisted. The game was over.

"Three cheers for Pancho," his teammates cried. Pancho's "strangeness" was now just a memory. Miss Brewster beamed. "This should be a lesson to us all," she remarked. But Pancho had no time to enjoy his triumph. He had promised his sister María to help her clean house for rich Mrs. Murdock.

The sturdy lad ran all the way up Maple Street and down Persimmon Place and into the banker's spacious driveway. Scarcely noticing the presence of Sheriff Trotter's car parked before the towering white columns, he hurried to the kitchen door. Little did he suspect the painful situation into which he was about to stumble.

That ended our chapter and I wasn't sorry. Like always, they then asked ten questions. Number 1 was, "Can you find a good example of foreshadowing in the pages you have just read?" I went looking for one but before I could find it, here comes my tutor. It was no blondie chick, to my disgust, but only Eddie Velasquez from Milflores Street. Eddie was no friend of mine, but in one way you had to give him credit. He was a big success at Audubon, president of this, secretary of that and a straight-A student with horn-rim specs to prove it, but not even Eddie could find any of that foreshadowing my book told me to look out for.

"Tell you what, Rudy," he said. "Get up there in class and ask your teacher what the question means."

"Ask her shit," I said.

"Hold it right there, guy." Eddie waved his finger back and forth in front of my eyes. "How dumb can you get? Ask a question and there's a question you won't have to answer. And teachers love it, Bontempo especially."

We all know the type that asks that kind of question, but why start an argument? So I sat on the bench and Eddie stood with one foot on it and told me the Secrets of Success at School. First, look neat and well-combed and always sit up straight and don't stare out the window. Have pencil and paper on you so you don't have to borrow. Put your hand up every chance you get and give your teacher a pleasant smile when convenient.

"Attitude," Eddie instructed me, "cooperation, guy, that's what gets you grades in English and Social Studies and all those bullshit courses. So let's look at your next question."

"What important lesson does this chapter teach us?" it asked.

. "Learn to catch barehanded," I suggested.

"Wrong," he told me frankly. "They expect something way bigger, like Attitude to Life."

Eddie studied the air.

"Here you go," he said. "That chapter teaches us you can't keep a good man down irregardless of his race, how's that? So don't holler if they discriminate you, just be patient and your time will come. Can you remember that? Okay, tell it to Bontempo and there's an A for you every time."

I could remember, but how could I recite it with Pelón in the classroom?

"I know a lot of you guys call me a kiss-up," Eddie went

on, "but give me ten years, then come up to my office and we'll see who's kissing whose? CPA, Rudy, Certified Public Accountant, that's where I'm heading. And how'm I going to get up there? Grades, buddy, grades. And school activities don't hurt you any when they're passing out those college scholarships. Like for instance, I'm making service points for tutoring you right now."

"Thanks anyway," I said.

"Take one tip from me," he said. "Cut loose from the Jesters. You'll never get nowhere with them guys, except dead or jailed."

I hated to admit it but it made you think. Shamrock had more than its share of early corpses and half our Veteranos ended up in the wrong class of college. Like old San Quentin U. On the other side, there was Eddie. The teachers loved him and right now he was running for Student Body president and had a good chance of winning, it was said, and some blondie chick would be his secretary.

The chainlink gates were open now. The yard was filling up with voters.

"Figure out those other questions on your own," Eddie told me. "I got to go associate. And hey, since I'm doing you a favor, do me one. Line up the Shamrock vote for me, I could do you guys a lot of favors if I get elected. See you tomorrow, Rudy, same place, same time."

And away went Eddie Velasquez, not walking cool and casual like us, more on the order of a diesel locomotive pounding down the track, one Mexican who was going places and I only wondered if I could go that road too. Yesterday I had done my bit for Shamrock. Today I would do it for me, myself and I, and Miss Bontempo's English class was my testing ground.

I'd hoped to be the first student there, to prove my Attitude but of course two Oriental guys were in their seats ahead of me. Possibly they spent the night in there. Miss Bontempo was at the blackboard writing down our Words-We-Live-With. Today they were solid ITES and IGHTS such as right and

write, sight, night and kite. She omitted fight, I noticed, and
was in a big hurry to finish her list before the class showed
up. She never cared to turn her back on us for fear things
might go flying.

Miss Bontempo was Italian and around twenty-six years old
or twenty-four and not too bad-looking when she smiled. The
only trouble was, her smile stayed glued on there too long. It
got to looking more like a scream. She was fresh out of teacher
college and how that lady had changed since the first day of
school. She started out preaching Democracy in the Classroom and Everybody Express Yourself, which was a big
change for Audubon after all those Don't-drop-a-pin-or-else
teachers we were accustomed to. Then one day somebody
stole $11 from Miss Bontempo's purse during Nutrition and a
couple of windows got broken by mistake. She still talked
Democratic ways but as soon as the discussion got interesting
she suddenly turned cop on you.

So anyway, I sat down very studious to copy out my word
list and when I caught Bontempo's eye, I flashed her a grade-
A smile. It gave her such a scare she dropped the chalk. When
the tardy bell rang, the usual stampede came through the
door. Books banged down on desks. A guy from Sierra yanked
all the windows open. A Shamrock banged them shut. Then
came the usual parade of pencil and paper borrowers till finally something more or less like quiet settled in.

"Good morning, people," Miss Bontempo started off. "And
how many of you bothered to read today's assignment?"

Half the hands went up, my own included, though I could
see Miss Bontempo seriously doubted me.

"Very good. Excellent. Now tell me, class, is reading just
some old-fashioned subject we teachers assign to make your
lives miserable?" I heard some yesses but my teacher didn't.
"Why is it we really need to read well and easily? Can I see
hands?"

A few went up, not mine. I hate that kind of question but
all the Oriental hands were flying.

"We read so we can get to college and make money."

"Very good, Wah, excellent. Are there any other reasons? Yes, Gloria?"

"How could we buy stuff at the store if we can't read the cans?"

"Like street signs too, man, not to get lost."

"My grandma can read Spanish even!"

"That's very nice, Linda," Miss Bontempo said, "and I only wish I could too. Those are all good answers. Excellent, but we read for pleasure too, do we not?"

Nobody passed any comments.

"A good book can whisk us off to India or deep into past ages, can it not? Reading takes us out of our little lives and opens whole worlds for us to roam in. Then too, there is another kind of book which gives us insights into our own daily problems and helps us solve them. Our text for instance. Young Pancho and his sister María, are they so very different from the boys and girls seated in this room?"

Slapsy Annie of the Sierra spoke up. "María's working and I wish I was!"

"What I mean is," Miss Bontempo said, "they're both Mexican-American young people like so many of us here. We can identify with them, can we not? And learn from their experience. For instance, from Pancho we can see how patience is rewarded when he proves himself. Isn't that the best way for us to deal with Discrimination? And far better than just sulking or shouting our heads off?"

She had just killed Eddie's fine speech which I was all primed with. I had to work fast and up went my hand.

"Yes, Rudy?" Miss Bontempo sighed.

"I don't get that first question," I told her. "What's all this 'foreshadowing' they ask you for?"

"Why, that's a very good question, Rudy. Excellent."

Pelón gave the back of his hand a fat juicy kiss. My face burned.

"I was hoping someone would ask that question," Miss

Bontempo said. "This is the first time we've met that useful word. Foreshadowing, can anyone tell me what it means? Class?"

Wah said it meant like sunset when it throws your shadow in front of you like walking up Broadway.

"Almost," Miss Bontempo agreed. "But here it means that our author is giving us a little hint that something very exciting is about to happen. He FORESHADOWS it. Open your texts to page forty-seven. Do you see the line, 'Little did Pancho suspect . . .'? That's how our author leads us on into the next chapter."

"He don't lead me on," Pelón said. "He turns me off, man."

"Yes, Richard," which was Pelón's other name. "We all know how hard you are to please."

"Oh, indubitably."

"You see," Miss Bontempo went on, "the writer is telling us to expect trouble ahead, though none of us can guess just what it will be."

My hand was up. I was following Eddie to the letter.

"I could guess," I proudly said.

Possibly it was the wrong thing to say because I was told to stand up and give the whole class the benefit of my wisdom.

"Well, that rich old lady, I bet she's lost her diamond bracelet so of course she claims María stole it and calls the cops on her."

Miss Bontempo's smile left her for far-off places.

"Rudy, I'm afraid you read the next chapter." I denied it. "Rudy," she sang my name, "you're not being very honest with us, and you're spoiling the story. Nobody could possibly guess that from the text."

I got quite hot. "Then how come the sheriff's car's in the driveway, huh?" I asked. "And how come in that other chapter Mrs. Murdock bragged about her bracelet unless somebody's gonna steal it? Anybody can guess what happens in these dumb books, where on the television—"

"You may be seated, Rudy."

Pelón was happy to take over. "Chato's right," he hollered. "And you know something else? Sturdy old Pancho goes and finds that bracelet right where the old lady lost it. In the toledo."

A big scream went up from the girls.

"In the what?" Miss Bontempo was stupid enough to ask.

"The toledo, Oheedo," said Pelón.

"Eeee, send him to the Vice, Miss, he's talking dirty about the restroom," Slapsie Annie screamed.

"Shut your big mouth," Boxer suggested.

Various others had other suggestions.

"Quiet! Class, settle down! I won't stand for this!"

"Look at Pelón, Miss," Annie yelled. "He just called me THAT WORD!"

"I did not."

"He made it with his lips. I seen him."

"Your mother!"

"La tuya!"

Annie was off in Spanish. Pelón said several things in both languages. The Sierra backed up Annie. We backed our buddy. A pencil flew. Somebody tossed a book. Miss Bontempo hammered on her desk to establish some kind of Law and Order.

"He found it in the toledo," Pelón repeated, "tucked away in a big old raggedy—"

Scream scream went the girls.

"—roll of toledo paper."

"Out!" said Miss Bontempo.

"Who? Me?" Pelón asked innocently. "Out where?"

"How come?" I asked. "He was only guessing."

"You too. Out!"

"You're discriminating, lady," Pelón told her. "I'm gonna phone the Mexican consul on you."

"Vice-principal!" was Miss Bontempo's answer.

She scratched angry words on pink slips and dealt them out to us. The trip was nothing new for Pelón, but believe it or not, this was my first time.

"You really set that Bontempo up," Pelón told me in the hall. "Little brother, you done it perfect."

I felt quite proud of myself but as we passed by Mr. Pilger's office it bothered me the way my new leaf had withered.

"Mr. Beaver is busy," the Vice's secretary informed us. "Wait in the hall."

The happy sound of the paddle could be heard. We waited on the mourner's bench.

"He'll give you a choice," Pelón advised me. "Either the paddle or else he'll send home a note. Take the swats. Beaver has a heavy hand but your father's hand is heavier."

Pelón popped one of his uncle Ruben's famous pills.

"Care for one?" he asked.

"Why not?"

"Did you hear the news?" he asked me. "We're gonna have it out with Sierra after school. Fat Manuel's gonna meet us across the bridge. He'll have the arsenal in the back of his car. Are we gonna slaughter them? Oh, indubitably."

Pelón's pill hopped around in my stomach like a frog. I coughed and almost threw it up.

"What's with you, guy?" Pelón inquired. "Did you swallow wrong?"

Chapter
9

BACK BEHIND COLETTI'S GROTTO was where I went to meet Pelón. It's across the street from Audubon, a good-time bar and grill with dancing for Italians every Friday night and Mexicans most other times, of the richer classes. I waited in the parking lot beside the long wall. You could see ten years of Eastside history spelled out there, our wars and peaces and our in-betweens. A thousand guys had scrawled their names from Chivi de Shamrock and Robot's older brother Turkey that became a barber, up to Kiko's ugly scribble which looked done yesterday. There were plenty of Con Safos too, meaning that if you add something to the signer's name like Fuck you, it will bounce back double on your private reputation. SHAM-ROCK and SIERRA took up most of the space with a few sneakers from AVENUES and one big splash of FLATS when they tried to invade our turf. Most businesses paint their walls over once a year or more. Not Tony Coletti. Either he didn't care to spend the money or possibly he was artistic-minded.

I waited and I waited, happy not to be sitting down. All 6th period my pants stayed stuck to my sitters after Mr. Beaver's paddle. At first I thought I might be bleeding but I was wrong. Your tried-and-true Vice-principal is very careful not to draw blood. Parents often get quite upset.

"Maybe Pelón won't show," I told myself. "I'll count a hundred then I'm cutting out for home." I counted, but those names on the wall got me nervous, so many of the signers were now in Folsom, or else dead. My incision started in to

ache. Would my number come up next? I started counting
faster but wouldn't you know it, Pelón showed up on 69.

"Where to?" I asked in the ruggedest voice I could manage.

"Blood Alley, where else?" he told me.

The heat was off the bridge. Not a cop in sight which was a
welcome sign. We went two blocks up Avenue 26, then turned
in where the railroad siding cuts between two warehouses.
You can drive in on the tracks with space to park behind, and
no spectátors. Around twenty guys were ganged up by Manuel's car, or eighteen. I found myself a little short of breath.
Would anybody bother to remember I was not a well man?

"Where's Milflores Street?" Gorilla growled. "Where's Gib-
son? Where's all our chickenshit allies?"

"In my day they showed, or else," Fat Manuel bragged. In-
my-day was that guy's favorite word. To hear him tell it they
were all man-eaters back in 1959.

"Let's GO, man," Buddha said. "Fuck the allies. Unpack
the arsenal."

"Two minutes more." Gorilla checked his wristwatch but
nobody came, only Boxer. "No chicks!" Gorilla told her.

"Free country," she said and untaped her zip gun.

"Time," Buddha insisted. He was very hot on account of
birdshot in his little brother.

Manuel unlocked the trunk. Thirty hands reached in ahead
of mine. Termite grabbed Kiko's pet 2-by-4 with the spikes
and wouldn't turn loose of it. Others fought for various old
favorites. I myself hoped for something long distance like another zip gun but a tire iron was the best I could come up
with. I swung it round to get the feel but it didn't balance
right. And how about Pelón's uncle's pills which were supposed to put you on your toes? They didn't do me nothing. I
felt down at the heels and looked around to see if others might
feel the same.

Not Buddha with his baseball bat. Not Hungryman with his
homemade bayonet. Lobo Villaseñor was an altar boy but he
looked ready for anything as he flicked his switch blade in

and out. And who could doubt Conejo Delaguerra who placed his faith in giant rocks? If anybody felt like me they didn't show it.

Gorilla's bike chain snaked around in the dust while he stood inspecting the troops. "Now hear this," he said. "Sierra goes home by Pasadena Avenue. They'll be close order for safety, maybe scouts out front, maybe not. We set the trap behind Sunshine Biscuits at the corner. When they come in sight we send out Pelón for bait. They chase him, right? and get all excited and careless? That's when we come roaring out and drive them in Goodwill's parking lot. No place else for them to go, no way out. And after that, to each his own. Okay. Move out!"

Who could doubt Gorilla's strategy? It would be a massacre. Except just at that moment a car cut into the alley and came skidding down the tracks right at us. We dove for the walls to save ourself. The guy hits the brakes, his tires throw dirt in our face, and it's Ernie Zapata from Boys' Club, who else? In all my life I never saw a happier sight but I tried not to show it.

"Son of a bitch!" Buddha yells, "who's the fucking big-mouth?"

But Ernie never needed stool pigeons. Any trouble breaks out in Eastside, and there he is. Ernie climbed out of his station wagon slow. He was shorter than most of us but so is a snub-nose revolver. We stood there with all our hardware on show but Ernie had a weapon worth our whole arsenal. Past history. There was not one of us he hadn't gone to bat for one time or another. Police, probation officers, vice-principals, judges, hooky cops, by night and by day he argued our hard cases with all of them. "Give the kid one more chance," he'd beg. "He's got troubles at home. He didn't really mean it. I'll be responsible for the guy." And got us off more often than you might expect.

"What a fine bunch of scarecrows," Ernie said in that knife-grinder voice of his. "What a credit to the Mexican race!" One after another he looked in all our faces and nobody had the heart to look him back. When he got to Fat Manuel he slapped him in the face, good and hard too.

"Bored with probation, Manuel? Want to go back to jail?"

"What did I do, man?"

"You know something, Manuel? Of all the stupid, dumb, vicious, chickenshit cowards I ever met, you're number one. Yes, you and all those other bloodthirsty Veteranos with your big talk. Just aching to see your little brothers mess up their lives like you did yours."

"Man, what are you talking about? I'm clean," Manuel complained and held up empty hands. "I'm going straight, man. Aren't I working steady?"

"Who got you the job? Who got you out of jail? And who can get you right back in again?"

Manuel folded.

"The rest of you punks, throw that garbage in my wagon," Ernie ordered. Last out but first in, my tire iron went clanging through Ernie's tailgate. Our other hardware followed. Gorilla was the only holdout.

"How come, man?" he hollered at Ernie. "What are we supposed to do? Let Sierra walk all over us? We got our pride, man." But the guy soon got bored of listening to himself. "Oh shit," he said and slung his bike chain half a mile down the tracks.

"How can you be so dumb?" Ernie told us. "Even the stupid cops are smarter than you geniuses. Yes and they're waiting for you right now, both ends of the alley. I had to go on my knees to the captain. They'll let you through, on one condition. You come with me to Boys' Club. Sierra's there already. We're holding a peace conference and this time it's going to stick!"

"Peace conference, my ass," Buddha yelled. "They shot my kid brother, man."

"Is he dead?" Ernie asked. "Was that his ghost I threw out of junior game room last night for stealing Cokes?"

No more arguments. Those that fitted piled into Ernie's

station wagon, those that didn't rode with Manuel, including me. We went sliding down the tracks with our bumper nearly touching. The riot squad was there to give us fish looks at the corner. Once they were out of sight, Manuel raged and pounded the steering wheel and fucked everybody's mother all the way to Boys' Club. As I was getting out he grabbed me by the sleeve.

"It's you," he yelled at me and shook me good and hard. "Shitty little stool pigeon, don't tell me no. Ass-licking up to Ernie Zapata like always. Just you wait!"

He landed me on the cement, then took off leaving rubber. I was too mad to find my voice. And this was the rat who'd be my sister's partner at the wedding Saturday! "Liar, liar," I yelled after him too late. It was Boxer helped me up and held my hand, to my surprise.

"Don't take it hard, Chato. Nobody listens to that asshole," she said and walked me round to cool me off.

Boys' Club used to be my heaven back in the old days. Twelve years old and eleven I used to go there after school and Ernie even rode me home when my asthma was acting up. They had a lot of books up there with color pictures of every kind of monster and dinosaur which I went crazy over. I even got so I could draw them very true to life, everybody said so. But marbles was my main activity.

Out back they had a dirt place which they kept it rolled and watered and you could draw your marbles ring out there. Olympic games don't have it better. I stood there three hours a day just practicing. Or sometimes guys would drop by and challenge me. Too bad for them. I cleaned them every time, older guys too, and made money selling them their marbles back, till Boys' Club made a rule, No playing for keeps.

Then came the All-City. Ernie entered me in the Twelve And Under. I beat the best from Flats, and Brooklyn Avenue, Midtown, Hollywood and San Fernando Valley. They barely gave me competition. My father even came to watch me once or twice and Lena was a regular. And then came the finals and a crippled colored kid from Watts. He was good, but not too good. Shamrock was there solid and others from Eastside irregardless of their street. It was a windy day, that's what threw me off. Without the wind I could have stomped that guy, but somehow he won and they gave him a $50 bond and his picture in the paper. Ernie Zapata really had tears in his eyes for the Mexican race that day. He wanted me to keep practicing for next year but who wants to waste their time on kid stuff like that?

So much for memories.

The peace conference was held in the auditorium. Sierra was bunched up on the far side and we sat down leaving plenty of room in between. Robot and a couple others were seated at the long table on the stage and Ernie made Gorilla go up there with him.

"No shaking hands," Robot stated.

"I want Buddha up here for counselor," Gorilla said, "and Chato you come too so you could write it all down and there won't be no arguments after."

They brought me pencil and paper. I wrote down the date in the upper right hand corner in my best handwriting, then let my eyes wander around. Nothing was changed over the last two years, not even the paint. On the wall by the door I saw an old dinosaur picture of mine. It seemed 1,000 years ago when I painted that picture but it still looked pretty good. From there my eyes cruised over the crowd and found Boxer. She was staring at me and no mistaking it. She even smiled. Her face was on the bulldog side but she was looking a lot prettier lately I noticed. Her shape was something I'd often dreamed about, from the neck down. Then Ernie started talking.

"Where's Farmer?" he asked. "Dead with an ice pick in his brain. Where's Li'l Augie? Same place. By God, I've had enough of it. Up to now I've shielded you hoodlums from the cops. 'Who shot Midget?' I dummied up. But now I have a little announcement to make. From today on, my friends, I'm stool pigeon number one. And I don't give a damn who started it. I'm not here begging you to make a truce. I'm telling you. Now talk. I'm listening."

"Let's settle it by a fair fight," Buddha suggested. "Put up your best man. Pure fists."

But Robot shook his head. Who did they have to go against Gorilla? So they yelled instead.

"When did Shamrock ever fight fair?"

"Took six of you cowards to stomp Blackie."

"And how about my sister's house party that you busted up and broke the record player and it costed $500."

"And hit a girl!"

It took Robot quite a while to quiet down his troops.

"Then how about my uncle?" Hungryman pointed out, "which you shot him in the back?"

"I'm real bored of your uncle, man, dead or alive. He's ancient history, man. 1956, that's ancient history."

It took two of our guys to hold back Hungryman, and finally all beefs before last year got ruled out of order. So then Forney Playground got brought up which was our territory but they were marking up the walls. And where do you draw the line on Broadway? And what about zip guns? And how long a blade is it okay to carry to clean your nails with? Everybody talked and talked. I got very bored and Pelón got thrown out for snoring. It was almost six before we could agree on the peace treaty, and Robot and Gorilla dictated me the following:

1. No Sierra at Forney Playground, or if so, don't chalk it on the walls.
2. When we give a house party, you stay away.
3. Broadway is Shamrock turf below Bailey Street.
4. Nobody controls Boys' Club.
5. Zip guns will be de-commissioned.
6. No smart remarks to chicks on either side.
7. If Flats invades we get together and unite.
8. See Gorilla or Robot if you have a beef and settle it democratic.
9. No two against one, no matter what.

Ernie suggested number 10 should be "All Mexicans are brothers," but it got voted down. So then various people had various ideas but nobody liked them, till finally I got brave and suggested, "When the Veteranos say 'In my day,' we either shut them up or else quit listening." It passed unanimous because of dinner time. So we adjourned.

I was in a hurry to catch up with Boxer in hopes to walk her home in the dark, but her father was waiting for her in his car, wouldn't you know? And did he offer me a ride, or any of us? Forget it. He was well known for being very strong against boys or men or whatever. So I stood on the curb and watched Boxer wave goodbye.

Never mind. I'd see her at school tomorrow, and Saturday she would be at Espie's wedding. Fat Manuel would be there too in his damn tuxedo, Fat Manuel with his fat cupid lips and chickenshit mustache which all the girls went crazy over. All the way home I thought of ways to get that guy but none of them sounded what you might call practical.

Chapter
10

NINE NEW-WASHED CARS were parked across the street with
flowers taped on, one car per bridesmaid. Veteranos and older
brothers lounged around the sidewalk suave as dukes in their
snowy tuxes with violet ruffles on the shirts. Raggedy kids
raced their bikes up and down the street hoping to call attention to themselves. Mothers stood waiting at front fences to
see the bride, and their daughters, that yesterday were crows
in curlers, clattered up and down front steps in their bridesmaid dresses like a bunch of parrots.

"Hurry up! It's gonna be nine o'clock!"

"Who busted my bouquet?"

"That damn priest don't wait for nobody, where's Lena at?"

I stepped inside to check.

"Look at this damn buzzard nest!" my sister yelled into her
mirror while she twisted curls and jabbed more hairpins in
her upsweep. Since 6 A.M. everything went wrong. Seams
split, zippers jammed, ruffles tore. My poor little mother ran
round on her knees like a squirrel straightening hemlines
with her mouth full of pins. But now at last, Lena put on her
tiny princess cap with the pearls and diamonds and posed for
us.

That dress of hers had everything you might ask for, lace,
ruffles, tucks, gathers, pleats and 1,000,000 buttons with no
place to go. The style was Scarlett O'Hara, Lena informed us
and the color was Mermaid Green which was the latest thing
in Alvarado's Bridal Shoppe. And there on our old cracked

linoleum stood my once rowdy sister, unless by mistake somebody dropped us down a queen instead.

"Where you been all my life, Majesty?" I asked her.

It was Lena's first wedding, because my father always told her No before. "Those bridesmaid dresses put itchy little notions in young girls' heads," he claimed and even if Lena had money of her own, she had to hunger-strike three days to get his consent. Looking at my sister now I felt on my father's side. She had a certain little sparkle in her eyes I didn't like the looks of, and besides, the chamberlain that would be her partner was Fat Manuel.

"See you don't smoke none of his funny cigarettes," I ordered as she went running down the steps.

My father was working with Chuchu that particular Saturday and he left me instructions not to let my sister out of sight so I followed her across the street and got there just in time to see the bride. Espie came out her front door like a white cloud. Timid, with mousy little steps, she edged down the creaky stairs as if they might be a tightrope, and everybody said Ahhhh. She held her puffy skirts tight with one scared brown hand to dodge them past the rusty nails on her front gate. After her came Don Tiburcio, in his blue suit and tie with a carnation pinned on him. He was her father and his eyes looked washed in wine. Up the street there was a big banging of car doors as bridesmaids climbed in for church. I ran to Manuel's car which was last in line. Lena had promised me the front seat beside the driver.

"How about it?" I yelled at her.

"Ask Manuel," she told me.

Fat Manuel? I wouldn't ask him shit. I had my pride. And where did it get me? A lonely place on the sidewalk is where, with a nice view of their car as it took off down the street. And I had been told to guard my sister. Maybe she might be safe from Manuel in church but how about later? How about that crazy ride they'd take all over Eastside with horns honking? Who knows what liberties that rat might take?

It was three o'clock before I heard horns honking up Milflores Street. The parade swung into Shamrock from the track side, came racing down the street with all flowers flying and screeched their brakes in front of Espie's house for the reception. I went over to inspect my sister. Her Scarlett O'Hara was all rumpled, her little nose-length veil was torn and that famous upsweep of hers was falling down her neck like some old mop.

"Where you been?" I asked her crossly, "to the tornadoes?" Lena only laughed.

"Hi, Chat," Fat Manuel told me and put an ugly hand on my shoulder very buddy-buddy. I flicked it off and didn't hear him, but my sister took his arm into Espie's house. They looked too damn friendly for my taste. It was already crowded in there and people kept coming and coming till you wondered how the house could hold them. Right away the record player started to blast and through the open door you could see couples dancing. For myself I joined my fellow Jesters hanging on the fence. We were not dance-minded.

"You should of been with your sister in Manuel's car, man," Gorilla scolded. I knew I messed up but I hate critics to point it out, and now there were a dozen of them.

"You know those cigarettes of his, and they drive girls crazy."

"Lena don't smoke," I pointed out.

"Or he could of put some special drops in her punch at the wedding breakfast."

"And besides, there's one certain place you can touch a girl and they can't tell you no."

"Where's that?" I asked.

Various guys had various ideas.

"You should go inside," they told me and pointed at the dancers through the door. "Look how Manuel's holding her."

"Bullshit," I told them. "Go dance with her yourself."

Some went in. Others cruised round the house to the backyard where the beer was, hoping. I leaned on the fence disgusted and Gorilla kept me company.

"Trucha!" somebody called.

That word might mean trout in the dictionary, but to us it has a different meaning. I looked down the street. A black-and-white had just turned into Shamrock and now it came prowling up the street. A black-and-white on Shamrock is like a cloud passing across the sun, it chills you. Loud guys get quiet, quiet guys get loud. Some walk casually into backyards, others start flaky conversations and everybody feels Wanted For Murder. The cops raked the sidewalk with those glassy eyes of theirs, and I stared right back at them. They don't like that.

"What's going on?" they asked.

"Funeral," I told them.

"Don't get smart with us!"

They came walking over like a Frankenstein.

"Hands on your head," they said. "Spread your legs wide. Check his eyes," they said. "The son of a bitch is stoned."

"You're crazy," Gorilla told them.

"You too, hands on head."

They patted us both down between our legs to shame us publicly and went inside our pockets. I felt 50 eyes from Espie's house, then heard a well-known voice.

"That's my brother!" it said. "Take him to jail and you'll take me too."

The cops knew better. Pull in a bridesmaid with 100 people watching? You better call the riot squad.

"As you were," they told me.

"Him too, he's my cousin," Lena shouted, for Gorilla.

"Then get him back to the zoo before closing time," they said and prowled off up the street.

"Come inside, you hoodlum. You bore me, always making trouble." Lena tried to drag me in the house but I shook her off. Various Jesters came from the backyard to give me medals for courage under fire and we kidded around.

"Look, look! A movie star!" Pelón pointed up the street.

It was Boxer, but not the Boxer any of us were acquainted with. Her hair was permanented to the teeth and she was wearing her sister Angie's last year bridesmaid dress which was Flamingo pink. It had been chopped at the knees, possibly by a meat cleaver and around her hips those pinky threads hung onto each other for dear life since Boxer was twice Angie's size. What's more, she had painted her face ten shades lighter and here she came stumbling towards us on her sister's spiky heels. Pelón let out a screech.

"Dearie me, if it isn't Pinky the Shrimp! Yoohoo, darling! Oh you're cute and teensy-weensy! Oooo, I could just hug and kiss my little blondie sugarplum half to death!"

He went skipping and dancing round her like some queer gone crazy.

"Cut it!" Boxer growled and showed him a fist. He grabbed and kissed it before she could let fly, then ducked out of reach.

"And to think I once took you for a lowdown Mexican, silly little me." The guy had us rolling. I laughed too. I couldn't help myself. Then Boxer made it worse by trying to catch him which nobody could ever do. On her first step a heel broke off and she fell on her knees. Pelón was halfway to Main by now. I went to help her up but she slapped for my face.

"Hey," I told her.

"Puto," she yelled and picked up her busted heel and carried it limping up the street. I tried to talk to her and beg her pardon for laughing which I couldn't help, but she didn't listen and into her house she went and never came to the party after, not even in her familiar blue jeans.

"I need a drink, man," I told Buddha.

"They're guarding it like gold," he reported. We were headed for the backyard and Fat Manuel passed by right then with a foamy pitcher in his hand.

"Chato, man," he told me, "you look dry as a bone, man."

Again I didn't hear him, even when he held out the pitcher.

"What's wrong, guy?" he begged me, "what I said at Boys' Club? Forget it, man, I was all upset. And hey, how come you

didn't ride with us to church? I was expecting you." And more
like that.

It's hard for me to keep a grudge and that's the truth, so after
Fat Manuel apologized, I let him shake my hand. There was
a bunch of Veteranos around us at the time and Manuel
couldn't say enough about how I said "Funeral" right in those
policemen's teeth. For once those older guys treated me like
one of them and put their beer pitcher in my hands to serve
my buddies.

We found ourself a cozy little spot out back behind the
lemon tree. How rich that good brew tasted, my first since the
hospital. I could feel it cruising fine and mellow through my
blood, and what a fine backyard Don Tiburcio had made for
himself, like Knott's Berry Farm Fruit trees? You could reach
up and pick the oranges, and big beds of yellow flowers along
the fence, and everything so neat and clean, no dry dead grass
or rusty bedsprings or loaded clotheslines to be seen. So I had
another glass and another glass out there in the warm sunshine with my friends and the music came rolling out to us
from the open doors and windows. Till we got interrupted by
a scandal at the barbecue pit.

"Please, Father-in-law," Memo begged, he was the groom,
"with all respect, it's time to take out the meat. People are
starving, and besides don't forget who bought and paid for it."

Poor guy, the meat wasn't all he paid for. There was Espie's
wedding dress and her bouquet, the priest at church, the wedding pictures. Then too there was the hall he rented for the
dance tonight and the orchestra and the beer, even if the
chamberlains kicked in their share. Eight hundred dollars this
wedding would cost him if it costed him a dime, which is why
so many guys these days wish they could get married American style where the bride's father is said to pay for everything.
But Memo's 800 meant very little to Don Tiburcio compared
to his favorite daughter.

"It's my land," he was shouting, "and I pay the taxes. And
it's my barbecue hole which I dug myself and lined with
bricks. And you don't touch that hole till I give permission."

So he swung a shovel at Memo's head. Who ducked. So
Espie then made love to him, he never could say No to her,
and Don Tiburcio more or less calmed down. He agreed to
dig up the meat but only if all those putos in tuxedos went far
far away. Which they did, so then we Jesters pitched in and
helped him shovel off the dirt and take out the barbecue. It
could weigh 100 pounds and what a smell!

In the ordinary way we would be the last served but Don
Tiburcio decided we were good boys since none of us ever
tried to steal his daughter, and gave us the first and finest cuts.
Who cared for paper plates or potato salad? We ate by hand
and the happy juice ran down our sleeves. Manuel brought
another pitcher to go with the barbecue, so we downed it, so
then I went for tortillas in the kitchen which was full of
bridesmaids serving plates.

"Here, take this one to my mother," Lena ordered me, who
couldn't leave the house in public till her forty days were up.

"Take it yourself," I suggested. "I'm a very busy man, so
give me tortillas since I have important business matters to
attend to."

"Lemme smell your breath," she said.

I quick ducked out of there and lost myself among the dancers.

"Lover boy, let's cut a rug!" Elva shouted and grabbed me
by the hand. For all her 300 pounds she was quite some
dancer with a few beers in her, and before I could get away
she had me twirling, Pachuco style, then she hugged me tight
against those enormous chichis till I could barely breathe. We
cleared the floor, and I was laughing and Elva was laughing
and everybody was laughing at us in a very friendly way, and
then Elva gives me such a spin I go flying through the door
and out onto the porch and had to hang onto the post till my
brains quit whirling. So then here's Fat Manuel who has now
become my best of friends, and here's a half-pint of Seagram's.
"Down the hatch," he suggested so I hatched it and everybody cheered. "One more to keep it company!" Who was I to
tell my best friend no? So I hatched that too.

Then it seemed there were Veteranos all around me and they were saying something about those damn braceros and TJ's that are all the time stealing our girlfriends and sisters when everybody knows they have wives and kids on the other side. And somebody better start doing something about it. So they got quite hot. And I got quite hot thinking of my sister Lena and how those son of a bitches might take advantage of her over at X-Cell Packing and elsewhere. So then it seemed we went down some steps somewhere. Maybe I fell because somebody picked me up. And right there in front of me, wouldn't you know it, there's a whole herd of those TJ's at Espie's gate as if invited. And they're all jabbering that Mexico City Spanish which goes so fast it makes your ears hurt, rolling their damn fucking R's like those announcers on the Mexican radio. And now they're actually coming through the gate till I blocked it.

"Con permiso?" they asked me politely in their Spanish.

"Fuck off," I told them in my English, which they failed to understand.

"Got a match?" I demanded.

"Qué dice? Qué quiere? No understands."

"Torcha, trola, fósforo, macha, cerillo," I informed them in various brands of Spanish.

Oh yes indeed they had a match for me. One even flicked a lighter. He was wearing checkered shoes which I couldn't stand.

A cigarette I asked for next.

The Veteranos stood back laughing their heads off. The TJ's looked at each other, then decided to laugh too. Not having papers does wonders for people's disposition. So they handed me a cigarette and lit it for me and I blew the smoke in their face.

By now we had collected quite some little attention. Bridesmaids hung off the porch and scolded but the chamberlains were solid on my side, Fat Manuel especially, and he had a laugh on him like a burro, my good friend Fat Manuel. So then, they told me later, I made a very patriotic speech, I forget the words myself, and followed it with a roundhouse swing on Checkered Shoes which landed on the gate instead because it seems my feet went out from under me. How good that old dirt felt! Who wants to get up when you've got good old dirt to keep you company and everything else in the world is whirling.

Someone picked me up. Someone carried me across the street. Do I remember checkered shoes on him? I remember my sister scolding me all the way, and my mother with a washcloth, and falling onto Lena's bed. I wanted to get up very badly. It was my duty. To guard my sister at the dance. But then she had Fat Manuel to guard her and Fat Manuel was my friend. The best thing was, get a little sleep, treat yourself to a little shut-eye, then you could get up later and attend to all your duties. So I shut my eyes and hung onto the mattress with both hands to keep it from going round and round and round.

Chapter
11

LIFE PASSED ME BY that Sunday morning. I couldn't wake and I couldn't sleep. I heard Chuchu's whistle out front and my father stomping out the door. Whenever I lifted my head off the pillow they hit me with a 2-by-4, whenever I opened my eyes daylight poured into my brains like boiling water, and the early-bird freight train which I seldom noted went rolling in one ear and out the other. And now here's Lena banging in the door.

"Hi," I said from the grave.

She looked through me like chicken wire.

"Some hoodlum I got for a brother," she told her mirror, "Shut your eyes," she told me.

I heard rubber snap and the rustly noise of Lena's dress sliding down over her hips. A zipper scratched. Stockings slid up silky. Heels stomped.

"You can look now."

My sister was dressed for Mass.

"How come?" I asked. She seldom went if ever.

"To pray for my drunken brother."

"Hey, what happened at the dance?" I called.

"Wouldn't you like to know?" Lena cut out. Her diary might possibly answer my question. Slowly, slowly I climbed out of bed and nearly fell through the window before my feet woke up. Outside it was raining and I saw Boxer in the rain. She was picking soggy paper flowers off Manuel's car to make herself a souvenir bouquet. Last night I dreamed her. She was fist-fighting with Lena. Blood was flowing. The referee wore checkered shoes. I scratched that dream and headed for the bureau. No diary. Even the tape was gone.

What happened last night? I had to know. Lena often did her writing last thing in the toledo. I checked there first. Behind the water box? No. I tried the kitchen. And saw the gunny-sack of beans. Maybe she'd plant her diary there, but she hadn't and I made a mess.

"What you want?" my mother asked.

"Something I lost last night."

"Yourself," she said.

"Well, I didn't throw up at least."

"That's right, go brag about it," my mother scolded. "Now hold this baby so I can pack." .

Her forty days would be up next week and she was off to Mexico on her famous bus ticket, I remembered. And hated it.

"Probly it might be raining in the desert," I pointed out, "roads washed out and all. You better put it off."

"Tuesday," she said, "if I have to swim." And banged a pile of diapers in the corner of her paper suitcase.

"How long you gonna be gone?" I asked.

"Till I get back."

My mother was no easy thing to deal with today.

"No doubt I'll take to drinking regular," I sadly told her. "End up in the Juvy or worse. 'No wonder,' they'll say. 'He comes from a busted home.' " I looked over at her. No sympathy. Nothing. "And how about my father? What's he gonna do without you."

"Plenty!"

The way she spit that word out bothered me. Could there be mysteries in my home I didn't know about? But before I could lead my mother on I heard Chuchu's truck out front.

"Tell them I'm asleep," I begged and ran for Lena's room, but they came in anyway to inspect me.

"Poor boy, the peritonitis is bothering him quite bad today," my mother explained.

My father sniffed. I held my breath.

"It has a very familiar smell, that Peri-what's-its-name." His fingers went for his belt buckle. "Answer me, did you drink beer?"

Thank God for Chuchu. "And whiskey too, I bet," he said. "Remember your first time, compadre? And your father whipped you good? Mine sure did me, for all the good it did for either one of us. So anyway, let's cure this boy first, then we can beat him later. Arriba, Méjico!"

Chuchu picked me up like a baby, ran me to the kitchen and sat me at the table. Then he spooned out a bowl of menudo, which is every drinker's Sunday breakfast. Greasy islands of pigs' feet floated round bumping into sliced-up stomach and bloated grains of corn.

"Shut your eyes and eat," they ordered.

For a wonder it actually tasted good and everybody tried a bowl and I could see I was forgiven. Chuchu had made the menudo himself, he was well known for it. And sitting around the kitchen table it got to be like a party with Chuchu telling stories of his most famous hangovers.

"That's right," my mother complained. "Make a hero of this little borrachito so he'll grow up just like you. Eeeho but you men really bore me."

"Tortillas, vieja," I told her in my father's voice, so everybody had to laugh and they turned on the radio. "No vale nada la vida, la vida no vale na—a—ada." The mariachis from TJ sang and Chuchu sang along with them but in a different key. It soon got too loud for my poor ears and I went looking for quiet.

The shed had always been more or less my private property. Nobody else came in there except to drop off a three-leg chair or grab a shovel and that was where I went and made myself cozy on last year's busted mattress. Perhaps I might inspect my personal gallery of hidden pinups and see which one I was in the mood for, but I noted certain bed springs had been moved since my last trip. No doubt to ditch a certain diary. I

reached under but what I came up with instead was an unfamiliar suitcase. It was streamlined and silver-color.

"Hey!" I thought.

Stolen money was my first idea. Which some bank robber
stashed on his getaway? Or drug king dropped? I shook it. Not
a rattle. No small change in there. Just dollar bills, possibly 3
million. The case had a lock which a hammer quick took care
of. Before opening it I said a prayer but to the wrong saint
because clothes proved to be the contents, men's clothes.
They were exactly what some wetback would buy in hopes to
look native-born American. On top was a sport shirt covered
with baseball players and the Statue of Liberty. Underneath,
a suede vest with woolly red sleeves and it had gold chains
instead of buttons. Then a checkered tie and handkerchief
which exactly matched my memory of last night's checkered
shoes.

Damn! Who was that guy? And why did he park his suitcase
in our shed. Detective work was called for. A little book
caught my eyes. "Immigrant's Guide To Useful English, 5
pesos," it translated. "Will you please direct me to the closest
Golf Court?" it asked and answered in two languages. I
passed it by. What's this? Pay slips from X-Cell Packing?

Oho!

Gorilla's warning came back to me. Was this rat banging my
sister in my own shed? I kicked that suitcase. I stomped that
checkered tie in the dirt, and that matching handkerchief,
then caught my breath. Play it cool, guy, I told myself. Get
the evidence. No doubt there's a wife in Mexico and kids,
which Lena might not even know about. I went through a
pack of letters but they were all from the rat's mother and
begged for money. Which is typical. They make big promises,
those braceros, I'll send home every cent I earn, they swear,
but once they're across the line all they know to do is play
pool, go to the dance and dress themself like peacocks. Adiós,
Mamacita, and see you later.

Armando de la O. was the guy's name, if you could call it

one, and Swede's Hotel over on Milflores Street was his address, practically in our backyard. I went through his pants pockets but that tightwad hadn't even left a nickel, only a crumpled pack of Luckies which I lit one up to calm my nerves. And then heard Lena calling me from the house. I slid the suitcase out of sight and settled myself down on the mattress to cat-and-mouse my sister.

"What you doing?" she asked quite cross.

"Smoking," I informed her.

"I'm gonna tell my father."

"I doubt it."

She looked at me very hard, to read my face.

"And now," I told her lawyer-style, "it might be a good time to talk about a certain silver suitcase."

My sister was not acquainted with any suitcase, she said.

"Okay," I told her, "then no doubt my father will recognize it."

Lena broke.

"I was only doing a favor for a friend," she claimed. "Aurora's friend, her cousin in fact. I barely know him. Maybe we danced a few times, you know, or whatever."

"Uh-huh," I said.

"So anyway, last night, at the dance, there was a little argument between him and Fat Manuel, I forget what about, so then Manuel gets mad and phones the Immigration, says Go raid Swede's Hotel—that's where Aurora's friend lives, you see, so me and him and Aurora we took a cab and sneaked his junk out of the hotel before La Migra could get there. So then, naturally he can't walk the streets at midnight with a valise, so then I hid it for him, and what's wrong with that?"

"Nothing," I said. "And it's only right for you to go out of your way for Aurora's friend, or cousin or uncle possibly." Then I put my five fingertips together the way they do. "And you met him last night at the dance?" I asked.

"Yes. Well, I seen him two weeks ago, at another dance."

"Never happened to bump into him at work?"

"Jesus Christ! Shit! Who are you, the FBI?" Lena yelled.

"I just happen to be your brother," I informed her.

"You're a snot-nose metiche. Get out of my life!"

I guess I should have slugged her. Knuckles are the only language a woman understands, or girl, but I wasn't in the mood.

"And don't expect me to kiss your ass!" Lena shouted. "Go ahead! Tell my father, you little snitch-baby!"

· She busted out of the shed like dynamite, and left me behind with the evidence. One word to my father was enough to hang her. He'd beat her up and lock her in her room. He'd go roaring out after this Armando de la Whatever. And Lena would break out and marry the guy, if he was still alive.

But who wants to be a stool pigeon? I found myself remembering how Lena used to nurse me when I was sick with the asthma which was often. She'd stay home from school and tell me fairy stories made up out of her own head. Witches 7 feet tall with green faces and long teeth. And el Cucúi. And La Llorona that goes wailing through the night after her dead babies. And those coloring books she used to buy me with her own money.

Face facts. Lena was going to be 18. All her friends were marrying. Soon she'd get married too, and what would our house be without her? I didn't care to think about it. But marry with some bracero who'd carry her off to Mexico or who knows where? This I would have to stop. But not by telling my father. I'd have to settle it my own way. Somehow.

It was getting chilly in the shed. I went back to the house. Chuchu had gone but the radio was still blasting out rancheras and paso dobles. My father kept time with a spoon. Lena just sat, and my mother was busy packing her stuff into that pathetic paper suitcase of hers, the one she brought from Mexico 100 years ago.

"Hey," I told her. "Empty that old thing and throw it away. I can get you a better one and almost brand-new."

Lena gave me such a look.

"Where?" my mother asked.

"At Goodwill," I coolly said, "or the Salvation Army, if my father will loan me $5."

Lena switched the radio to her favorite rock-and-roll, and grabbed my little mama by her waist and spinned her round the floor. "Shake, rattle and roll, Mamacita," she shrieked. "Tomorrow I'm gonna take you to the beauty parlor and we'll give you a permanent so you could show off for those natives down there at my grandma's." My mother freed herself and Lena danced alone on our kitchen floor. "I'm so happy!" she sang. "Why am I so happy?"

Chapter
12

"HEY HEY, look who's all dressed up like a princess," I told my baby sister. She kicked her tiny arms and legs at me and nearly smiled. It was that same Sunday night and I noted an open Sears box on the bed. "Don't tell me you're gonna baptize her in Mexico?" I asked for a joke, but what else could such a dress be meant for, all ribbons and lace?

"Why not?" my mother answered.

I was shocked. "You mean all by yourself? Without my father or none of us?"

"My mother will be there." She stripped the little dress off Dolores and hid it in the bottom of her suitcase. "Now get out," she said. "I'm sleepy. Quick! Pa' fuera, out!" And shut the door on me.

Whenever my mother mentioned my father, her voice got edgy, I wondered why. I never remembered them what you might call lovey-dovey but in the old days they weren't like this. Maybe even at that age married people had their little secrets. There were too many secrets in this house of ours and I didn't care for it at all.

Dr. Kildare cured his patient of the week on the TV, and I was on my way to bed when my father came charging up the steps. "Where's your sister at?" he yelled at me.

"How should I know?"

He grabbed my arm.

"A brother guards his sister, that's how. In Mexico, even the lowest knows that but up here you don't know nothing."

He turned me loose and yanked open the bedroom door.

"Where's my daughter?" he yelled into the dark.

My mother groaned herself awake.

"In the crib," she said. My father swore at her and shook the bed. She came out pulling on her robe. Her eyes were still asleep and her mouth and hair.

"Maybe she's over Aurora's house, I think," my mother yawned.

"Liar!"

"What's this big noise all about?"

"Public scandal's what," my father shouted, "and with one of those bracero devils, those no-good son of a bitch rapers."

"Who says?"

"Never mind who, it's all over town. But what do you care? Do you know where your daughter goes at night? No, not you. Just turn her loose on the town!"

"Calm yourself. Drink coffee."

They were in the kitchen now. I heard a slap and a coffee mug went rolling, but from my mother not a sound. She was too proud to scream like most. And now she came on real strong.

"You bore me," she said. "All you damn men. Think you're king over us because you got that ugly thing that dangles down your pants. A bull's got bigger, or a burro."

SLAP.

"Hey, cut it out," I called. What else? If I went in there it only made things worse. I felt sympathy for my mother but tonight, in another way, I was on my father's side. This so-called romance of my sister should have been stomped before it got started and I had a feeling my mother knew more than she admitted. Lately there had been a lot of misterioso whispering between those two women and our house was split down the middle, where back in the old days Lena was always Papa's little girl and used to sit at his feet and trim his rocky toenails.

"What you want in there?" my mother called.

My father was in the bedroom now, racketing through the closet. For the .45? I wondered.

"You'll never find it," my mother promised him.

My father knew better than to try to beat it out of her. He would have to kill her first, she was that kind of Indian. I heard the closet shelf come crashing down. Dolores woke up and yelled. My father's face was wild wild red and his teeth were grinding. His fists looked like battlaxes. My mother tried to stop him.

"You'll only make a scandal."

He brushed her off his sleeve and banged out the door. I ran after but already he was in the Buick and gone. I shook all over. My father's voice set me on fire. I couldn't sit home doing nothing. I had to find them and save my sister even if I had to kill the guy. But that Armando was twenty-four years old, his papers said. I went for my baseball bat. And what about the cops? Which always show up when you need them least? And what about their smart remarks? "Well well, if it isn't the home-run king," they no doubt might say. "Climb in and we'll drive you to the ball park." No. A knife was more private. I grabbed the chicken-killer from the kitchen drawer and slided it inside my pants where the belt would hold the handle. My mother sat at the table, eyes shut, touching her bruised face here and there with her finger tips.

"Are you okay?" I asked.

She didn't say she wasn't, so I went running down Shamrock and up Main to Huxley Street. Lots of apartments there rent to braceros, and junky old hotels. Behind any one of those closed doors that rat could have my sister. Possibly he got her drunk or gave her some kind of pill. I could see him riding her with his pants shoved down over those checkered shoes. Raging all the way, I cut into yards and listened outside suspicious windows but all I heard was televisions and snoring. I kept tight hold of my knife so it wouldn't slip down my pants. This would be my first time to stab into flesh. "Don't stab high," everybody always told me. "Drive in for the

belly." I needed practice. Lucky for me, it was garbage night.
I stabbed paper sacks and plastic bags and ripped them from
the navel up. I left a fine trail of garbage up Huxley Street and
people might hate me in the morning, but by the time I hit
Broadway I was quite expert with that blade.

From Webster & Ponce's Funeral Home on the corner I
cruised down toward Bailey Street, but they would never risk
all the bright lights of Broadway, no, they would be locked
into some dark bedroom which there were hundreds of in
Eastside if not thousands.

I was just going to turn back when by some miracle I saw
them at the Mexicatessen. It's the least dark place in town.
Neons shoot red and blue arrows and bulbs wink on and off
till your eyes can't stand it.

They were sitting outside at one of those cement tables
where you bring your food from the service window, the only
ones out there. It was wet from today's rain and a cold wind
was blowing but they didn't seem to notice. They didn't even
notice when I walked up to them. My hand was folded round
the knife handle ready for anything, and under my pants the
blade froze my skin.

"My father wants you," I told my sister, very rugged.

That bracero jumped up like electrocuted, not Lena.

"This here's my brother," she told the guy as calm as if
she'd been expecting me. He held out his hand. Automatic,
my own hand reached out like an idiot. I pulled it back too
late. The knife slid down my pants leg and rattled on the
cement. We all inspected it. I made a grab but Lena's foot got
there first.

"Jees Christ," she yelled. "Do you want to kill somebody?"

"Why not?" I said.

She whipped the knife into her bag and started scolding,
but to my surprise the guy took my side.

"If it was my sister, I would do the same," he said. "What
does your brother know of me and my intentions? Rodolfo,"
he seemed to know my name, "I swear to you by my mother

that I am honest and sincere with your sister. Never once did I touch her the wrong way, or even suggest it."

"Sit down, little brother," Lena told me. She yanked my wrist. My knees seemed watery and there I was on the bench facing them.

"Permit me to buy you a hamburger," Armando begged, "or even a steak sandwich."

To sit at the same table was bad enough. To eat was going too far.

"Rodolfo," he sang in that decoráted Spanish they use down there, "I am not like those others from my country who come up here to take advantage. Pure brutes they are, for the major part, and lacking in cultura and educación." Where he himself had gone one year to the Politécnico and his family was highly respected, to hear him tell it, with a licenciado for a cousin and a far uncle that was a priest. But his mother was a widow and life was hard down there so every week he sent his money home. Oh yes, I knew all about his "money home" from that lady's letters. But I didn't mention it at the time.

I knew it was my place to hate the guy, but he was so polite, what could I do? Especially since I'd lost my blade. While he talked I inspected him closely. He was light color, as light as Lena and more the Latin type than Indian. His pearly teeth were the first thing you noticed. They were on view all the time, a whole mouthful of them. He had narrow eyebrows that met over his nose which was thin and straight and even looked okay from the side, and not like mine. Girls would no doubt call him very handsome. And his hands were like a woman's. You knew he wore gloves to work.

"Rodolfo," how he loved that name, "I confess I am here illegal. I wanted to come the right way but the list was too long. My Mexican papers are all in order." He pulled out a letter which stated he had a good character and had never been in jail. It was from his Chief of Police, as if that might make a hit with me. "What else can I say?" he said, "except that I have fallen honorably in love with your sister, not only for the beauty of her face but for the beauty of her soul and for her gentle quiet ways."

Quiet ways? Lena?

I looked at her and she winked. Wait till the guy heard her banging around the kitchen, so anyway he respected my sister and my mother and my father and me. He didn't mention the baby but no doubt he respected her too.

"Shall I show him something?" Lena asked the guy in Spanish, then held out her wedding finger and there was a ring on it with a tiny sparkle that could be a diamond.

"We're gonna get married by church," Lena told me, "just like Espie's wedding only I've decided on yellow for the bridesmaids because it's cheerfuller and we're gonna have twelve instead of eight."

"Qué dices?" Armando asked her.

My sister had slipped out of her Spanish. It seems she was giving him English lessons but if so he hadn't gotten very far. So then I had to sit back and listen to them rave in both languages, how the chamberlains would wear those new King Edward style tuxedos and they would hire a Cadillac convertible to drive to Church and have mariachis at their reception and a rock band for their dance, and of course, Mexican style, Armando would pay for everything.

"What's he do?" I asked my sister. "Rob banks?"

It seemed that temporarily Armando was making the potato salad over at X-Cell Packing which he did in a cement mixer, feeding in the potatoes and hard-boiled eggs by shovel and the mayonnaise by hose.

"But my true career is artista," Armando said.

He only had five lessons more to go on his draw-by-mail course and would soon earn up to $200 a week in his spare time. To prove it he opened up his sketch pad which he always carried with him. The first page was a big head of Lena. I have to admit it was very pretty but you would hardly know it for my sister, the way he had tamed down that fighting nose of hers. He showed me other pictures too, all dollies in bikinis with left legs crossed over for stylish. They were quite sexy too, except no hands or feet because that would be covered in the next lesson. Till finally I got bored of pictures and threw them the one big question.

"What about my father?"

"I will pay him a formal visit," Armando promised, "to ask for your sister's hand."

"And he'll give you both fists."

"If I treat your father with respect," Armando thought, "he will respect me too. I would let him set the wedding day. We could wait six months, one year even, and both save money till the happy day when I stand beside the altar and your father leads your sister down the aisle with a carnation in his buttonhole."

I seriously doubted any of us would live to see that day.

"He's looking for you right now," I told Lena. "He could drive by any minute."

That stopped the conversation.

"I am not afraid of him," Armando boasted, "I am a master of Kung Fu," but Lena dragged him off in the shadows to say goodnight. She tried to kiss the guy but he didn't let her, possibly out of respect for me.

"Now shake hands with your future brother-in-law," she ordered me.

I hated to but to please her finally I did, keeping fingers crossed behind my back. So then Armando went his way and we went ours which was down Huxley Street.

"How come all this garbage?" Lena asked after stepping on a grapefruit skin. "Did Jack the Ripper pass by here?"

I changed the subject.

"My father's gonna murder you."

"Oh well," she said, "you only live once."

Lena hung lovey-dovey on my arm like I might be her boyfriend, but all she could talk about was Armando and what a fine dancer he was and how he talked like poems, besides being so polite and well-dressed.

"Oh sure," I said. "The guy's a prince and no doubt his little wife in Mexico thinks the same."

Lena threw my arm away.

"There's no little wife!" she yelled. "I asked him. And besides he's very Catholic-minded."

"He's only marrying you to get immigrated."

"Thanks a lot, little brother. You make me feel real charming."

"There's plenty of guys from up here and you've known them all your life," I pointed out.

"Fat Manuel? Your friend Gorilla?"

I named various others.

"A lot you know," she said. "All they ever want is just one thing. 'Come on, honeee, let's make out, huh?' And 'Ooooo,' and 'Aaaaaah,' and 'Eeeeee,' like some dirty kind of animal. My toes get sore from kicking shins. Where with Armando, holding hands is good enough for him, and he talks to me so fine, 'My little green-eye orchid of the jungle,' he calls me in Spanish."

"What do you call *him*? My potato salad?"

Lena blazed and slapped. There was no room beside her on the sidewalk after that. Single file we passed the brewery and the Aztecs' club. On Shamrock my sister's feet started dragging and I didn't blame them. "Maybe I won't tell the whole truth exactly just yet," she said.

The Buick wasn't home yet. Still, the lights were on in the house and possibly he could be waiting.

"I'll go first just in case," I said.

My mother was alone, at the kitchen table. Her left eye was turning black.

"Mama, look at your face!" Lena screamed, then turned on me. "And I suppose you just stood around as usual!"

I ignored her and went outside to watch for my father. I turned off the porch light and sat in the shadows and their voices came rattling through the screen door.

"But I gotta face him sometime!"

"Not tonight. Tomorrow he'll be grumpy but mornings he doesn't slap. Or better, wait till the afternoon. He'll cool down at work. Go spend the night at Virgie's."

Lena groaned. "Why not Aurora's?"

"Because he'll bust in her door which he wouldn't dare with my comadre. And after work tomorrow I'll phone you what mood he's in. And I'll make him chile verde which he loves and hand over Dolores for him to play with . . ."

On and on they went like that. What politicians! My dumb innocent little mother had my father figured to his slightest sneeze. They may claim Mexicanas are slaves to their husbands, but sitting out there on the porch and listening to those two, I wondered if I myself would ever dare to marry with any member of that tribe.

Chapter 13

THE FRONT DOOR woke me up. It was possibly 3 A.M. My father's face was cut and bleeding. The Buick was missing from out front.

"Did you wreck?" I asked him.

He shook his head and went in the shower. He was still bleeding when he came out so I got out my L.A. County first aid and made him sit. I used plenty alcohol, he didn't even blink, and 10 yards of bandages. I wrapped him good. There was a cut on his wrist too, a deep one like from a knife.

"How come?" I asked.

"A little argument," he said.

He didn't say who with, or what about.

"So where's the Buick?"

It wouldn't start, he reported, so he left it over there on Forney Street. "Me and Buddha could go for it after school," I said. The guy was good with cars and had a driver's license too, so my father handed me the keys. To my surprise he didn't mention Lena but fell asleep in the chair instead while I lectured him on infections, X-rays and possible internal injuries. And of course he went to work at seven, bandages and all. Miss work? Not my father, he went the day after he lost his knuckle and no doubt would go with one leg cut off.

I sweated through school with the car keys rattling in my pocket. Forney was no kind of street to leave the Buick on, dead or alive, so at the last bell I cut out for there. Buddha had come down sick but maybe I could get it running.

Most houses are 4-plex on Forney Street, paintless wonders
with a line of front doors side by side and porches upstairs
and down. There's no fences on the yards because over there
who cares whose is what. Winos, whores, small-time pushers,
that's what you find, plus illegals, plenty of them, and no
doubt that's why my father's chase ended up there.

The curb was lined solid with junky cars as usual, sides
caved in, radiators gone, or roosted on milk-bottle crates waiting for the right transmission to turn up at the junk. I spotted
the Buick right away. For a wonder all wheels seemed present
and hubcaps even. It was parked beside a certain low-class
bar, the Arco Iris was its name and its famous rainbow window was busted in 10,000 pieces which was no doubt where
my father had his little argument last night.

I turned the key in the ignition. Nothing. Battery cables was
my first idea so I opened up the hood and scraped the connec-
tions, which were very rusty, and pounded them back on. I
tried the key again. The motor took right off. Did I dare to
drive it home without a license? Why not? I was just closing
the hood when some lady hollered at me from a second-story
window. She had a voice on her like a diesel.

"Pinchi cabrón, get your ass out of there," she yelled, "or
else I'll call the cops on you."

"It's my father's car so go ahead," I answered her.

"You wait right there!"

It took her a while to come down. Possibly she'd been laying around naked. They often do on Forney Street, it's said.
And what a dump she lived in. The yard was solid washing
machines, every make and model and all dying of rust or already dead. Finally here she comes tromping down the stairs.
She was a plump little woman, on the dark side, and possibly
around thirty-four years old or thirty-two. Some kind of rumpled nightgown hung down below her skirt and her blouse
was only half-buttoned up the front and buttoned wrong.
There was something wrong about her face, too, like lopsided,
and her hair was scrambled like just out of bed.

"If it's your father's car what's his name?" she asked me.

"Mr. Rudolph G. Medina," I told her proudly.

"Oh yeah," she said, "so you're his Junior. I remember you from over there on Shamrock. You used to be that sickly kid, huh? I lived across the street, Soco Gutiérrez."

I remembered her when I heard the name. She was famous on Shamrock for daytime boyfriends and nighttime battles with her husband till finally he threw her out and took the kids. Back in those days she was really something to look at too, but now here she was, tossed up on Forney Street with all those rusty washers.

"Who bust the rainbow?" I asked and pointed.

"Your father, with his head, poor man. And it took three of them, young guys too, and no peanuts neither. They were welters at the least, light-heavy maybe. But oh that father of yours, what a man! I seen it all from start to finish. I work there, see, at the Arco Iris, you know, making enchiladas, serving beer and all, so in comes your father which I hadn't seen him in years and he walks over to the table of them three guys. Asks, is anybody by chance acquainted with his daughter? He asked real polite too, but they gave him a dirty answer, no respect. So then he says this and they say that. His back's to the rainbow, huh? And when he looks the other way they charge him and down he goes and busts the glass with his poor head. Quit? Not him! Did you ever see a tiger? That's him. Bounces off the floor and piles all over them."

She was acting it out now throwing lefts and rights. "This one's on the floor but he gets up. Saaahhhs! Your daddy kicks him in the belly. Adiós. And grabs the other two and knocks their heads together. Then here comes number four charging from across the room, but I hit him over the head with a bottle. So then it was quite peaceful."

"Did the cops come?" I asked.

"Nah, we handle these things on our own. And them three promised to pay for the rainbow, and they will too because we know just who they are and where they work. Eeeho, what a man, that father of yours, you should be proud of him. They don't come like him these days."

She sighed as if she meant it, then checked me over up and down. "Hey," she said, "look at you way up there, how you've grown. I'm a shrimp beside you. How many years you got?"

"Sixteen," I said and stood my tallest.

"Well well, what do you know? You don't look much like your daddy but maybe you take after him in other ways. Got a cigarette?"

By good luck I still had Armando's Luckies. I gave her one and she steadied my match with her hand. This was the first lady or woman I ever lit up for and we stood there smoking on the curb quite cozy and I found myself noting how she filled up her clothes. Those buttons on her blouse looked ready to pop any minute and spill out the contents. Some might call her a little old and beat-up, but then I saw the only thing wrong with that lady's face was eyelashes, very long and sexy on one side but naked on the other. If I concentrated on her better eye I could see her quite gorgeous the way she used to be on Shamrock. Maybe she noted how I looked at her.

"I lost half my beauty down the toilet this morning," she explained, "so please look the other way. Would you care for a Coke or something? I got one cold upstairs."

"Thanks anyway," I told her. "I got to take the car home."

It was out before I knew it. If only I'd said Yes, we could go upstairs together. It would be dark up there.

"You sure you got a driver's license?" she asked me.

"Oh sure," I said. "Why else would my father give me his keys?"

I banged down the hood and swung myself into the driver's seat. "See you round," I casually called. In the mirror I saw her looking after me. "A Coke," she had said. "Or SOMETHING." What kind of something? Up in that room of hers there was no doubt a bed. The covers would be thrown back and trailing on the floor. She would reach that plump little hand into the refrigerator. "I'll have a beer myself," she'd say. "Me too," I'd say. "Well happy days and nights," I'd say and clank our bottles. Skin would touch skin. Why not? You know what they say about those divorciadas, they can't ever get enough of it. And prefer young guys too.

"Just relax," she'd whisper. "Don't get excited. Trust me."

I dreamed myself in heaven. But why, oh why didn't I at least ask her for a raincheck? How could I be so dumb? Cars honked and cut around me, I drove so slow. I took forever crossing Main. When I pulled up at the house I smelled rubber. Damn, I'd driven all that way with the handbrake on. Oh well. I ran for the shed to cure my shakes. I couldn't wait but there was Lena calling from the porch which ruined everything.

"Lucky you didn't kill nobody." She stood drinking coffee with not a mark on her. I went in the kitchen. My mother's eye was swollen shut. And my father had gone to work with cuts all over him from the Arco Iris, while there stood my dear sister that caused all our troubles forking herself casual leftovers from the frying pan.

"That's right," I told her. "Stuff your gut and to hell with everybody."

"What's wrong with him?" Lena asked my mother.

"My father fought and bled for you last night," I yelled. "Don't that mean nothing to you?"

"Was it my fault I suppose? Did I ask him to go raving round the town?"

I spoiled my sister's little snack and spoiled it good. In detail I described the battle at the Arco Iris, adding extra braceros for excitement, and extra blood till even Lena got scared and anxious.

"You better not be here when he gets home," I warned, but to give her credit, Lena stood her ground. In the bedroom my mother was carefully unpacking her suitcase. "How come?" I asked her. She didn't say but we all knew it was for Lena's sake.

My father's feet sounded heavy on the front steps. I got ready to duck but his face showed nothing except that he had ripped off all the fine bandages I put on it. I expected him to slap my sister good and that would only be starters. But he didn't. My father was full of surprises and his voice when he finally talked was like every day.

"With any other father in the world you'd be already on the floor and begging for mercy," he told Lena. "And I hope you appreciate it."

"You could hit me, Papa," Lena answered very humble, "if it would make you feel better."

"All I want is the truth," he said, "right from the beginning."

"Well, Papa," Lena said, "I met Armando on the Main Street bus, only I didn't exactly meet him there, see? but that's where I saw him first. I was just getting off at the corner, see? and I had my little gift for Espie's shower. That was last month, remember? It was towels I got her, real pretty ones with roses on. Well, he got off the bus too and started after me. It was dark so I walked faster. I even went running in Espie's gate but here he comes right behind me. Do you happen to be following me?' I tell him. 'Absolutamente no, señorita,' he says. 'Liar!' I was gonna let him have it with my shoulder bag only Espie opens her door right then and it seems he's a far cousin of hers, and he's bringing a present for her too. Eeeho, was I blushing? So anyway we talked real fine about crazy coincidents and all. Armando's very polite, Papa, and very educáted too. You should hear his Spanish. So anyway, after that we casually started seeing each other here and there, from time to time."

"Without permission," my father pointed out.

"Kind of," Lena had to admit. "Papa, I really love him and he loves me too and what's more he wants to marry me."

To me it sounded more or less like the truth, only it was a different truth from yesterday's. And I was happy that Lena had omitted me and the suitcase and the Mexicatessen.

"How long pregnant are you?" my father asked.

Lena screamed. "Papa, I'm not like that! And besides Armando respects me!"

"He's kissed you, don't deny it."

Lena didn't.

"And put his hands on you here. And here. And here. 'Just one little touch, honeee. And come to my room and prove you love me.' "

"Jees Christ, shit," Lena screamed and buried her face.

"I don't care to listen to that kind of talk," my mother said, "your own daughter too."

"It's only Facts of Life I'm talking," said my father. "I know all these little tricks of theirs."

"I bet you do," my mother told him.

He started playing with the sugar, scooped it out with a spoon, dumped it back in the bowl, then he sighed and wiped what could be a tear from his left eye.

"All my life I've tried to be a good father. I've put the roof over your head—"

"Who paid for it? I did!" Lena interrupted but he didn't hear.

"—Were you ever hungry? Clothes? Buy anything you need. At night I used to pick you up when you dreamed those witches and took you in to sleep with us. But now you're seventeen years old and bored of us. Maybe you could help your mother with the baby, but no. Forget it. You've found some slick suave stranger that talks of roses and pets you like a cat. So it's 'Goodbye, Papa, adiós. He's the one I love, not you.' Why not? Forget it. What else is new?"

Lena always cried when my father played the violin and now her tears came rolling down. "I'm not forgetting you, Papa," she bawled. "And I'm real thankful for what you done for me in my life. But it's only human to get married someday. And we're not gonna move away or anything. We plan to live real close by and Armando will love you like a son if only you'll let him."

"By the way," my father asked, "what happens to be his family name?"

"He's Armando de la O.," said Lena proudly.

"De la O.? That's no name. De la O-what? de la Zero? de la Orina?"

"Stop stop, stop!" Lena wailed. "He comes from important people. It's an antique Spanish name! ... Oh, why can't we be like those Americans on the television where a girl can bring her sweetheart home to dinner and they talk things over civilized?"

"Because they don't give a damn about their daughters, those gringos. They're so glad to get rid of them they even pay for the wedding if you can believe it."

"I give up," Lena said.

"Where does he live right now?" my father casually asked.

My sister opened her mouth then shut it.

"I don't trust you, Papa."

"Do you think I want to harm him? Not me. Never. I'm a law-abiding man," my father claimed. "And if this Armando No-name is brave enough to call on me I would be glad to listen to him. And now with your permission—"

My father stepped out back humming a happy little tune.

"Do you believe him?" Lena asked my mother.

"No," my mother said.

"Watch him out the door," Lena ordered. "I gotta phone Armando. He's coming over right now. I told him no, but he's very headstrong."

"He better be," I said. "Or else wear a helmet."

My sister dialed some number. The phone rang and rang. "Please, somebody answer, please!" They did, and Lena started shaking and stamping her feet on the floor. "No!" she said, then, "No, no!" again, then hung up the phone and started wailing.

Because the Immigration had picked up Armando in the morning, him and all his friends. And shipped them back to Mexico.

"What's all this noise?" my father came back and asked.

"It's all your damn fault," my sister screamed at him and ran into her room and slammed the door.

"What now?" he asked.

"La Migra," I explained. "They got him."

My father smiled the brightest smile I'd seen on him for years.

"Well now," he said. "I'll really miss seeing that young man but I hope he'll be very happy down there in Mexico with his wife and kiddies."

Chapter
14

THURSDAY NIGHT when everybody was asleep, cardboard signs went up on Shamrock Street. They even nailed one to the telephone pole by our house. I saw it in the morning on my way to school and in the afternoon my father dragged me outside to translate for him. Lena was our usual interpreter but since Monday she wasn't speaking. The sign seemed to say something about the S.P. Railroad and Zone M-1 and then there were a gang of numbers, 800 feet this way, 1,200 feet that way. It was a mystery to me.

"Speak up! You're nine years in school so prove it," my father said, which was one of his most favorite sayings.

"It's only a lot of boring railroad business," I explained. "Something about O'Higgins's tracks." But my father remembered that O'Higgins from somewhere and went rustling in the closet and brought out the house papers to compare.

"Railroad nothing!" he said. "O'Higgins tracks that's us, so interpret me that sign from the beginning.

"Eeee," I told him. "They don't even got those words in Spanish."

Lucky for me, Chuchu passed by right then. Fifteen years in construction he knew all there was to know about real estate. Twice he read the notice to himself with both lips moving, then cleared his throat and let us in on his discoveries.

"It's City Planning, compadre," he said. "S.P. wants Shamrock zoned M-1. I forget just what that M means but probly it's Meat-packing or Motels or something like that."

"Manufacturing," Virgie pointed out. Trust her to show up whenever she could demonstrate her high school diploma, so Chuchu left.

"What it is, compadre," she explained, "they want to take over Shamrock to put up factories. That's good news for you, compadre. They'll give you a good price, and all cash too."

"I don't sell," my father stated.

"Be reasonable, compadre. Who can stop S.P.?"

"I pay my taxes," my father shouted, "and nobody don't put no factory on top of me. In Mexico, yes, they do like that, but we got justicia in the U.S.A. like it said in my citizenship book, even if I missed the examination."

"Oh, it'll all be legal, compadre. Go to the hearing next week at City Hall and talk. They'll listen to you but in the end those City Planners vote just like S.P. wants them to. This is no time to be stubborn, compadre. You can get twice what you paid. I've even heard 8,000."

Virgie talked my father up the steps and into the house. To my surprise he even listened which he seldom if ever did to any woman and it froze my blood. New friends? New neighborhood? New school? Why not die better? But Virgie went on and on. "Think of Lena, compadre. That darn bracero won't stay in Mexico forever and when he comes back Lena's gonna marry him. She'll be eighteen. Open your eyes, compadre, is this any place for an artistic-minded girl like her? Where if you bought a nice new home she could pick out the rugs and drapes and decorate for you. Take it from me, compadre, with a chance like that she'd soon forget all about that Armando guy. And it just so happens there's a darling little house for sale across the street from our new one. And Saturday when we move in you could meet the salesman and talk it over."

"How much down?" my father asked.

"Only 1,500, compadre, and oh you can't believe how beautiful everything is out there, so new and up-to-date. Even our doorbell don't just go buzz. It plays a real pretty tune and just wait till you hear it."

I hoped that day would be never, but Saturday Arturo had to be at their new home to meet the truck from Sears with the furniture, so of course my father volunteered me to help load their old junk onto the trailer from the Rentals. Most generally, when people move out, there's a lot of fine excitement. Stuff gets lost or smashed, kids get slapped. Not Virgie. She lined up her kids, gave them their orders and off they scooted like on tracks. Debra, Dennis, Denise and Darwin were their names, possibly for Discipline. At school they were famous for A students but on Shamrock they were nothing. You barely noticed them for good or bad.

To save money for her dream home, Virgie rented out the front house and lived in the little shack in back, one tiny bedroom with her four kids sleeping sideways on the mattress. Her living room was so cozy you had to put the armchair on the porch to open up the couch at night. So we cleared out the furniture, me and my father doing all the heavy lifting. When we got it empty that little home looked very pitiful with only Arturo's Mexican-hero pinups hanging tattery on the walls. My father looked back in and sighed but you didn't notice Virgie spilling any tears.

"Overstuff goes to the dump, compadre," she told my father, "and pillows and mattresses. There's sure to be cucarachas in the stuffing and for once in my damn life I'm gonna turn on my kitchen light and not see a single devil running for his crack. Darwin, bring the Bug-go."

Virgie was very scientific. Before anything could go into the trailer she sprayed it good, the chrome dinette set, the pots and pans and groceries and even the wet wash off the line. She sprayed the TV through those little holes in back and even the antenna off the roof. And how that Bug-go stank!

I liked better Chuchu's X-terminator which he brought to our house one night after the bars closed and woke us up and herded us into the kitchen. It was a demonstrator model, he announced and fully guaranteed. Then he opened a box. A young duckling it turned out to be, and when the light went on you should have seen that duck go for the cucarachas, slipping and slapping on the linoleum and quack-quacking with excitement while he fielded them right and left in his noisy bill. Survivors climbed the walls but in Chuchu's big hands the duck snapped them off the plaster like a pro. It was a comical sight and for a week that duckling was our main event. It took the place of television till finally the poor thing died. Too much roach powder next door was my father's idea because your cucaracha is a constant cruiser and you never know if the roach you kill is your own or belongs to poison-minded neighbors down the street.

So anyway, when we got the trailer loaded and all roped down, my mother brought the baby and Virgie stacked in her kids till the Buick was packed solid, even without Lena who had to work.

"Too bad there isn't any room for me," I was happy to point out.

"Debra can sit on your lap, Junior," Virgie ordered, "if that won't kill you."

Debra, how thrilling! She was around my age but too skinny to pay attention to, plus she wore those big round lenses that made her eyes look like a couple of turtles swimming in their bowls, but when Debra got out to let me in under, I noted improvements. New glasses, number 1, very long and snaky that turned her quite Oriental and mysterious. Also there were certain pleasant little bulges here and there which I had never seen on her before. So I quit arguing and shoved into the front seat next to Virgie and Debra slid onto my lap.

"Hey!" I thought. Because she sat just right. My father got us rolling and right away something started to take place in me. I did my best to argue with it. "This chick is a dead fly and you know it," I told myself. "Besides there's a time and place for everything and sitting next to her mother is definitely not it. So quit!" I ordered, "Lay down. Take it easy." But who can fight against Mother Nature?

"We should Americaníze ourself, compadre," Virgie announced. "Just because we're Mexicans by blood is that any reason for us to crowd up together on the wrong side of the tracks? We discrimináte ourself, and you should think about it."

I could settle better for romantic music but we got Virgie's commercial instead. I tried to think seriously about discrimination. I really concentráted on what was coming in my ears but I was going crazy in another place. Maybe I even jiggled around some.

"Am I too heavy for you, Junior?" Debra asked me kindly.

"It's okay," I said in what came out a very funny voice. We fitted together like lock and key. Didn't she feel something going on? What if suddenly she hollers rape? But strange to say, she didn't so I gave up trying to fight myself. Every little bump took me to heaven, till finally I got quite reckless.

"It's shorter by Zonal Street," I casually told my father.

"Too bouncy for the trailer," was his disappointing answer.

When we turned onto the Freeway I fell in love. Debra's hair blew softly over my cheek, her little hand perched like a canary on my arm. My rocket busted and showers of sparks coasted slow and gentle through my blood while we cruised out east, just gently swaying, and Virgie talked and talked.

"And I'll tell you something else, compadre," she told my father. "The schools are better out this way too, all grass and trees like in a park so our kids could take advantage of their studies and go on to college even and amount to something in the world."

I shut my eyes and made movies. We would move out and live across the street. Every night Debra would help me with my homework while we held hands, and other things. Debra would turn over my New Leaf for me which I couldn't on my own. And I would round off some of her square corners. I saw us walking lovey-dovey at Nutrition through all that grass and trees. And bushes, we would sit behind them and she would light my cigarette like in commercials and I would light up hers which was one subject I could be her teacher in, and drinking beer was another. Who knows? Virgie could be right for once. Back on Shamrock I might easily end up in jail or dead, where if my father bought that cute house with the red door I could well end up doctor. And Debra would be my nurse.

"Calling Dr. Medina," the squawk box would shout.

"Piss off, Mabel, I'm in surgery," I would inform them with my scalpel in my hand. But oh those weekends! We would never leave our well-appointed bedroom or put on clothes. "Where did my father and mother go wrong?" I asked myself. Always fighting or snoring, they forgot the Best Things In Life. They wasted twenty-three hours and forty minutes out of every day. Possibly no education was the answer unless it was old age. And the Buick floated on out east along the Freeway.

"Where's it at? In Arizona?" my father finally asked.

"There's our sign," Virgie pointed out. "Hacienda Allegro, that's us."

"I only hope their houses are better than their Spanish," my father grumbled.

Through Debra's blowing hair I peeked out at where my future might be located and saw miles and miles of new white roofs.

"Just think, compadre," Virgie said, "a year ago there was nothing out this way, only orange trees."

We drove down a curvy street with all new homes which matched exactly except the doors. Lawns like carpets to the curb. Could anyone believe our good old Virgie would actually live out here? Sure enough, there was Arturo with his familiar beer can, leaning on the mailbox.

"Welcome to the North Pole," he shouted, and hugged my father as if he hadn't seen him in 100 years. Debra hopped out like a butterfly but I climbed out slow and sluggish.

"Hurry up, Junior, what's wrong with you?" Virgie told me.

"I just had a heart attack," I said mysteriously in Debra's direction.

"Take your hands out of your pockets, dummy, unrope the trailer," my father ordered.

"Debra, hang the wash on the line," Virgie directed. "Dennis and Denise, take Darwin to watch Little League so he won't be pestering. The field's only a block away, comadre. Everything is so close and convenient out here."

"How far to the Aztecs' club?" Arturo loudly asked, and reached into his mailbox for another beer.

"You've had enough, Arturo," Virgie stated.

"Call me Arthur if you please. I have been promoted. I am a very big man out here among the Eskimos." And he pointed to his name spelled American on the mailbox. "Nobody talks out here, compadre. They must be deaf and dumb," he told my father. And stated he'd already seen the house when Virgie tried to coax him in. Anyway she herded us up the walk and rang her famous doorbell so we could hear the music.

We stepped inside on solid carpet wall-to-wall and softer than a bed. In all my life I had never been in a really high-class home like that one. I'd seen similar on the television but Americans always lived in them. And could you believe our Virgie owned all this? My mother's comadre from her familiar shack on Shamrock? Beside me was my father bulging out of his air-condition T-shirt and my timid little mother and me, and we all seemed out of place.

Believe it or not, that living room was 20 feet long or 18. One end was solid glass with a glass door you could drive a car through, and it slided sideways if you just barely touched it. The walls were rich creamy avocado color and not one crack or patch in all that plaster, no light bulb swinging from the ceiling here, just standing lamps and sitting lamps with lampshades bigger than umbrellas. And the furniture had not once been sat on.

"All my life I've lived with second-hand," Virgie preached, "first my father's house, then my own. Salvation Army and Goodwill, they were my department stores, and sometimes the city dump. Day-olds from the bakery, dented tomato cans, sunburned shirts from store windows. Never two chairs alike and lucky if one shoe matched the other. To me the prettiest thing in the world is a price tag without a Fire Sale on it. Compadre, from twelve years old I worked for those American ladies back there in Tucumcari. Why shouldn't we live like that? We're as good as them, or almost anyway."

We looked and turned and looked some more.

"I'm Cape Cod outside," Virgie explained, "but indoors I went all the way with French Provincial. That's how come all the curly chair legs. The decorator from Sears explained us everything, she was so nice, and showed us where each piece of furniture should fit and color-coordinated the whole house from the carpet up."

The coffee table was paved with a thick slab of glass and through it you saw monster fish with curly tails but from the waist up those fish were naked women with bright red nipples, which was Arturo's idea, Virgie said, then led us to the kitchen.

"Notice all my built-ins, even the broom's got its little house, and all pure knotty pine. Of course it's All-electric and Step-saver—designed by Spacial Engineers. They thought of everything, comadre."

"How many steps to the restroom?" my father asked, "or do I go out back in the corral?" Virgie escorted us to the Master Bath, they had two if you can believe it, all gleaming green tile and the toledo wore a fuzzy overcoat which was color-coordinated with the rug. When Virgie touched the handle it flushed quiet as a Cadillac and the water came down blue like the Pacific Ocean.

"What if I shoot something in there that's the wrong color?" my father joked.

"Ai, compadre!" Virgie closed the door on him then toured me and my mother to a pink bedroom with silver dancing girls and lattice on the wallpaper. There were twin beds for Debra and Denise that always slept on a mattress with Dennis and Darwin. "We picked Old Rose for our basic color here," Virgie said, "on account of the high school pompoms. They're chocolate and chartreuse so they'll contrast nice hanging on the wall when Debra goes out for drill team. But just try the beds, comadre. Sit down, make yourself at home."

My mother was careful to dust her skirt before perching on

the satin spread, and kept Dolores safely on her lap. The spread had lace too, like bridesmaids.

"Can't you just see Lena in a room like this?" Virgie asked.

I couldn't. Through the wall I heard my father's firehose stream splashing in the toledo. It seemed the wrong noise to be hearing in Debra's bedroom, but Virgie covered it up with talk. "And there's another thing for you to think about," she told my mother. "A house like this is what my compadre needs to keep his nose to the grindstone instead of banging round the town and drinking beer and you know what all else. The payments, comadre, they'll make him save and be responsible. The payments will make a new man of him, like they have Arturo."

Bored of Virgie's voice, I cruised the living room, stroking the new upholstery and petting the deep-pile rug. Till I saw myself in the gold mirror. I looked just like a thief. Keeping myself in sight I tried to casually saunter round as if I owned the place and even sat in an armchair and stretched, but I failed to be persuaded that I belonged in all this luxury, or ever could.

Where was Debra? Possibly she might convince me. I found her out back hanging up the wash. She threw me a mysterious little smile. I searched for something suave to say but "Hey man, some pad you got out here," was all I could come up with.

"Will your father buy across the street?" she asked.

"I hope."

We were all alone between the sheets. They flapped gently round us on the lines. Debra reached into the basket for a towel. I reached too. Our skins touched and sparked. My hand came up with Virgie's workday underwear. It was full of ugly holes in all the worst places. I quick dropped it back and felt around for something tastier. My fingers passed by Arturo's flannel shirt, then struck gold, which could be nothing less than Debra's pink panties. While fumbling with the clothespins I stroked their silky net, not in any dirty way but with respect. If Debra noticed, that might tell her what my feelings were towards her, and she might tell me hers for me.

But, "You could sign up for Little League," is what she told me.

She took the panties from my fumbly hands and hung them up as if they could be some old rag to mop the floor with.

"You'd be senior division, of course," she said, "and out here in Hacienda Allegro they buy you real pretty uniforms, and give gold trophies too, And there's a Pop Warner team for football season."

How could she be sports-minded at a time like this? But Debra who never had a mouth before talked and talked and wouldn't quit talking while she hung out the wash. "I'll tell you one thing," she said. "And I'll tell you something else," she added. Along with, "I hate to say it, but—"

She turned into Virgie Junior. That dead fly had me cutting my hair in Paddy style, and Stand up straight and Look people in the eyes when you talk to them. And no more speaking Spanish, plus two dozen ways to improve my personality. She had me mowing lawns to develop my muscles and my bank account, attending summer school to improve my grades. Then I could run for Class Vice-president and maybe have surgery on my nose to look more refined. Finally, in the middle of one of her sentences, I headed for the kitchen.

"Where you going, Junior?" she asked me quite surprised.

"To get fitted for my uniform," I informed her in my most sarcastic voice. Whatever I felt for her in the Buick had all leaked out of me.

"Oh, Junior," she called after, not too sweetly, "in case you'd like to know, those panties you made love to, they're Denise's." But already I was gone.

After we unloaded the trailer, Virgie put out food for us but nobody seemed in the mood to eat. All I could taste and smell was Darwin's Bug-go. Suddenly my father of all people had to go to the toledo in a hurry, and I went running to the other one. I fell on my knees in front of Virgie's sky-blue water and heaved and heaved. Till I got a feeling somebody was watching me. I quick looked around. Nobody. And the door was locked. And then I saw my audience. He was an old familiar friend from Shamrock Street, but not in the best of health. He could barely drag his six skinny little legs across the color-coordinated carpet, so I helped him along with my finger to where the rug ended and watched him scuttle down fine and safe and dark under the toledo.

"Go with God, little cucaracha," I told him in Spanish. "Go find yourself a little wife."

We soon left Virgie's house.

"Aren't you gonna talk to the salesman?" she asked my father.

"Maybe next time," he said to my relief. Arturo begged to ride with us to the Aztecs' club but Virgie changed his mind for him.

"Come see us," Virgie called and waved. "You know where we live. Come real soon."

So we drove back to good old Shamrock Street sick at stomach but glad at heart and the empty trailer rattled along behind us.

Chapter
15

WHEN WE CAME from Virgie's, a fat envelope was waiting in the box. It was from someplace called Nayarit, Mexico, and was addressed to Lena in a flowery hand which could only be Armando. My mother quickly hid it till my sister came from work. "He still loves me," she privately reported. "Only he plans to spend a month down there with his mother, darn him. And asks me to send down his clothes." So she went and got them from his rooming house and spent all day Sunday making love to Armando's shirts on the ironing board while Aurora read to her from *True Romance* magazine and both of them rained down tears.

Under my father's glaring eyes, I was busy hammering my weekly nails in the front porch steps when Chuchu ran through our gate gabbling unfamiliar words, "Respected planners of L.A. No, honorable. Honored City Plan Committee. Bring paper and pencil quick before I lose it." I ran for them. "You know that lawyer, I been putting in a carport for him? Mr. O'Gara is his name, I showed him that M-1 notice and he says get petitions signed. Says get people to City Hall on Thursday. Says maybe he'll even come himself, and gave me the right words to use, if only I can remember."

Chuchu dictated and I copied him down the best I could. "We the undersigners all live on Shamrock Street, L.A., which also own our own home ... Taxpayers!" he suddenly remembered. "We got to get Taxpayers in there someplace. We the undersign Taxpayers—"

In the middle of the word he turned his head and whistled. A brand-new emerald green Pontiac convertible flashed by with Pelón's Uncle Ruben at the wheel. He was in the rackets and part-owned the Arco Iris, and he screeched his tires in front of Elva's house which he also owned, it was said. And who stepped out of that motion-picture car but that Soco lady from Forney Street? Today she was fixed up like Elizabeth Taylor, killer-eyelashes on both sides and a shape on her to raise the dead, possibly from girdles. She swept her eyes across us as if we might be garbage cans, then paraded into Elva's house with a glittery little handbag swinging from her pinky finger.

"What's that one want on Shamrock?" Chuchu wondered.

"The crows always come back," my mother said from the screen door.

"Let's get on with this petition here," my father ordered. He was the only one who hadn't bothered to look.

"Where was I?" Chuchu asked me.

I couldn't remember, my head was suddenly so full of that woman. I could barely breathe. And how about that rain check I forgot to ask for? And that "Care for a Coke, or something?" So Chuchu went back to the beginning and I finally got it copied in my best handwriting. It was quite pretty to look at, all admitted, but not real businesslike, so they asked Aurora to do it on the typewriter.

That Sunday and every day till Thursday Chuchu and my father carried petitions house to house. Everyone signed up, homeowners and renters too, except several absent landlords who could not be reached. All promised to attend, but when Thursday came this one was sick in bed, that one couldn't miss work and there was my father climbing those City Hall steps alone except for his translator which was me.

From Shamrock Street, City Hall always was a pretty sight. Standing up there in the west it was a big part of all our sunsets and our night skies too, but on that Thursday when we stood there in its teeth like a couple of ants I didn't care for its looks at all.

"What did you bring me for?" I asked my father. "I can't do you nothing."

"You could interpret me and quit whining," he said.

We climbed and climbed those steps. My father pointed at words in stone over the monster doors. "Fiat Justicia" they seemed to say. My father recognized justicia but not the fiat.

"It's a tiny car," I patiently explained. "Big mileage but no horsepower. They come from Japan or someplace."

"American's best," my father said. He was very patriotic over automobiles, so in we went.

To show respect for the city, my father was wearing his complete blue suit and vest and tie and Snappy Tiger hat. He handed me the sign from our telephone pole. It was almost worn out from beery fingers pointing at various words but I could still make out "Room 201." I looked around. No doors. Only long long halls.

"Ask somebody," my father ordered.

Who for an instance? All I could see were the busy business type and their heels clicked and clacked on the marble floors. Ask them a question and they'll freeze your blood. I spotted some few others that were more our kind but they looked lost too. And of course there was a cop with a gold badge.

"Ask the policía," my stupid father said.

So he could ask me back what was I doing there during school hours? And no doubt the name of my probation officer? I went to the candy stand better and bought Life Savers.

"Through the rotunda, then left, then right," they told me.

"Come on," I told my father.

We went.

"What's a 'rotunda'?" he asked me.

"How should I know?" I told him crossly.

We marched up and down the halls. They were a city block each way and had every 200 number except 201. Till finally my father noted someone more or less his own shade of brown who happened to be pushing a broom. They had quite some little conversation. It seemed the man came from almost the same little town my father was born in, so he dropped his broom and escorted us to the right door and shook hands and introduced himself, and we went on in.

Room 201 was big enough to hold a church. Two-story black marble pillars went parading up one side and down the other. There were rows of high-back churchy benches, mostly empty, then up front a fence where the altar should be with a monster table and men sitting back of it like judges. Not to call attention to ourself, we went on tiptoe down the near-side aisle.

"Where's that damn Chuchu?" my father asked in his thunder-whisper. It had been decided he would speak for us and then my father would stand up to say "Me too," along with others that had signed the petition but on all those benches we couldn't see a single friendly face to sit beside, so my father picked an empty row down front, and accidentally kneeled and blessed himself before sliding in.

"City Planning Commission," a block of wood said in gold.

There were nine planners present, each one with his private sign, such as La Kretz, Torvaldsen, Kleinburger and other all-American names. You don't see much Gómez up there at City Hall, or García, at least not without a broom in hand. The Planners sat listening in fat green chairs and passed the time by putting their glasses on and taking them off. Of all those 18 hands there was not a single missing finger which would be a world record for any 9 of our people. A tall, gray-haired, S-shape man was preaching from the pulpit in front. Mr. Cockburn they called him, which seemed a very crazy name to me, even for an American.

"What's he talking?" my father asked.

"All about a bunch of slums someplace," I answered. "They didn't get to Shamrock yet."

But I was wrong. Mr. Cockburn snapped his fingers and they splashed a very familiar picture on a big movie screen. My father gasped like shot. It was our own home, and how mean and ugly we looked up there between those marble columns.

"Don't get mad, compadre, or we're dead," Chuchu whis-

pered and slid in next to us. He'd come straight from the job
and he pulled our petition from his pocket and blew a cloud
of cement off it, then cleared his throat so loud everybody
turned to look. Chuchu waved and smiled at them. "Mr.
O'Gara will fix 'em, just wait and see," he said.

"Crack!" went Mr. Cockburn's fingers and another picture
flashed up on the screen and then another. He showed us a
parade of Shamrock houses from Main Street to the tracks,
except he skipped Don Tiburcio's pretty garden, I noted.
While the picture show was going on, he talked building
codes and welfare families and dropouts from school. He
preached Broken Homes and busted sewer pipes, trains passing day and night and no foundations to the houses. Too many
kids to the bedroom caused TB and worse, he claimed. Mr.
Cockburn had figures on everything, arrests, probations, jails,
sick and dead. And how he loved to add up all our troubles
and all our little mistakes.

"Qué dice? What's he say?" my father kept asking me.

But how could I keep up with all those ugly numbers? Was
I deprived and disadvantaged like this man said, or desti-
túted? My father worked steady. I had never been sorry for
myself before, except maybe two Christmases back. And here
I was living in The Slums and never knew it, because by the
time Mr. Cockburn added it all up, even a cucaracha would
be ashamed to admit Shamrock Street was his home address.

Next, Mr. Cockburn told what a fine place Shamrock would
be with all our little homes torn down. M-1 zoning would
bring 1,000 new jobs, so he said, and millions in tax dollars
which seemed to cheer those city planners up. And finally, he
said, this rezone was in accordance with the City's own Master Plan for more up-to-date L.A.

"Describe the exact land use," they asked him.

The S.P. would put a giant parking lot on top of us, he said,
for their piggy-back trucks which would be loaded onto
freight cars and speed up deliveries and reduce traffic on the
freeways.

"What about the people who live there now?" Mr. Klein-burger asked. He seemed quite concerned.

"They will receive fifty percent above the market price for their houses," was Mr. Cockburn's answer. "They'll move to better neighborhoods with lower crime rates, good schools, nice homes. We are actually paying them to trade up into the American Standard of Living. Some have made the move already."

Was he meaning Virgie, I wondered?

The planners seemed quite pleased with the picture. "Are there any opposed?" they asked. There was a big noisy silence. Chuchu looked round for his lawyer friend and so did we.

"Then if nobody objects—"

"Me," Chuchu got up and said. "Me and eighty-three others of us." He waved our petition. Kindly bring it forward. He did. Was there any statement he cared to make? There was. Then please use the microphone.

"Mr. Chairman, respected public . . ."

There stood Chuchu in his overalls from work and cement dust in his hair, and he looked out over that sea of neckties. And then Chuchu that never lost a word before, ran out of gas. Possibly his voice booming around that big hall bothered him. I held my breath and prayed. The planners smiled down very patiently to prove how much they loved the Mexican people and no doubt even generously ate a taco or two from time to time, when bored of hamburgers.

"Check his list against the tax roll," the head planner told the clerk. Chuchu looked at us like a drowning man, then finally found his voice.

"Knock on the walls," he said, "we're pure lath and plaster down there on Shamrock, no cheap wallboard. I'm twenty years in construction, Laborers' Union 802. They're good little homes. Don't tell me earthquakes. Nothing ever fell with us but Hibernia Street school, the whole damn roof and it was builded according to so-called building codes, lucky nobody was in there. Says we're overcrowded? Too many kids? Not in families that get along and most of us do. Eight kids? Twelve? They'll fit. I've seen big homes overcrowded with two persons. Me, I was born in Sonora, Mexico, you should see the house, dirt floor, tin-can roof, carry the water, but we got by. And Shamrock, it's heaven compared to that."

The planners started coughing and checking wristwatches. The clerk interrupted to report only 22 out of our 83 names were on the tax rolls.

"Where did you get the other signatures?" the head planner sternly asked.

"They live on Shamrock, every one of them," Chuchu answered.

"But not taxpayers."

"Sure they pay their taxes," Chuchu said, "if not on homes, then on cigarettes, beers, cars, underwear, the works."

That brought quite some laugh.

"Are we ready to vote?" the planners asked.

"May I first say a few words?" Mr. Cockburn asked and turned to Chuchu. "Mr. Madrigal," he said, "we of the S.P. railroad consider you folks our very good neighbors. Many of you are in our employ. Rather than depriving you of your homes we're opening the door to a better and a richer life—"

Mr. Cockburn never finished because a new voice came booming from the back of the hall.

"Yes, you love your neighbors so much you're ready to gobble them up all the way to their bloody bootstrings!" From the sound of him, I expected at least a 10-foot giant to come tromping down the aisle but what came was a hunched-up monkey of a man on wheels. He came spinning down between those benches and pulled up by the microphone on squealing rubber.

"Must I stand before this distinguished body?" he asked and clattered out a pair of crutches.

"You may remain seated, Mr. O'Gara, as usual," they sighed.

"Mr. Cockburn sir, I listened with concern to your depressing statistics but there is one pertinent figure you seem to have overlooked. Tell me, Mr. Cockburn, just how many young men from Shamrock died on the bloody fields of Europe and Asia? You don't *know*, Mr. Cockburn? Tss tss, perhaps my client Mr. Madrigal can tell us."

"Seventeen," Chuchu said, "not counting Augie Martinez."

"Seventeen, Mr. Cockburn!" and how that man made those numbers ring. "And can you tell me, sir, how many died for their country on your own street in Beverly Hills? And you propose, Mr. Cockburn, to drive these patriotic citizens from their homes, the little homes they've managed to buy out of the peon wages the S.P. railroad is famous for?"

"We're buying their houses, not driving them out," Mr. Cockburn shouted. "And we do not pay peon wages—"

"Tut tut, Mr. Cockburn, please keep your shirt on. Wages are not in question here. However, since you brought them up, please tell me why with all the hundreds of Mexican-Americans in your shops, not one has ever been promoted to machinist? Too stupid, Mr. Cockburn? Too untrustworthy? Bright enough only to die in the uniform of their adopted country?"

I machine-gunned the Spanish to my pop-eyed father.

"An Irish?" he said. "San Patricio come again?" And banged Chuchu on his knee and shoulder, who grinned back at him. Meanwhile that Mr. O'Gara went rolling on like the Sunset Limited.

"Gentlemen, let's fill in a little background," he said. "It was the S.P. railroad built that little street. Very convenient to have a pool of cheap labor so handy to the tracks. That labor was Irish first which is where the 'Shamrock' came from. My own great-uncle lived there. Next it was Italians till they wanted better wages and now it's Mexicans. Oh, very convenient, but alas, gentlemen, times have changed. S.P. must modernize its operations to compete with the trucking industry. It needs space to park its trailers on, acres and acres of space. It's a whole new omelet, gentlemen, and whose eggs get broken? Why, there's old rundown Shamrock Street. Nobody much lives there except a bunch of Mexicans. And we can buy them out for peanuts. They refuse to sell? Never mind, we have ways. Oh how well I know those ways. Threats, intimidation. Mr. Kleinburger, you used to call yourself a Democrat, were you honestly going to vote these honest workingmen right out of their homes? It won't look good on the record, Mr. Kleinburger, if you run again for any office. My good friend La Kretz, aren't you on a committee dedicated to Minority Rights?"

"Move to study the problem in committee," said Mr. Kleinburger.

"Second," said Mr. La Kretz. "It's getting late."

There were a bunch of protests and a big commotion but in the end those planners couldn't get out of there fast enough.

"What happened?" my father asked outside in the hall. "Did we win?"

"Indubitably," I told him. But Mr. O'Gara wasn't all that hopeful. "It's only the first round," he told us. "They'll raise their price a few dollars. They'll flash cash in your faces. They'll send in building inspectors, try to condemn your homes. The question is, will you stand together?"

"We'll stand," Chuchu boasted.

"Do you want me to represent you? Then I'll need a retainer. Just sign these papers with your address. I'll send you a letter of explanation in the morning."

Chuchu signed and then my father and Mr. O'Gara shook hands all around, me too. What a grip, he was more bonecrusher than my father even. All shoulders and arms he was, the rest of him was shriveled up and twisted round with steel braces here and leather harness there.

"And now I've got to run," he said. "Don't talk to anybody. Refer them all to me." And he whirled away down the long long hall and into the elevator.

"Son of a beechie," my father said looking after, "where has that man been all our lives?"

Chapter
16

FROM THAT DAY ON, my father talked about el señor O'Gara and nothing else till my mother got very bored of the name.

"You didn't sign nothing at least?" she hoped.

"Yes I signed something, Indian. And so did Chuchu and the others. We're gonna teach S.P. a damn good lesson for once in their life and maybe we'll sue the City too."

We were on the front porch. It was a Saturday. The sun was shining bright on City Hall.

"Sue THAT?" my mother asked and pointed.

"This for that," said my father and stuck his second finger in the air.

"You trust the gringo? Madness!" My mother banged in through the screen door. My father ran in after.

"How about that Mister Sam?" he shouted. "When I walked tracks in Nuevo Méjico who loaned me $20 and no interest and no nothing? Mr. Sam is who, and this lawyer he's got the same face exactly only his legs are not as good."

"I never saw his pretty face," my mother said, "but I heard his voice when he called you on the phone and it was raw and ugly."

"Because he's man-to-man is why. None of your 'Muy bien, Señora Medina.' " My father went into his well-known coyote whine. " 'El gusto es mío, señora, y aquí puede Vd. comprar con toda confianza.' Yes, that's your type, the snaky kind like that cockroach Mendivil over there in Tucson that sold us the guaranteed bedroom suit. And didn't the mattress bust before the second payment? And the spring next year? And weren't we three years paying for it? But you trusted him because he was a Mexican and so soft-spoken."

"Oh yes?" my mother said. "And how about that Meestair Smeeth that owned ten thousand acres and his scales were ten pounds short on every hundred? But he puts his paw on your shoulder and calls you little brown brother. And then when you're away he puts his paw on me another way, only I never told you because you wouldn't believe nothing bad from your good American friend."

"And who was the contratista got us that no-good job? Your own uncle, that boot kisser."

"He was only a far uncle," my mother said.

I learned a lot of family history that day. My father recalled every Mexican that ever cheated him and my mother every gringo till finally she put her hands over her ears and slammed out back to tell it to her little birdies.

My father stood very hot in the kitchen. "Women!" he told me. "Whatever God made them for, it wasn't conversation. Scream, stamp, lose their temper! Where with a man you can sit down muy pacífico and argue with logic and justicia. And another thing, you'll find it out some day, they have a certain ugly little smell, women do, and never lose it, not even after showers, not even sprayed with perfume. . . . I'm going to the Aztecs," he hollered at my mother through the door.

Left to myself, I wondered what my father meant about that little smell which I would learn about it later? Lena always smelled sweet to me, and my mother was my mother. Girls at school, they smelled like everybody else when sweaty. That lady on Forney Street, it's true there was a certain little odor on her, was it perfume, or the other thing? Either way, I liked it and now I could almost taste her smell inside my nose.

The truth is, that lady had been on my mind for days. Maybe she even witched me because one night I dreamed her and woke up in a puddle. If I shut my eyes in Social Studies there she was on the inside of my lids. All my life I heard good things about these older ladies and how they favor us young guys because we can go and go and go and never get tired out. A lot of my friends learned their ropes from them. Maybe it was not as romantic as some young chick your own age, they reported, but those older types don't make demands on you, where your junior high or high school girl is all the time begging, buy me this, take me there, and don't you dare look at any other girl. Besides, they regularly get pregnant too.

It was high time for me to become a Man. Most of my friends were there already, unless they were lying, and how they loved to talk about it! Some, with married ladies you would never suspect, but divorciadas were the best, they said. No crazy husband to worry about.

That lady from Forney Street could be my solution.

Except, what if she told me No? I hate that.

Or screamed about Insulted?

Or phoned my father?

But she didn't seem the tattletale type.

So why not?

What have you got to lose?

It won't kill you to get turned down.

She might even take it for a compliment.

I already had a clean shirt on. Underpants I'd changed this morning. So I combed myself and cut out for Forney Street. My feet failed to behave just right. I stumbled quite a lot and had that tight-chest feel you get when stealing things in stores. It was knocking on that lady's door that scared me most, and no rain check to start the conversation with. "Hi," I might say, "and how's every little thing this morning?" Or, "I just happened to be passing by and being I was thirsty—" Neither one of them pleased me so I walked on past her door to the Arco Iris. Their rainbow was still busted but they put plywood over. And then God was good to me because I saw her down the street carrying a heavy bag of groceries from the market.

"Hey, lemme give you a hand," was all I had to say.

I followed close up her exciting stairs. She wasn't all fixed up like when I saw her last on Shamrock Street. Curlers in her hair with a scarf tied over, but who minded little details like that? On the top step she turned around and kicked her door open like a mule, and took a disgusted look inside.

"Lazy little bitch," she yelled.

Who? Me?

"Elvira!" she shouted down the hall, then told me to put the groceries on the damn sink and stomped off to pound on her neighbor's door. There was no room for a cucaracha even on that sink of hers. It was stacked three stories high with pots and big black enchilada pans full of greasy water, so I unloaded on the table. From down the hall I heard angry conversation. To pass the time, I inspected the lady's room. A big brass bed took up most of it with covers thrown back and dragging on the floor, but what a bed, man! It shined like gold with pearl-shell flowers and stars worked in here and there. In the middle of the mattress was a deep cozy valley that almost made my heart stop, and when I stroked the sheets they felt like silk. The lady almost caught me at it.

"That damn snot-nose! Promised to clean house for me," she complained, "and I already paid her a dollar. Which reminds me, here's a quarter for carrying up my junk. Take it, take it! Socorro Gutiérrez always pays her way. . . . Gone visiting her grandma, little slut, and leaves me with all this mess to clean up, and eight dozens enchiladas to make tonight. I sell 'em at the Arco Iris," she explained. "A girl's gotta live somehow." She dropped onto the bed and fanned her face with her fingers. "Ai, I'm beat. Care for a Coke or something?"

At last!

From the bed she reached in the refrigerator and pulled me out a Coke and one for herself. So we started drinking. "Where do I go from here?" I asked myself. She was on the bed already but not in what you might call a romantic mood. I coolly upended the Coke the suavest way I knew and set it on the table. Perhaps she would offer beer for seconds.

"So tell me what's new, Rudy Junior," she said. "How's your father and everybody?"

"The same," I said.

"What's all this I hear about S.P.'s buying Shamrock Street?"

She seemed very interested in our real estate so I told her about the hearing and all.

"You mean they're offering 8,000 for those old shacks?" she asked, and whistled. "And your big-shot father won't take that kind of money? And all cash too? Where's his brains at?"

She mashed the Coke can in her fist which I had never seen a lady do before, or woman, and lobbed it across the room to the waste basket. "Well," she sighed, "back to my pots and pans."

"I could wash them for you," I quickly said before she could dismiss me.

"Rudy Junior, you're a dreamboat, that's what you are."

I rolled up my sleeves and she tucked a towel into my belt. Her fingers made my stomach shiver, and she gave me a friendly little hug besides.

"You're cute, Rudy Junior. I bet all the girls go crazy over you, huh?"

"Aw," I said.

"Don't deny it," she teased. "Sit in the back row at the Starland? I remember, hold hands, play little finger games. Oooo, don't touch me there. Am I right, Rudy Junior?"

My drums began to beat. The hot water in the sink seemed running through my blood into my face. My eyes went misty. I could barely breathe, and finally, when she laughed and ran her fingers through my hair, I turned around and reached. I couldn't help myself. Her juicy chichis are what I touched and sunk my fingers in.

"SHIT!"

Where did that yell come from? What hit me after? I was laying on the floor. The maddest female face I ever saw was glaring down at me.

"Puto, sinverguenza, filthy animal," she yelled in Spanish. "Chingada madre, take me for a whore do you? Think I want that ugly little worm of yours?" And more like that, and kicks besides, until she got her breath. I didn't dare get up.

"Now, you go home and send me back your father."

What's that she's saying?

"Yes, your damn father, that's what I said. You heard me. He knows the way. He's been here. He's been here plenty. Knocked me up, the son of a bitch and now won't even talk on the phone. Yes, you heard me right. Your fucking baby brother is what I got inside my belly where you wanted to go poking."

I slided toward the door. Was that a knife she had?

"Now get out of here, and tell your father just one thing for me, he better come and quick and bring money with him, son of a bitch or else I'll have a lawyer on him. He don't leave Soco Gutiérrez pregnant with his bastard and not pay plenty for it!"

I flew down those stairs like a roller coaster, ran down the street till a tree got in the way. I pounded it with my fists, no matter blood. People looked. Go someplace, behind the Pepsi sign. Tall brown weeds back there, busted bottles back there, beer cans. Kick and stomp them. Dirty stinking whore that leads me on and tells me No. Her and my father on that brassy bed. My respected father, my father the preacher, "Kiss the hand that feeds you. Do like I do and you won't go wrong."

How could I be so stupid? The signs were everywhere. Those deaf-and-dumb phone calls lately to our house. Say hello, they hang up. That battle at the Arco Iris, what took him there? Virgie's little whispers. My mother's indirectos. She knew, they knew, the whole town knew, except only dumb stupid me. I banged myself a good one on the jaw.

And now what?

Go home and throw it in my father's face. But first lead him on. "A certain person wants to see you, a certain lady, if you can call her that. You know the one, you knocked her up and now she's got your brat inside her belly." Oh, to see his face. Let him kill me, who cares? I stormed out from behind the Pepsi sign and stomped on home. The Buick was gone from out in front.

"Where's my damn father?" I yelled from the door.

My mother maybe knew something from my voice. She was ironing and didn't miss a stroke.

"Gone to TJ with his friends."

"I have to see him right now."

"For what?"

My mother looked up from her iron. She could read me even when I turned my back. "What did you expect?" she asked. "He's a man, isn't he?" She folded his pants very neatly and laid them on the chair. "Who told you?"

"They did," I vaguely said and blushed and then got mad. "And what's more, she's pregnant from him."

"That too? Well well."

She picked up a rumpled shirt of mine.

"Don't you even care?" I yelled.

"Oh," she said. "I stand it. Or else who'll buy the groceries?"

Suddenly I saw something I should have seen before. "Is that how come your trip to Mexico?"

"No," she said and thought about it. "Not really."

I saw my sister coming up the walk. "Does Lena know?" My mother nodded. "And she let him preach to her and never threw it in his face?"

"It's not Lena's business," my mother said, "or your business either." She tossed my shirt at me. "I've ironed this old rag of yours for the last time. Did you bring tortillas?" she asked my sister coming in.

"God damn!" I yelled. "Don't anybody give a damn but me?"

"What's with him?" Lena asked.

My mother petted my arm. "It's not the end of the world," she told me. "Go take a shower and you'll feel better."

Chapter
17

I WAITED UP that night to catch my father but he didn't come. I stood home and waited all day Sunday. I didn't care to leave the house. My friends would see the story in my face if they didn't know already. Sunday night I fell asleep around eleven. Who knows when my father got back from TJ? He was already at work when I woke up Monday and I went to school with my message still rumbling round inside me.

It was one of those hot November days you don't expect. The air was dead and slimy, it erased everybody. We had a big time in Math multiplying fractions and in Social Studies learned the principal products of Peru. Bontempo's class was back with Sturdy Pancho after a week of punctuation drill. Of course Pancho found the missing jewelry, only not exactly in the toledo where Pelón predicted, so now, after scolding rich Mrs. Murdock, here's the sheriff driving Pancho and Maria home and Slapsy Annie is reading aloud to the class.

" 'Did you ever arrest a real-live murder?' Pancho inkerd."

"What's that last word?" Miss Bontempo asked.

"Inqueered?" Annie guessed.

"InQUIRed, Annie, we had it on the blackboard yesterday. Proceed."

" 'Oh I have arrested them by the dozens,' retorted Sheriff Trotter with a jolly laugh which bellied his words."

"BeLIED," Miss Bontempo suggested. "Rudy, your turn."

"Where's the place?" I asked.

Miss Bontempo gave a brief lecture on It Pays to Pay Attention, and pointed with her finger.

"I got a sore throat," I said.

She marked me zero for the day and Wah took over. "By now they were crossing the railroad tracks. The houses were quite run-down in that section but one tiny home stood out proudly from its neighbors. It was freshly painted in a jolly pink and as luck would have it, the children's father was just now coming home from work, a bright red bandanna tied about his throat to add a touch of color to his grease-stained overalls.

" 'I'll be a monkey's uncle,' Sheriff Trotter cried, 'if it isn't my old buddy Charlie García from the Fighting 69th.'

"What a reunion! The two men pounded each other excitedly on the back, and in less time than it takes to tell, all were happily seated about Mama García's groaning board."

"Groaning board," Miss Bontempo interrupted. "What do you suppose that means, class?"

"A board with a nail in it," Wah suggested.

"That's a good try, Wah, but no. It's what we call a Figure of Speech, can you remember that, Class? and means a table piled high with good things to eat. Proceed."

Wah proceeded. "Enchiladas were the main course." They were the first that Sheriff Trotter had encountered.

" 'Which end do you start on?' he joked.

" 'The end that goes over the fence last,' Pancho's father retorted in kind."

Some dumb girl's hand was flag-waving.

"Hey, Miss, Miss, enchiladas don't go over no fence, Miss."

"It's a joke, Darlene," Miss Bontempo pointed out. "As if they were turkeys, you know."

Nobody managed a laugh, not even Wah, who went on reading.

" 'All of which reminds me,' remarked the sheriff as he washed down his first Mexican meal with a cup of good strong coffee, 'I'm looking for a new Deputy Sheriff, a good steady man I can rely on. Would you like the job, Charlie?' "

"BULLSHÍT!"

I couldn't help myself. I said it right out loud, but the bell rang just then so Miss Bontempo failed to hear, only the guys in the near seats, which made me their hero for the day, but I wasn't in any mood to stick around and enjoy it. I cut out through the nearest gate. To hell with 6th period, which was Phys. Ed.

Walking home, I held rehearsals. I'm sitting on the front steps waiting. My father comes through the gate. I deliver him my message right out in the open air. "Your whore's pregnant and how do you like that?" No matter neighbors listening in. And then what? Can I look him in the eyes? Will the right words come to me? I began to doubt myself. Better to come home late, after dark even. He'll start preaching. I'll look at him very calm and cool and let him have it. Maybe.

"ONLY 30 DAYS TILL XMAS," the sign at Five Points read. All those wide-awake merchants down Bailey and up and down Broadway were already stringing up their Santas and their Merry Christmas bells. It bored me. In the good old days Lena used to take my father to Sears and shop for everybody and pick out the tree, but this year with the mood our house was in, the best I could expect was a pair of socks or maybe underpants. I turned off onto Pasadena Avenue, they're not so patriotic over Christmas down that way.

"JUNIOR!"

I jumped. It was my father's voice but Pelón is all it turned out to be.

"What you doing off your chain?" he asked. "Let's go someplace and do something. How much money you got on you?"

"Seventeen cents," I reported.

"Honestly?" he asked and bugged his eyes. "Or are you only bragging?"

I flashed my roll, one dime, one nickel, two no-good pennies.

"What we need's a transfusion, man. There's a horseplayer owes my uncle $10, so let's go, manito."

Manito, little brother, he hadn't called me that in ages, not since that night he ran away from my father's house for good. I only wished I'd run with him. What a life he had, compared to mine, no father to be scolding him and making rules, only his grandma, and Elva hardly cared. Day or night he could be anywhere he choosed while I stood cooped up like my father's chickens. Maybe it wasn't too late. Today could be my Declaration of Independence, why not? And just let my father try to scold me. Suddenly I found myself lighthearted and ready of anything.

The horseplayer wasn't home, of course, only his daughter that's around nineteen and ugly. We tried to fool around with her anyway but she slammed the door on us, and standing there on the steps I knew what I really needed, a woman, or girl, or whatever.

"Hey," I said, "let's go visit that sixth-grader aunt of yours." For months Pelón had burned our ears with tales of that chick and her lively little ways but nobody had ever seen her in the flesh.

"Not a chance," he said. "She keeps it in the family, man."

"We could try Artemis," I suggested.

"Which one?"

"Lives over there on Mozart Street," I told the guy. "She's in my Social Studies class, you should see her movement. And takes off her clothes if you feed her wine."

At least that's what guys claimed. Only, in the first place just how much wine would seventeen cents buy, if they would sell us any in the second place?

"Don't worry about it," Pelón said. "I know a certain place they give it away, let's go."

We went.

"Not the SA-VU market!" I said when we got opposite.

It was well-known for the most suspicious in all Eastside. They planted pipes in the cement at the exit with barely room to squeeze yourself between, but your cart never. SHOP-LIFTING IS A FELONY was the biggest sign you saw inside, plus they had snoopy assistant managers spying through the alleys and round mirrors staring down at you from every cor-

ner. TV cameras too, so they could take your picture in the
act. I never cared for that place at all.

"How we gonna manage?" I asked, quite nervous.

For answer Pelón fished a paper from the gutter and handed
it to me. It was the tail end of some dumb kid's science report.
"Ice is mostly mad of snow," it informed me. No wonder the
kid tore it up.

"Huh?" I asked Pelón.

"That's our grocery list, Stupid. We just moved into the
neighborhood and our mommie's so busy killing cucarachas
she sent us to the store for her, and we need a big supply of
everything."

Maybe my mouth was open.

"Wake up! A couple guys go cruising empty-handed
through the market, they spot you right away, but good cash
customers with loaded carts, that cheers them up and they get
careless."

In we went.

I was never much for acting. In 3rd grade they fired me
from the Pilgrim Fathers and put me with the tongue-tied
Indians.

So I handed our so-called list to Pelón.

"You talk, I'll wheel," I said and grabbed a cart.

Pelón tossed in a box of salt and a can of lard, a 10-pound
bag of rice and the biggest sack of beans they had.

"Get chiles," Pelón ordered. "Jalapeños and that other kind
Mom likes, around three dozens if you can count that high."

I went for them.

"And a sack of potatoes," he hollered after me, "and a couple lettuces. Don't bring no brown ones like last time. And
tomatillos or else my mother will murder us."

I dumped the order in the cart, then got real brave and
snatched eight French rolls on my own.

"Don't overlook the eggs," I yelled across.

"Did you get the toilet paper like I told you? Pink, remember."

I tossed in a 4-pack. And why not paper towels too? And napkins. I picked out yellow ones for cheery.

"They'll match the kitchen exactly," I loudly pointed out. At the meat counter I grabbed off two pounds of hamburg, three of hot dogs and for luck tossed in a juicy T-bone steak, but every time I passed by the wine shelf I felt eyeballs burning holes in my neck. I was happy Pelón was taking on that assignment. By now we were pushing the heaviest basket in the market. There could be $60 worth in there or 50, and I was feeling very fine except for one small worry. How would we ever get out of that place alive? A manager trotted by and flashed us his friendliest smile to guarantee our future business.

"Hey, mister," Pelón asked, "is this roach killer any good? We just moved in over on Manitoba Street and my mom's going crazy with the bugs."

The manager carefully selected us a can of Bug-go and suggested the large economy size and we politely thanked him. So then Pelón squinted at our list.

"That's got it," he said. "Let's check out."

"How?" I asked in a very skinny voice.

We headed for the cash registers and shoved our cart in line. Then he started yelling at me. "Dummy! Stupid! You forgot the rabbit food! Do you want the poor things to starve to death? Get empty sacks."

I grabbed some.

"Señora, please save our place in line," he told a lady and I rolled our cart to the back of the store after him, wondering what next? Pelón went banging through the swinging stockroom doors. "Mister," he hollered in, "could me and my brother take some carrot tops for our bunny rabbits, huh? And maybe rotted lettuce leafs?"

The man pointed at the trash box.

"Leave the cart where it is, dummy," Pelón ordered and I followed him through the swinging doors. Absentmindedly he had a big sack of celery under his arm. I poked through the trash. Was it ever rotten? That stingy SA-VU hardly throws anything away, but I managed to fill one bag.

"They got a bigger trash box in the parking," Pelón said. So we squeezed past a truck backed up there for delivery and nobody cared or noticed. We jumped off the loading dock and cut around the corner. Pelón was whistling quite happily.

"Okay, clown," I told him, "so where's the wine at?"

He handed me the sack of celery and it gurgled. I peeked in between the leaves and saw two fine fifths of muscatel, a carton of cigarettes and three wineglasses off the notions rack, with those long legs which people drink from them on television. I patted Pelón on the back and almost kissed him.

"Oh, indubitably," he said. "It's no doubt the heist of the century."

We took off for Mozart Street, crunching celery as we went and I wished we'd stolen salt to give it taste. Halfway there, Pelón thought he better piss first so we ducked down the basement steps at the Methodists' church and baptized them in the Catholic religion. It then seemed a good idea to sample the muscatel. It was SA-VU's own brand and tasted real good, almost like cherry soda. We clinked our stylish glasses and Pelón winked at me across the rim. My worries and my damn father were 1,000,000 miles away and I was zooming out into Pelón's chancy world which had no fences and no clocks.

"Where we gonna take this Artemis to strip off her clothes?" Pelón asked.

"She takes us, right inside her house."

"How about her father?"

"Don't worry about it," I told the guy. He seemed quite anxious all of a sudden. "Her father works two jobs and her mother the same, and they got an automatic record player and TV and full refrigerator, everything."

At least that's what Hungryman reported.

"I can't stand it when they tell you No," Pelón said. "And she better not call me Shortie."

I screwed the cap on our muscatel. "Let's go," I said. I

seemed to be the leader in the Artemis department, and we left the Methodists behind us.

The houses along Mozart Street are way bigger than on Shamrock with grassy lawns and two-car garages in the back. Italianos live there mostly and they demand the best. Any Mexican family that moves in there has to hustle to keep up. Everything was very high-class on Mozart Street except that Artemis, and there she was in full view at her gate like waiting for us to happen by. Maybe she might be a little skinny for my personal taste. She had those hard little apples up front where I'm a grapefruit man myself, and I didn't care too much for her eyes and nose, but then you can't have everything.

"Hello-o-o-o," I told her, dragging it out very suave the way I had heard Fat Manuel speak the word. "And how's every little thing on Mozart these days?" I leaned across the gate into her cloud of perfume but kept my head. "We just happened to be passing by," I told her, "so I thought, why not let's do our homework together?" I said it quite suggestive. "This here's my friend Pelón," I said, "and he's real good at homework too. And we brought you a little present," I said and flashed the muscatel at her. According to Hungryman it was now time for her to invite us in.

"Well well," she said instead, "this is a surprise and aren't you the Man About Town?"

She petted my hand like a baby.

"Don't take it personal, Rudy," she said, "but lately I seem to prefer the older type. Right now I'm waiting for my boyfriend. He's McKinley High," she proudly added.

"What is he over there, the custodian?" I asked. I was getting ready to slap that Artemis for her big-shot lies, except they turned out to be the truth, because here's a horn blasting behind my back, and there's a big ugly monster in his letterman jacket. He could be eighteen at least and his car was a near-new Plymouth which he had flamed it, so what chance was there for Pelón and me?

"Just a couple of kids from my Social Science." Artemis

explained to her boyfriend and swung her famous ball-bearing hips into the seat and away they went, leaving rubber.

There we stood, flat-footed on the sidewalk.

"Oh well," Pelón said, "probly no doubt she's got the clap anyhow."

So we smashed our wineglasses on Artemis' front walk for souvenir and headed for Main Street disgusted. When you got no wheels you're noplace in L.A.

Chapter
18

A CERTAIN WIND visits L.A. from time to time, and the Santana is its name. It comes roaring in hot off the desert like a raging bull, and so dry your mouth tastes full of sand. Women snatch washing off the line before it goes flying over the next-door roof. They scream their kids off the street, spank them for nothing, then turn up the television to drown out the world while the beans burn black on the stove. Men do worse things. Everybody seems to hate that wind. Not me. It stirs my blood around till I'm ready for anything, and the harder it blows, the better I like it. It could blow L.A. into the ocean for all I care.

Well, we barely walked one block when that Santana grabbed Mozart Street. The palm trees took it first. Way far up you heard those big leaves scrape and rattle and claw and now a dead one comes twisting down through the air. It's 12 feet long at least and hits the pavement like a pistol. We stood looking up. How those palm trees swung and swayed, it was exactly like Artemis when she walked and if you touched the trunk you could feel their pulse. And now the Santana came swooping down to rip the hair right off our heads. It was easier running than standing still.

"Come on," I yelled, "maybe she'll blow us some chicks from Lincoln Park." We raced round the corner and down the street and had to grab a lamppost to put on brakes, but the park was already blown empty. Not a single chick in sight.

"They're inside patching up their permanents," was Pelón's idea. "They'll creep out later, only we need a cozy little coupe to scoop them up in. Let's check the used-car lots. Maybe we could pick up their seventeen-cent Special of the Week."

The Santana blew us on down Main to Railroad Avenue. It is famous for 10th-hand cars, famous too for being paved with broken bottles and bumpy dirt, most of which was now flying in the air. You could barely see 10 feet. The usual line of wrecks was nosed in against back fences, hoods gone, motors absent, two-wheel cripples and total basket cases. Cars live on there for years after they should be dead and buried and from time to time people drop by to cannibalize them.

"The price looks right," Pelón said, "only where's all the salesmen?" We cruised along kicking flat tires and slamming dented doors till we came to a '47 Nash with all wheels present, and the tires were even full. Pelón got curious about it. "What are you doing here, darling?" he asked. "Cruise on down the line," he told me. "Maybe you could find a near-new Hudson or an Essex even."

"Or possibly a covered wagon," I suggested.

So we had a little slug of muscatel to wet our dusty mouths and I walked on down the block checking the wrecks. At the corner I turned around and came back, but where's Pelón? Through the dust I spotted him finally at the wheel of that Nash and he even had the motor running.

"Our seventeen-cent special," he announced.

"You crazy?" I told the guy. "That's G.T.A."

"Who says we're stealing it? Joyriding, man, that's no worse than curfew violation and here's a little Xmas present I found for you." He handed out a hard hat which he'd found two of in back. It fitted me perfect. I'd always wanted one.

"Okay," I said, "let's take the hats and split."

"By foot?" he asked. "With Larceny perched on top of your skull and Breaking-and-Entering right behind you? Shit, man, let's take the car. Couple of laborers driving home in our beat-up old Nash, who's ever gonna stop us?"

"Only the first cop," I said. "You look like a peanut behind that wheel."

He pulled a toolbox from the floor and sat on it to look more or less man-sized. He gunned the engine. It had a piston slap but not too bad. I looked around. Nobody could see us with all that blowing dirt. Oh well, I thought, there's got to be a first time for everything, so I climbed in. Grand Theft Auto, here we come.

"Don't worry about it," he said. "I know the owner very well, only what's his name again?" He tore the registration off the wheel. "Joseph P. Bugliosi," he read. "Hurray for Italy. You should never never steal from a brother Mexican if you can help it."

And away we went. I looked back. Nobody came running. Nobody hollered Robber. We left a dust cloud behind us as high as City Hall. Pelón was a carefuller driver than I expected. We full-stopped for the signs and drove down Mission, not too fast, not too slow. The wind was really howling now and I pitied those poor little old ladies on the sidewalk wrestling the Santana for their skirts, while we lounged back so fine in our rugged old Nash coupe, a couple of hard hats from the building trades looking to find ourself a little flesh. Only one thing was missing. The radio wouldn't work.

"An Italiano without his música? You're crazy," Pelón said. He twisted knobs and pushed buttons and felt for loose wires. Nothing. "And no damn gas either," I pointed out. The needle hung below the Empty.

"Damn Buglousy and his no-good car," Pelón shouted. "Let's unload it for a later model. Charlie Chueco will give us 50 bucks at least."

I coolly lighted up a souvenir cigarette from SA-VU. I felt very free and easy in my mind and helped myself to muscatel. This joy-riding was well named. To save gas we took the short cut up Zonal with County Hospital shining up above us where God saved me from death on the 11th floor. I doubted if He spared me for Grand Theft Auto. Oh well, tomorrow I would

get back to my Book of Bones, but today I would swing with
Pelón. You can't study all the time. Everybody needs a little
sunshine in their life.

"Look, look. Nursies!" Pelón pointed out. Their skirts
whipped up around their elbows. The guy stared so hard he
took a wrong turn and we headed up the ramp marked EMER-
GENCY VEHICLES ONLY. And no backing up. An ambulance was screaming right behind us. Nothing to do but drive
up. And into that walled-in parking lot which is Misery Headquarters for L.A. Whatever wasn't ambulance was black-and-
white. Right there I dropped my sunshine.

"What's that smell?" Pelón asked. "Did you shit your
pants?"

We were boxed in. Cops with bleeding prisoners went by
close enough to touch us. And here comes the Chief with his
gold badge and that big Police Positive swinging off his belt.
"You got a patient in there?" he asks Pelón. No doubt I looked
like one by now.

"Is my mother still alive?" Pelón bawls. "Did the ambulance bring her from the wreck yet? Mrs. Rodríguez?"

What an actor. The cop patted his arm. "You'll have to ask
at the desk, son," he said. "Park your car down below." He
made the ambulance pull up and waved us through the traffic
and down the ramp. "A mother is still a boy's best friend,"
Pelón remarked, and we rolled through the hospital grounds
and up State Street and across the Freeway. Just short of First
Street we turned into an alley.

On our right there's the rear end of Dante Inferno's two-
story nightclub and on our left 8 foot of wood fence with
barbwire on top. It was dark like a tunnel. Even the Santana
seemed scared to blow in there. Till suddenly here she comes
with a big whoosh, grabs a giant refrigerator carton and chases
it end over end till it smashes against our bumper and hangs
there with big black letters painted on the side. G.T.A.? No.
G.E. was all, but what those ugly letters did to my digestion.

"Charlie Chueco's palace," Pelón announced. He pulled up
in front of garage doors. I was quite slow getting out. "What's

wrong with you?" Pelón told me. "Or don't you care for easy money? I been here a hundred times with my Uncle Ruben. Charlie's a fine guy—and full of jokes."

I opened the gates and Pelón drove in. It was a long, low shed with a bumpy iron roof over that banged and rattled in the Santana. Boxes of parts stood around, stacks of wheels and hubcaps, old transmissions and rear ends. What looked to be a paint spray stood over in one corner. A work light hung above a cable spool and a fat man in his undershirt and a slutty-looking woman were playing greasy cards there. Both of them had their tits practically hanging out.

"Hi, Charlie," Pelón called. "Remember me?"

The man got up but he was taller sitting down. He came at us bent over and shuffling like some kind of animal. Stretched out straight he might be 6 feet but he had to bend his neck back to look up in our faces. If this was Charlie Chueco he didn't look too full of jokes to me.

"Me and my friend, we got one car too many," Pelón said.

"And one pinkie slip too few, huh?"

The whore came over to inspect us. "A genuine living Nash automobile," she said, "and my favorite color too, shit green. You're cute, baby," she told me and patted my cheek.

"One bill takes it," Pelón said like a pro.

Charlie Chueco made a noise like a dog.

"50?"

"Radio works good? AM, FM?"

"Naturally," Pelón lied.

"Not no more it don't."

Charlie Chueco snapped off our antenna and whipped it past our faces. "Listen good, punks," he yelled. "Charlie Chueco don't contribute to the delinquency of no fucking minors."

"Bullshit," Pelón told him. "You bought a dozen bikes off me."

"Big mouth, snot-nose car stealers, tear up the street, run down women and babies. Can't even see over the hood. Don't tell me, I seen it happen. Kill them dead, no driver's license

even. Now get your assholes back in that piece of junk and
drive it round the first corner and dump it there!"

He backed us into the Nash. His whore came over to my
side. "Don't mind Charlie, kid," she told me. "The wind
fucked up his paint spray. Bring us something newer and
you'll get a price, only not when the damn Santana's blowing."

We backed into the alley. Charlie Chueco slammed the antenna on our roof. "Be glad I don't tell your uncle," he hollered. "He'd stomp your ass all the way to San Diego."

"Cripple motherfucker," Pelón yelled but the gates had already slammed on Charlie Chueco and his easy money and
all those funny jokes of his.

Pelón cruised down First Street and threw a left onto Boyle.
It's all dead millionaires' homes along there but now they're
either Insurance or Sisters of Mercy or Foot Hospitals. We
pulled into a vacant lot where they'd torn out the house and
down an old brick driveway. There was a bunch of scraggly
bushes for privacy from the street.

"The Butcher Shop," he announced. "Headquarters for the
cheap meat trade." But there wasn't any meat around, cheap
or dear. We had the place to ourself.

"I need refreshments," Pelón announced so I got out the
muscatel and we took turns drinking.

What a vista of L.A. We looked down over the Projects and
S.P. tracks and Santa Fe and the L.A. river with busy Downtown on beyond. There was the Fifth Street bridge to the left
of us and the buzzing Freeway below our street. The sun was
going down and angry clouds paraded past San Pedro. Red
sharks chased purple elephants. Ribs like on a skeleton
dripped blood. It was a very scary sky if you took it serious.

"This wine don't do me nothing," Pelón complained and
dug in his pocket for Speed and swallowed down a few. The
guy looked half-asleep.

"Remember when your old man caught us in the shed?" he
told me suddenly. "Red-handed, pants down and everything?

Swore he'd chop off our marbles? You didn't even have hair on you yet, remember?"

I wasn't likely to forget.

"Suppose he never caught us? I might still be your brother living in your house, with Lena combing through my hair for bugs." Could it be possible that Pelón for all his free-and-easy life might envy mine? Some people never know when they're well off.

"Let's dump the car and walk home," I suggested. That Charlie Chueco had drained off my electricity.

"Put your hard hat on," he ordered. "We're cruising."

"What you plan to use for gas?" And then it came to me. The needle could be lying. I found a stick and stuck it in the gas tank. It came out 4 inches wet. Pelón banged me on the shoulder. "Come on, brother-genius," he told me. "East L.A., that's where the action's at. They got one million lively chicks out that way. Let's go, man, go."

And we were rolling again.

East L.A. is the Mexican capital of California, with four taco stands to the block. There's bars, haberdash, jewelry stores and Ladies' Clothes with English never spoken. They even print the STOP signs in Spanish or else the streets would run with blood.

The Santana is different from any other wind. It doesn't quit when the sun goes down. All the way out Whittier Boulevard, it shook our Nash like a cat. A couple of blocks short of Atlantic the traffic started to get thick. The sidewalks were jammed too, what for? There was a big glare of light up ahead, possibly a fire. People were running. Cars were packed solid. Pelón pulled over to the curb.

"It's painted red," I warned him.

"So Buglousy gets a ticket and who cares?" he pointed out.

We joined the runners on the sidewalk. What we found at Atlantic was better than a fire. Two Saints were having it out on the corner, Santa Claus vs. Santa Ana, and the Lady from the Desert was taking every round. Because it seems those generous East L.A. merchants had strung up a life-size sleigh and reindeers across Whittier, not just cutouts, mind you, but genuine lifelike rounded plastic, the real thing, searchlights and all. Possibly last night it was a cheerful sight and no doubt coaxed a lot of lazy dollars from unwilling pockets, but now the whole big show was flying wild. Santa and his deers whipped up and down and round and round. Wreaths, bells, giant candy canes, Merry Xmases and Feliz Navidads went sailing off into the night like rockets. Here's a reindeer hanging by his neck and every time he whirls around blue sparks shoot off the power line. It was Christmas, Fourth of July and Halloween wrapped up in one.

"I told you," Pelón yelled. "East L.A. is where the action's at!"

But trust the policía to put an end to any free entertainment. They screeched in by the dozens to clear the streets. The County Sheriffs they have out there are even worse than LAPD if you can believe it. Down goes one poor old man because he can't move out fast enough to suit them, and they shoved ladies too in a very dirty way. People were running all directions and we ran too.

"Care for a ride home?" Pelón asked a couple of chicks that were going our way.

"On what?" they said. "Your handlebars? Get lost!"

We ran ahead to our Nash. "Just wait till I cruise by and give them the finger," Pelón said and pulled out from the curb.

"There's sheriffs behind us," I pointed out.

"Possibly just by chance."

We cruised down the street. The sheriffs cruised after us. I forgot about the chicks. "Maybe we're on their hot list," I said.

"For this old clunker? Bullshit."

They flashed their reds.

"Son of a bitch," Pelón yelled. "What they picking on me for? I didn't commit no violations."

They gave us a growly blast on their siren.

"Pull over," I begged the guy. "You could make up some story."

Instead Pelón gunned it. We took the corner on two wheels. The siren was really yelling now.

"They shoot out here," I begged him.

The street was parked solid on both sides. Pelón drove down the middle, no room for them to pass. He hung another right. The paving was all torn up, sawhorses, red blinker lights, a ditch along one side and potholes everywhere. My head hit the roof and bounced back off the dashboard. And then another right and now Pelón's aimed at Whittier Boulevard and what looks like solid traffic. Fifty miles an hour, a stop sign ahead in two languages and the guy's laughing like a crazy man.

"Slug the muscatel and say two Hail Mary's," he shouts at me and hits the horn one long solid blast as we slice across the boulevard. I shut my eyes but I could feel headlights burning into me from both sides and hear brakes scream. How we got through all that traffic, I'll never know, and there's the sheriffs hung up at the corner half a block behind.

"Dump the car and run," I yelled. "They'll never recognize us."

But he turned off our lights and whipped into an alley. We raked a fence. Boards played the drums along our fenders. A fat man hollered at us from a porch but we're gone already. Two blocks Pelón ran that alley, dodging trash cans all the way, then turned down the next street, flicked on his lights and slowed to very law-abiding. There's no red lights behind us now. I could hear the sirens but they're way back someplace.

"God damn!" I banged the guy's shoulder. "Son of a bitch, you lost them. You really did!"

I was never in my life so happy.

"Nothing to it," Pelón said modestly.

Now we could cruise free and easy to the bridge across the Freeway. On the other side it's City and the sheriffs got no jurisdiction. My legs were still jumping around like rabbits. Sunday I would definitely go to church and say those two Hail Mary's there was no time for on Whittier Boulevard. I might even crawl to the altar on my knees. But not in my own parish, who wants to start a lot of gossip? I'd go to La Placita where I'm not known, and besides it's an older church and holier too. I made my vow right there but I never kept it because there were those racing red lights again.

"Oh no," I moaned.

"Shit, man, just four more blocks. Come on, baby!"

He floored the gas. The street's solid branches. They crack under the wheels and bang the fenders. The Freeway's just ahead but high up above us. Wrong street. This one is dead end. We missed the bridge. Red lights shine on Pelón's eyes. He quick twists the mirror. Curbing ahead and a steep bank. We skid screeching broadside. A tree snaps off. The doors pop open on their own. Those red lights are too damn close.

Pelón yells, "Split up, to each his own."

He dashes one way, me the other. It's uphill and against the wind. I can barely move. They're yelling at us. Squashy green stuff under my feet. I hear firecrackers. They can't be shooting. Not at us. And then I fell flat and laid there. That squashy green stuff had fat fingers. I dug my face into them and prayed, let them not see me, let them pass me by. But they didn't.

I got dragged to my feet and cuffs snapped on. I saw search-lights but no Pelón, just cops over there in a huddle, two standing, one kneeling down. "Send an ambulance," they hollered, or something like that. It all seemed out of place. Nothing made any sense, like suddenly switching channels on the television.

Chapter
19

THEY TOOK MY PRINTS at the Sheriff station. They searched my clothes and found my comb and seventeen cents. They got disgusted and took me to a tiny room down the hall. It had a chair but no window.

"Your name!" they asked me for the third time.

You have to tell them something. It's the Law.

"Rudy M. Chato," I told them.

"That's no name, asshole," the Mexican cop yelled.

They slapped me around to shake out the facts. Let them kill me, my father was never going to know. Better he thought me dead. And when they asked Address? I gave them a number in the middle of the river.

"Probly got a mile-long record on him," they guessed.

"Hold up your head."

"Profile."

"Full face."

"Look me in the eye."

I looked into so many eyes, blue, gray and green, that I got seasick and threw up on the floor. They threw me a rag and left me alone to clean it up. Through the door I could hear talkers. One sounded nervous. "I saw the little bastard reach for his pocket," he kept complaining. "How did I know he didn't have a gun? And besides, I aimed over his head."

"You could still lose two weeks' pay," they told him.

By now Pelón would no doubt be taking it easy on a clean white bed at County Hospital. What's a little bullet hole? It's nothing. Fifteen minutes and they would have it patched. I would be happy to trade places any day. Finally the report came back on my fingerprints. None on file so they put the cuffs on me again and sent me off to Juvy in a black-and-white, with two friendly sheriffs to cheer me up.

"Wait till those horny bloods climb into him," one said.

"Naw, he's too ugly."

"Not for bloods. How they love that Mexican ass!"

I barely bothered to listen. They drove back on Whittier, took a right on Soto and dropped down into the little hole where Juvy's hidden from the public view. In front they dress it up with grass and trees and a flagpole for your parents' sake, but I was driven around in back where it's pure cement and iron bars. They pressed a button. The gate rattled open then rattled shut behind me, just like prison but a Hall is what they call it, and remember you're not arrested. You're detained, and you're not a prisoner, you're a ward. Nothing goes by its right name at Juvy. It's like those mortuaries with Slumber Rooms for corpses.

A medium-pretty lady behind a window gave the sheriffs a receipt for me, then begged quite motherly for me to phone my family. I was almost sorry to tell her No Thanks. So then they processed me down the corridor. First stop, they took my valuable seventeen cents and my belt, and gave me a claim check. Second stop, the uniform, black tennies, sweatshirt, khakis and a towel with free toothbrush and paper comb. The shower was number 3.

"Be sure to wash your hair," they told me.

It was a big green-tile room, quite cheery. You could shower two dozens at once in there with plenty of hot water, and take your time, where at Aubudon Junior High they run you in and out like pigs. Only one other guy was present, a crybaby blondie that kept collapsing so they got their sleeves all wet holding him up. Compared to him I was quite popular. So then I dressed myself. To my surprise those clothes fitted me perfect, except my khakis had no press in them and I hate that. The nurse came next. She took samples of everything I had and asked, "Syphilis or Epilepsy, honey?" Then they took me down another corridor to cell 57 which was solitary I was glad to see, and locked me in.

"Well well," I told myself. "You finally made it, man. Nobody can criticize you now for chickenshit."

Cell 57 had all the modern advantages, my own hot and cold water, my own private toledo, except no toilet seat for fear you might hang yourself in it, no doubt. The mattress was better than my couch at home and there was an iron desk with a swinging stool attached. To do my homework on?

"Don't write on the walls," they told me when they locked me in. It was far from my thoughts but now my fingers itched for a pen or pencil or even rusty nail so I could sign in with all my past brothers-in-trouble whose names they'd painted over but still you could read them. But what to write with? I tried to file my toothbrush to a point on the cement but it wouldn't file. My fingernails were too short and my comb was paper. Somewhere there's got to be something, I told myself, and finally I found it, stuck with chewing gum to the bottom of the swinging stool, an empty needle with a busted end.

I started on my R but that was my father's name and I wanted no part of him so why not go to CHATO? That was the name I would make famous, not my damn father's. I was starting on the C when the lights went out on me. Never mind, I'll finish up tomorrow. I looked out the window. It had iron gratings on it. So did the one across the way, and all the others. Possibly there might be some mean hombres behind those windows, like those horny bloods the sheriffs bragged about, or guys from Sierra, White Fence or Flats. What would happen when I told them I was Shamrock? I really wished I had Pelón with me then. As frequent visitor he would know just how to act.

What time it was, I had no idea, possibly midnight or beyond. I didn't bother to make up the bed and kept my clothes on, tennies too, in case of unexpected company. I laid down and pulled a blanket over, but when I shut my eyes I got caught up on those If Onlys. If only we shook the cops when

Pelón turned down the alley, if only we didn't drive to East
L.A. Or the Nash didn't start. Or Artemis was what Hungryman reported her. I went back through my whole day scratching off one If Only after another.

Knocking woke me up. It was morning already and somebody was letting himself in with a key. He was black and so
big he had to duck his head coming through the door. I backed
into a corner expecting you know what, but it was my counselor, he said, and Bill Bozeman was his name. He folded
himself onto the top of my desk and planted his shoes halfway
up the wall opposite. They were big enough to go swimming
in. For a wonder he didn't stare into my eyes like all the
others. Instead he got very interested in a cracked place in
the plaster. He reached across the room and ran his fingernail
down it, which was pink to my surprise.

"Rudy M. Chato," he sighed. "Mr. AKA Nobody. Probably
you got reasons to dummy up, hey baby? Couldn't blame
you," he said. "Who wants out when they got a nice clean jail
like this. Why go home when home's all busted up, unknown
uncles kick your ass around the block for nothing. Welfare
food, welfare clothes—"

"Not my home," I interrupted. "My old man works steady."

"Then why didn't you call him up?"

I didn't say.

"He have a heavy hand, your daddy?"

"Pretty heavy," I admitted.

"My daddy had the heaviest hand in Watts," he told me,
"but you know what? When I had my little troubles, about
your age too, police and all, that daddy of mine never laid a
finger on me."

Mr. Bill Bozeman unfolded himself and rested his hands on
the roof and looked at me. "Well, Mr. Rudy Medina Junior
Nobody, I won't waste no more of your time just now."

"Huh?"

"Formerly of 114 Shamrock Street? And will be again if
your 650 release goes through."

Where did they nail me from? Pelón would never talk. Would Lena call police? Never.

"I rather stay here," I doggedly said.

"I'll make a little note of that," he told me. "But now it's breakfast time, Mr. Medina."

He dropped me off at a table on the newcomers' side. They were separate like in a restaurant. I saw the blondie from the showers, hardly anybody else. Maybe business was slow last night. Before I finished eating, a Mexican guy around my age tags me on the shoulder to follow him. He's got a blue scarf around his neck with a gold L printed on it, he didn't say for what.

"Esé, where you from, guy?" he asked.

I told him Eastside, not caring to say too definitely.

"You walk like Shamrock," he said. "I'm Flats myself but everybody's brothers here in Juvy. What they got you in for?"

"G.T.A.," I proudly stated.

"I'm Rape, myself," he told me, "and with a deadly weapon."

He didn't look it.

A gate stared us in the face. They checked our pass and unlocked us through. In the Day Room a dozen guys sat on long green benches goggling like goldfish at the television. They seemed half asleep.

"Reds," the guy from Flats explained. "Reds, whites, yellows, Mary Jane, whatever you use, it's cheaper here than on the outside. You ought to stick around, guy, join the club and get yourself rehabilitáted."

We were outside now. I saw a football field and a gym and a brick schoolhouse with roaring stone lions in front. They had my father's face exactly. "We got an Olympic pool too," my friend reported. "And three times a week there's a dance in the gym. They throw us those little runaway whores from the girls' side. Eeee, you can practically screw them right there on the dance floor."

Everything was very groovy down in Juvy according to my

guide. He gave me the complete conducted tour till a guard happened to look at our pass and ordered us to chase ass to IDC where we belonged.

"What's that?" I asked.

"Intake Detention Crisis or something like that. They decide to either turn you loose or else they don't. Me, I'm a lifer here myself. Ten Foster Homes last year and I busted out of all of them."

More gates unlocked for us till we came to a big room full of glass cages with ladies pounding typewriters. We passed down the aisle between and at the far end there's a door with a window in it.

"Through there, Shamrock," my good friend told me.

When I peeked in he kicked my ass so hard it nearly popped out of my mouth.

"Compliments of Flats," he called and was gone before I could revenge myself.

Through the window I saw three very familiar backs. I wanted to run straight back to cell 57 but the American sitting at the table in there motioned me in. My father didn't even turn his head but Lena jumped up and threw her arms around my neck. "We were up all night," she wailed at me. "Then Elva came over. They called her from the hospital. She's there now with Pelón's twin. Why didn't you phone us?"

I tried to keep a stony face and sat down by my mother. She took my hand which she seldom or never did in public. The walls carried pictures of various colorful mountains and valleys but they failed to cheer me up. I kept swallowing and swallowing.

Mr. Poynter was the American's name, don't ask me what he looked like. I kept my eyes on the table. His voice had a friendly sound but maybe a little bored. He told me all I'd done wrong which I knew already, like taking things that belong to others and drinking wine in cars and endangering lives by running from cops. But was it our fault those sheriffs chased us? Was a $50 Nash worth all that action? That question came to me but I didn't choose to bring it up right then.

So then Mr. Poynter asked me was I sorry for what I did, and I said Yes. And would I ever do the same again? And I said No.

"Rudy," he said, "of all the thousands of youngsters we get here, not one in a hundred conceals his name. Can you tell me why you did that?"

I couldn't, so he told me. It indicated a serious breakdown in interpersonal relations within the family group, he said, a basic failure to communicate. He went on like that and who could understand him? Lena tried to translate for my father but soon gave up.

"Now," said Mr. Poynter finally, "let's see our staff report." He picked up a paper and read: "When interviewed, subject revealed that he comes from an economically viable household, in which, however, the father's role borders on tyranny. Far from being a stabilizing influence, it is perhaps the major cause of this boy's antisocial behavior. If incarcerated the prognosis for rehabilitation is poor. Release in custody of the boy's parents will prove more productive but only under close supervision by the probation department. A stern warning to the father is indicated. Signed, William P. Bozeman, Counselor."

I jumped. Was that black giant some kind of mind reader? And how could he write those high-class words when he talked like somebody you might run into in a pool hall? While I tried to puzzle it out, Mr. Poynter got busy touching his fingertips together. He made a little tent of them, then peeked inside to see what he might find there. It didn't seem to please him.

"Mr. Bozeman adds a P.S.," he told me. "He quotes you as stating you don't want to go home. You'd rather stay here in Juvenile Hall. Do you still feel that way, Rudy?"

I opened my mouth and shut it. I thought about those night dances in the gym, but how about those bloods the sheriffs mentioned? And my good friend from Flats? Then I thought about Lena, and about my mother, and about my friends on the street.

"Speak up, boy," Mr. Poynter said. "Are you ready to go home?"

"I guess so," I mumbled.

He turned to my father. "Mr. Medina, we don't like to come between a father and his son, but in certain cases we have to. I want you to understand that Rudy, if released, will be a Ward of the County of Los Angeles." Lena translated the best she could. "You are not to inflict physical punishment on him, do you understand?"

"Yes, mister," my father said with head hanging down.

"Neither will you shout at him or scold him for what you yourself are in part responsible for. If the boy trusted and loved you, why would he deny his name? This is something you must ask yourself."

Mr. Poynter went on and on like that and I didn't care for it at all. No doubt Lena felt the same because she quit translating. Maybe my father had his bad points but who was he to throw it in my father's face? And would they ever dare to if he was anything more than a Mexican? Then finally Mr. Poynter turned to me.

"Rudy, I want you to understand probation. You'll report weekly to your probation officer. You'll attend school every day and come straight home. I want you to cut all ties with the Shamrock gang, do you understand? Within five days there will be a hearing in Juvenile Court. I think the judge will go along with our recommendations, but a serious crime has been committed, and the final verdict depends on who actually stole that car and who drove it. The police reports are vague. Was it you or the other boy?"

How could I answer that? Pelón was already on probation. It would hurt him worse than me.

"I forget," I said.

"Forget? How can you possibly forget?"

He almost shouted it. Americans go by different rules than us. I kept my mouth shut, but not Lena.

"My dumb brother," she yelled. "He can't even drive a car."

"Shut up, how do you know?" I yelled back at her.

Mr. Poynter looked at me and sighed. "All right, Rudy. Hang tough, if you insist. Probably the other boy has already made a statement."

He phoned the sheriffs and read out the case number. It was a long one. Then he played the drums with a pencil while he waited forever. Finally they came back on the line.

"Oh, Christ," he said. "Will you repeat that?"

He listened again, then hung up.

"The other boy died this morning," he said.

It was very quiet in there till Lena started screaming.

"The boys were running," Mr. Poynter told her. "It was dark. The cops were angry. They're not supposed to shoot but sometimes they do. They're only human."

"It could of been my brother!" Lena screamed.

Chapter
20

SOMEBODY KNOCKED. I opened the door and nearly yelled. Pelón's face was staring up at me with something black as death around it. Then I recognized his twin in a raggedy, old-woman shawl that hung down to hide her big belly.

"My uncle wants you for pallbear," she said.

Already that was too many words for her. Yes, No, Maybe was the most anybody ever heard her speak. And she was chewing gum which I never saw her chew before, and clacking it between her teeth.

"The wake's gonna be Thursday night," she said, "if you're not too busy, and my uncle's gonna buy me a black dress and a new suit for my brother too, and the best coffin they got. He won't cut no cheap corners, my Uncle Ruben says." The twin couldn't stop talking. "And he's hired the Master Chapel at Webster and Ponce's Funeral Parlors. A lot of Italian people might even come, my uncle says. At the hospital they had my brother in a machine. He couldn't even recognize us. Police was there too. Then the machine stopped and they told me kiss your brother because he's dead. My Uncle Ruben cried and cried and my grandma too. They were real nice up there at the hospital and gave me chew'n gum."

Lena came and hugged her and made her sit for coffee.

"Could I hold the baby?" the twin asked, "for practice-like? I've hardly held babies. She's so cute, and I'm gonna call mine Dolores too if she's a girl."

"Eat something," my mother told me.

"I'm not hungry."

"Then go sleep in Lena's room."

"I can't sleep in the daytime," I told her crossly, but I went in there. "I wish they shot me too," I called back and shut the door.

At school everybody knew about Pelón. Wah even cut out the story in the newspaper but it didn't mention my name. They never do with Juveniles unless you're dead. Everyplace I went, kids pointed me out and showed respect. Teachers didn't trouble me with questions and chicks that never knew I was alive before seemed proud to stop and talk.

"You were right there, huh?" they asked.

"Did you see the bullet go in?"

"Was he going steady with anyone?"

"What were his last words?"

Even the Sierra came to me and sympathized.

"That's too much, man," they told me, "shot dead for a clunky Nash. That's like murder, man."

"They never shoot no Paddy kids, I notice."

"Shamrock should take some action on that sheriff, man."

They never said what action but all promised to attend the wake.

"I really hated that little guy," one of them admitted, "but like a brother, man, like a brother."

And some kid I never saw before wondered about the fifty cents Pelón owed him for lunch money.

Going home I walked up beside Gorilla instead of my usual spot. There was no clowning round today. We walked down Broadway to be seen by all. People got out of our way, no doubt wondering what happened to Shamrock suddenly? Back on the street, Pelón's Uncle Ruben screeched his Pontiac convertible alongside of us. We lined up on the curb.

"Get your ass off that fender," he told Kiko. "Which ones are pallbears?"

We stepped forward, six of us.

"Now listen," he said. "I don't want to see no shitty khakis on you at the wake, or blue jeans. Dark suits with pants to match, entiendes? And you," he told Gorilla, "get you a shave and cut your hair. This funeral's gonna be run the right way for once," he said. "I loved that little son of a bitch."

He started crying, then blasted his 400 horses and took off down the street scattering ball players right and left.

"Do me a favor, Chato?" the twin asked later. "They gave me my brother's key, but I'm scared to go down there all by myself."

Pelón always kept his room padlocked. It was under Elva's house in back with slanty doors you walked down through. Nobody ever got invited in that I remember. I wouldn't blame the twin for being nervous. It was black as tar down there.

"He's got a light if you feel around," she called down the steps. I found a string and pulled it. A radio started playing and a heater glared on. There was wall-to-wall carpet but you could feel bumpy dirt under and rocks. In one corner the rug was wet where water dripped down the steps. But what a pad.

Pelón had all the comforts of home. Lined up beside the radio was a 12-inch TV, a coffee maker, waffle iron and electric toothbrush even, each one brand-new and with its price tag on from Thrifty's Drugstore. What an artist that little guy was, in that oversize jacket he always wore to go shopping in. And on top of the toaster was the fat dictionary which my father once bought when he was drinking. So that's where it disappeared to and that's where Pelón got all his big words from.

"Could I come down okay?" the twin called from up above. She was heavy coming down the steps. Whoever she got the big belly from nobody could guess. She hardly left her grandma's house except for school, and she was in 5th grade there. When they were handing out brains her brother got them all.

"You like my brother's stuff, huh?" she asked. "You could take anything you like, Chato. He always said you were the best friend he ever had."

My eyes got wet and starry. If I was Pelón's best friend why didn't he ever let me know? How come I was his special victim when he wanted laughs? After looking round I took the dictionary which the twin wouldn't ever use, or her Uncle Ruben or Elva either.

The day after you get out of Juvy is not the best time to beg your father for a new suit of clothes. So far he hadn't scolded me even one time, perhaps because of Mr. Poynter, but I didn't want to give him any openings so my mother asked for me.

"They want Junior for pallbear," she casually mentioned. "It's going to be at Webster and Ponce's."

"Those bandits," my father said. "Who pays?"

"The uncle."

"That rat," was my father's comment, and when a black suit was suggested he banged the table so hard his beer went flying.

"A suit!" he yelled. "Let him go ask the County. They'll give him a suit, yes with black-and-white stripes and hand-cuffs to match!"

But later Chuchu brought me his Número Uno blue suit to try. It fitted me almost perfect with a few pins here and there. Why couldn't he have been my father? I almost wished.

When you die, Webster & Ponce's Funeral Home is the only way to go. It's the prettiest home in Eastside, everybody points it out, with those tall white columns like George Washington. My father drove us over. In back was a big wreath he bought for $50 to my surprise. "Rodolfo M. Medina y familia," was pasted on the ribbon in fat gold letters. "He was my godson after all," my father said. "If only that boy had taken after my poor dead compadre. I never had another friend like him. And what a clown he used to be at work. He made eight hours go like ten minutes. But as a father, no disciplina. He never hit that boy one time, and now look what's happened."

"I'm gonna faint in there, I know it," Lena said and held

my hand tight. We could barely get her out of the car. Virgie
was there of course with all her tribe. She was specialist in
funerals and would travel 100 miles any day to see a corpse.
"Poor little Richard," she sighed. "I always said he'd end like
this. Hi, Lena, hi, Junior, how fine you look. Did you hear, my
Debra's got her a steady boyfriend already, some fast worker,
huh? And he's a gringo too, on the Jewish side, I think, but
where's my comadre?"

My mother had no use for death. If she showed up for her
own funeral I would be surprised. So then my father went in
to sign the guest book with Lena hanging on him and I went
back to the office where Pelón's Uncle Ruben was waiting for
us. The other five had managed suits too and Gorilla had
shaved himself. He looked like a peeled coconut.

"Now listen," Ruben told us. "A lot of important and re-
fined-type people are coming tonight, business associates of
mine, Italianos mostly, and I want everything kept dignified,
entiendes?"

We said yes.

"Crying's okay," he said, "and even a little wailing from the
women, but no fucking screamers! Anybody starts that, drag
'em out to the parking lot. And don't let nobody start hollering
about cops and murder and all that shit. I'm gonna attend to
that policía myself in person. I got plenty friends at City Hall,
and I'll have his badge and his ass too."

Privately we doubted it. Sheriffs aren't City Hall, they're
County, and for all his big talk and his Pontiac convertible
Ruben was said to be no more than box boy for the Italians.

The chapel was packed solid. All Shamrock Street was
there, Veteranos, Jesters, Pee-wees, parents and so on down
to babies. A lot of the guys showed up very casual with T-
shirts and Ruben threw them dirty looks. Audubon came too,
especially the most gorgeous of the chicks, 10th-graders even,
dressed in their best, hair let down and all. You didn't see a
single curler peeking out from any scarf. Artemis wore black
like a widow. Hipócrita, she tried to touch my hand but I

passed her by. If it wasn't her fault Pelón was laying in his coffin, then whose fault was it?

The ceiling was blue with twinkling electric stars like heaven. Long, sad gray curtains hung to the floor and they were real velvet. The benches had cushions and padded kneelers too. Sweet organ music hung heavy in the air. It felt as holy as any church but more comfortable. In front was a big statue of the Holy Virgin, not dark-skin Guadalupe, too many Italian customers for her, but one of those blondie Virgins, I don't know her name, but her face was in full bloom like a movie star and she smiled down on Pelón so sweet and sad, it made me want to cry.

The coffin had an innerspring mattress and Never-Leak seals and costed $1,750, Ruben informed us. You never saw so many flowers, baskets, sprays, made-up wreaths standing on their own three legs. The Sierra sent a cross of all-white flowers, but not as big as the big red bleeding heart we pitched in and sent from Shamrock. We told them to write KILLED BY COPS on the ribbon but they wouldn't, so we settled for WE WILL NEVER FORGET YOU EVER, PELÓN, except the uncle changed it to RICHARD for more dignified.

Doña Eufemia said the Rosary. She was a church rat from Milflores Street and her old voice scratched and whistled like sandpaper, too fast to hear the words. I mumbled my responses, the ones I could recall, and said buzz-buzz on all the rest. So after that was finally over, Ruben signaled us to pass by the coffin first and take our places just behind it. When I walked up those two soft-padded steps and past that velvet rope, I suddenly couldn't breathe, maybe from all those flowers. When I got to the foot of the coffin I shut my eyes, afraid of what I might see till Kiko pounded my arm and I forced myself to look.

If Pelón died hurting, he wasn't hurting now. The bullet came out through his jaw, they said, but you would never know it. Maybe they used body putty. The guy was laying

there so cozy on those silky quilts, so suave in that blue suit
his uncle bought him which was the first full suit he ever had
in all his life. There was a sad little smile on his lips, which
were pinker than I remembered. His complexion seemed a
few shades lighter too. You really have to give Mr. Webster
credit and Mr. Ponce or whoever does their work. They may
charge a lot but they do a whole lot for you.

I watched while people passed by the casket.

"Eeee, how lifelike," they whispered.

"He could be sleeping," they said.

"He was the best, man. He was the best there is."

They passed by in ones and twos and families, so mournful,
but how many of them cared for my friend alive or even bothered to say Hi to him? They called him hoodlum, trouble-
maker, bad influence and "Get your ass out of here, punk,"
but now, lying in his coffin and fine clothes he was everybody's number 1.

Ernie Zapata passed and held my arm tight but I didn't
want to look at him. Gorilla's mother passed with the uncle-
of-the-week, and Buddha's little brothers. Chuchu passed by
and cleared his throat that way he had, and Virgie and Arturo,
then my father holding Lena's arm. She was so pale, and
leaned down and kissed Pelón on the lips. It made my tears
start rolling. What if it might be me lying in that coffin? I could
feel myself on that lacy pillow looking through my lashes into
Lena's eyes. I could see my father crying over me and begging
pardon for all the wrongs he did me in my life. And after,
would come a big parade of beauties from Audubon and elsewhere, dropping tears on my cold cold cheeks. I found myself
envying Pelón. No more school, no more worries, dead in the
flower of my early years and the whole world remembering
me forever. Till Charlie Chueco's ugly face woke me up. "I
told you, asshole," he hissed, and spidered past me and out
the door.

By now it was mostly women in the chapel. The men and
guys would be in the parking lot smoking, hugging long-lost
friends, passing half-pints and memories from hand to hand.

The family still sat in the side room back of those gauzy curtains. People came and went in there reciting those "Te acompaño en tus sentimientos" and the other things you are supposed to say. Elva was crying steady. Tears ran off her big face like Niagara Falls. I'm ashamed to say I kept looking for that 6th-grader aunt which Pelón used to brag about, either she didn't come or else she was a fairy tale. Among all the cousins crying, aunts and far uncles, the twin still was tearless and quite casual. She was wearing the new black dress her Uncle Ruben bought her and when she came up to the coffin her belly stuck out like Mt. Baldy. And she stood looking down quite a while, busily chewing on her gum.

"They parted him wrong," she finally said. "Got a comb, Chato?" When she reached in to comb him her hand touched Pelón's forehead. And right there she broke.

"He's too cold," she started screaming. "That's not my brother! They put a dummy in there with his picture on it." People pushed up the padded steps to see. Guys heard the scream and jammed in from the parking lot. "They murdered him and stole his body," the twin was screaming. We tried to drag her outside as instructed but suddenly her Uncle Ruben's fighting with us, eyes rolling like he's gone crazy.

"Pinchi policías," he's yelling. "Hijo de la chingada! Baby-killers!" He hammered on the coffin with his fists. He clawed down the blanket of flowers that costed him 200. Mr. Ponce tried to drag him off.

"Quiet! Silencio! Show respect!" he hissed.

"They didn't respect my brother," the twin screamed.

"They shot him because he was a Mexican," somebody yelled.

That did it.

A wave of people came crashing through the velvet ropes. Girls screamed and shrieked. Guys yelled all kind of crazy things, me too, don't ask me what. Women got pushed and fell. Blows got thrown. The uncle swung at anyone in reach. Wreaths came crashing down, the white cross of Sierra, the red heart of Shamrock. It was a wonder the coffin didn't go rolling. And then it all stopped, just the way it started, with a scream, a scream like none that went before, a scream that cut through all the yelling like an ice pick.

Pelón's twin was rolling on the floor. Her eyes turned up till all you saw was whites, and kicking with her feet and beating on the floor with her fists. Somebody hollered Doctor! Mr. Webster and Mr. Ponce carried her outside. Somebody had a car. It drove off fast. I looked around. Busted wreaths, smashed flowers, girls with dresses torn and hair in tangles hugged each other in little bunches. Guys had sleeves ripped off, torn shirts, bloody noses.

"Indians!" Mr. Ponce yelled at us. "Hoodlums! What a scandal! Look at my flowers!"

We helped him set the wreaths back up. Somebody had put a fist through the Sierra cross, perhaps by chance. We apologized. They took it the right way.

"Everybody go home now, immediately," Mr. Ponce ordered.

"How about the Slumber Room?" we asked. We had planned to spend the night in there with Pelón.

"No slumber room for gangsters. Look at my velvet curtains. No respect! No cultura!" We stood around the coffin to say goodnight, the pallbears and some few others. Pelón still had that little smile which the undertakers put on his face but now it didn't look so saintly or so sad. It seemed more on the happy side. I doubt if he was sorry for what happened. All his life that crazy guy cared more for excitement than he ever did for velvet curtains or respect, or cultura even.

Chapter

21

NEXT MORNING WE LINED UP by the coffin. They handed us white cotton gloves and carnations for our buttonholes which they picked off Pelón's flowery blanket. Those who wanted one last look had already passed by, the family last, except the twin. She was in the hospital, it was said. When the chapel was cleared of all but us, Mr. Webster lowered down the coffin lid.

"Split, guy," I prayed. "Get out of there."

I seemed to feel a little breeze pass by my face, or was it imagination? Mr. Webster screwed down the bolts. Mr. Ponce gave us our signal. Three and three we walked beside the coffin while it rolled on shiny bike wheels down the ramp to the hearse. Mr. Ponce opened the big side door and pressed a button. The coffin-catcher buzzed and swung out. We put Pelón on its silver tracks and it buzzed him back inside.

Father Dos Casas stood waiting at the church in his purples. Father Dos Casas was from Spain and never let you forget it. In catechism, Pelón used to kill us laughing when he imitated those *th*'s the father used, till he got excommunicated from the class. A lot of Shamrock stood waiting for us too. My father even missed work for the day and so did plenty others, and they made an opening for us at the curb and we wheeled the coffin down the aisle with rubber tires whispering on the floor.

Father Dos Casas raced the mass. His altar boys could

barely keep up. When they rang those bells for the Divine
Mystery of the blood and bread, I had a different mystery on
my mind. Where was Pelón? Was he inside that box or out of
it? I preferred to see him invisible, perched on the coffin lid
and enjoying the service, and when the father threw Holy
Water he squinted up his eyes and asked, "Do you also fur-
nish towels?" which in life he used to ask those wet-spray
talkers. What I didn't want to see was Pelón inside and
scratching to get out. Better he should be flying around to try
out his wings, and tickling the chicks on the backs of their
necks and other places. Why not? because across the aisle I
saw a couple of them scratch their armpits.

After the mass, Father Dos Casas preached down at us. "I
was acquainted with the defunct," he preached. "Yes, I knew
Richard, if all too briefly, this same Richard who now lies
before us dead, dead of a violent and a terrible death, his
young life cut short before he was confirmed. And yet, who
can doubt the mercy of Our Lord, Jesus Christ? For at this
boy's final breath, time was granted to confess himself to a
priest of the church, and to receive absolution, so who can
doubt that Richard will be found acceptable in the eyes of
Our Lord."

Father Dos Casas doubted it. You could tell from his face
which looked like a sour green olive. And then he took aim at
the pallbear's bench. "O young men," he preached in his
Spanish Spanish, "young men whose faces I seldom see in
church but often on certain street corners, let me warn you of
the deadly path you follow. That scandal which took place last
night, I heard of it and I grieved. Shameful, shameful! Violence and rage in place of sorrow and Christian hope. Young
men, I know of your sins, who does not? but never from your
own lips in the confessional. O my children, I beg you to come
to me, to fall on your knees and ask forgiveness for your evil
ways, to dedicate yourselves from this day forward to a holy
life, a Catholic life. Learn from the tragic death of your young
friend, let it be the occasion for your own redemption. Or one
day soon I may be speaking these same sad words over you.

Ask yourselves, will I be next? Will I be struck down in the
very act of sin? Will I be damned to spend eternity in the fires
of Hell?"

I tried not to listen. That other father at the hospital came
to mind. God had spared me then, he said. Now He spared
me a second time. Would he spare me from death number 3?
How many chances do you get? Last night Lena sat me down
after the wake and begged me to mend my ways, but how?
What did they want me to do besides homework?

"Give up your sins, young men, give up your lawlessness
and savage rage," Father Dos Casas urged. "Remember that
those who pick up the sword will surely die by it."

"What's all that sword-talk?" Gorilla whispered to me. "A
thirty-eight was what they shot him with."

Looking back, I counted 17 cars with funeral stickers and
headlights burning, but Hungryman claimed 20. We were
next behind the hearse, in Mr. Webster's Cadillac with the
two jumper seats and Kiko up front with the driver. The cop
raced his motorcycle to stop the traffic on Main, then waved
us through and ripped ahead to catch the next stop light. He
was an imitation cop, for funerals only, but he wore that ugly
uniform and I prayed for him to wreck, but he didn't.

"Look what somebody handed me at church," Buddha said.
"Looks like some kind of poem only who could read it?" It
was crumpled up and the writing was sloppy and smeared
but finally I managed it out loud. "ADIÓS PELÓN," was the
title.

We will never hear your happy laugh again
And that is why I now pick up a pen
To say goodbye to my dear friend.

With your cheery smile and big brown eyes
You used to turn our gloomy days to bright blue skies.
But you are gone now, you are dead
At 16 years old, shot through the head
By some County Sheriff's murdering hot lead.

We will never forget you, Pelón and we swear
Our prayers will follow you upstairs
Till some fine day by a lucky chance
We'll all get together and shake hands
'Cause there's sure to be another Shamrock in the sky
And we'll meet you on the corner there and tell you Hi.

Kiko found his voice first. "Eee, man, that's a real fine poem only who could ever write it?"

"Some chick," Buddha thought. "No guy could find those words or say 'dear friend' either."

"Boxer," was Hungryman's idea.

"Too dumb, man."

"Not if her sister helped her."

"That 'Shamrock-in-the-sky' really gets to me, man," Gorilla said and blew his nose.

I volunteered to copy it out for everybody.

"Use red ink," they said, "like in blood."

We floated past the hospital on that famous Cadillac ride and up Marengo. On our right was a big muddy gash I'd never seen before, like scraped bare with a monster hoe. Detroit Street was gone and Decatur too and all those others, I forget their names. Bulldozers were hard at work filling dump trucks. It was an ugly sight.

"I had an uncle used to live down there," Kiko remembered. "He had a real nice little home too, only the roof leaked."

"What they gonna do there?" somebody asked.

"Freeway," somebody answered.

A dump truck roared up out of there and tried to cut in behind the hearse, then changed his mind. We shook fists out the window and called him everything. "Is Shamrock gonna end up like that?" Buddha wondered. He was the anxious type.

"Never," we told him. "Never while we live, man!" And our funeral trailed on toward Soto Street.

You drive slantwise into Calvary between two stone pillars with iron gates between. First come the offices where you put down payments on your plot. Next you pass by a street of marble houses big enough to raise a family in with all-American names carved up over. From there if you look up the hill you see a big flock of marble angels, life-size or better, and that's Italianos. On the other side, on the left, that's where the Mexican class of people go, Gómez, Gonzales, Rivera and all like that. It's all grass there. The stones are laid so lowly you could barely see them from the car.

"My old man's over by that tree," Gorilla said. "We used to put fresh flowers, me and my mom, but not for a long time now."

"There's for Pelón," Buddha pointed out.

It was like a sudden garden in the grass, solid flowers. The wreaths and sprays circled it like fruit trees in bloom. You knew that in the middle was that ugly hole cut into the dirt but they didn't let you see it, and I was glad of that.

"Put on your gloves."

The coffin-catcher swung out buzzing for the last time. The ground was too bumpy for the silver cart. We carried Pelón, which would be nothing, the guy barely weighed 100 pounds, but that coffin was heavy like a battleship. Kiko kept stumbling. I heaved up tighter on my handle to take the weight. It hurt my shoulder and I wanted it to hurt. Mr. Webster led us up the slope. He was very careless about stepping on people's gravestones but we did our best to walk between.

They had like a machine with pipes for rollers and we set the coffin on them. And then I saw the hole. They tried to hide it with blankets of false grass but between the rollers you could see straight down in and it was black black. I looked away and saw a little hill. It was covered with false grass and flowers casually tossed on top, but underneath would be a pile of dirt and I knew where that dirt came from and where it was going back to after.

Pelón's uncle could barely sit in his chair. People held him. His eyes were purple like a bruise and he made noises in his throat. They brought a special heavy-duty chair for Elva. The family sat. All others stood. We made a circle. Father Dos Casas said his words. He threw more Holy Water on. This time I couldn't hear Pelón asking for any towel. I looked up in hopes to see some sign from him. A bird flew down from a tree and landed on the grass but it didn't prove anything, it was just any bird going about its particular business. Pelón never cared much for birds besides. He used to go for them with a slingshot. No use hoping any more, Pelón was locked into that coffin and no way out. Last night I almost envied him. I didn't envy him now.

We marched by the coffin first.

"The gloves," Mr. Ponce whispered. He signaled us to drop them on the coffin which we did, except I slipped one glove in my pocket to keep forever. People followed us and dropped their handful of dirt as they passed by. Some broke and moaned. Others didn't. I hardly payed attention. Father Dos Casas cut out with his altar boys. Old women in black trailed off behind him.

"Come on, man," Kiko told me, "hurry up, they're waiting for you."

"Please," Mr. Ponce hissed at me. He wanted his Cadillac for another job, and his hearse. I didn't hear him. Suppose Pelón woke up in his coffin and clawed for air and banged his fists against the sides. And nobody to hear him, nobody to holler help and crash that lid and rip it off. Somebody had to stay. I was the last to see him alive and running. I would be the last to see him dead. That's what a friend is for, or brother.

"Crazy guy, what's wrong with you?" they argued, but finally the pallbears left without me. I heard cars driving off. Let them go. I'll wait till they strip that false grass from the hole. I'll watch them hook the coffin and take away those rollers. I'll watch them lower it in the hole. And then I'll watch them shovel the dirt back on top and stomp it down with their big feet. Then maybe I'll go, maybe not. And every

Sunday I'll bring fresh flowers and sit beside my friend. My eyes got cloudy. I reached in my pocket for a handkerchief and found the white glove instead. I wiped my eyes on it, till a heavy hand closed on my shoulder.

"Time to go," my father said.

"He's inside there!" I argued.

"It's only dust."

With arm around, he moved me down the hill and past a grave I didn't see before. They had made a picnic there. A bottle of beer half-empty was standing on the headstone and a bitten-into sandwich and a piece of birthday cake with pink icing. Two cigarettes, one part-smoked, and matches. It had rained on them yesterday.

"If it's only dust down there what's all that for?" I asked.

"They make a party," my father said, "and leave a little bit behind, just in case. But it's only superstition."

He bent down to inspect the stone.

"Francisco X. Aragón," he recited. "Dead five years. They got long memories in that family."

Chapter
22

ON TUESDAY MR. PILGER CAUGHT ME between Spanish and Social Studies to ask about the Coroner's Inquest. They held it the day after Pelón's funeral. So I told him.

"You mean to tell me," Mr. Pilger shouted, "you mean to tell me two weeks' suspension is all that killer gets?"

"Without pay," I added.

"And then goes back in uniform to shoot some other kid. And nobody protests? Nobody brings charges? Where's the ACLU? Where's the Mexican Political What's-its-name? I'm going to bring this to the attention of the B'nai B'rith," he promised, whatever that was.

You could see sparks in his all-electric hair. Everybody in the corridor turned to gawk at us.

"They claimed they found a gun on him after," I explained. "They claimed I might not be telling the whole truth, or else maybe I didn't know what my friend had in his pockets."

"I can't believe it," Mr. Pilger said. "Not in this day and age!" I wondered where he had been living all his life. It took him quite some time to cool down. The warning bell rang. Guys were running now but Mr. Pilger held me. "Your probation officer came this morning to see your records. Mr. Fujita. Very thorough. Told me he was once a student here himself."

"I better get to class," I said.

"Rudy," Mr. Pilger said. "Rudy, God love you, try not to hate. Hate will poison you."

I said okay and joined the stampede. I barely made it before the tardy bell.

At my other hearing which was yesterday the judge placed me on one year probation the way Mr. Poynter suggested. I hoped to be assigned to the Big Bill Bozeman type but Mr. Fujita was what they gave me. Don't think I'm prejudiced against the Oriental class of people, but if this Mr. Fujita ever went to Audubon Junior High it would be only human for him to pay back the Mexicans for the rough times they gave him there. He was due to call at our house at 4:30 and by the time 4 o'clock rolled around I found myself quite nervous. I put on a fresh white shirt and combed myself. My mother was busy waxing the linoleum to shine.

"Should I make him a taco, maybe?" she asked.

"They only eat raw fish," I informed her.

"Qué barbaridad!"

Lena tried to hand me Dolores.

"It'll look real good if he finds you holding the baby," she argued. "Is my hair okay?"

"Very comely," I told her out of Pelón's dictionary that used to be my father's.

Could Mr. Fujita be early? We heard someone on the porch and Lena went but it was Gorilla. He blushed at her as usual.

"I only wanted to say," he said, "that there's a certain person on the street and I heard her talking to Elva on the porch."

"Oh yeah?" Lena said.

"She's talking dirty things about your father. Says, 'I'm gonna take him to court.' Says—I don't know what all. Says, 'I'm gonna tell him off in public.' Maybe it isn't none of my business but you ought to know about it. And she's drinking too. I gotta go now. But if you need any help—"

Gorilla went stumbling down the stairs, all heels.

"Eeeho," Lena said. "That's all it takes to make life perfect around here, a Jap probation officer and that big-mouth loose on the street."

"Should we ought to tell my father?" I suggested.

"Never," my sister said. "He's nervous enough like it is, but I'll tell you one thing, if that bitch comes over here to make trouble I'm personally gonna kill her."

My father came from work early to change clothes.

"Not your funeral suit," Lena begged him. "Be more on the casual side." So he put on his green shirt with the pineapples. My father was not in the best of moods. "They got no right to come in a man's house," he mumbled. "Ask questions, peek into closets. Are you real proud of yourself?" he asked me.

I didn't say.

"And see you interpret good for once," he crossly told my sister.

Nobody could ever predict my father's English. Sometimes he even could understand politicians on the TV. Other times you had to translate "Where's the fly-swatter?" And when he spoke English he sounded just like Sitting Bull. Where my little mother that could understand every English word was too timid to say even "Buenos días" in anything but the Spanish language. So anyway, there we sat in our corner waiting for the opposition to step into the ring.

Mr. Fujita came on the dot of 4:30. He was Ivy League with rimless glasses. He had a very polite and gentle voice but his words were so exact they sounded chopped out of ice.

"I must ask some very personal questions," he told us after shaking everybody's hand. "Please don't think of me as a policeman. Our departments are quite separate. Regard me as a counselor, or family doctor. What we are dealing with here is a kind of illness, a social illness I shall call it, and we must understand its causes before we can expect a cure."

He waited for Lena to translate. When my father said "Sí, señor," he proceeded on. "With many boys," he said, "the family situation is so hopeless that I have to recommend foster homes, but I hope that won't be necessary in this case." Then he turned to me and rapid-fired his questions. Did I have my own private room for sleep and study? What did I eat for breakfast because diet was important to mental health as well. How many hours did I watch television? While I tried to answer him, Mr. Fujita's eyes moved round the house like tiny black cameras snapping pictures all the way. Did I have a weekly allowance? No. Regular chores around the house? Yes. What were they? And how about girls? Was I going steady?

"Don't act so sullen," Lena mumbled at me in that rapid-fire Spanish you use with English-speakers present. "And smile once in a while," she suggested, "and tell him Sir." My mother wondered if she might serve him coffee at least, but I shook my head. It might look like a bribe. A lot of very private Spanish got whispered into the cracks between Mr. Fujita's 1,000,000 questions.

"Now tell me, Rudy," he asked next, "would you consider yourself a regular member of the Shamrock gang?"

My father understood that without translation and got quite excited in English. I bit my teeth and tried to shut my ears.

"I telling him hundred time, you stay 'way from those sinvergüenzas. Smokee, drinkee, make much trouble alla time. You end up dead maybe or in la prisión. Every day me telling him but he no pay 'tention."

Mr. Fujita turned his cameras on my father. " 'Telling' a boy is often not productive," he said. "Neither is threatening him or shouting at him. Mr. Medina, do you ever sit down for a straightforward man-to-man discussion with your son? Do you discuss his problems at school and with his friends? Do you really listen to his point of view?"

I hated it before with Mr. Poynter and I hated it now. My father might have his faults here and there but how could the Oriental type possibly understand them? But he went on and on. When did my father enter the country? Had he ever been in jail? Or on the welfare? And why had he not applied for American citizenship after all these years? Till Lena couldn't stand it any more.

"Lemme tell you something about my father, mister," she interrupted. "Maybe he don't speak English good and maybe he don't got his citizenship but he works hard like maybe you never had to. You're educated. But my father, you should see him after work, tired, disgusted, grease all over him. And you expect him to study a bunch of history books and go to night school? He even works weekends, mister, in cement, to bring a little more money home."

Mr. Fujita was very patient, to give him credit. He didn't try to argue, just sat back and listened while my fighting sister raved on. Up to now she stuck fairly close to what you might call the truth but now Lena got carried away, she was like that. "My father is a very good father," she bragged. "He takes us to the circus and the zoo and the ball games and to look at all those bones in the museum over there in Exposition Park." Her voice got quite dreamy while she carried on about our saintly father but possibly there's a punishment for lying, even if it's lying in a good cause because right then a commotion broke out on the street. A certain very ugly female voice from our front gate came banging through our doors and windows.

"Oiga tú, pinchi cabrón! Tú sabes a quien hablo! Sálgase de aí, culón!"

She dared my father to come out. She called him everything. He sat frozen in his chair, but to Mr. Fujita it might have been just a passing train, and my sister didn't seem to hear.

"Evenings," she went calmly on, "my father's friends come by. 'Compadre,' they tell him, 'let's go someplace and have a brew.' 'Not me,' says my dad. 'If I want a beer or two I'll have it right here at home with the family.' "

From outside came, "Sinvergüenza, hipócrita, leave me pregnant with your brat, will you? Not Socorro Gutiérrez! You gonna pay up, entiendes?"

Thanks be to God she stood in Spanish.

"My father even helps my brother with his homework when he can understand it," Lena went on. "And if we need a few dollars for anything, all we have to do is ask. Yes, Mr. I-forget-your-name-excuse-me, we got a real warm and loving family here, no problems."

"Then why," Mr. Fujita asked, "did your brother steal that car?"

Lena blinked like just waking up.

"What car?" she asked. It took her a minute to come back to earth, meanwhile that voice outside couldn't seem to quit.

"Chinga tu madre, tu vas a pagar and pay damn good. Entiendes? Do you hear me? Yes, even if you gotta sell your damn house to do it."

It was Spanish still but my sister had enough of it. "Excuse me," she said to Mr. Fujita. "I'll go quiet down that poor crazy woman outside. She's a Metodista, you know the type and comes here once a week to preach at us Roman Catholics. If I give her fifty cents she'll go away."

Lena went through the kitchen instead of out the front, I wondered why. I saw her through the side window headed for the gate. And recalled that famous battle at the Arco Iris, and Soco's arms that were strong as hams. She outweighed my sister 30 pounds or more. Should I go out there? But what about my probation officer? And if I showed myself who knows what that woman might bring up from my past history? So I just sat, I'm ashamed to say. Mr. Fujita looked at his watch. With 117 cases on his list he couldn't spare more time, he said, and handed me a County pamphlet. "Do's and Don't's of Probation," was its name and he handed another copy to my father in the Spanish language.

Exactly what my sister said or did out there at the gate I'll never know, but the next I heard of Soco's voice it came from far away across the street. It had a lot of cops and murder in it but you could barely hear them. And in a minute Lena tripped in the front door like fresh from the beauty parlor.

"Where were we in our conversation?" she sweetly asked.

"At the end," Mr. Fujita said and again shook hands with everybody and reminded me to come on Thursday to his office. And then, just as he started out the door he turned to Lena. Some question seemed to be on his mind.

"Dígame, qué dijiste a la borrachita?" Mr. Fujita asked in

perfect barrio Spanish. "Cómo la corrió?" Meaning what did she say to that drunken lady to get rid of her.

Lena answered, "Huh?"

Others caught their breath.

We watched Mr. Fujita off the porch and down the steps.

"Mexican stepmother," he called back. "Five Mexican step-brothers, for ten long years." So then he waved his hand in the air, climbed into his car and adiós.

My father's face was a sight to see.

"How dirty!" Lena yelled. "To listen in and not admit it." Then she relaxed and even laughed. "Eeeho, at least it's all out in the open now. With all he knows of us I guess Mr. What's-his-name is a permanent member of the family."

"Only for one year," I said.

"You hope," she said.

"What did you do outside?" I asked.

Lena showed the chicken-killer knife from the kitchen drawer. Nobody made any comments. My father sat holding his head in both his hands, squeezing it tight as if it might be a nut.

"Well," Lena finally said through the family silence, "Hurray for the Medinas!"

Chapter
23

"WOULD YOU BE HAPPIER in a Foster home?" Mr. Fujita asked.

"What's the Fosters like?" I asked him back.

It was my second visit to his office and while Mr. Fujita explained those Foster homes I thought about my own. The house was like holding its breath. There were no loud arguments or even quiet ones. Ever since Soco made her scandal on the public street, my father hardly went out except to work. Now and then Chuchu tried to drag him off to the Aztecs' club but my father preferred to drink his beers at the kitchen table, like living out my sister's lies.

"The damn street's a cemetery," Chuchu complained, "not only you, compadre, nobody talks no more. S.P. may be getting to them, no matter their names on the petition. Every time I go out real-estaters are knocking on my neighbors' doors. Oh, the hell with everybody. I'm off to the Aztecs' even if I'm the only Christian there."

My father sat at the TV with his cowboys. My mother was the same puzzle as always, but after the lights went out I heard rumblings and grumblings through the bedroom door and last night my mother left my father's bed and slept with Lena.

"There's no disgrace in living with another family," Mr. Fujita finally said. "In my own case I would have been better off. And it doesn't have to be permanent. A few weeks, a few months, while your parents settle their differences. So think

about it. Anyway," he said, "I'm glad to see your attendance
record is good at school. Next week then, Rudy?"

Yes, I went to school every day for all the good it did me.
In class I couldn't seem to stay awake and when I went to bed
at night I couldn't sleep. Every minute I found myself expecting something, I don't know what. And one night it finally
came.

It was the anniversary of Pearl Harbor day, they announced
in Social Science. That night my mother was in Lena's room
as usual. She spent a lot of time there on Women's Secrets.
My sister was fighting by mail with her darling Armando. Fat,
angry envelopes came and went every day, all about which
did he love best, her or his damn mamacita? From what I
could manage to read while Lena took her showers. My father
was in the living room with his cowboys when the phone
rang. Like always I had to be the one to answer.

"Wrong number," I said disgusted and hung up.

"Who did they want?" my stupid father asked.

"Some dumb Eleanora or something like that," I told him.

"Pendejo," my mother screamed from Lena's room, "that's
my name!"

I had forgotten it completely. Her friends all called her
Nellie. So right away came the third degree. Were they in
Spanish? Did they sound excited? Where did the call come
from?"

How was I supposed to know? There was a lot of buzzing
on the line and some idiot operator I couldn't understand, and
if people were so particular why didn't they answer the phone
themself, I complained.

My mother slapped my face which she never did.

"It's Mexico. They want me. My mother's dying!" Lena
hugged and baby-talked her. My father woke up finally.

"That old witch," he grumbled, "she'll live ten thousand
years."

If my mother's guess was right this would be her first call
from down there. They didn't even have a telephone in that

little town of hers, it seemed, or even electric lights or faucets. Letters came twice a year which started out, "Hoping you are well in health and disfruiting the perfect happiness in company with your esteemed husband." Then would come four lines of Who died and Which got married and How bad the crops were, as usual. It was always a big day for my mother when those letters came and she used to carry them around all week in her apron pocket.

So my mother sat holding the phone and praying they would call again. They soon did, which proved her only halfway right because my grandma was enjoying the best of health. But it was going to be her seventieth birthday; so couldn't my mother possibly come down? She cried all over the phone and said yes-yes-yes.

"You got to go right away," Lena told my mother when they hung up. "You already got your bus ticket." My mother looked at my father.

"Go," he said. "Didn't I already give permission? Stay a month, a year. We'll get Señor Fujita in to cook raw fish for us." At least he finally knew my probation officer's name.

"If I was you I wouldn't be so sarcastic," my sister told him, but it failed to shut my father up.

"Don't forget to say hello for me to that Faustino which was your sweetheart before I busted his guitar over his hairy ears."

"He's dead," my mother answered.

"May he rest in peace. And say hello to all those others, the one which looked like a frog, and old Monkey-face and Thomas the badger. Your mother had a whole zooful of novios down there."

"Eeeho," Lena sighed, "you really take the prize for jealous."

And then Lena suddenly said "Hey!"

She looked around at us, from face to face.

"Why couldn't we all go down there?" she asked. "Papa, you could drive us in the Buick so it won't cost nothing except a few pennies for gas, and you said yourself the motor needs exercise. Well, how 'bout it? Papa?"

I expected a world-record No. Instead my father stared at her. You could see wheels turning in his head. One of them might be named Soco, another Mr. Fujita, and possibly there were dozens I'll never know about.

"Come on, Papa, don't I get to see my little grandma once in my life at least? And all those uncles with the funny names? And find out the truth behind all those lies you been telling us forever, Señor Vaquero Medina? Would you really get on a crazy bronco and ride him round, Papa? I bet he'll toss you in the river."

"Ten dollars," my father said with money in his hand. For the first time in weeks he grinned. Whenever we begged him to ride for us he claimed the horses were no good and didn't speak Spanish besides, where on the other side he was Buffalo Bill, to hear him tell it. Personally, if I had ten dollars I would have covered him.

But my mother had not been heard from. "What you so quiet about?" Lena asked her, "Don't you want us, or what?"

"I was only planning to take the baby," she said. "Of course if everybody wants to go, and if your father promises to act right around my mother. . ."

"Your mother treated me like dirt and don't forget it, her and her whole tribe. Black, like the Blancos people used to say, black of skin and black of heart, with all their acres here and their hectáreas there, but never a peso to buy you beer with."

"You see?" my mother said.

"I'll sew up my lips," he promised. "And besides, if I say anything wrong no doubt those Indians will scalp me. Only I wonder," he said, "how many of those proud relatives of yours are driving Buick automobiles today? I wonder how they'll look, walking the roads behind those high-class burros of theirs when I come driving past."

My father got him a beer. By now he was in the best of moods.

"Don't think I'll act big with them," he informed us. "No, señor, I'll be real democratic. 'And how goes life with you, Rodolfo?' they'll ask me. 'Oh, not bad,' I'll say. 'I still work for the railroad driving their locomotives when I feel like it but mainly I live off my rentals. And here,' I'll say, 'have an American cigarette. Take the package, man, only tell me, how can you smoke those dog turds they sell down here and call it tobacco?' "

"Eeeho," my mother sighed, "we'll never get out of there alive!"

My father raved on. He talked us all straight across the border as if the whole thing was his idea in the first place, till I mentioned my probation officer.

"I'm still your father. I say where you go and where you don't."

"He'll never let me miss school."

"It's gonna be Christmas vacation," my sister pointed out, "and you could talk to that Mr. Pilgrim that you claim is on your side. He could get you off. I'll meet you in his office tomorrow."

"Am I a baby or something? I could ask for myself."

"You!" Lena said and broke out one of her well-known imitations. " 'Look, man,' " she mumbled around, " 'it's more or less this way, more or less. My old man wants to take me on some kind of crazy trip to Mexico, or something like that, but you wouldn't let me miss school, huh?' "

"I'm not like that!" I yelled at her. She had her head hanging practically between her knees and got my father laughing, and my mother even.

Laying awake that night I didn't know just how to feel about this Mexico. Was it possible my family could be born again down there? My mother would at least for once be happy. And my father? Suddenly he seemed like his old self. It seemed he'd already put that woman behind him, but she could still make trouble with a lawyer, or maybe even pay some hoods to chop my father off at the knees. She was a friend of Ruben's and his well-known Italianos. Was that what kept my father off the streets? Or was it shame? Either way Mexico could be his savior. And maybe down there, he would at least be out of reach and who knows, he might even start getting lovey-dovey with my mother like in the old days. But how about myself?

I was all against it when the subject first came up. I hate the way they talk Spanish down there, who can understand them? And I'd be surrounded by a whole gang of Indians, as my father called them. And yet, on the other side, I had always wondered about Family. I had none living in L.A. on my mother's side or on my father's either, where all my friends were loaded down with them. "What's an uncle like?" I used to ask. "Once in a while they might bring you presents," would be the answer. But what I really had to know is, how do you feel toward your aunt or your cousin or your grandma for instance? Does blood call to blood? And always I envied my friends when they went out to Montebello to baptize a far cousin with all their family present. So yes, I finally decided, yes, I'll go, and give Mexico a try.

And how about those little dark-skin girls, those morenitas that my father spoke of and his friends? Those plump and generous ones? Possibly they would find me quite thrilling coming down there from the city of L.A., California, to visit their dumpy little village. And how about my father's big stories of the cowboy life down there? Why not take a chance? I asked myself, and just before I fell asleep that night I dreamed of riding fiery horses with my father, cutting through the wind.

And how about those interesting snakes they have down there?

Next day during Nutrition I was at my counselor's door where Lena promised to meet me. She was late as usual and I was glad of it.

"My father wants to take me to Mexico," I told Mr. Pilger, "if you could persuade Mr. Fujita it's okay. I'll have to miss a little school." I explained about my seventy-year-old grandma and the place she lived and how it didn't have phones or anything. I soon got bored listening to myself.

"Who was Dolores Hidalgo?" Mr. Pilger interrupted.

"Search me," I said.

"Porfirio Díaz? Benito Juárez?"

Suddenly it came back to me. "He was the Mexican Lincoln," I proudly stated. "He freed the slaves."

"Hurray," Mr. Pilger said. "Good for him!"

"We had all that stuff in the B-Seven," I told him, "and our textbook had a cactus on the cover with a burro and some beardy guy in an iron suit up the clouds someplace."

"What a memory!" Mr. Pilger said. "But from inside the book all you know is, 'He freed the slaves.' And they call it Education."

Lena slipped in then but Mr. Pilger was too busy shouting to notice her. "Six whole months you wasted in that class! One day in Mexico will teach you more. God love you, son, of course you can be excused and Max Pilger will stick out his neck for you. What an opportunity, Rudy. The temples of your ancestors, the land of your fathers, you'll see them with your own eyes."

He was charging around the office now and suddenly he bumped into Lena. "Who's this?" he asked.

"His sister," Lena admitted.

"Why, what a pretty girl," Mr. Pilger said like surprised. "Sit down, miss, sit down. Son, did I ever tell you I once followed in Moses' footsteps, by jeep of course. The Red Sea, Sinai, the Promised Land, yes, Max Pilger banged his head against the Wailing Wall and learned to be a Jew again. Go thou, Rudy and do likewise. Find your roots! Discover your identity!"

He ran his fingers through his hair to calm it down.

"I'll square you with Mr. Fujita, don't worry," he said and snatched a guidebook from his desk. "Read it," he ordered. "And mind you, don't miss the pyramids. Remember, we Jews had ours. Egyptian, yes, but by God we hauled those rocks."

"You see?" I told Lena in the hall outside, "who needed you?"

"I still can't believe him," she said. "All my counselor ever knew to say was 'Take Home Economics.' Maybe he's a little crazy in the head but he likes us and how they hate that! They'll fire him sure. So come on, I'll buy you a Coke. Do they still got the machine where it used to be? Or is it busted as usual?

My little mother that hardly used to leave the house now started going every day to Goodwill over on Avenue 19, or the Salvation Army. She brought home so many sacks of clothes she might be shopping for the Republic of Mexico.

"How come?" I asked her, "if your family's rich like my father says?"

"Your father!" she said. "They're poor like you never saw up here. They live and die in rags. For once they're gonna wear something pretty in their lives."

She dragged out her treasures to the washing machine.

"Look at this blouse." She held it up. "Like new except for bloodstains."

"Hey," I asked her from curiosity. "How about my father? Was he really a big-shot cowboy down there like he claims?"

"Juan Charrasqueado."

"Like in the song?" I asked. They played it all the time on the Mexican radio, all about this scarface cholo that grabbed off all the pretty girls in town and shot their husbands, till they killed him.

"The same exactly," she said, "except your father's still alive."

But who could ever tell about my mother, if she was joking or on the level?

This seemed to be our week for phone calls. The next was Mr. O'Gara for my father. He had looked things up in his books, he said and we had the Law on our side, but he needed $25 more for his expenses.

"I've already got S.P. on the run," he boomed. "They've raised their price to $10,000. Do you still hold out, Mr. Medina?"

My father did.

"Good, what about the others? I've heard rumors you'll be seeing building inspectors. You've got to let them enter, it's the Law, but don't talk to them and don't argue. Just call my office. I'll handle it. Nothing to be afraid of."

After Mr. O'Gara hung up my father was ready to burn more candles on his altar.

"Did he want more money?" my mother asked.

"Twenty-five and what's that? Nada. I went to borrow 300 from the Union and they let me have 500." He forced 50 in my mother's hand to do her shopping with. Her bus ticket was already spent. "If we're gonna play Santa Claus to all those Indians, let's do it right," my father said.

By nine o'clock next morning my mother was beating on the door at Goodwill. She shopped the As-Is department mostly, fishing through boxes raw off the trucks before anything was washed or fumigated. That way she stretched her $50. Good sturdy shoes were a quarter, which might cost seventy-five cents at least when sold at the store up front. She bought men's old-time double-breasted suits with Superman padding in the shoulders for $1 or less and work pants for a dime. They were busted at the knees but could be easy patched. And underwear and sweaters and coats and dresses years out of style but down there who would know the difference? And kids' clothes she bought especially in all sizes, and babies'.

My mother dragged them home by bus, somehow. Some days I helped her. My father was too proud to be caught shopping in such places. And then till 2 A.M. the washing machine sweated on our back porch and Virgie's borrowed Singer kept it company while Lena helped my mother patch and mend and hang.

Our backyard turned into a spiderweb, so many clotheslines you had to crawl on your knees to feed the chickens. In order to save space, nothing got ironed. My mother rolled the clothes up as tight as iron pipes with rubber bands around and stuffed them into paper sacks, dozens of them, the Buick was piled so high with junk it looked like Mount Everest. You should have heard my father holler.

"It'll never fit! Do you want to bust the axles?" But by push and by pull and hammering with fists and by my father jumping up and down on the trunk we finally got the lid to catch, and went to bed. But around one in the morning I woke up and heard somebody messing with the Buick. I sneaked the front door open. The hood was up. It was my father taping his .45 underneath the battery.

"How come?" I asked him.

"Shut up and don't tell your mother. Baltazar gave me the idea. He goes back and forth all the time and makes money both ways. Customs will never find it here, if only the damn tape holds.

"But what for?" I asked.

"You don't know those Blancos, so now get back to bed and keep your mouth shut, understand?"

Chapter
24

MY FATHER PLANNED on leaving at 4 A.M., to cross the desert before the sun got hot. By 3 A.M. everybody was milling around like angry ants, but I never saw Dolores in a happier mood and held her up to inspect the moon. She seemed to enjoy it. By 3:30 Chuchu was at the gate with his fat cousin Emilio, who would guard our house till we got back in January.

"Take your time over there, compadre," Chuchu said. "Emilio will look after everything."

"What's in the refrigerator?" Emilio asked and yawned.

My father still was nervous about building inspectors but Chuchu pacified him. "Get rolling, compadre," he ordered. "Don't you worry about a single thing."

We climbed into the Buick and I do mean climbed, because our personal junk was stuffed behind the front seat to make a solid bed in back for the women. There was a valise and three sacks on my side in front. My father's feet were the only ones that touched the floor. He stepped on the starter. Emilio came out on the porch chewing on a pork chop my mother left behind.

"Some house guard," my father muttered. "He'll eat up all my chickens probly if not your damn canaries too."

"Drive careful," Chuchu called.

He waved and we waved and away we went.

We rolled through Yuma eating burritos on the fly. The back seat was full of giggles while my sister played games with family names. "Lemme try once more," she said. "Your oldest brother, he's my Uncle Jesús."

"No no no," my mother told her. "Jesús is your Aunt Chuy."

Lena squawked.

"I'll never get them straight. There's my cousin Cuca and my cousin Kika and Lalo and Lola and Rosario the boy, and Rosario the girl and my Uncle Benedicto that the priest put a curse on him for what he done in the bell tower."

"Idiota! Benedicto is the saint. It was Bentura in the tower. He's only a far uncle, but double because his cousin's aunt's daughter married with my grandpa's nephew's brother-in-law."

It sounded like a rabbit farm to me.

"One mile to the border," I pointed out.

"Oh, those bandits in the Customs," my mother moaned. "You heard what they did to Virgie's cousin."

"Quit worrying," my father told her. "I'm still a Mexican citizen. They're our brothers."

"Hermanos!" he shouted at the soldiers as we crossed the line, but they only waved us to a little dusty parking lot in back and my father took his papers into the office.

"Give them $5 in a nice way," my mother suggested.

"Not one penny," said my father.

We waited. It was hot. The baby vomited. Lena cleaned her up. My mother prayed. A raggedy soldier in what looked to be a secondhand Boy Scout suit came with a rifle, looked at us, then went back inside. At last here comes my father like the rising sun, waving the car papers in his hand. An officer came after and stuck a gold star seal on the trunk and waved us on our way.

"How much was the bite?" my mother asked.

"What bite? All we gotta do is show our papers at the Customs Station in the desert and they'll pass us through. Where if you énter the U.S.A. they search the holes in your teeth for contrabando."

We drove into town, San Luis is its name. It looked more

American than Whittier Boulevard and I was disappointed but
not my father.

"Mi tierra," he laughed and cried. "La patria!" And
couldn't wait to kiss the ground, but where? We couldn't find
a parking space till this kid comes running up to pat our
fender.

"Parky carro," he yelled and led us to a space, except it was
paved solid with broken bottles.

"You crazy?" my father yelled at him in Spanish.

The kid waved his finger in front of our face the way they
do down there, ran for a broom and swept the glass under the
car behind so we could park. Right there my father fell in love
with him.

"No lively ones like that in L.A.," he said. "No, señor,
they're all too busy watching television."

I took no notice of his remark. The kid opened the door for
us like kings. He reminded me of that famous Pepe that stole
Dr. Penrose's $400 watch in Acapulco except this kid had
three front teeth missing where somebody had no doubt
kicked them down his throat. I could quite easily have done
the same except the guy was only twelve years old or ten so
where would be the glory?

"Changie money?" Showing off all his English the kid led
us to a window where my father traded 100 U.S. dollars for
the biggest bundle of pesos you ever saw. "Now where's mariachis?" he asked. The kid whistled and they came running.
He seemed to have the whole town organized.

"Méjico Lindo," was my father's request because it always
made him cry.

"Oh no, not that song again," Lena howled. "I'm starving."

Parky Carro knew just where to eat, a little café advertising
Tacos Higiénicos—so the women went there but I stuck with
my father. He sang along with the musicians and we drew a
big crowd of down-and-out music lovers. So after $10 worth
of songs we stepped into the nearest bar and left the kid to
watch the Buick, which I was sure he would, all the way to
the local Charlie Chueco's.

"No beer like this in the U.S.A.," my father bragged and ordered a round for the mariachis and a bottle for me too which I appreciated but to be honest I like our Lucky Lager better. On his third bottle my father got quite confidential.

"You're my son," he told me.

"Sí, señor."

"We men got to stand together and I'm counting on you for your help. This trip is more than just a holiday. Are you listening?" I was. "Número uno, your grandma's rich, you'd never know it to look at her, but she's rich rich, terrenos, fields, houses, cattle, goats and likely gold buried in the ground someplace, they're like squirrels, those viejas. Okay, so now she's seventy years old and even witches got to die sometime, entiendes?"

I did.

"Número dos, it so happens that your mama is her favorite, and that's good. But I'm not, and that's bad. The old woman hates me. But I'm gonna change all that. Just watch how I kiss her ass in public. You know how those viejas are, they're fools for flattery. Now understand, I don't do nothing illegal or even against the Church. Everything's on the up and up with me and all I do is see the old woman's money goes to your mother, which is exactly what the old woman wants herself."

"Where does the Forty-five come in?" I asked.

"The uncles," he explained. "It's disgusting the way they're all so greedy. They'll try to run us out of there, but we don't run, entiendes? No, señor! We sit there solid till the will is written and everything's arranged. It might take a while but I got months of vacation time coming from S.P. You might have to miss a little school, so what?"

So these were some of the unknown wheels that went spinning round in my father's head that night the phone call came. "And then, muchacho," he went on, "after the old woman finally passes on, we'll live like kings, like emperors! No more slaving for the damn S.P. Down here we could be gente! Rich!

I might raise horses like the Castillos. But what's wrong with you? The beer make you sick or something?"

Maybe I was pale.

"Leave Shamrock?" I said. "Live in a foreign land?"

"It's the land of your blood, muchacho. It's your Patria and you're gonna love it here."

My father took me outside for air. Lena and my mother were waiting for us across the street by a jewelry store. "You okay now?" my father asked. "Remember what I said is confidential between you and me. It's for everybody's good but don't tell it to the women. They don't understand nothing." We crossed the street and he put his arm around my sister. "See anything pretty in there?" he asked. "Here's money, go buy it."

But Lena wasn't in the mood so we walked back to where we left the Buick. To my surprise it was still there, hubcaps too, don't worry I checked them, and Parky Carro had even washed the car. My father handed him a bill.

"Ten dollars!" I said.

But it was only Mexican money, so then we drove off. My father couldn't quit talking about how solid-gold that kid was, so thoughtful and polite.

"Anybody could be polite for money," I remarked.

"For hunger," my father roared at me, "which you don't even know the name of." He made up a whole sad story about that kid, how the mother was a widow with twelve mouths to feed and if it wasn't for Parky Carro they would no doubt be dying from starvation. It was a very boring story.

"Life's a wrestle down here," my father went on. "Work or starve and that's what builds men. You'll see, the next hundred years are gonna belong to the Mexicans and that kid's proof of it."

I shut my mouth. We headed east on what they call El Camino del Diablo mainly no doubt because nobody else seems to use it, hardly another car, or house, or fence post even. You could see for miles but what was there to look at?

Sand and prickly bushes and jagged mountains. Till Lena spotted a little signpost and made my father stop to take its picture. "LOS ANGELES 1 KILOMETRO," it said beside a burro path that led off to nowhere.

"Don't laugh," my father told her. "They got a bigger population than us, ten billion ants and scorpions."

It seemed a good time for everybody to go someplace so I walked off down the path to piss in private. The dirt was red and cracked all over. Everything that grew had wicked prickers on it, or snaky arms with fingers like dipped in blood. One type was round and fat and 10 feet high looking like a giant macho you-know-what. All it needed for a picture was a burro and some clown with a big hat over his eyes. If this was my father's famous Mexico, you could give me the U.S. any time.

The sky was bigger than I remembered it back home and the sun was closer. What if I got left behind all by myself? No doubt I would lose my mind and run screeching through the desert till the hyenas got me, or the cobras. I quick zipped up my fly and hurried back to the friendly Buick. My father was busy showing Lena all those thrilling cactuses. "This here's the Barrel," he pointed out, "cut it open and you'll find drinking water. And that other one—" But he lost Lena. She was vomiting all over the rocks. When she finished we drove on. We'd be in Caborca for dinner, my father said. He had been driving twelve hours already but when he saw the Mexican flag flying over the Customs Station he gave it a big salute. It was a pretty sight out there in the desert, with the wind flapping it out almost flat and the snake and eagle dancing around like alive. We stopped in front and two soldiers with rifles stepped out on the porch to look us over. And an officer came down the steps.

"I smell a rat trap here," my mother warned. "Get ready with $10 at the least."

"You women don't know nothing," my father told her. "I'll handle this my own way. Buenas tardes," he told the officer. "Here you are, my captain, all papers stamped and signed."

"I am not a captain," the officer informed us. "I am Inspector Solís of the Department of Importaciones."

He circled the Buick as if it might be a tarantula.

"I'm gonna be sick again," Lena moaned. "Where's the place?"

My mother hurried her round behind the station.

"What's this gold seal doing on the trunk?" Inspector Solís barked at us. He was short and fat with goldfish eyes and his lips puffed out like a trumpet.

"They put it on at the border," my father said.

"Against regulations! And how much did you bribe them for it, hah? Yes, I know all about those pesos that pass from hand to hand. But not here! No, señor! Contrabandos do not pass by Inspector Solís. Open up that trunk! What's all this stuff inside?"

"A few little Christmas presents for the family," my father said.

"You think I'm stupid? You're no private visitor. You're comerciante. Load up your car with junk to sell down here. Make big profits from poor ignorant people that buy any piece of shit if it's got the U.S. label. So take out those sacks and empty every one of them on the table for inspection."

While we unloaded, my father growled and raged inside. We watched a brand-new Chrysler station wagon stopped in the next lane, full of blondies. Even their dog had yellow hair. Inspector Solís glanced casually at their papers and waved them through.

"Why not search *Them*?" my father asked.

"Because they are honest tourists coming down to spend their dollars while you come to rob your brothers. Everything out! Hurry up!"

By now the wind was blowing very angry. Half the desert seemed to be moving across the highway. Sand stung our faces. The clothes flapped and blew. Dresses fluttered loose, skidded under the car and stuck there. Empty sacks took off across the desert like jet propelled.

"It'll all blow away!" my father shouted.

"Is that my business? Do I make the wind? Put rocks on top. Everything must be counted down to the last snot-rag. Then I will assess the impuestos."

While we made piles of shirts and pants, Lena came staggering back to the car. She fell into the back seat and held her hands over her face. Solís counted our junk and added figures in his notebook.

"You will pay 1,200 pesos duty," he informed us.

My father really yelled.

"And there will be a fine on top of that. Now empty out the inside of the car." He pulled the door open. My father slammed it shut.

"My daughter's sick in there," he shouted. "Keep out!"

"Are you challenging my orders? Rafaél! Porfirio!"

The two soldiers came down with rifles.

"What you gonna do?" I asked my father.

He was too crazy-mad to speak, just kept dragging air in between his teeth while his hands made fists, and stood backed up against the car door daring them to open it.

"This is a penitentiary offense. I will give you one more chance—"

"Solís," somebody called very bored from the porch. "Basta! Let them through!"

It was the head inspector with ropes of gold braid on him.

"But they're contrabandistas!"

"Oh shut up," Solís was told.

What happened next was my little mother. She came walking down the steps like a queen with Dolores in her arms. My father stared at her and so did I.

"Let's go," she said in a very boring voice.

"What did you tell them?" my father asked. "What did you do inside there?"

"Pack up," my mother ordered.

We rolled the clothes up again and stuffed them back in the trunk.

"My best red dress!" Lena called.

It was stuck in the bushes across the highway. My father crossed to get it, and then I noticed something missing from my mother.

"Where's your earrings?" I asked her.

They were big gold hoops with parrots perched inside. She wore them always. She never never took them off.

"Shut up," she told me. "Just shut up," she told me very hard.

My mother's earrings weren't the only things that turned up missing. When we stopped in Caborca my father's .45 was missing too. You could see where the duct tape had been cut with a knife. My father raved. Who? When? Where? Till I mentioned his good friend Parky Carro. Who else? And after that, on our long road south, my father never saluted the Mexican flag again, and he talked more English than I ever heard him speak in L.A., and louder too, in gas stations and other public places.

Chapter
25

"Viva Méjico," my father growled through the steering
wheel.

The Buick jumped like a rabbit, then came clanking down
on the axle. The highway was 4 miles behind and we were
slugging along the road to Titatlán. Dust swarmed in through
the windows, too thick and hot to breathe. Loose rocks raced
round between the wheels and crashed our tailpipe and my
father had a bad word for every one of them. Then finally the
road turned sharp around a tree, slid down a little hill and
dived into the river. You could see it climbing out wet and
muddy on the other side.

My father hit the brakes.

"What you stopping for?" my mother asked. She couldn't
wait.

"I don't drive 2,000 damn miles to get dragged into town
behind your brothers' oxes."

My father got out to inspect the river and I got out to help
him. It was too muddy to tell how deep.

"Mama, bring paper!" Lena called from the bushes. Those
tacos higiénicos were still at work. At a farmacia we bought
fat black pills. They put her to sleep, but when she woke up
she had to go again. "Her grandma will cure it," my mother
said but my father swore no old witch was going to touch any
daughter of his. Across the river bushes bloomed with skirts
and shirts and faded pants drying in the sun. A skinny girl was
busy pounding her rags on the rocks.

"Same old washing machine like always," my father said. "Lifetime guarantee."

He spit in the river.

"How deep, muchacha?" he called across.

"They cross," the girl called back.

"On burros probably," my father grumbled, "and swimming with all six feet."

"Afraid the F will grab you?" my mother teased.

She used to tell the story when I was little. It seems there was this certain ghost or devil called El Fantasma which it was bad luck to name in full, and since before the Spaniards, this F had been grabbing people in the river, especially young girls after dark. But my mother when she was fifteen years old came one night to dare him, and she waded in the river till she felt like a claw grab her ankle. Her heart stopped, she said, but she pulled loose and ran. When the story got out, it ruined her reputation and costed her three sweethearts. That's what she claimed at least, but I had trouble seeing my mother all that brave or fifteen years old either.

"Well, say your prayers." My father eased us down the slope, then hit the gas, and we tore across throwing spray and skidded up the other bank. Through the trees and across the fields I saw a white little town with a tower pointing its finger at the sky. From there on my mother couldn't quit talking. She called off every house along the road and who lived in it, and every tree and most of the rocks. Soon the houses began to crowd each other till finally they touched and we drove between solid walls. They opened up into a plaza and my mother pounded on my father's shoulder.

"Stop, stop! My little church! I made a vow!"

My mother was never the religious type except on Ash Wednesdays but she walked up those stone steps on her knees like an Indian, then stood kneeling, both arms stretched out with palms turned up. Her lips were racing but you couldn't hear the words.

It was spooky to think my own mother had spent half her life in this foreign place and this was the church she was

baptized and confirmed in. Which would be the temple of my
ancestors, like Mr. Pilger said. I studiously inspected it. It
was solid rock—all carved by hand, with rock flowers and
animals and rock people who were no doubt saints but most
of them had lost their heads. Rocky vines went twisting like
spaghetti up the bell tower where my famous uncle once did
something bad, I wondered what. It was quite some monster
church for a town this size but old dead grass grew between
the steps and over the door, where our parish church in L.A.
was always spick and span and got fresh-painted every three
years.

I looked off across the plaza. It was completely dead except
for the wind chasing leaves and dust around. They didn't have
a grocery or a drugstore or filling station even. The only car in
sight was a rusty old Ford truck with three wheels. In the
middle of the square a bandstand was falling to pieces, with
cement walks around and rusty iron benches. Nobody was
using them except one old man bent over to count the ants,
no doubt. So this was our famous Titatlán.

"What do they do around here?" I asked my father.

"They work around here," he told me crossly, "so go clean
the bugs off the windshield. Don't be so lazy."

"We could go now," my mother said in a tiny voice.

She didn't tell us what she had prayed for.

We drove round the plaza and out on the far side. The road
was sunk 10 feet below the houses and full of boulders. When
it rained a river ran down there, my father said. One short
block and already we were out of town, dusty fields on both
sides with dead cornstalks sticking up. Houses stood here and
there but most were empty, roofs caved in and walls melted
down like ice-cream cones where the water had licked into
them.

"Oh! Aí! I'm gonna faint!"

My mother's hand flashed by my face to point up ahead at a
square adobe box. That's what it looked like anyway. There
were two windows but they were bricked in solid. Behind
was a round pointy hutch of sticks like made by cannibals.

Out front half of Titatlán was waiting for us, fat old ladies in dusty black dresses that dragged the dirt, skinny men with various straw hats, young guys with funny haircuts and 1,000 kids running back and forth across the road and screaming. My father blasted out a happy little tune on the horn. We jumped a shallow ditch and coasted into the yard and everybody swarmed us. Hands reached in. My mother hung out the window kissing aunts and cousins, and tears were everywhere.

"Ojitos verdes," they screamed at Dolores. Green eyes were no doubt quite something down there, and my baby sister disappeared into a sea of unknown faces. Now a tiny little old lady came walking, with people falling back to make room. Her face was black and wrinkled like a prune with white braids wrapped around it. Could this be my grandma? Our old picture showed her round and fat but now she was all shrunk in against her bones. My mother swallowed her up in her arms.

"Mamacita, you're so tiny now!"

"They left me out in the rain too long," my grandma said.

She kissed me on the mouth. Chicken claws dug into my shoulders. Her lips were leathery and her breath was hot and dusty on my neck. And after her came uncles, aunts and cousins, hugging, kissing, shaking hands. They all knew my name but I couldn't tell one from the other and they tossed me back and forth between them like a football till finally I slid out of reach in front of the Buick. I stood there with an idiot smile pasted on my face till it came to me to open up the hood, and lean in under. It smelled of good old L.A. and home. I frowned at the motor, felt the fan belt for slack and pulled the dipstick out to check the oil. It stood full which was no wonder since I had checked it when we got gas an hour ago.

By now I was feeling more or less like myself. From under the hood I watched various girls pass Dolores from hand to hand like a china doll, screaming Qué chula, how pretty, and what a darling little dress! I couldn't see my mother for the aunts bustling round her. My father had his own crowd, no doubt the uncles who once chased him with guns but now they seemed in a very pacific mood, and the tequila bottle passed from mouth to mouth. I checked the chicks too, in hopes to find a plump little morenita among my cousins but they all wore those farmery braids and no-style skirts that hung around their ankles like gunnysacks. Possibly one or two might pass if you dragged them to the beauty shop but where would you find one in Titatlán?

"Le Gusta Méjico?" some cousin asked me, leaning in across the motor.

"It's okay," I said, then remembered and switched gears to Spanish.

The cousin's name was Hector Blanco. He was around my height but with big shoulders on him and a big mustache. Possibly he was nineteen years old but even so he treated me with respect. He was a schoolteacher too, it seemed, and was crazy to learn all about automobiles, which was the first schoolteacher I ever heard of who wanted to learn anything.

"How is that thing called?" he asked and pointed.

"El Sparky Plug," I told him. So then I yanked the distributor cap so he could see the points, and explained him how they sent the juice through. I didn't know the names in Spanish but still we had quite some fine little conversation. He wanted to know how you say No in English which surprised him that it was the same word. But he couldn't manage Yes. The closest he could come was "Yex," which made me laugh, but in a nice way.

"Hey, quit showing off! Open up the trunk."

"In a minute," I told my father in my most boring voice.

"Pendejo, what you doing?" my mother said and slapped my hand off the lock.

"Why wait?" my father asked. "Time to play Santa Claus." But my mother snatched the key and put it down her neck.

"It's my family and you don't throw presents out like slops!"

Cat and dog they faced each other behind the car. Never before had I seen my mother like that in public, but lucky for her, my little grandma interrupted.

"Nothing for me?" she whined. "No pretty little presents from the U.S.A.?"

"Later, Mamacita," my mother told her.

"But the nights are so cold. Teodoro brought his mother a big woolly sweater from Tejas and it had pearly buttons too. Not even one little American cigarette for your poor old mamacita?"

My father held out his pack to her. She took one, then snaked out another with a giggle and stuck it behind her ear. She stretched out her neck like a turkey to my father's match and puffed deep and fast, holding the cigarette with all four fingers for fear it might run away from her.

"Very good for the lungs," she said and coughed a rattly one. "A good strong North American cigarette burns away all that nasty green stuff inside."

"Sure, Mamacita," my father agreed. "All the doctors recommend them, so here, take the pack."

My grandma stuffed it up her sleeve and hopped away before he could change his mind. My father gave my mother a very hard look. "Okay for this time," he told her, "but you watch it, baby. Mexico's no place for a woman to start acting smart in."

"I'm not smart, I'm crazy," she said. "I'm one crazy Indian from Titatlán and I've got a witch for a mother." She slapped my father very friendly on the shoulder and off she went to bury herself in family.

"Look at the woman," my father said. "She don't belong to us no more, she's all Blanco."

"Where's the restroom at?" I asked.

We walked round the house and past a well with a rope and bucket like in Chinatown where you throw your pennies in but this one you drank water from. A stone wall was just beyond with a tired old horse-chewed gate that scraped the dirt. We went through and I looked around.

"Where?" I asked.

"Here, there, anyplace," he said and opened up his fly.

I couldn't believe it.

"Right out in the open?"

"God's way," he said. "No plumbing bills."

"But everyone can see you!"

"Only from the waist up."

My father's fat stream splashed loud and heavy like a horse. Nobody was exactly watching but I could see the backs of girls' heads and womens' too. Three burros and two skinny goats stood staring at me. Turds in various shapes and sizes, human, animal and whatever lay casually around in the dirt. I shut my eyes and strained my muscles. All that came was a skinny little trickle but my father seemed right at home and very talky too.

"It's working out just like I planned it," he told me. "Your little grandma, she's in love with me already, and it only took one pack of Lucky Strikes. Tonight at dinner she'll have me sitting by her elbow, and I'll cut her meat real fine so she can gum it down. We'll be los preferidos, muchacho. Who was the big mustache you were talking to?" he asked me.

"My cousin Hector. He was real friendly."

"Don't trust no Blancos," my father warned. "Oh sure, those Indians are very friendly with one face but they got two and you didn't see the ugly one yet."

"You were drinking with them real fine," I reminded him.

"Sure, drinking, but all the time like this." With one finger he pulled down his cheek to make the Big Eye. "So you keep yours open too."

"Don Rodolfo," they were calling from across the wall, "the President is here to see you."

"Of Mexico?" I asked with both eyes popping.

"Mexico, Inglaterra, who knows?" my father coolly said and zipped up his fly and I followed him out of the gate. The President that was waiting turned out to be the Presidente Municipal, which they call the Mayor down there. He was a dry little man in a dusty blue suit but no collar and no tie, and my father gave him an abrazo that lifted him off the ground. It seemed he used to work for the Castillos like my father, only where my father ran the horses, that one added up the moneys and paid the bills. So their talk was all about the good old days.

"Remember, muchacho," my father told me, "all those stories I told you on the Castillos and I doubt if you believed them? Well, here's somebody can call me liar if I don't tell the truth. One hundred purebred horses we had in those stalls and I was chief of all of them, am I right?"

"Exactamente, Rodolfo," said the Presidente Municipal.

"They'd come to me for mounts, Don Serafín and his guests, and what guests they were, muchacho, General David Camacho, the President's cousin, singers from the opera, milionarios from Nueva York, dukes from Russia, ballerinas from París, ambassadors from who-knows-where, they all came to the Castillos for holidays, and for horses they came to me. 'Don't ride Attila,' I'd say, 'he's stone-bruised on the cannon. Ride Moonbeam better.' And they listened to me. On the trail rides I'd eat at the same table with them. 'Another slice of venison, Rodolfo?' they'd ask. 'Another glass of champagne? You've earned it, hombre, the horses are tiptop today.'"

"Precisamente, Rodolfo," said the Presidente Municipal. "Like you were a member of the family."

"And what wineglasses they had! They were thin as soap bubbles. Aí, those handsome young men, those beautiful women, the court for tennis, the Roman bath, that whole fine noble life, all gone now. Where's those Castillos now?"

"Dead," said the Presidente Municipal. "Dead, or drunk in the capital, and who lives now up there in the big house except owls and snakes, snakes and owls and goats?"

"Hallo!" my father said, and pointed. "Who's that?"

It was a horse. Two men were barely holding him while he kicked and pranced around.

"Meet Attila's great-grandson," said the Presidente Municipal. "I brought him over by halter so you could take a little ride."

"What you breed my Attila to, grasshoppers?" my father complained. "He was seventeen hands and this one's no bigger than a squirrel."

He looked big enough to me.

"Don't worry, Rodolfo," the President said. "He'll give you some entertainment."

"I haven't been up in twenty years," my father said. "These things are out of style in the U.S.A. Don't I know that saddle? I should. I polished it often enough. Look, muchacho, see all that silver work, pounds and pounds of it. Come over here, the horse won't eat you."

He had very hungry eyes it seemed to me. My father stepped up to the front end. Attila Junior showed his teeth and reared. My father grabbed the reins and gave him a good one across the nose with a board. That cooled him down a little.

By now we had quite some audience, everybody begging my father to climb aboard, except my grandma.

"Don't do it, son-in-law," she begged. "He's too strong for you. And besides, you're not the man you used to be."

"No?" said my father, and up he went. For all his big belly, he barely touched the stirrup. Attila Junior waited one long minute, then jumped up in front like kicking at the sun, and away they went. Over the wall, over the fence, across the field, across the road, turning, bucking, twisting, throwing rocks and dirt till they were just a speck off in the distance. The commotion brought Lena out of the house.

"Look look!" I proudly pointed.

Now they came racing back. Blancos flew right and left, me too, till my father put on the brakes and Attila skidded to a stop right in front of my grandma and stood there shaking.

"Your servant, Mamacita," my father called down to her.

"Oh, where's my damn camera?" Lena wailed.

I didn't need one. I still carry that picture in my head, my father mounted on that outlaw horse and looking like a king. It was possibly the closest to heaven he ever came in all his life. I forgave him everything, and so did the Blancos, the way they yelled and cheered. My mother was his only critic.

"El bobo" is what she called him, the boob.

Chapter
26

MY GRANDMA'S HOUSE was just one big room with a wall-to-wall dirt floor. No TV I was expecting, but no stove, no sink and no refrigerator? That was too much. And not a chair worth sitting on. All you saw was a couple of rickety iron beds with boards for springs, an old tin trunk and various pegs in the wall with faded clothes hanging from them like dead bodies. There was a patch of sun by the door but in the corners the shadows were so solid they must have been there since Columbus. And chickens paraded in and out as if they owned the place. If my grandma had money like my father said, she sure wasn't showing it.

"Come kiss your pretty cousin," Lena called me from the bed. "Rebeca's been looking after me like a hen, and you know my red party dress that's in the Buick? I'm gonna give it to her for a present."

Lena rattled on and on.

"If only she'd drink her grandma's yerba buena," my mother whispered, "but your fine father told her No."

"We should get a doctor," I insisted.

"Your grandma's one."

"A real doctor."

"You too?" My mother got cross and said, "Get out and let your sister sleep."

I cruised the yard looking for my cousin Hector. The cannibal hutch of sticks turned out to be the kitchen and there was a big gang of aunts sweating like devils over various char-

coal fires and others grinding chiles and patting tortillas. They
all started chattering at me. I couldn't understand a word and
quick got out of there. Then, around in back I ran across a
chick I hadn't seen before. She was kneeling on the ground
and stirring something with her fingers and she flashed me a
big-city look.

"What you stirring there, cousin?" I asked. "Hawaiian
punch?"

It was that color but the smell was different.

"Blood," she informed me.

"Whose?" I asked.

"From the little goats," she said, "to make the little pud-
dings."

Everything was always little down there in Titatlán.

"Do you have to use your little fingers?" I asked disgusted.

They were better than spoons to keep the blood from scab-
bing, she informed me. I squatted down across the bowl and
her eyes played games with mine. Her plump little arms were
red to the elbows and when she bended over to inspect the
blood her chichis hung like cantaloupes. My heart took a
bounce. This could be my little morenita.

"Lemme help you," I said and started to reach out.

"Oh, no, cousin, this is woman's work."

I was sorry about that because our fingers might touch
cheek to cheek and we could even end up holding hands in
that bowl of blood which might be quite exciting. So I gave
her a look even Fat Manuel would be proud of.

"What grade of cousins are we?" I asked. "Not too too close,
I hope?"

"Ai, Rodolfo," she scolded, then blushed which is more
than you ever get from those chicks at Audubon. Smart remarks is all they know. Remedios her name was, but before I
could make my next move they were calling for her blood
from inside the hutch of sticks. She picked up the bowl and
scuttled off with a certain little smile like she might soon
come back. While I stood waiting, Hector trotted by with

water for the cooks which he carried it on a pole with 5-gallon cans swinging from the ends.

"How do you say, 'I carry the water' in English?" he asked.

"You don't," I told him. "You get it from the faucet."

After I explained the joke he died laughing and called over various friends and cousins so they could laugh too. I was very cómico they all agreed so we went and parked ourselves against the Buick. I asked them how they made it with the chicks down there in Titatlán. It seemed the system was what they called El Paseo which takes place on Saturdays. The music plays, they said, the chicks walk round the plaza one way and the guys walk opposite, and if you really like some girl you could give her a flower.

"Then what?" I asked.

Then nothing, it seemed.

"Hot spit," I thought. "How thrilling." But I didn't say it. Who wanted to hurt their feelings? So then of course they asked me how it was on the other side.

"Take any average Sunday in L.A.," I said, "we start things off by drinking ourself a brew or two or possibly blowing some of that good Acapulco gold to get our horsepower up. And then if the weather's good we take us a carful of lively chicks to the beach and play Hide the Weenie."

My listeners slapped legs, shook heads and whistled at the American Way of Life. I was their Man from Mars and they paid me a lot of respect.

The dinner was supposed to be at three o'clock but it seemed my Uncle Borroméo the butcher lost himself with mezcal so my aunt had to kill the goats so by four o'clock they were still roasting in the pit. A long table of boards on sawhorses was set up in the back with fancy tablecloths that hadn't been out of the trunk in years. In the middle they piled up a mountain of breads, all kinds, regular and sweet. It was 2 feet high and 5 feet long which proved that food was not lacking in that household. Every little kid in town stood staring at it while the women ran back and forth and shouted orders at each other and nobody listened.

Being a foreigner they put me at the first serving along with the oldest and most respected uncles and the Presidente Municipal. My little grandma sat in the middle with my mother beside her, which were the only women seated, and my father sat opposite. Hector served tequila in tiny little copitas and there were beer bottles in front of everybody so I helped myself. Talk was very lively till the loaded plates came, then POW! Silencio. You have never seen such serious eating. Before you even emptied your plate here was one of the cousins or lesser aunts to fill it up again. When I was through my dish looked like a goat graveyard. So then people called for my father to stand up and deliver a discurso. Around our house he never said much you cared to listen to, but evidently he was famous for public speaking down there in Titatlán.

"Friends, brothers, estimado público," he started off. "Let me first drink a toast to my well-loved mother-in-law. But no! That's the wrong word because I feel to her like to my own dear dead mamá. Yes, in the old days we had our little difference, me and her, but that's all over now and I've driven two thousand long miles to prove it. Mamacita, this is your seventieth birthday, so salud y bien provecho, and I for one would gladly surrender up my life to give you seventy birthdays more and I call on everybody else to do the same."

The uncles shouted and clapped hands and I felt quite proud of my father and his golden tongue. So then he started telling funny stories like the one about that certain tourist which stops his car beside this humble peón. He's low on gas and asks how many kilómetros to Mexico City? The humble peón doesn't know too much about kilómetros, he admits, but between three men on burros it takes them exactly four litros of tequila to reach the capital. So everybody laughed forever and repeated the words over again. And then my father got real serious. He said he was a Mexican first, last and always, even if he lived in the U.S.A., because there were no boundaries high enough to divide La Raza Mejicana. And here with his beloved mamacita and in company with her family he felt himself among brothers ever united in pura confianza and amistad. And if any of them should ever cross the line, his house was always their house at número 114 Shamrock Street en la ciudad de la Reina de Los Angeles, California EEUU."

Their tears went rolling. So did my father's, and all those murderous Blancos, so-called, clapped hands and pounded the table with fists and beer bottles. By now it was beginning to get dark so they hung out a couple of gas lanterns from the big tree, one owned, one borrowed, and the more honored uncles got up and the less honored sat down along with the oldest aunts for the second serving.

"Where you going?" I asked my father. He was headed for the Buick with the Presidente Municipal.

"Lawyers' business for your grandma," he told me. "I'm driving the President over to San Marco.

"Take me too," I begged.

He signaled me secretly aside. "You've got to stay here, son. To guard your mother."

"From what?" I asked disgusted.

"From Blancos. Did you believe all those pretty things I preached? I hope not. You don't know this people. They take advantage of a lone woman, by force if they can't get her by lies. Then too, you know yourself how crazy your mother's been acting since we got here. So mind you keep your eyes on her. Guard her good."

My father slapped my shoulder, got in the car and raced the motor. The headlights flashed across the table and the eaters stared into them like owls. Then the Buick jolted across the ditch and onto the road. I watched its taillights go bouncing across the valley till they went out of sight.

In one way I hated not to go along, but in another way I was quite proud that my father trusted me. All during dinner I had made big plans for my little cousin Remedios but now she seemed to have disappeared someplace and anyway tonight that little matter would have to wait. I had more important work to do.

On my way back to the table Hector came up to me. "Maybe I shouldn't say it," he said, "but tell your father, Watch out for El Presidente."

"How come?" I asked.

"Nobody's trusted him yet who didn't get hurt by it," he said. So there I was, a million miles from home and who do you trust? It was black night now, of a black you don't see in L.A. Not a ray of light anyplace except that single yellow cave of lamplight round the table. It was now the third serving and my mother sat on gossiping with my aunties. I found myself a dark shadow by the corner of the house and stood guard.

I had seen my mother's face every day of my life, seen it leaning over a stove or washing machine or the baby, but never before did I see it like tonight. For one thing, she looked younger and livelier than I remembered. Her lips were riper red and her eyes had that Oriental slant which now looked quite misterioso. I barely seemed to know her. Her dress was unfamiliar too. It was ivory silk and low-cut with arms bare and there were big splashy orange flowers here and there. Lena made her buy it for the trip and it showed my mother's shape the way those old rags she wore on Shamrock never did. Maybe I shouldn't say it but if some girl or woman looking more or less like that came up and smiled at me I'd be proud to go along with her anywhere.

Next to my mother, the aunts looked like old crows in their rusty dresses and dark rebozos. I checked over the men, one by one, to see if they might be eying my mother too. They were younger now than at the first serving but they all seemed very timid and farmery to me and small competition for my father. Then I heard hoofs. They came racing down the road and the showiest Mexican you ever saw came crashing into the cave of light around the table. He looked fresh out of the television tube with his mariachi-style hat pulled down over his eyes. He had a rifle too and his horse couldn't quit dancing its feet around.

"Amador!" my mother called up at him.

Cousin Amador? Uncle Amador? Sweetheart Amador?

What was he to her? She stood up and he leaned down to take her hand. They smiled and laughed too much for comfort, it seemed to me, so I cruised over there. What he said I couldn't quite catch, something about the good old days. Did I hear When? Where? Later? I wasn't sure because everybody was talking at once. My grandma begged him to eat but he couldn't stop. He was on the trail of sheep-stealers, he claimed, so my mother handed him up a big meaty bone. He ripped off a hunk in his teeth, waved it around his head for goodbye, then off he went like Jesse James with my mother staring after. And I knew right away this was the Blanco I had to watch out for.

The party broke when the last belly got filled. Kids were collected, uncles and cousins shook my hand very formal and asked my permission to go home which I was happy to give them. All were careful to wrap serapes over their nose to protect them against Los Aires which are some superstitious class of devils said to climb into your lungs and tear you up after dark. Then finally the uncle that owned lantern number 2 took it down from the tree and they all moved off down the road, bunched up close around their precious ball of light.

But where was my mother?

Gone off with her Amador while my back was turned?

I ran to the hutch of sticks. Not there, only two aunts scrubbing pots by candle. The corral? No. I shook all over. My father had given me his trust, and I messed up. Not in the house either. And then, thanks be to God, I finally found her kneeling down beside the well.

"What you doing?" I asked crossly.

"Washing diapers like always," she said and found a rope to hang them up on.

"Who's El Cowboy?" I casually remarked.

She looked at me. "Are you your father's little watchdog?"

"Just curious," I explained.

Somebody carried the lamp to the house. It shined across my mother. I saw her pretty dress all splashed with water and in the face she was the same bored old mother I had known all my life. I felt myself relieved, and yet a little disappointed too, don't ask me why. So then she followed the lamp into the house and I waited outside with Hector for the women to get to bed. Way off where the mountains were, lightnings flashed on and off and flamed the edges of the sky.

"It wants to rain," Hector said, "but it's forgotten how."

Above our head the stars were brighter than in L.A. and closer too, which was no doubt the altitude. They seemed fastened to the branches of the big tree like Xmas lights. Hector knew them all by name and pointed out Polaris and Jupiter and Vega to me, which no doubt they named a certain class of Chevies after. Even if he was a schooteacher I couldn't help liking the guy. Maybe he was on the serious side but then we can't all be witty. Was he two-faced, like my father said? I doubted it. Then too, he had my mother's nose exactly, and Lena's. Maybe it's true what they say, blood calls out to blood. So anyway, we talked of this and this and that till I asked about my cousin Remedios.

"Stay away from that one," he warned me. And wouldn't answer when I asked him why.

The women were all settled down now for the night. Two skinny girls giggled at me when we went inside. They were in their underwear and pulled the blanket over their skinny chests, as if I cared to look. Hector took a log and braced it against the door for lock. He showed me to a narrow cot they borrowed for me, since I was a high-class American. Then he unrolled his petate on the floor and laid down on it with his serape over. The Virgin's candle flickered low in its glass. I rolled round till I discovered all the tricks that no-good cot knew how to play, then I fell asleep.

I woke up with a snap, I don't know when but it was late. My father hadn't come yet or I would hear him snoring. Instead I heard secret rustling noises like a woman makes when she puts on clothes. I saw something white with darker spots on it creeping toward the door. The dark spots could be big orange flowers.

"Hey," I whispered not loud enough to wake people up.

Either my mother didn't hear or else she didn't want to. She lifted the log from the door, the hinges whined and she was gone. It could be she only needed to go to the corral. But it could be something very different too. I clawed my shoes out from under the cot. My shirt and pants were already on. I slid to the door, careful with my feet for the sleepers on their mats. The moon was up now, an old moon rotted on one side. It threw long hot purple shadows. Across the road I saw white moving. I ran after. My mother was walking fast, almost running. Where to? She was pointed away from town. There were no more houses on that side if I remembered. My feet found the path she was walking on. It ran beside a stone wall.

Why didn't I call out to her? Because I was hungry to know the Truth, no matter how bad it might be. Up ahead I could see a line of trees, silver on top but dark and gloomy under. I ran faster, tripped on a rock and fell on my face. By the time I got to the forest my mother was out of sight. I swore at myself. Whatever happened now would be my fault because I could of stopped her if I had only called.

The path took me sliding down a bank. Branches brushed my face but I swatted them off. The air was colder. It had a wet green smell. Up ahead I could hear whispering. I stopped to listen. It was the river.

I went sliding down a muddy bank till there was only water ahead. Now it was hopeless. My mother had turned off on another path. Somebody was waiting for her there. He would jump her to his saddle and ride her off. The chills took me very bad. It was a spooky place, like no kind of place I had ever been before.

And then I saw my mother.

She was upstream in the water, wading in it where the moon came through the trees. One hand held her shoes and hoisted up her skirt to keep it dry. She waved the other hand for balance. The water cut past her legs in silver ripples. My chills left me and I was only mad.

"Hey, what you doing there?"

It wasn't any kind of voice to call your mother in. More like yelling at some pesty kid. My mother only ran her fingers through the water and flipped the drops away.

"Can't you talk?"

She turned now and waded back to me. Her legs got longer as she came into the shallows.

"Who knows?" she said quite cheerily, "maybe you saved your mother's life. Maybe if you didn't come, the F would grab my leg and carry me off under the water and under the ground to whatever place he calls his home."

"Is that what you came for?" I asked her very rugged.

My mother sat on the bank and put her shoes on. I threw a rock in the water to hear it splash.

"Or maybe I'm too old for El Fantasma now," she said, "too old, too ugly and too damn pregnant."

Chapter

27

It was not the best of mornings. Lena was vomiting again, my father still hadn't come home and they didn't have Corn Frosties for breakfast or even Cheery Oats. Instead I got handed two raw eggs in a glass, which is a big treat down there. They stared up at me like a crocodile but I had to swallow them to satisfy my little grandma. Right away they started doing flip-flops in my stomach. I stuffed down a tortilla in hopes to smother them.

The house was full of aunts so I went outside and found a hot patch of sunshine to sit in while I watched and worried for my father. Here we were 2,000 miles from home in a crazy country full of two-faced Blancos and Fantasmas and bandits and who knows what? My poor father could be robbed, shot, stabbed, drowned in the river, killed in a wreck, or worse. And how about that Presidente Municipal that Hector warned me not to trust? I sat there a long time and made various promises to the Holy Virgin till finally I saw the old friendly Buick crawling along the road from town with a long raggedy squirrel-tail of dust dragging out behind.

It clunked across the ditch, rolled into the yard and wheezed to a stop. The headlights had half-moons of dust. The radiator was steaming and there was an evil smell of oil. Oh-oh, I thought. My father eased himself out, balancing his head like a melon which might fall off and pop open on the ground.

"Flat tire," he mumbled.

No use mentioning the motor in his condition. He staggered off toward the house. At the door he aimed a giant belch at the sun, then stumbled inside. Aunts scattered. I steered him to my cot. He fell on it and before I could take off his shoes he was snoring. My mother tapped me on the shoulder.

"Get his keys." I fished them from his pocket. "Open the Buick," she ordered.

"What about my father?"

"My sisters can't wait for Santa Claus."

My father's flat tire was no lie. Everything in the trunk was trompled on. I carried sacks to the table where we ate last night. More aunts had come, from where, I couldn't guess, unless possibly they had been roosting in the big tree. They stood in a buzzardy circle wearing their dusty blacks and brown. And how their eyes gobbled up those fine feathers from the U.S.A., those pink blouses and bright greens, those blue dresses and lively reds and yellows, those checks and stripes and all-over flowers such as no doubt my aunts had never seen. No uncles were present. I could guess why. I felt uncomfortable myself.

"Rosario, Martita, if you please, Antonia, Soledad."

One by one my mother called them up by name and apologized for nothing being ironed. She issued according to size partly, or how close by blood, or how many kids, or which families she knew for the neediest. When the aunts came forward for their clothes they never looked in my mother's face and she didn't look in theirs. The handout was very quiet. Little gasps and giggles were all you heard, and each lady fired quick looks around to measure her take against what her sisters got. The only fun came when my little grandma snatched an elephant-size brassiere and danced it round in front of her, what a clown.

When the table was empty, the aunts and cousins could barely wait to get home and try on their fine clothes. They said quick thanks and scooted off hugging bundles to their chest like nursing babies. And then, just as the last were leaving, here comes Lena hanging out the door, her hair sweated to her face. She was bare-arm in her rumpled slip, and her eyes were wild.

"Where's my red party dress? Did you give it away?"

My sister wasn't exactly screaming but it wasn't any whisper either.

"Look under the car seat," my mother told me.

It wasn't there.

"Those bandits stole it at the border," I suggested.

But my sister had seen it since and she wanted it this very minute for her cousin Rebeca. Lena was yelling now and throwing her arms around. Nobody could calm her down till my grandma that lately was a clown, suddenly turned witch. Three times she clapped her hands in front of my sister's face.

"Cállate la boca!"

Lena's mouth was open for a scream but no scream came.

"Get this girl inside. Lay her on my bed. She's burning up!"

Lena folded up like an empty sack and my mother dragged her inside.

"Run boil me water," my grandma ordered. "Bring tortillas, hot ones." Rebeca went bouncing to the hutch of sticks. "Lie flat, little one," my grandma sang to Lena. "Lie still, little one, pretty one."

My sister did as told, and I would do the same if ordered in that sleepy singsong voice. "What a pretty little shape," my grandma hummed. "What cute little chichis that stand up like soldiers, so straight and brave. It's myself exactly at her age, and you were the same," she told my mother. "There's nothing of his in this girl except green eyes."

Her hands moved over Lena just barely touching her slip here and there. "Where does it hurt you, little love?" she asked.

"My head. And oh–h down there. Like a fist."

"Come on," I told my mother. "Let's go for a doctor."

"I'm doctor enough," my grandma said. "Give me a cigarette."

She lit it from the Virgin's candle, then puffed smoke on Lena's body. It seemed to hang to her, then slowly, slowly it twisted up through the candle flame and my grandma watched the smoky curls as if they might tell her something. She nodded finally, then without a word spoken those women went to work. They rolled Lena on her belly. My mother sat on her legs, my grandma dug skinny fingers into her neck. Lena yelled murder but then a long easy sigh came out of her, while my grandma's fingers moved down her spine and up again. Rebeca came running with a steaming cup of water and a napkin of tortillas. Take the baby away, they ordered her, and rolled my sister on her back and plastered hot tortillas on her belly. Next, my grandma bit open a little sack and shook powder into the cup of hot water and held it under Lena's nose.

"It smells like caca," Lena yelled and fought it off.

"What is that junk?" I told my mother. For all I knew, it might be poison. My mother spoke some long word that wasn't Spanish and it wasn't English either, some word full of attles or ottles or something like that. "Don't drink it," I warned my sister, but she did, then pitched sideways to vomit, only nothing came up.

"What do you know?" she mumbled, "it don't taste like shit, more like pee." And quietly lay down and shut her eyes.

"The hotness will leave her now," my grandma said. "Two hours and she'll wake up cured." She lifted the tortillas from Lena's belly. They had sucked out the disease, she said, but don't feed them to the chickens. Bury them in the dirt better.

Heavy and quiet was how Lena slept. Maybe it was imagination but I thought I could see color come back into her face. I sat with her an hour maybe, or longer, till finally my father snored himself awake, called for a bottle and ran to the corral to get rid of last night's beer. I took him a new one and he drank it off like putting out a fire. Then he started in to rave. My grandma was his subject.

"Queen of the son-of-a-bitch two-faces," he shouted. "You saw her last night so lovey-dovey at the dinner table, called me her yanqui caballero. Do you know what she calls me behind my back? El Marrano, the ugly pig." I found that out last night from El Presidente. Rewrote her will even so we'll never get one penny out of her, dead or alive. A la chingada! Who wants her damn money? Dried-up old witch, I hope The Cancer gets her. Let her try her witches' tea on that one."

"It cured my sister," I informed him.

"It What?"

I tried to explain but he banged the empty bottle on the wall and ran inside with the jaggedy bottle neck in his fist. I ran after. There stood my grandma waiting for him.

"Something wrong with your beer, mi caballero?" she coolly asked him.

He saw the busted bottle in his hand and threw it past me out the door. "What did you do to my girl?" he yelled.

"Cured her of the Hotness," she told him.

"With these?" There were cigarette papers stuck to Lena's temples on both sides. My father snatched them off but Lena still stood sleeping. "And what do you mean 'The Hotness'? Where's your thermometer? Where's your earphones and your X-rays? If you mean a fever, say so. And tell me which one? Malaria? Typhoid? What?

"Who cares about names as long as Lena's better?" my mother asked, quite bored.

"Who says she's better? What does that old witch know about medicine? My boy knows more and he's only fourteen years old. What Lena needs is an injection and she's gonna get one, so please explain all that stuff to your grandma, Junior."

I really didn't care to, especially not in Spanish, but there was my father shaking my arm and my grandma with her glittery little eyes. "Do what your father tells you, boy," she ordered. "Teach your poor poor old grandma about these famous injections and save her from La Ignorancia."

"Well," I said, "it's more or less like this—" I recited what I could remember from various Life Science classes, how every sickness has its own special little bugs, or worms, or whatever, so tiny you can't see them. Only some look like corkscrews and others more like dots and dashes. Then I ex-

plained how when you're sick all those bugs get together inside you and make bug-babies, but other times they just split.
And when you get too many, then you're sick. So the doctor,
he shoots dead bugs into you by needle and the dead bugs eat
up the live bugs till finally you get well, more or less.

"That's my Junior," my father proudly said. "And I only
hope you paid attention. Maybe you might learn something."

"Without me," my grandma yelled, "half the women in this
town would be dead today, yes and the men, I cure them too,
but I'm always sorry after. Once I cured you of the empache
and don't deny it. Yes, when you were howling you were
gonna die."

"I never asked you to," my father shouted back. "And from
now on, keep your claws off my family. They're American
citizens from the U.S.A. where it's against the law to go
around curing people without a license."

"I've got a license. From the Estados Unidos de Méjico."

"Are they giving them to witches now?" my father asked.

My grandma dug fiercely in a box and pulled out a paper.
In big letters you could see the word PARTERA.

"Midwife!" my father jeered. "That's no kind of doctor. My
girl don't need a midwife, thank you."

A wicked little smile twisted up my grandma's lips.

"You hope," was all she said. But it was enough.

"What you mean by that?"

"Don't ask an ignorant old woman. Ask that educated muchacho of yours. No doubt he knows all about these scientific
worms that crawl into a young girl's belly."

"Mamá!" my mother scolded. "Don't pay attention!" she
begged my father.

My father stood there like an angry bull that can't decide
who to drive his horns in next. Could my grandma possibly
be right about Lena, I wondered. A month ago Armando got
deported, and wasn't Now just the time she would be getting
her sickness? But if I doubted my sister, my father double-
doubted her. With fiery eyes he stared at Lena where her slip

pulled tight across her belly, till finally he couldn't hold back the words.

"Are you or aren't you?" he yelled down at her.

Lena's eyes flickered. "Hi, Papa," she said in a lazy voice. "Did you say something?"

"Answer me. Did you vomit yesterday in the morning? Did you vomit today?"

My sister couldn't seem to quite wake up.

"Was it any secret?" she yawned.

"So you're pregnant! And don't deny it!"

"Me? How?" Lena was wide awake now. "Off some damn toilet seat? Has he gone crazy?" she asked.

"That fucking bracero nailed you."

"Do you wanna bet on it?" my sister yelled. "How much? Ten dollars? Twenty? Coward!"

And then, as if the fire wasn't hot enough already, my grandma threw on another log. "Ask him a few questions," she shrieked at Lena. "Ask your fine father about that little dress that's missing."

"What dress?" my father roared. "Who cares about some damn old red rag at a time like this?"

"Ask him about the little whore he gave it to last night, which the whole world already knows about."

"Liar," my father said.

But if so, how come he knew the dress's color? My mother looked through him as if he might be a dirty pane of glass. My sister didn't look at him at all. But my little grandma had words enough for everybody. Twenty years of hating him came charging out.

"Hypocrite," she told him, "you with your Mamacita this and your Mamacita that. Make me fine speeches when all you want is my money and my family's lands. You'll never get it, ni un centavo. Then you get drunk with your little whore, yes I know the one, don't worry, and she's my own blood and your daughter's blood. Think I don't know? I got eyes everywhere, ears too. I can walk right now to that girl's house and bring you back the dress. If anybody wants it. Is that any way to respect my family? And now you dare to come into my house and speak ugly words to my nieta when she's sick. Treat her like the whore you had last night. Basta! I've had enough of you. Out! Get out of my house!"

If there's any deadlier insult you can throw a man with in Mexico, I don't know it. My father started to shout words back but changed his mind.

"Pack up your junk," he told my mother. "We're leaving."

She didn't move.

"Right now," he said.

I was scared. Of all the bad things that ever happened in my family this was the worst. My father waited one-half minute in silence. He looked at Lena. She turned her back. He looked at me.

"Come on," he ordered, and walked out the door. I couldn't move. Outside I heard him slam the trunk lid shut which I left open. Possibly he noticed it empty. Anyway I heard him pound it with his fists. He blew the horn three times and waited. Then I heard the Buick limp away.

"What do we do?" Lena asked. "Is he really gonna leave us here?"

"He can't go far," I said. "The motor's blown."

"And that ain't all," said Lena.

Chapter
28

I WAS RIGHT. The Buick quit just outside town. They pushed it back to the President's house and sent to San Marcos for a mechanic. That was the story we got from our runners. What a system my grandma had. No bird shitted in Titatlán but she knew all about it.

"The Hell with Him and his Buick," was my sister's idea. "I'm not gonna let Him ruin my visit."

My father had been Him for some hours now.

"Excuse me for asking," I asked, "but how do we get back to L.A., if ever?"

"Armando could come for us."

"Oh yace," I said, "in his private plane no doubt." It was the first time his name had been spoken for days. I even began to hope he was already part of my sister's famous Past.

"Why go?" said my grandma. "This is your house. I have enough. You won't starve."

Everybody seemed too tired to think about it, especially my mother. Do you know what they do at night in Titatlán? They go to bed, is the answer, and so did I, one hour after the sun went down.

It was still dark when I woke up. Yesterday I had disobeyed my father to his face for the first time in my life. Today the sky might fall. To pass the time I went plowing with my cousin Hector. The oxes spent the night with an uncle so we

tromped over there and rousted them out. I let Hector attend
to the details.

"They won't do you nothing," he said. Possibly not, they
had big loving eyes but long sharp horns. So the four of us
went walking up the mountainside. Oh how they walk down
there, not slow and suave like us, with them it's a footrace all
the way. I could barely keep up. The higher we got, the more
rocks till you could hardly see dirt between.

"By rights nobody should plow up here," Hector said,
"but you have to eat." The plow looked to be from the Old
Stone Age, all wood except the blade. Hector laced the yoke
to the oxes' horns, poor things, but he said they didn't mind
it.

"Why not get a tractor better?" I suggested. "My grandma's
rich enough."

"Oh sure," he said, "if rocks were dollars."

The field was so steep that Napoleon stood 2 feet higher
than Waterloo which were the oxes' high-class names. Hector
dug in the plow blade and followed them, by foot on one side
and by knee on the other. Two rows and the guy was sweating
all over.

"Care to try?" he asked me.

"No thanks," I told him. It looked more like a spectator
sport to me. On the next row the blade hit a monster rock and
the handle busted off, so we sat down to wire the pieces together. The sun was coming up fine and hot, which was the
blanket of the poor, I remembered. Below, the sierra was red,
like scraped raw and bleeding, and down in the valley the
church tower was all you could see of tiny Titatlán. Before
Columbus the town used to hold 25,000 souls, Hector told
me, but it seemed they weren't Aztecs the way I'd thought.
Our particular ancestors were a different breed of Indian
and the Aztecs stomped us, and after them, the Spaniards.
My cousin was very proud of those ancestors of ours, who
were very educated and peace-loving, he said, and famous
all over Mexico for the clay pots and idols they made back
there one thousand years ago, but to me they were a big

disappointment. Who wants his grandpas to be losers every time?

"They used to irrigate the valley by canals," Hector went on, "and they terraced up the hills to hold the soil but all that fine world of theirs fell to pieces under the Spaniards and the priests. Now every year the corn scorches, the wheat rusts and the people starve. The government does nothing for us, nothing."

My cousin taught me a lot of history up there on the mountainside. His big dream was to save the valley by Agronomía which I don't know its name in English, only he would have to go to college four years and each year would cost the whole harvest. The poor guy was quite hopeless about everything till suddenly it hit me.

"Hey, why not come to the U.S.A.?" I told him. "You could go to school free up there." I got so worked up over getting my cousin to L.A. that I completely forgot about my father and the Buick and how would we ever get back our own selves? "You could live with us," I told the guy, "and it wouldn't cost you a cent, and weekends you could work with Chuchu and buy you a car even."

"Who would work our fields?" he said. "Who would teach school?"

By now the plow handle was patched. Hector tried it again but it busted right away so we turned the oxes loose in the corral, threw them some cornstalks and walked back down. To my surprise Hector took hold of my hand.

"What's this now?" I asked myself, but as we walked along there didn't seem to be anything wrong about it. It even felt quite warm and brotherly. Suppose my father leaves without us, so what? I thought. With a little practice I could get used to those oxes. No doubt too I could learn to ride around like El Cowbóy shooting wolves and panthers in the night and then just before dawn snuggle into a warm bed with my little morenita, who could turn out to be my far cousin Remedios of the bloody hands. And wouldn't that be more of a life than Aubudon Junior High School and Mr. Fujita?

Except, right then, as if God was telling me something, I saw her. We were passing by a tumbledown shack just outside town and there she was, just coming out the door.

"Hi, cousin, how's every little thing?" I called.

Maybe she didn't hear me. Maybe somebody called her from inside, because she ducked back in.

"She's not for you," Hector told me and dragged me on down the road.

"How come not?" I asked.

He didn't say. I looked back over my shoulder. In the back yard I saw a red dress hanging on the line, a red party dress which was once Lena's dress. And finally Hector talked. "She belongs to El Presidente," he said, "and to El Presidente's friends. Her family was of the poorest. Now at least they eat."

So we walked on by. To hell with Titatlán, I told myself. It's like the rest of the world. Somebody else always gets there first.

"How do you say 'casually' in Spanish?" Lena asked me.

"Who knows?"

My grandma was off on her burro delivering babies. My mother had tagged along. I had my sister to myself. What I wanted was a War Council but all she could do was chatter. "Eeeho," she said, "but they sure talk real crazy Spanish down here. Mercado for marketa, camión for troque, and I had to act out lip-stique, if you can believe it. And guess what, my grandma wants me for her assistant witch, if only I promise not to get married. Says I'm just the right age like my mother was before she run off."

"She's pregnant," I interrupted, "in case you didn't know." That stopped my sister at last.

"Huh?" she said. "Who? Not my mother! Already so soon? How cute!" Lena's craze for babies stole her wits as usual.

"My mother don't think it's cute," I said.

"Does my father know?"

"She made me promise not to tell."

Lena chewed on her knuckles which she learned to do after

Armando criticized her fingernails. "I knew something was wrong. 'What are you gonna do?' I asked my mother after breakfast, 'go back to Him? Or do you rather stay here with my grandma?' She didn't give me any answer."

"S'pose he leaves without her," I pointed out. "Then how about us? How much money you got?"

"Thirty-seven dollars. We could hitchhike. No, I wouldn't care for that down here. Well, Jesus Christ, you're supposed to be so smart, suggest something!" Thinking always made my sister cross. "I'll have to get a job," she finally said.

"Doing what?"

"I could baby-sit for bus fare. But then they carry babies with them, huh? And don't go noplace besides. Maybe I could work in a store."

"El Presidente's? It's the only one."

"No thanks. Don't they got canneries? Or garment trade? I could do power-machine. Aren't there no hotels? No offices to clean? Eeee," Lena said, "how do they get by down here?"

"They milk each other's goats," I told her.

"Well," I finally suggested, "we could try talking to my father."

"Not me," Lena yelled. "Never. But you could. Why not? Yes, you go and be a missionary."

"A what?" I asked.

"Missionary, stupid, like what they send to Paris to make peace or something. And besides," my sentimental sister said, "it's only three days till Christmas so how could my father possibly tell you No?"

A grasshoppery little man with grease in his mustache was buzzing round the Buick. He had pulled the head, and nuts and bolts were sprinkled in the dirt as if it might have rained them. He was singing too, if you could call it that. "This little nut here, that little nut there," he sang, "y el tercero end el baldecito." And he tossed it in a bucket. I looked for his tool-box but all I could see was a crescent wrench, a pair of rusty pliers and two screwdrivers. Even Gorilla had more tools and better. If this was my father's big-time mechanic from San Marco, God help the Buick.

"Where's my father at?" I asked him.

"Ask your little mamacita," he sang.

"The man that owns this crate," I said disgusted.

"Adentro, amorcito," he sang again and waved a screwdriver toward the President's house. But I was in no mood to go inside that place. Maybe my father saw me through the window because he came out. "Buenos días," I told him. He passed me by and went to his mechanic.

"How goes it, maestro?" he asked.

"Perfecto, magnífico, estupendo," sang the mechanic.

"Is he from the opera?" I asked my father in English. He ignored me. "Did he bring the right gasket at least?" I asked.

"He'll make one. From cardboard."

I thought I had heard everything, but 2,000 miles on a paper gasket made by a canary? I waited for my father to talk. He didn't.

"When do you plan on leaving?" I finally asked.

My father looked at his mechanic.

"Pasadita mañanita, patroncito," the maestro sang, meaning day after tomorrow.

"Do we get invited?" I said.

"I asked you once," my father said and started back inside.

"My mother's pregnant," I said just-like-that. I had sworn not to tell him, but there it was. The news stopped my father in the door. He showed me his back for quite some time. "So. Now she needs me, hah?" my father said. "What does she say? Does she want to come home with me, yes or no?"

"Yes," I said. To be honest I wasn't sure, but I said it anyway.

My father showed me more back.

"Then be ready day after tomorrow at 7 A.M., American time, understand? Tell her to have her junk all packed and waiting on the road. Not in that house, entiendes? Not in that yard even. In the public road."

"Sí, señor," I told him and cut out.

"Dummy," my sister yelled. "Day after tomorrow is Christmas. Nobody travels on Christmas. Did you remind him?"

"Be your own missionary if you don't like it," I told her.

Lena grumbled but when I told her nobody gave presents in Titatlán till January sixth which is King-Magicians' Day, she calmed down. Now the problem was to get some kind of answer from my mother. She wasn't in the mood to give us any till finally we got impatient.

"Are you coming back to L.A.? Speak up?" we asked her.

"Why not?" she said, very casually it seemed to me.

"Mamá," Lena scolded, "how can you be so offhanded? This is a real serious decision for you, maybe the biggest in all your life. If you want to stay down here with my grandma nobody can say it isn't your rights after all He's done. Me, I've got to get back for Armando. And my brother for his school. But don't bring us into it. We could get by up there without you. So then, how about it?" my sister asked.

"Don't get so excited," my mother told her. "Why wouldn't I be coming? Who else could look after my little birdies?"

Chapter
29

Lena opened her eyes at last. "Merry Christmas, everybody," she announced.

"Don't mention it," I told her. The rest of us had been up for hours. Rebeca and her tiny sister had Dolores out back kissing the goats goodbye. Hector was out front guarding our junk on the road, from who, I couldn't guess, unless it was the coyotes. Last night they had come down from the mountains and stirred up every dog in town. The burros sang, the goats brayed, the roosters crowed. La Noche Buena was a big night in Titatlán.

I stepped outside. The lopside moon hung from the big tree like a pumpkin left over from Halloween. The only other light was a charcoal fire in the hutch of sticks. Hoping for coffee I went in and found my grandma jabbering that rattle-tattle language of hers while my mother sipped a steaming cup.

"Gimme a swallow," I begged and promptly spit it out. "What's that for, the measles?" I asked.

"Your curiosity," my mother said and downed the cup. She seemed almost cheery for a change. "How long since we got here?" she rambled on. "Four days? Three? Oh well, here today and gone tomorrow. If only we could have baptized in El Templo. That was the main reason we came down."

"Who needs the Templo?" said my grandma. "Our well water's just as holy and much cleaner. I can baptize here and now."

"Would it be legal?" my mother wondered. "Can you get the priest to come?"

"Him! He sleeps in San Marco and you couldn't get that one out of bed for the Resurrection. There's extremedades when you have to take the Church into your own hands," my grandma said, "like the sick babies in the mountains. What should I do? Let them die in sin?"

My mother convinced easy but not my sister. "What about my father? We can't baptize without him."

"Do widows' babies get baptized, yes or no?" My scrappy grandma asked.

Who could stand up to that old woman? She called Hector from the road and the girls from the goats. "He's gonna be real mad," Lena grumbled, "and I wouldn't blame him."

"Only if he knows about it," I pointed out.

They stripped my baby sister and put on the pretty dress my mother had brought from L.A. Hector lit the lamp and we all gathered by the well. It was solemn as any church, and the burros stared at us over the wall, and the goats. "In the name of this one and in the name of that one," my grandma raced the words like an old pro and poured on water with a generous hand, then blew cigarette smoke over for incense.

"The Pope's not gonna like this," Lena whispered in English, but she was the only critic. My grandma dried the baby and gave her a bottle.

"One more little Blanco saved from sin," she sighed. "How many of these have passed through my hands? Dozens? Hundreds? I baptize you, I bury you, I witness all your little idiocies in between. It gets so boring I often wish Death would give me a vacation, but what would you ever do without me? Who would pick up my load? Twenty years I waited for this daughter of mine to come back. She came. Now she goes away again. Who cares? Qué importa? In another twenty years this baby here will come back and take her place. Don't laugh. I'll still be here. Reach seventy years in Titatlán and you go on forever."

What a crazy old woman, but standing there in the dawn

who could doubt her? I walked out to the road to wait for my father. On top of our pile of junk I saw a handmade box of sticks stuffed with straw, which was Hector's Christmas present to me. It was football size but way too heavy. "One of my grandma's million-dollar rocks?" I guessed, but Hector insisted, "Don't open it till you get home." I argued with the guy. If there's anything I hate, it's mysteries, but just then the Buick came rolling down from town and nailed us with its headlights. I listened to the motor. It sounded better than I expected. Without any words my father handed me the key out the window. I opened up the trunk. Hector helped me load. Now, with all our presents given out, there was plenty of room for all our personal stuff. At least on the road home all our feet would touch the floor.

"Write me," Hector said, and I promised to. My mother came from the house carrying Dolores. The baby was in plain clothes, her baptism dress safely tucked away. Lena looked everyplace but at my father. We climbed into the Buick like strangers on a bus. Nobody came outside to see us off. Four days ago we rolled in there like the Three Magic Kings. Today we were scuttling off in the dawn like the cucarachas.

"Is it gonna rain?" I asked for conversation.

"No," my father answered.

That did it for the weather. As we drove past the Templo I wanted to ask exactly what my disgraced uncle did in the bell tower there, but all topics seemed full of booby traps.

I sneaked little looks at my father muscled down over the wheel. What was on his mind? I recalled those big plans of his, how he would twist my grandma round his finger and we'd all get rich. Instead, she twisted him, and this visit to Mexico that was supposed to unite the family had ended by tearing us apart, maybe for good.

When you're a kid, your father is like the sun in the sky. Your whole family circles him like a bunch of planets. He gives you your winters and your summers, your good days and your bad, and it's black night when his back is turned to you. But we had disobeyed him. We had shamed him in public and now our Gravity was all gone. The only thing that held us together was the Buick.

We splashed through the river. We went bumping along the dirt road and not a word among us, but when we climbed back onto the main highway, my father let out one of his famous sighs. After all that silence everybody jumped. "What this family needs," he said, and his voice was almost friendly, "is one big party. When we get home we're gonna invite the whole street over."

"I could cook the dinner," Lena interrupted, happy to make peace. "My cousin Rebeca gave me the recipe for goats, if only we can buy them already dead."

"I'll dig a barbecue pit in the backyard," my father said, "and the occasion will be Dolores' baptism."

I prayed.

"But Papa—" Lena said. I tried to interrupt her, but not in time."—isn't it a sin to baptize twice?" she asked.

My darling sister! Once her mouth was open who could close it? Thirty seconds and my father had the facts. "Behind my back?" he yelled. "My daughter baptized by a witch?" He slammed on the brakes and we skidded to a stop. "Out!" he hollered. "Out of the car, all of you."

Nobody argued. We stood facing him from the shoulder of the road. "Do we walk from here?" my mother asked. For answer he took off down the highway leaving rubber. We were in the middle of nothing. Except right opposite us were three wooden whitewashed crosses. "All we need," my mother said, "is make a tiny one for Dolores."

"Quit looking at me like that," Lena yelled. "It IS a sin to baptize twice. I remember it from catechism or someplace. Do you want your baby sister sent to Hell?"

"Who's looking?" I said. "Now what?" I asked my mother.

"He'll come back," she said, quite bored, and he did.

"Get in," he ordered, "and don't nobody talk."

We didn't.

My father drove like a tiger. We barely stopped for gas. We bought food and ate it at 80 miles an hour. To pass the time I

fished Mr. Pilger's book out from under the front seat. It had
pictures of the pyramids with well-dressed Indians going up
and down, very fine and all in color. It showed canoes full of
flowers and bloody battles with the Spaniards. I got quite
interested and even read some of the words here and there.

Late in the afternoon we hit Mexico City with its one million trucks and killer taxis and crazy walkers. All horn and no
brake, my father gave the right of way to nobody. I saw a
highway sign.

"Over there's the road to the pyramids," I pointed out. "You
promised we could see them on the way back," I reminded
him.

"The pyramids can go fuck their mothers," my father said.

He drove all night. In the morning you could barely see his
eyes. The highway was one long straight stretch now but he
kept weaving off on the shoulder. Three times I had to grab
the wheel.

"Who's asleep?" my father shouted.

"You drive before he kills us all," my mother told me at the
gas station. To my surprise my father let me. In ten seconds
he was snoring. Free and easy at the wheel I hung my elbow
out the window as if I might have been driving all my life. It
was mostly desert now but even in the most deserted desert
you saw people, waiting for a bus, walking through the cactuses, hacking something with a machete or digging something with a shovel. All turned their heads to watch us. What
else was there to do? And while we cruised north so fine and
cozy in the good old Buick I really pitied those poor Mejicanos which in all their life would never drive anything bigger
than a burro.

My father slept and slept. I drove and drove. The border
started getting close. I passed that den of thieves where they
made us open up the trunk but they don't bother you going
north.

"Stop at the first gas," my mother ordered.

"We still got a quarter tank."

"Never mind."

"It'll be cheaper in San Luis."

"Just stop," my mother said.

I stopped.

The women scooted for the rest room. I checked the oil. It was full and I took back all the evil things I thought about the singing mechanic from San Marco. And then we waited.

"Are those women gonna be in there all day?" I complained to my father. He had woken up a little alleviated.

"It's no good criticizing," he told me. "Never criticize an Indian or a mule or a woman, it's a waste of time." Then my father threw an unexpected arm around my shoulder. "I guess you drove pretty good," he said. "At least we got here but I better drive across the line."

When my mother finally came out she had changed her dress.

"Did you take a bath in there, or what?" I asked her.

My mother didn't say. She wasn't looking good. At the border, the U.S.A. side was almost casual with us until their dog spotted Hector's box of sticks and started barking at it.

"What's that?" they asked and almost drew their guns.

"A Christmas present," I said. "I didn't open it yet."

Could it be my cousin had given me a kilo of Mary Jane? But he didn't seem the type.

"Open it up right now," they told me.

I did, and dug into the straw.

"Wow!" the officers said.

"Oooo, how ugly," Lena screamed and covered up her eyes.

It was a plump little woman 8 inches high and naked all the way down. She was made out of red clay that shined like polished except for patches of dirt stuck on here and there. What could she be but an idol of my ancestors?

"Is it legal?" my father timidly asked.

"With us," they said, "but lucky for you they didn't spot it on the Mexican side. National treasures they call these things and you can't take them out. They're even worth a lot of money, if you can believe it."

So they passed Hector's present, but we had to burn the straw she was packed in, for the Agriculture. I got out a towel to wrap her.

"Quit touching her that dirty way," Lena scolded.

"Who cares? She's a thousand years old," I said.

"That only makes it worse."

"Our grandfathers probly prayed to her," I said. "Like to the Virgin."

"She's no Virgin, that one," my father pointed out, "not with her you-know-what wide open."

Lena snatched my little woman and made a dress for her out of Kleenex and danced her round on the back of the seat and there we were, all laughing for the first time since we left Titatlán, except my mother.

It was around five o'clock when we came rolling down those last brown hills before L.A. Afternoon was up above us but it was night below. I could count more lights down there than they've got stars in Mexico, and as we slid down into the valley there were interesting sights to see after those long empty deserts full of cactus. The good-natured old Kentucky Colonel with his fingerlicking chickens, and Mobil's Flying Horse, and all those gorgeous blondies 15 feet tall in their bikinis that begged me to drink their vitamin-rich milk or else to meet them in Las Vegas.

I leaned my nose out the window and sucked in the good old ozone from L.A., tasty and solid-packed like plasma, where down in Titatlán what they called air was so thin you could barely smell it. We rolled on past San Berdoo and Covina, past La Puente with four wide lanes to choose from and the Buick floated at an easy 70 like an oil. Past Rosemead and San Gabriel, and then at the Soto Street exit we dropped the Freeway and turned down Marengo onto familiar turf. I felt as if we'd been away a century.

"Look look," Lena called, "there's the corner those cute sailors tried to pick us up, me and Aurora when I was just thirteen. Papa, remember how you chased them? And was I ever furious with you? And there's your hospital, manito, where they saved your life. Eeee, it's so pretty all lit up."

On every corner the lights turned green in front of us, for a lucky sign. We went sailing across Mission Road and from Bailey turned down Main. There was The Brewery like a castle with a feather of steam waving off the tower. There was Frankie Martin's on our right with the handball courts lighted up behind. At the well-known Aztecs' club we hung a left and here was good old Shamrock waiting for us after all those 4,000 rolling miles. Up ahead, the S.P. signal tower winked red and green, and on beyond City Hall still scraped the sky. It was all the same, nothing changed. Crazy Kiko's house was dark and Gorilla's too, but the night light at the Miracle Market proudly shined down on all those ten big padlocks it took them one hour to unlock in the mornings. And finally here was our home, lucky number 114, the same old saggy fence and cranky front porch steps.

Maybe Life was giving us one more chance.

My mother was first out of the car and raced to her birdies. They were fine, all of them. Even the chickens were all present and accounted for. And the refrigerator was full of eggs, which we least expected from Emilio. There was good news for my sister too, in a big fat envelope from Armando. He was back in the U.S.A. at last and with a phone number she could call. But there was one thing extra. I didn't notice it when we first came in. A sign had been tacked up on our front porch. They had nailed it to the 4-by-4 and it looked official.

"Read it," my father told me.

I turned on the porch light. There was a lot of puzzling fine print but in big black letters what they said was, the house was condemned and we had thirty days to get out in.

Chapter
30

EMILIO SLEPT in Lena's bed. Lena slept on the couch. I slept in the Buick. If my father slept at all, I doubt it. Chuchu came at seven, talking all the way. "You're not the only one, compadre. Shamrock's solid with those signs, my place too. Did you read the fine print? Put in foundations, tear down the shed and porches, new sewer line, don't tell me, compadre, I know it all by heart. And did you see about the chickens? Suddenly they're illegal in the city limits."

Lena fussed with her hair. "They can't really mean it," she informed us. "Go down to City Hall, talk to them real fine—"

"Shut up," my father told her.

For once she did. If there were any troubles in the world my sister didn't care to hear about them today. And from her lively steps as she tripped off to work, I knew Armando would be waiting at the X-Cell gates.

"We could bring you up to code," Chuchu raced on, "put jacks under, lift the house, build forms, ease her down on concrete, but after, there's rewiring which I don't trust myself to do. Compadre, just the materials would come to 1,500, and don't mention banks. They're not making loans on Shamrock now."

"Where's our damn lawyer?" my father asked.

"Out of town, wouldn't you know? But I called a meeting tonight at the Aztecs', it's good you're here to talk to them. Those homeowners respect you better than me. Maybe we can hold them together, at least till O'Gara gets back."

"I don't sell never," my father said. "They'll kill me first."

"Me and you, compadre, but don't be too hopeful for the others. Two or three won't look me in the face these days."

The S.P. whistle blew. My father shook his fist at it.

"Emilio, we're gonna be late," Chuchu yelled. "Pouring slab out there in Tarzana, compadre, and I gotta run."

They left and my father headed for the Buick.

"Where you going?" I asked.

"Buy me a rifle. Thirty days and they'll find me waiting for them on the porch."

"The stores aren't open yet," I reminded him.

"Not from no store, dummy. Ruben."

Ruben sold a little of everything.

"Buy two," I told my father man to man.

He looked in my eyes. I looked him back, then he patted my shoulder and away he went. I stood looking after him.

Did you ever hear of Los Niños Héroes? They had their statue in that history book Mr. Pilger loaned me, guys around my age and they fought the whole U.S. Army down there at Chapultepec. Their elders all gave up but they stood on, and not one lived to tell the tale.

Could we do the same for Shamrock Street?

At last I knew what God had spared me for.

I saw myself on the front porch with my father. Loaded rifles in our lap. The showdown is set for 9 A.M. A big crowd's collected up and down the street. There's television cameras on top of the Miracle Market. Reporters want to interview us but we don't talk to nobody.

In the kitchen my mother boils water and makes bandages. The baby is at Virgie's. Lena guards the back door in case they come that way. Who knows where Armando is? The sun shines hot on our faces which is the blanket of the poor, but we are cool and collected.

Here comes the City's official car with two black-and-whites behind and two in front. Mayor Yorty steps out and reads a proclamation. "Hear ye," it says. "The City of L.A. vs. Rudolph Medina & Son, Mexicans. You are defying the Law of the Land. This is your last chance. Your house has been condemned so get out or suffer the consequences."

"Never," my father tells them in two languages.

"We will fight on to the death," I added.

"Then may God have mercy on your souls."

The mayor cuts out. They blow a bugle. Cops come from everywhere. Lead starts to fly. We duck inside and use my couch for shield. We mow them down. They keep on coming. My gun barrel is too hot to touch. Lena hands me a spare rifle. The street piles up with cops's corpses. Behind my back the phone rings. My mother answers.

"The President of Mexico wants to talk to you."

"We can't come right now."

"He says, 'Stand firm for La Raza. All Mexico is behind you on the television.' "

"You're bleeding pretty bad," my father points out.

"It's only a scratch." I empty blood out of my shoe. Now they're coming too thick and fast for us. I give the signal and Old Shamrock comes charging down the street. Gorilla's got a Tommy gun and Los Jesters take the enemy from the rear. On all sides cops run for their life. The S.P. whistle blows like a dying bull. All over town sirens are screaming. In the breathing space a reporter crawls to us with a microphone.

"This is the house which I was born in," I tell the world. "Even if I am a Mexican, the S.P. railroad's got no right to throw us out."

"But you're doomed," the reporter tells me.

"Who wants to live forever?" I tell him back.

The battle ended in various ways. In one they brought artillery and we're looking into cannon barrels as wide as trash cans. I pick off four cannoneers, my father three, but it's not enough.

"I guess this is it," I admitted.

"Arriba Méjico," my father shouts.

The first shell blasts the roof. The second goes right through my chest. I look down and see bloody stumps of ribs and my poor heart just barely beating.

"Adiós," I tell my father. "If ever in my life I did wrong, I'm sorry for it."

"My son, you are a man at last," he sobs, just before my lights went out. . . .

What a funeral.

The whole city came. Mr. Pilger draped my coffin with the Mexican flag. "Farewell, my morning glory," Mrs. Cully told me from 6th grade. "This boy would of made a distinguished doctor," said Dr. Penrose. Luscious girls from Audubon High filled Shamrock Street with flowers, and where our home once was they put up a monument with letters of gold. "A terrible mistake was made here," Mayor Yorty stated at the dedication.

I wiped tears from my eyes. Mobilize the gang. That had to be my first move.

Fat Manuel's battle wagon perched on milk boxes as usual. Buddha was squeezed in under and all the guys were there advising from Gorilla down. When they saw me they clustered round and gave me a big Welcome Home.

"Did you hear the news?" they asked. "The War Party's taken over Sierra. Robot's out and they've declared on Avenues!"

Another time that kid stuff might of seemed important.

"How about those Condemn signs?" I asked.

"Oh yeah," they said like they barely remembered. I was disgusted.

"For your information," I informed them, "my father just went to buy him a rifle. 'Buy two,' I told him."

That woke them up at last.

"How about your old man?" I asked Buddha. "Is he gonna hold out?"

"When I asked him he flattened my ears for me."

"He better shape up," I warned. "Chuchu's called a meet-

ing at the Aztecs'. My father's gonna be there and if anybody
turns traitor I really pity him."

"Don't worry," Gorilla said. "We don't let nobody tear
down Shamrock Street. City, County, State or Washington,
D.C., we're ready for them. As War Minister, go tell your
father he's got his troops. Is anyone opposed?"

Nobody was.

"What rifle?" my father asked when he came home to eat.
I reminded him.

"Do you think Ruben keeps rifles in his house, dummy?
Tomorrow or next week he'll have one maybe, plenty of time.
You know that's quite some showplace Ruben's got over there
on Mozart Street," he told my mother. "All the advantages,
with his personal bar eighteen feet long. Record player that
lights up in colors, slot machines, and you should see the
pictures on his walls, vieja." He patted my mother on the rear
which he hadn't done for quite some time, and she nearly
spilled the chile. But since when, I wondered, did he get so
buddy-buddy with Ruben Sandoval that he always used to
hate?

"And another thing," my father said, "I hear S.P.'s raised
their offer to 10,000 on our homes. Ten thousand dollars all in
cash too, those son of a beechies."

I got uncomfortable and changed the subject.

"When the showdown comes," I said, "the guys will all be
with us and they'll bring hardware too."

"Did you talk my business on the street?" he yelled.

"Do you have to shout?" my mother asked.

"Who's shouting? And if I am, this is my house, correcto?
It's not my mother-in-law's house or anybody else's house,
correcto? And I'll shout in it any time I like."

Nobody argued when my father brought out his correctos.
The food was on the table so we sat down to eat.

"Where's the beans?" he asked.

"We got rice," my mother pointed out.

"I didn't say Rice, I said Beans."

"You're bored of them you said."

"Bored or not I want to see Beans on the Table." My mother ran to heat some on the stove. "And put them right here so I could look at them." To show the exact right place he banged the table with his flat hand, and the plates jumped up and down.

"Did someone drop their handkerchief?" Lena asked, fresh from work. My father turned his head and stared at her.

"Oh-oh, did I say something wrong?" my sister wondered.

"What's that you got smeared on your mouth like a little whore?"

"Oh, not that again," my sister wailed.

"Go wash your face."

Lena was happy to get out of there. I got up too.

"Sit down," my father said.

"I'm through eating."

"No you're not. Clean your plate. I don't buy groceries for the garbage can."

"Here's your beans," my mother said.

He didn't bother to look at them. I pushed rice around my plate. My sister came back from the washroom.

"Now," my father said, "with everybody present I'll give you some advice and hope you take it. Lately this family has been running wild. That's over now. We're home and let me remind you of the rules. Número uno, respect. Número dos, respect. Número tres, respect, respect, respect. Entiendes?"

"Yes, Papa," Lena said, "and does that rule go for you too?"

"What Do You Mean?"

"Oh shit, I've had enough of this," my sister said. My father bounced up from the table. And found my mother in his road.

"One side. Don't think just because your're pregnant—"

"I'm not," she said, "so go ahead and hit me."

"Liar. Tomorrow I take you to the clínica—"

"There's no baby." For once my mother shouted. "I lost him down the toilet."

"It's true," Lena said. "I seen it happen."

At the gas station where my mother changed her dress? And how about at my grandma's, that ugly-tasting tea?

"And if you want another, go someplace else for it," my mother said.

After that, the air collapsed. What was there left to argue over? My father picked up his hat and left the house. My mother ate his plate of beans. I went out on the steps where I sat this morning with that rifle in my hands. I shut my eyes but I couldn't make that rifle come again. Still, for all his bad temper my father had gone off to the Aztecs' club to rally the troops. And I recalled how Pancho Villa had his little personal failings too.

I watched while they stripped my sister's room.

"It's kind of sudden," Lena apologized, "but Armando said now or never."

Armando had brought the ex-Featherweight Champion of the Mexican Navy along to help them. They were in quite a hurry even so.

"Would you please bring us some paper sacks, brother-in-law?" Armando asked me.

"No thanks," I said.

My mother was in her room with the door shut. Maybe she didn't care to watch. Lena ran in there at the last moments. "Mama, give me your blessing if you please. It's for the best," she begged. "My father'll murder me if I stay here longer, or me him. We'll marry by court in the morning and tonight I'll sleep with Armando's cousin that's a girl. So everything's on the up and up. I love you, Mama, and I always will, only there's no time to say it now."

Boots came pounding up the front steps. Everybody jumped, including the Mexican Navy, but it was only Chuchu for my father.

"He's at the Aztecs'," I explained.

"I just come from there. Everybody's waiting. Did something happen to him?"

Chuchu looked from one of us to the other. I did my best. "Well," I said, "he SAID he was going. Right after you left this morning he drove over Ruben's place—"

"Ruben Sandoval?"

"—to buy him a rifle he said."

"Rifle shit!" Chuchu yelled. "Vendido! He sold us out!"

Chuchu had papers in his hand, petitions, notices, things like that. He threw them on the floor. Then picked them up. "Excuse me, comadre for bad temper, but in case you didn't know it, Ruben sold Elva's house out from under her. He's S.P.'s number one boy to deliver up the others. Damn all these brave talkers, these big-mouths." He threw his papers in the trash basket. "Oh well, who knows?" he said. "Maybe it's all for the best, there's plenty other streets in L.A. to live on but I sure hate to kiss old Shamrock Street goodbye."

Chapter
31

"WELL WE DID IT," Lena announced on the phone. "Your big sister's Señora Tranquilina de la O., how fancy, huh? At least by court. My father's gone to work, I hope?"

"He never came home," I said.

"Oh-oh."

"Oh-oh's right," I told her. "Oh-oh is just exactly where he is right now, with the Buick parked in front."

"She-it," Lena wailed. "Why does everything always have to happen on my wedding day? How's my mama taking it? Lemme speak to her."

As usual my mother held the phone 6 inches from her ear, possibly for fear of getting electrocúted. You could hear Lena all over the house.

"Mama, be serious! What if he don't come back to you ever? Talk to Virgie, Mama, she knows all about these lawyer things." My mother didn't want to bother anybody. "But Mama, Virgie loves you. A lot of people love you if only you'd believe it."

"How could they love me when I don't love myself?" my mother asked.

"Mama, please don't start on that again, gimme my brother back." Which my mother was very glad to do.

"By law he's forced to give her half if he sells the house," Lena told me. "You got to wake her up so she could get her rights. . . . Please, Armando, I'll only be a minute. . . . We got no phone yet but here's our address so write it down. We're

way out in Montebello but you could take the P bus, or is it
the H? . . . Oooo, Armando, what are you doing? Not right
here in City Hall! . . . Look, manito, I gotta run so see you
behave yourself, father or no father, hear me? Go back to
school and . . . eeee, Armando, can't you wait?"

Evidently Armando couldn't. The phone clicked and
buzzed.

Thursdays were Mr. Fujita's days at five o'clock. Fuck him,
I thought. Let them come and get me. What's so bad about
Forestry Camp? It could be a change at least. But who would
look after my mother? So I took bus fare from her purse.

"Did you have a good time in Mexico?" Mr. Fujita inquired.

"Oh yes," I said. "We saw the pyramids and everything."

"Nothing new at home?" he asked.

"Oh no," I said. "Everything's fine and dandy."

The table was set for one. I was the man of the house now
and my mother rustled round the stove. She had just washed
her hair and it hung down loose to dry. You would never take
her for a mother from the back.

"Aren't you gonna sit with me at least?" I asked.

My mother rather not.

Chiles rellenos she served me, my favorite.

"Hey, these are real good," I told her.

"That's good," she said.

"Just right, not too much fire."

"I prefer them braver myself," she said.

We went on like that. So polite. Talk kept dying on us.
There were too many unmentionables.

"I hate to eat all by myself," I said.

"Here's company."

She plopped Dolores on my lap. When she bent down to
tuck in blankets, her long damp hair floated across my cheek.
I reached up and petted it.

"Let's me and you run off," I suggested, "run off someplace
no one could ever find us."

It was an old game we used to play when I was ten, but my mother grabbed the baby and reared back as if I'd pinched her in a dirty way.

"Hey, what you so jumpy for?" I asked.

My mother didn't say.

"So go back down there to my grandma!" I yelled at her. "What's keeping you? It won't kill us. Go ahead. Leave tomorrow!"

"Put your dishes in the sink," my mother told me. "I'm going to bed."

At 7:30? She took Dolores into Lena's room. She'd moved her junk in there already. Lena's door had a bolt on it and I heard it click. Against my father in case he should come home? Against me? Or what?

The first Monday after New Year's my father went back to work. Sometimes he came home, sometimes he didn't. But he never let us run out of money. That same Monday I went back to school. During Social Studies it came to me to write L O V E on the knuckles of my left hand and H A T E on the knuckles of my right. When I made fists everybody laughed so they sent me to the counselor. It wasn't Mr. Pilger any more. They fired him at Christmas which my sister had predicted. The new one scolded me for defacing myself and warned me to cooperate or my probation officer would hear of it.

"I guess you know I sold the house," my father said.

We were driving down Avenue 20 with my mother in the back. He had insisted on taking us out to dinner for a celebration. Now we knew what we were celebrating. "I gotta drop by the Real Estate to pick up the deposit," my father said, "then we'll eat." He stopped in front of what used to be a bank. It was solid shining white bathroom tiles with a round roof over like Washington, D.C.

"Come in and get your free gift," my father told my mother.

We shook hands with Mr. Luigi Calabrese. He spoke Spanish almost like a native but with spaghetti sauce on it. "How the world changes," he said. "I myself was born on Shamrock Street but we've all got to make way for progress, so if you'll just sign here, Mrs. Medina?"

"For what?" she asked.

"A technicality since the property's in your husband's name, but you know how particular these lawyers are."

"Don't do it," I told her. "Remember what Lena said."

My mother picked up the pen.

"Don't you even care?" I asked her.

"No," she said and signed.

"Don't expect me to sign nothing," I told my father.

"Oh no," Mr. Calabrese laughed. "That won't be necessary."

"This is one stubborn boy," my father said, "but I like him for it. I was like that myself at fourteen years."

The deposit money was $1,000 and my father waved the check at us. "Anything you need," he said, "like clothes, or even a trip someplace, there's plenty here."

"No thanks," my mother said.

Her free gift was a pretty calendar with Cuauhtémoc on the front, which Mr. Calabrese handed her on our way out.

"Comadre, why not move in with us?" Virgie asked. It was her first visit in a long time. "You know how I love your birdies. We got plenty of room for everybody, even Junior."

"Not me," I quickly said.

"And there's a lawyer lives down the block," Virgie rattled on, "and his daughter's in Debra's class, so he could go to court and get your money from the house. Comadre, please come with us, what are friends for anyway?"

"I'm going home," my mother said.

So there it was at last.

Next day when I got back from school, the cages were gone from our back porch. My mother sent them out to Virgie by Arturo after work.

The bulldozers came to Milflores Street on February 12 and
we all cut school to watch. What a racket those old houses
made when they ripped them up. I had no big love for Milflores. The guys were Shamrock allies but they never showed
up when we needed them. And the people over there always
claimed they were better than us. Still, their backyards nes-
tled up to ours and their sheds and clotheslines were old
friends. We looked very naked in the rear when they were
gone. Beyond our back fence was pure desert, busted boards
and holes and smashed cement but the cats were the worst.
My father's chickens didn't last a week.

My sister had been sick which was why we hadn't seen her
but she kept in touch by telephone. She was looking still quite
ghosty that day she stopped by after work.

"Mama, are you sure you want to go?" she said for the tenth
time. "Don't you care if my baby sister is raised down there
without the advantages? And how about my brother?"

"I'll get by, don't worry," I informed her.

"Of course you could move in with us," she offered, "only
Armando's kind of the jealous type and—"

"No thanks," I interrupted.

"But how could you stand to live alone with Him?"

"There's plenty of room in Juvy," I told her, "or I could
always try the Fosters."

My sister busted into tears which was maybe what I
wanted. "What's this son-of-a-bitch world coming to?" she
yelled. "I'm supposed to be happy. This is supposed to be the
happiest time of all my life. Where did we go wrong?" She
buried her face in the couch and pounded on it with her fists.
My father came from work while she was still pounding it.

It could have been the Battle of the Century but my father
didn't bring up Armando and my sister overlooked his
woman. Nobody talked Divorce or Money. Everything else
had been said too many times already, and after a while we

were all sitting down to eat together, which was for the last time.

In all my life I never had more happy dreams. Whatever was taking place in them, I was in charge of it. Doctor, lawyer, captain, you name it. One night I even dreamed myself a movie star. It was only while awake that I was bothered.

My mother's bags stood packed by the front door. She was only taking two. Everything else she gave away. My father would drive us to the bus station. Lena would meet us there. The bus would leave at 7 P.M. We were always coming up 7's lately.

I hate that special sing-songy voice you used on babies, but I used it now. It was the least I could do for my little sister after all those big promises I once made to her. "I been a bad bad brother," I crooned, "but I'll make it up to you. Just you see, I'll come sailing down in my Cadillac and take you swimming over there in Acapulco."

Who knows how many lies I might have told her except I heard my mother on the phone in English. English? Her? I almost dropped the baby.

"Please send a cab right now," she said and gave them the address and directions how to get here. Shamrock Street is not well known with taxis.

"Hey," I said. "Congratulations, you sounded like a pro. Only how about my father?"

"I'm taking the early bus," she said. "Who needs a thousand words?"

I held my sister in the cab. She waved her hands at passing telephone poles, the same ones I passed that long-ago morning coming from the hospital with my father. When would I see her next? She would be a big girl then no doubt and wouldn't even know me, perhaps a woman even. "This is him, Dolores, meet your big brother." And what would I look like then?

The buses were lined up in the parking lot like a herd of dragons. We found the one marked YUMA and threw the bags in its belly. There was barely time to say goodbye. I found my mother's window and stood under it, waving my hand and smiling like an idiot. Then the bus pulled out and swung into traffic and away my mother went. I didn't hang around to explain it to my father and my sister. Let them find out for their own self.

For company that night I unwrapped the little clay woman Hector gave me and inspected it. Her skin was reddish brown, almost the color of my own. Who was she supposed to be? Some grandma of mine that died back there before Columbus, like a mummy? Or was she more like a god for them to say their prayers to? What cute little sitters she had and chichis too, so nice and plump. Only why did they put that ugly earring in her nose?

On Shamrock, Boxer's family was the first to leave. Her father was moving them to Bakersfield and while his back was turned, Boxer that before had only been shaking hands, threw both arms around my neck. She whispered Chato, Chato in my ear till it sounded like the sweetest music.

"Violeta!" her father scolded, which was her baptized name.

She didn't look back when she climbed into the truck. You never know anything till it's too late, do you? But then what did it mean anyway? Everybody always loves you when they say goodbye.

It was the month of March on my mother's Cuauhtémoc calendar and our neighbors packed their junk and moved away. Some were careful to lock their doors. Others left them wide and swinging. Either way, a certain class of men came and took those doors and door frames too. "It's the genuine Victoria," I used to hear them scream. Another class racketed through the houses after dark, unscrewed pipes and tore out plumbing, salvaged lumber and dug up bricks. And of course the last of the Peewees busted all the windows.

I got very bored of telling friends goodbye.

"We'll be seeing you, guy," they said, "and here's our new address so don't go lose it."

"We got a real fine new home," they said, "three bedrooms with a tiled bath even, and man, you should see the chick that lives next door."

"But there'll never be another Shamrock, never."

Remember the time Pelón this?

Remember the time Gorilla that?

"So long, Chat," they said. "One of these days we'll all get together for a big reunion.

"Well," they finally said, "when you gotta go, you gotta go."

And away they went.

They moved out Brooklyn Avenue or it might be Whittier Boulevard or else down Soto toward Olympic. Nobody seemed to stay in Eastside. Some moved to Maravilla, or La Puente or Alhambra and one to high-class Glendale where Mexicans never used to live. Kiko's family moved to Chicago, Illinois, way over there on the other side of the world. And Gorilla ran away and joined the Navy because he always liked to swim.

But we stayed.

"Why get out?" my father said, "when we can live rent free?"

He did his best to be a good father to me. He spoke politely and not in his old way at all. He was usually quite cheery. At night he mostly watched his cowboys on the television but he would usually turn up absent in the morning when I got out of bed. He cooked some and so did I. We ate a lot of hamburgers out.

I went to school for my five days a week and saw Mr. Fujita every Thursday. There were more SIERRA signs everywhere you looked. One night they came to Shamrock Street and what a time they had. They scratched their SIERRA on every house and even stole our street sign for souvenir which used to be on the corner of Main.

The bulldozers came for us the end of March. They started out across the street and down the block. The first day they ripped out Chuchu's house and Don Tiburcio's that was Espie's father. They tore out his lemon tree that generously used to feed the street. They leveled the lots and then worked up toward us, but before they got halfway it started in to rain. It rained three days solid. The bulldozers sunk in the mud and stuck there. A truck turned over in a pool of water. They left it laying on its side, and old familiar Shamrock Street looked like the end of the world.

I prayed for more bad weather. I prayed it would rain and rain and never stop.

How does a punching bag feel when you punch it in the face? Does a sidewalk hurt when you stomp all over it? What does a nail think of hammers? Who knows if ants shed tears? How would you feel, man, if they came onto your street and tore it down. What would you do?

Chapter
32

IT WAS 7 A.M. AGAIN.

The sun was shining on my face. Nobody had answered my prayers for rain. I lay there asking myself What next? What next? and the minutes ticked on by. I heard the Buick stop out front. My father came in to check on me the way he always did before he went to work.

"Time to get up," he announced, which was no news.

"I'm quitting school." It came out just-like-that.

My father was in a happy mood. "Come now," he says, "don't you want to be a doctor so you could cut off my leg for nothing?" I could be dead and he wouldn't take me serious. "Don't you want to be a lawyer so you could defend the Mexican people? How will you support me in my old age?" he says, "or will you marry with a rich old woman that owns a pool hall?"

"I'm cutting out," I shouted. "You'll never see my face again." But already he was out the door.

It was eleven o'clock when I woke up next. I could sleep forever in those days. I woke up thinking, This will be a red-letter day for me, don't ask me why. Something big is going to happen, don't ask me what. So I put on clean underpants and socks and the whitest of my T-shirts and the sharpest of my jeans. I combed myself extra-careful and ate two boxes of Cheery Oats. "Because who knows when you'll eat next?" I said out loud, "or where?" My voice sounded funny so I quit talking. I took down my jacket and put it on. I looked around one last time, then walked out of my house and slammed the door behind me.

It's enough to make you cry to see Shamrock Street, the way they murdered it. Don't tell me houses have no feelings. You should have heard them scream when the bulldozers ripped them down, boards splitting open, plaster crashing, nails hanging in there for dear life. I had to hold my ears. And now all that's left of us is a cracked cement walk that leads to the hole where Gorilla's house used to be, and Kiko's home is an ugly pile of busted lumber, twisted pipes, jaggedy scraps of well-known linoleum waiting to get hauled off to the city dump.

"Stop and look even if it hurts," I told myself. "Look hard so later you could testify."

I looked long enough, then slogged on down the street through holes and puddles where the trucks rolled across the sidewalk and busted it, past ugly piles of rubbish. And here's a flattened fork and here's a no-tooth comb, and there's a red Crayola with a little life left in it so I picked it up. The floater bulb from somebody's old toledo caught my eye. I slung it skidding down the street to make some kind of human noise in all that quiet. Then, feeling like some kind of graveyard ghost, I dragged myself along to Main Street. The Aztecs' club that my father used to be King of was boarded up with plywood, and it came to me, Why not sign myself there and prove somebody's left alive at least? Or else why did I pick up that red Crayola?

A lot of names you see in public places are written very sloppy. Not me. Like Mrs. Cully said back there in 6th grade, "If others will see your work you owe it to yourself to do it right." So I took my time. I didn't sign the name I got from my father, I wanted no part of him. CHATO is what I wrote on the Aztecs' club, CHATO de SHAMROCK in big curly free-and-easy letters. And stepped back to inspect my work.

"Hey," I thought, "this is more or less like living."

So I crossed the street to Dino's market and helped myself

to more Crayolas, and two boxes of chalk, all colors. They had gotten quite careless there at Dino's since the Shamrocks moved away. I only wished they carried spray paint but they didn't, so I cruised on down Main, writing all the way. I wondered should I write "Down with the S.P. railroad"? or "Chato will revenge you"? Things like that, news, but I decided No. Just write your name and keep them guessing.

Forney Playground was our turf for 100 years but now the Sierra had their ugly name scribbled all over it. "Ho ho," I said, "let's see about that." I scratched their SIERRA out and wrote SHAMROCK over. I autographed the tennis courts in giant letters and decorated the gymnasium. I left a fine trail of Chato de Shamrock in rainbow colors to blast the Sierras' eyes. Most places I used chalk. It shows up better on bricks and on cement but here and there I decorated with Crayolas. I'm telling you by the time I left, I was quite famous over there at Forney Playground.

Next stop, Broadway.

It's the living heart of Eastside, solid businesses for blocks and blocks, everybody goes there for everything, what a showcase. I crossed the street and got ready to begin when something new and different hit me. You know how you put your name on your tennies or your baseball mitt and that proves they belong to you?

"Well, how about that now?" I asked myself.

I signed myself on Morrie's Liquor as new owner and on Flaco's Tacos and García's Short Change Department Store so I could drink and eat and dress in the latest style. I signed myself on the Mexicatessen for Lena and old times. Nobody seemed to pay attention. I could have been the Invisible Man. I kept my eyes open for cops of course, but they were all someplace else and I cruised up Broadway getting rich. I took over Blackie's Barber Shop to get my haircuts free for life, and Cashen's Haberdash and the E.Z. Credit Furniture in case some day I might decide to get married and settle down. I signed the Firehouse for laughs and the Telephone Company so I could call up all my girlfriends and keep my dimes. Till suddenly there was Webster & Ponce's Funeral Home staring me in the face.

"No thanks," I said.

But then I thought how we all gotta go sooner or later so I put my name on all six pillars. Now I can live like a king, have a big time all my life then kiss you all goodbye and give myself the biggest funeral in history and it won't cost me one single cent.

My funeral followed immediately. Almost. Just as I was putting the K on Shamrock here comes the Sierra, twelve or eight big, ugly monsters from Van Buren High, parading down Broadway with that high-kick walk which is their stupid trademark. Don't call me Coward. Getting stomped is nothing to me. What I hate is those blades they carry which are like a piece of ice cutting into your belly. I ducked into the parking lot and hid behind the hearse.

God was good to me. The Sierra passed me by. I was close enough to hear their voices. It was me they were after, no doubt about it, or soon would be. I watched them out of sight and then to be on the safe side I cut over to Boys' Club. They don't let anybody get you there, no matter what street you live on. To pass the time I shot some pool on those famous no-bounce they got upstairs, then watched television, but it was very boring. Why not autograph the picture tube? Which I did with a borrowed squeaky pen. How fine those cowboys looked with Chato de Shamrock written all over them in purple, everybody enjoyed it, till of course here comes the Assistant Honcho. They're always spying on you up there at Boys' Club, and he drags me to Ernie Zapata's office where I most especially didn't want to go.

"Well well," says Ernie, "if it isn't the last of the dinosaurs."

Very funny, and meaning Shamrock is dead as lizards, I suppose. Anyhow he didn't scold me much. He only talked. Oh how they love to talk up there at Boys' Club. All about Too bad they tore up your street only you'll get over it, and here's your chance to make new friends and straighten yourself out. Do your homework. Take an interest in sports. Be a credit to the Mexican race. So I could end up a well-paid barber if lucky? Or make big money in upholstery no doubt? And then he asks me about school which is always his most favorite question.

"I quit. I can't go there no more. They'll get me."

"The Sierra's forgotten you're alive," he tries to tell me.

"Then how come they mark my house for Death? They wrote it on the front gate even."

"Did they? When?"

I hate those eyes of his. He thinks he can see right through a person and who is he anyway? Just a Mexican like everybody else.

"So you write on the TV in the game room to get even. Come on, Chato," he says, "what you trying to prove?"

"Who's proving? I just like to write my name, is all."

"So do dogs," he tells me, "on every lamppost."

"Bow-wow," I said for no reason.

He was upset. "Lemme look in your eyes," he tells me. "You're on something. Reds? Whites? What?"

I only smiled.

That upset him more.

"I'll drive you home," he says.

"Where's that?" I asked.

Then he remembers murdered Shamrock.

"I'm living with my sister now," I finally told him. "She's married in case nobody told you. Lives out there in Montebello. They got a real nice house with lemon trees and a two-car garage so I better move along. She's picking me up on Broadway."

I cut out of there quite proud at leaving Ernie in a puzzle. Outside was all smog now, only not smog exactly, more like some kind of yellow, gray, brown wetness that came up out of the ground. It was getting to be night, you could barely see, which suited me fine for smoke screen.

My ammunition was running low by now. My chalk was nearly gone and most of the Crayolas. "How about a spray can?" I wondered. There was a paint store quite close, at Five Points, but it had eagle eyes. No doubt they would call the cops if I even looked in the window. I passed it by. The street lights popped on right then and I followed my autographs back down Broadway to check how they looked by artificial light. Very fine, was the answer. The letters shined like neon. Till down by the Mexicatessen I stopped flat-footed. Somebody had drawn a big red heart around my name in lipstick.

To be honest, I didn't know just how to feel. In one way it made me mad to see my name molested, especially if it was by some dumb guy for laughs. But in another way, if some girl had done it, or woman, that could be more or less interesting. A girl is what it turned out to be. I caught up with her in back of the Taco house, drawing her red heart around my name. She had a very nice shape on her too. Right away my blood started charging around so fast it shook me up all over. I thought all kinds of things, but then she turned around and it was only Crusader Rabbit from my Social Studies class. That's what we called her, after the television show, because of those teeth of hers.

When she sees me she takes off down the alley. In 20 feet I grab her and go for the lipstick but she whips it behind her back. And she's giggling the way they do. I quick-reached round to pull her fingers open but my hands are sweaty and her breath is splashing on my face and now we're glued together till I can feel everything she's got all the way down. We wrestled a while till we lost balance and fell into a bunch of garbage cans. After that I got the lipstick away from her quite easy.

"What right you got to my name?" I told her. "Who gave you permission?"

"You sign yourself real fine," she informed me.

As if I didn't know that already.

"Come on Chat," she says, "let's me and you go write together. We could do a lot of crazy things."

I'm ashamed to say I almost told her Yes. To go writing with a girl might be quite some change. We could be very private

out there in the dark, and decide where would be the best
locations for our work. And her writing wasn't too bad either,
at least in hearts. But then I came back to my senses. Me and
Crusader Rabbit? I had my reputation to consider. Somebody
would be sure to spot us. The story would get out and they'd
be laughing at me all over Eastside, so I told her off.

"Run along, Crusader," I told her. "I don't want partners
and especially not you."

That stupid girl called me everything, and even spit in my
face, but missed. I didn't bother to argue. I cut out, and the
first sewer I passed by, I tossed her lipstick in it.

Broadway and Bailey is possibly the busiest corner in Eastside. Pelón always went there to shine shoes in the good old
days and on Saturday nights Gorilla and a big gang of us
would display on that corner to prove who was king on Broadway. The Bank of America is there, pure satin-finish plaster
and they had given it a fresh coat of white paint. There was
not a single mark on it. My name would be Número Uno.

I picked the very best spot. I watched the passerbys. They
were racing home to dinner. Nobody looked at anybody. The
surface was perfect. My chalk floated over it like paint.

I hate to brag but that was the finest writing I ever did in
all my life, a 4-color job with letters 2 feet high outlined in
gold. Under the street lamp my name sparkled out into the
night like a jewelry store. I stood to one side and watched The
Public as they passed by inspecting it. With some, I couldn't
guess their feelings but with others I rang bells. There was
one older man, very well-dressed, the All-American type.
When he saw my name it was like a gun aimed right at him.
He nearly put up his hands.

"Who is this Chato?" that man no doubt asked himself.
"And what's his name doing on my Bank of America?"

Possibly he was their vice-president. Anyway he bought a
newspaper from the coin box then drove off in his Lincoln
Continental. My name will follow that man home like the

toothache. It will haunt his sleep and tomorrow it will still be scrambling around inside his head. And he won't be my only victim.

By now I was shivering and my fingers were too stiff to write. I had no chalk left and only one Crayola and it was shitty brown but standing there on the corner of Broadway and Bailey The Message finally came to me, The Message I'd been waiting all my life for. "I don't need to be any fancy kind of Lawyer or Doctor or Big League ball player to make my mark in the world. All I need is plenty of chalk and some Crayolas, or better, paint cans which I'll mobilize tomorrow. L.A. may be a monster city but give me a month and I'll be famous all over town. They'll do their best to stop me, the Sierra and everybody, but I'll be like a ghost, mysterious and I'll print my Chato de Shamrock on every wall with fiery rays and darts shooting out like from the Holy Cross."

"Well well," I heard. "If it isn't him at last."

"The 'Writer,' " they said.

It was cops of course. They spread-eagled me and rambled through my pockets and found my last Crayola stub.

"What's the charge?" I said.

"Defacing public property," they said.

"Wrong," I said. "I decoráted it."

And pointed proudly at my wall.

"Wowie," they said on the sarcastic side. "This genius has just commited a masterpiece."

So then they invited me into their black-and-white and away we went.

Chapter

33

THREE DAYS LATER they took me back to my Bank of America.

"Scrub that wall clean," they said and handed me a brush. I slung it into the middle of Broadway. A truck ran over it. They were not pleased. "Do what the judge ordered," they said, "or else we'll lock you up and throw away the key."

"Throw it," I told them.

So back to Juvy. In my spare time I decoráted it. Various doctors asked me various questions. One of them handed me a red spiral notebook to do my writing in. "Show me your pages next week," he said. He was not too crazy about them, but they can't keep you in jail forever. At that time my father was living with his woman on Forney Street. She was quite fat-bellied now. They couldn't send me there. My mother wrote from Titatlán. Somebody had just given her a parrot. She was quite happy with it. They couldn't send me there either, so finally they turned me over to Lena and Armando.

Poor old Shamrock was solid asphalt now from Main street to the tracks. That whole life was over so I began a new one in my sister's tiny house. It started out quite happily but soon turned out to be quite some barrel of snakes. In case you're curious, you could possibly read all about it someday. When and if I ever get around to writing it down, that is.

the end.

27 million Americans can't read a bedtime story to a child.

It's because 27 million adults in this country simply can't read.

Functional illiteracy has reached one out of five Americans. It robs them of even the simplest of human pleasures, like reading a fairy tale to a child.

You can change all this by joining the fight against illiteracy.

Call the Coalition for Literacy at toll-free **1-800-228-8813** and volunteer.

Volunteer Against Illiteracy. The only degree you need is a degree of caring.